*Acclaim for Jennifer Egan's*

# LOOK AT ME

"Ambitious, swiftly paced. . . . Egan writes with such shimmering élan that it's easy to follow her cast on its journey."  —*The Wall Street Journal*

"*Look at Me* is so engrossing, energetic, sharp, and funny, it reminded me of Ralph Ellison's masterpiece, *Invisible Man,* another novel that charts the modernist riddle of human identity."
—Maureen Corrigan, *Fresh Air* (NPR)

"Intriguing. . . . An unlikely blend of tabloid luridness and brainy cultural commentary. . . . The novel's uncanny prescience gives *Look at Me* a rare urgency."  —*Time*

"Egan has created some compelling characters and written provocative meditations on our times. . . . [She] has captured our culture in its edge-city awfulness."  —*The Washington Post Book World*

"*Look at Me* is a complicated novel . . . but the questions it raises are worth following a lifetime of labyrinths toward the answers."  —*Los Angeles Times*

"Prescient and provocative. . . . The characters . . . jump from the pages and dare you to care about them. . . . The prose is crisp and precise. . . . The pieces fit together at the end with a satisfying click."
—*The Philadelphia Inquirer*

"Propelled by plot, peppered with insights, enlivened by quirkily astute characterizations, and displaying an impressive prescience about our newly altered world, *Look at Me* . . . takes us beyond what we see and hints at truths we have only just begun to understand. . . . Few recent books have so eloquently demonstrated how often fiction, in its visionary form, speaks of truth."
—*Salon.com*

"*Look at Me* makes us think about our trust in the images that bombard us, and what we give away in the process." —*Chicago Tribune*

"Egan's rich new novel . . . is about bigger things: double lives; secret selves; the difficulty of really seeing anything in a world so flooded with images."
—*The Nation*

"Stunning. . . . This is more than a story, it's a thought-world, a novel of ideas brilliantly cloaked in the skin of characters." —*The Sunday Oregonian*

"Egan's take . . . is surreal and profoundly ironic and exaggerated, but it still rings true. . . . Beneath it all, she finds characters worth saving."
—*The Hartford Courant*

"Breathtaking. . . . Combines the tautness of a good mystery with the measured, exquisitely articulated detail and emotional landscape of the most literary of narratives. . . . Sure to leave readers thinking about these very real characters for some time to come." —*BookPage*

"An imaginative, well-paced read with serious questions about the elusiveness of meaning inside the gilded cage. Egan has intelligence to burn but plenty of feeling too." —*People*

"Part mystery, part cultural critique, [*Look at Me*] masterfully entwines the novel's secondary characters, building to a conclusion that is unexpected and disturbing, and making an incisive statement about our society's obsession with fame and glamour." —*San Francisco Chronicle*

## Also by Jennifer Egan

Emerald City

The Invisible Circus

# Jennifer Egan

# LOOK AT ME

Jennifer Egan is the author of *The Invisible Circus* and the story collection *Emerald City*. Her stories have been published in such magazines as *The New Yorker*, *Harper's*, *GQ*, *Zoetrope*, and *Ploughshares*, and her nonfiction appears frequently in *The New York Times Magazine*. Egan lives with her husband and son in Brooklyn.

For further information about Jennifer Egan, visit her Web site at www.jenniferegan.com.

**ANCHOR BOOKS**

A Division of Random House, Inc.

New York

Jennifer Egan

# Look at Me

A Novel

FIRST ANCHOR BOOKS EDITION, OCTOBER 2002

*Copyright © 2001 by Jennifer Egan*

All rights reserved under International and Pan-American Copyright Conventions. Published in
the United States by Anchor Books, a division of Random House, Inc., New York, and simultaneously
in Canada by Random House of Canada Limited, Toronto. Originally published in hardcover
in the United States by Nan A. Talese, an imprint of Doubleday, a division of
Random House, Inc., New York, in 2001.

Anchor Books and colophon are registered trademarks of Random House, Inc.

The Library of Congress has cataloged the Nan A. Talese/Doubleday edition as follows:

Egan, Jennifer.

Look at me : a novel / Jennifer Egan.

p. cm.

ISBN 0-385-50276-1

1. Traffic accident victims—Fiction. 2. Identity (Psychology)—Fiction. 3. Models (Persons)—Fiction.
4. New York (N.Y.)—Fiction. 5. Teenage girls—Fiction. I. Title.

PS3555.G292 L66 2001

813'.54—dc21

2001027152

CIP

Anchor ISBN: 0-385-72135-8

*Book design by Gretchen Achilles*

www.anchorbooks.com

Printed in the United States of America

10   9   8   7   6   5   4   3

In Memory

D. E. E.

W. D. K.

We walk through ourselves, meeting robbers, ghosts, giants, old men, young men, wives, widows, brothers-in-love. But always meeting ourselves.

—*ULYSSES,* JAMES JOYCE

# Part One

## Double Life

# Chapter One

*After the accident,* I became less visible. I don't mean in the obvious sense that I went to fewer parties and retreated from general view. Or not just that. I mean that after the accident, I became more difficult to see.

In my memory, the accident has acquired a harsh, dazzling beauty: white sunlight, a slow loop through space like being on the Tilt-A-Whirl (always a favorite of mine), feeling my body move faster than, and counter to, the vehicle containing it. Then a bright, splintering crack as I burst through the windshield into the open air, bloody and frightened and uncomprehending.

The truth is that I don't remember anything. The accident happened at night during an August downpour on a deserted stretch of highway through corn and soybean fields, a few miles outside Rockford, Illinois, my hometown. I hit the brakes and my face collided with the windshield, knocking me out instantly. Thus I was spared the adventure of my car veering off the tollway into a cornfield, rolling several times, bursting into flame and ultimately exploding. The air bags didn't inflate; I could sue, of course, but since I wasn't wearing my seatbelt, it's probably a good thing they didn't inflate, or I might have been decapitated, adding injury to insult, you might say. The shatterproof windshield did indeed hold fast upon its impact with my head, so although I broke virtually every bone in my face, I have almost no visible scars.

I owe my life to what is known as a "Good Samaritan," someone who pulled me out of the flaming wreck so promptly that only my hair was burned, someone who laid me gently on the perimeter of the cornfield, called an ambulance, described my location with some precision and then, with a self-effacement that strikes me as perverse, not to mention un-American, chose to slink away anonymously rather than take credit for these sterling deeds. A passing motorist in a hurry, that sort of thing.

The ambulance took me to Rockford Memorial Hospital, where I fell into the hands of one Dr. Hans Fabermann, reconstructive surgeon extraordinaire. When I emerged from unconsciousness fourteen hours later, it was Dr. Fabermann who sat beside me, an elderly man with a broad, muscular jaw and tufts of white hair in both ears, though most of this I didn't see that night—I could hardly see at all. Calmly Dr. Fabermann explained that I was lucky; I'd broken ribs, arm and leg, but had no internal injuries to speak of. My face was in the midst of what he called a "golden time," before the "grotesque swelling" would set in. If he operated immediately, he could get a jump on my "gross asymmetry"—namely, the disconnection of my cheekbones from my upper skull and of my lower jaw from my "midface." I had no idea where I was, or what had happened to me. My face was numb, I saw with slurry double vision and had an odd sensation around my mouth as if my upper and lower teeth were out of whack. I felt a hand on mine, and realized then that my sister, Grace, was at my bedside. I sensed the vibration of her terror, and it induced in me a familiar desire to calm her, Grace curled against me in bed during a thunderstorm, the smell of cedar, wet leaves. . . . It's fine, I wanted to say. It's a golden time.

"If we don't operate now, we'll have to wait five or six days for the swelling to go down," Dr. Fabermann said.

I tried to speak, to acquiesce, but no moving parts of my head would move. I produced one of those aerated gurgles made by movie characters expiring from war wounds. Then I closed my eyes. But apparently Dr. Fabermann understood, because he operated that night.

After twelve hours of surgery, during which eighty titanium screws were implanted in the crushed bones of my face to connect and hold them together; after I'd been sliced from ear to ear over the crown of my head so Dr. Fabermann could peel down the skin from my forehead and reattach my cheekbones to my upper skull; after incisions were made inside my mouth so that he could connect my lower and upper jaws; after eleven days during which my sister fluttered by my hospital bed like a squeamish angel while her husband, Frank Jones, whom I loathed and who loathed me, stayed home with my two nieces and nephew—I was discharged from the hospital.

I found myself at a strange crossroads. I had spent my youth awaiting the chance to bolt from Rockford, Illinois, and had done so the moment I was able. I'd visited rarely, to the chagrin of my parents and sister, and what visits I made were impetuous, cranky and short. In my real life, as I thought of it, I had actively concealed my connection to Rockford, telling people I was from Chicago, if I told even that. But much as I longed to return to New York after the accident, to pad barefoot on the fluffy white carpeting of my twenty-fifth floor apartment overlooking the East River, the fact that I lived alone made this impossible. My right leg and left arm were sheathed in plaster. My face was just entering the "angry healing phase": black bruises extending down to my chest, the whites of my eyes a monstrous red; a swollen, basketball-sized head with stitches across the crown (an improvement over the staples they'd used initially). My head was partly shaved, and what hair remained was singed, rank smelling and falling out in bunches. Pain, mercifully, wasn't a problem; nerve damage had left me mostly numb, particularly from my eyes down, though I did have excruciating headaches. I wanted to stay near Dr. Fabermann, though he insisted, with classic midwestern self-deprecation, that I would find his surgical equal, or superior, in New York. But New York was for the strong, and I was weak—so weak! I slept nearly all the time. It seemed fitting that I nurse my weakness in a place I had always associated with the meek, the lame, and the useless.

And so, to the bewilderment of my friends and colleagues at home, to the pain of my sister, whose husband refused to have me under his roof (not that I could have borne it), she arranged for me to move into the home of an old friend of our parents', Mary Cunningham, who lived just east of the Rock River on Ridgewood Road, near the house where we grew up. My parents had long since moved to Arizona, where my father's lungs were slowly dissolving from emphysema, and where my mother had come to believe in the power of certain oddly shaped stones, which she arranged on his gasping chest at night while he slept. "Please let me come," my mother pleaded with me over the phone, having assembled healing pouches full of herbs and feathers and teeth. But no, I said, please. Stay with Dad. "I'll be fine," I told her, "Grace will take care of me," and even through my croaking stranger's voice I heard a resolve that was familiar to me—and no doubt to my mother. I would take care of myself. I always had.

Mrs. Cunningham had become an old woman since I knew her as the lady who used a broom to chase away neighborhood kids trying to scoop the billowing goldfish from her murky backyard pond. The fish, or their descendants, were still there, visible in flashes of gold-speckled white among a snarl of moss and lily pads. The house smelled of dust and dead flowers, the closets were full of old hats. The lives of Mrs. Cunningham's dead husband and her children who lived far away were still in that house, asleep in the cedar-filled attic, which is doubtless why she, an old woman with a bum hip, was still living there, struggling up that flight of stairs when most of her widowed, bridge-playing friends had decamped long ago to spiffy apartments. She tucked me into bed in one of her daughters' rooms and seemed to enjoy a renaissance of second motherhood, bringing me tea and juice which I drank from a baby cup, slipping knitted booties on my feet and feeding me Gerber apricot puree, which I lapped down lustily. She had the lawn boy carry the TV up to my room, and in the evenings would recline on the twin bed beside mine, her waxen, veiny calves exposed beneath the hem of her padded bathrobe. Together we watched the local news, where I learned that even in Rockford, drug gangs had come to rule the streets, and drive-by shootings were the norm.

"When I think what this town used to be," Mrs. Cunningham would mutter as she watched, alluding to the postwar years when she and her husband, Ralph, had chosen Rockford above all American cities as the ideal place to make their home. "The most prosperous community in the nation," some erstwhile pundit named Roger Babson had apparently anointed it; Mary Cunningham went so far as to heft a musty tome onto my bed and jab her bent, trembling finger at the very quotation. I sensed her bitterness, her disgust at the grave miscalculation that left her now, in her solitude, obliged by memory and experience to love a place she had come to despise.

———

It was four weeks before I left the house to do anything more than herd my various limbs into Grace's car for visits to Dr. Fabermann and his associate, Dr. Pine, who was tending to my broken bones. When he implanted a walking plug in my leg cast, I ventured outside for the very first time in zebra-striped sunglasses Mary Cunningham had worn in the sixties, Mary herself at my side, to walk gingerly through my old neighborhood. I hadn't returned to this part of town since Grace had left for college, at which point my parents had bought a smaller place on a bit of land east of town, near the interstate, and a horse, Daffodil, whom my father rode until he was too short of breath.

By now it was late September; I had tracked the passing days in the obsessive belief that if I measured the time, it wouldn't really be lost. We stepped through a warm breeze toward the house on Brownwood Drive where I had lain in bed for several thousand nights, staring into a cat's cradle of Elm trees that were slowly expiring from Dutch elm disease, where I'd listened to Supertramp albums in a basement with orange indoor-outdoor carpeting laid over the concrete, where I'd stood before a mirror in a prom dress, my mother plucking at its petals of rayon—and yet, for all that, a house I'd thought of hardly ever since I'd left. And there it was: flat, ranch-style, covered with yellow bricks that must have been pasted on from outside, a square of crisp green lawn tucked like a napkin under its chin. So indistinguishable was this house from tens of thousands of others in Rockford that I turned to Mary Cunningham and asked, "Are you sure this is it?"

She looked puzzled, then laughed, no doubt reminding herself that my vision was worse than hers at the moment, that I was doped up on painkillers.

And yet, as we were turning to go, I had what I guess was a memory: this house against a dawn sky as I jogged toward it from my best friend Ellen Metcalf's house, where I'd spent the night. The feeling of seeing it there—my house, with everything I knew inside it. The experience of that memory was like being hit, or kissed, unexpectedly. I blinked to recover from it.

The next week, I made my way on crutches to the Rock River, where a park and jogging path meandered along the water's eastern edge. I gazed hungrily at the path, longing to visit the rose garden and duck pond farther north along it, but knowing I didn't have the strength. Instead, I used a pay phone in the parking lot beside the YMCA to call my answering machine; Mrs. Cunningham's phones were all rotaries.

It had now been seven weeks since the accident, and the outgoing message I'd instructed my sister to leave on my machine explaining my plight while not revealing that I'd left my apartment—lest it get robbed, which would really have finished me—had provoked a rash of messages from worried friends that Grace had been dutifully collecting. But there were a couple she hadn't retrieved yet. One from Oscar, my booker, who yelled through a polyphony of ringing phones that seemed otherworldly to me now, "Just checking in, sweet. Call when you've regained the gift of speech." He'd been calling every day, my sister said. Oscar adored me, though it had been years since I'd earned my agency, Femme, any serious money.

The second call was from someone named Anthony Halliday, who identified himself as a private detective. Grace had taken two messages from him already. Having never spoken with a private detective before, I dialed his number out of curiosity.

"Anthony Halliday's office." A wobbly, almost childish female voice. Not a professional, I thought; someone filling in. "He's not here right now," she told me. "Can I take a message?"

I wasn't giving out Mary Cunningham's phone number, in part because she was a kind old woman, not my secretary, and because there was something perverse and incompatible in the notion of New York and its inhabitants storming the mausoleum of her house. "I'd rather call him," I said. "What's a good time?"

She hesitated. "There's no way he can call you?"

"Look," I said. "If he wants to reach—"

"He's, ah . . . in the hospital," she said quickly.

I laughed—my first real laugh since the accident. It made my throat ache. "Tell him that makes two of us," I cackled. "Too bad we're not in the same hospital, we could just meet in the hallway."

She laughed uneasily. "I think I wasn't supposed to say that, about the hospital."

"There's no shame in hospitalization," I assured her heartily, "as long as it's not a mental hospital . . ."

Dead silence. Anthony Halliday, a private detective with whom I'd never spoken, was in a mental hospital.

"Maybe next week?" she said timidly.

"I'll call next week."

But even as I began my halting journey back toward Mary Cunningham's, I felt the notion slip from my mind like those lists you make as you're falling asleep.

Grace visited that night, pulling a chair between the twin beds where Mary Cunningham and I were ensconced as usual, watching *NYPD Blue*. When a man was pummeled in a restroom, his face beaten bloody, Grace covered her eyes and begged me to change the channel. "You change it," I retorted. "I'm the invalid."

"Sorry," she said, going sheepishly to the TV—apparently one of the last in the world to be controlled manually. "I shouldn't be the one crying."

"You're crying for both of us," I said.

"It just seems bizarre that you would come to Rockford without telling me," she fretted, flipping channels. She'd said this a dozen times, apparently in the belief that, had she but known I was on my way, I would have arrived without incident. And much as I disliked this line of questioning (or any line of questioning, for that matter), I vastly preferred it to the topic Grace didn't dare broach: What would I look like when all this was done? And what would become of me?

"I wanted to surprise you," I said.

"My, and you still don't remember what happened!" Mary Cunningham marveled. "Was it an animal in the road, dear, or were you feeling sleepy? Could you have dropped off at the wheel for a minute?"

"I don't remember. I don't remember," I said. For some reason, I covered my ears.

"Her memory's always been lousy," Grace said.

It was true—my memory was lousy, and Rockford was the place I remembered least. And yet the boredom and stasis of my present circumstances were driving me to retrospect in the desultory way that a person cooped up in an old house will eventually make her way to the attic and upend a few boxes. In moments, I found myself drenched in early childhood impressions of Rockford: a lush, sensuous world of sticky green lawns and violent thunderstorms, mountains of glittering snow in winter. In early adolescence, I'd done a school report on Rockford's industrial achievements, reading at the public library about a self-tying attachment for grain binders, a knitting machine that made seamless socks, the oil-lubricated "universal joint," whose purpose I've forgotten; the "side by side," a bookcase-and-desk combination; about lathes, reapers and their component parts. I remembered reading in a state of keen anticipation, awaiting the moment when Rockford would burst forth in triumph, the envy of the industrial world. I sensed this glory approaching with the invention of cars, for eleven Rockford companies had designed them, and one, the Tarkington Motor Company, built a prototype that was warmly received at an auto show in Chicago in the twenties. But no—the investors backed out, the car was never produced, and with this failure, my excitement began to congeal into something heavier. There was to be no limelight; Rockford remained a city known for its drills, transmissions, joints, saws, watertight seals, adjustable door bumpers, spark plugs, gaskets—"automobile sundries," as such products are known—and for its agricultural tools; in short, for dull, invisible things that no one in the world would ever know or care about.

After two days of reading, I had tottered from the library into the empty husk of "downtown," across the river from our house, nearly all of whose commerce had been leached away by malls far to the east of the river, out by the interstate. My mother beeped her horn from the parking lot across the street. But I held still for a minute, clutching my bookbag, letting the smallness and meagerness of this forgotten place pour in around me. Rockford, I now saw, was a city of losers, a place that had never come close to being famous for anything, despite the fact that again and again it had tried. A place revered among mechanics for its universal joint was not a place where I could remain. This was clear to me at age twelve: my first clear notion of myself. I was *not* Rockford—I was its opposite, whatever that might be. I decided this while standing in front of the public library. Then I crossed the street and got in my mother's car.

Our father owned a wholesale electrical supply company; he was a man who could push through walls to the hidden circuitry behind, who braided wires between his fingers and made the lights turn on. As a child,

I had ascribed magical powers to his work, and arrayed myself in necklaces he made me from bolts and washers and colored wire. But after the library, I began to imagine a perspective from which my father's life—and my mother's, too—were small, earnest, and futile, too deeply touched by this place where they both had spent their lives. I grew up waiting to leave. And Grace grew up cleaving to me, knowing that I would go and she would stay.

Now here I was, back in Rockford, fighting with my sister over who should change the TV channel, my head full of titanium bolts and screws invented here, for all I knew. I found this funny in a dark way, one of life's little ironies.

"The girls are dying to see you," Grace said, reviving our ongoing debate over my nieces. "Please let me bring them."

"They *think* they want to see me," I said.

"Charlotte, get over it," she said, and pressed my hand. "They love you so much!"

"Not yet."

It wasn't that I didn't want to see Allison and Pammy. In fact I hungered to snuff their mussed-up hair and feel them bump against me the way kids do without thinking. But to them, I was Glamorous Aunt Charlotte, the fashion model whom they sometimes found grinning, hand on hip, inside catalogues that arrived on their doorsteps unwanted (for that was the level I'd sunk to) or wandering through the background of a Tampax commercial. That was me hawking deodorant on the Coney Island Cyclone ("Now this. Is stress."); that was me in waders, wielding a fishing rod and declaiming the merits of antifungal foot powder. That pixiefaced brunette sprawled atop a Buick as if she'd fallen from a tree? The one in glasses, blushingly recounting the trauma of passing gas during a board meeting? Urging fortified granola on her freckled son? Those were me, too. It was far short of the transcendent existence I once had envisioned. But to my young nieces, I embodied a mythical ascension.

I would let them believe in me in peace, I told myself, unencumbered by my present grotesqueness. I was ashamed to be seen.

One afternoon, I walked to the Cedar Bluffs Cemetery and parked my rear end on a gravestone that was as near as I could recall to the spot where I used to sit with Ellen Metcalf. I lit up a Merit, my first since the accident, thus flouting Dr. Fabermann's warning that smoking impeded the healing of bone. Before dinner and after, too, sometimes, Ellen and I would lean against these stones among the legions of dead Swedes, Olsens, Lofgrens, Larsens, Swensons like myself, and smoke Kools, which we believed were a cure for the summer heat. We talked about losing our virginity— not losing it, though, with all the haplessness that word implied, but yielding it up in a blaze of ecstasy that would leave us permanently altered.

I tried to recall the sound of Ellen's voice. I couldn't, as if she'd been an imaginary friend, a projected figment of myself. Once, we had walked from East High School all the way to the pharmacy beside the Piggly Wiggly, then stopped before the section of plastic children's toys. Only to find, as we looked at each other inquiringly, that neither one of us knew what we were doing there; we had each been following the other.

After my next doctor's visit, I asked Grace to drive past East High School. A rather grand building, it seemed to me now, large and mustard-tinted, hundreds of canted windows juggling the sunlight. As I stood before its broad, empty steps, I had another jab of memory: seeing Ellen Metcalf for the first time outside that school, an olive-skinned girl with long black hair. Watching her there, exotic, alone, and wanting to become her—the feeling sprang from my fingers to my throat. Later, Ellen said, of spotting me that day, "I could tell you didn't belong here." The highest compliment.

Her father owned a large fertilizer business, and her mother was a quasi-invalid, cloistered in a darkened master bedroom, consumed by some malady whose exact nature no one seemed sure of. They lived in a copious house just a few blocks from my own much smaller one. Ellen existed in a state of lonely hauteur, like the last surviving member of a royal family; her brother, Moose, had departed the previous year for the University of Michigan. I knew about Moose. He was one of those high school boys whose athletic and romantic feats inspire the teenage equivalent of epic poetry, recited longingly in their absence. I had encountered him once, briefly, thrillingly, on a summer afternoon when I was practicing my golf swing on our front lawn and nicked a sprinkler head, sending a geyser of water into a red Mustang convertible that happened to be driving past.

The driver got out, shaking water from his longish hair: an older boy, tanned in a spotless white T-shirt, ambling over the grass like a person who had never hurried in his life. As I stammered my apologies, struggling to tamp the foaming crescendo of water with my foot, he scanned our yard and said, "Handle's where, behind that hedge? Turn it off and I'll take a look."

By the time I'd returned from that errand, he had removed the sprinkler head and was rattling its rusted parts in his hand like dice. His absorption allowed me to study him; a charmed, confident boy whose appeal was compounded, somehow, by the Neanderthal cast of his head. Twenty minutes later he had repaired the sprinkler, sauntered back to his car and driven away with a wave, and it was only then that an older girl from across the street stampeded over to tell me, breathlessly, in whose rarefied presence I had found myself.

But Moose was gone. Ellen was alone, marooned in a place that felt as bankrupt to her as it did to me. Everything good was gone from this crummy city, this home of reapers and ball bearings, and there was nothing for it but to plunder what few excitements remained. We talked about our lust—where exactly it resided within us; our stomachs, we thought, though Ellen said she felt it, too, in the back of her mouth.

By October, Dr. Pine had removed the last vestiges of plaster from my body. As Mary Cunningham raked her yard, I trailed behind her with a tube of green poison whose proboscis I shoved into the eye of each weed I spied, and pumped. Rockford was in the grip of a mania for jack-o'-lantern leaf bags; at least one grinning orange sack squatted on every lawn, fat with leaves. Stalking weeds, I tried to recall each one of my sexual quarries that sophomore year with Ellen. Jeff Heinz: a shy and statuesque football-playing senior, the sheer grace of whose movements set him apart from the sludge of players on the field. Jeff and I were in chemistry together, and I managed to insinuate my way into the role of lab partner, standing close, brushing his wrist as we puzzled over beakers full of colored liquid. Nothing. Meanwhile, Ellen had a boyfriend, Michael Ippen, with whom she expected to do it shortly. So I relinquished Jeff Heinz, who proceeded on to Brown University (an unusual step for a Rockford boy), whence filtered back the electrifying news, a year or two later, that he was a fairy. I would have loved to snicker over that one with Ellen, but by then we were no longer speaking.

Benji Gustafsen: blond, sweet, rippled muscles on his belly, the whole of whose intelligence, it seemed, was compressed into a knack for restoring small antique appliances: can openers, toaster ovens, vacuum cleaners. This was a boon for Benji's friends and neighbors; less so for anyone trying to hold a conversation with him. But conversation wasn't my goal, either, and I lost my virginity to Benji in his squalid basement workroom only two days after Ellen lost hers to Michael Ippen on his older brother's squishy bed.

We brushed snow from our respective gravestones and perched in the early dark, down parkas pulled tight around us, looking west toward the lights of the expressway that snaked alongside the Rock River.

"The bed had a scratchy blanket on it," Ellen remarked.

"There were tons of McDonald's wrappers on the floor," I said. "It smelled like catsup."

"Did it hurt?"

"Killed. Plus I bled."

"With all the catsup around," she said, "he probably didn't notice."

We passed our last Kool back and forth. Ellen slipped off the gravestone and lay on her back in the snow.

"Doesn't that freeze your head?" I asked.

"Yeah," she said, "but the stars."

I lay down beside her. She was right, the stars. After I'd done it with Benji, an awful sensation had come open in me—who was this guy, stretching like a dog so his spine cracked? But then I'd thought of Ellen, telling it to her, strategizing, and the feeling had melted into a kind of sweetness.

Marcus Sealander: a tattooed motorcyclist whose menacing black leather vest concealed, of all things, a potbelly. We did it standing up. Marcus had a nasty habit of shoving my shoulders against the wall as if it excited him to think of snapping my spine, so he got no second chance. Meanwhile, Ellen did it twice with Luis Guasto, a strange boy who'd pasted hundreds of beer cans to the walls of his parents' rec room with a glue gun. They did it downstairs, among the cans, and the first time Ellen thought she might almost, just barely feel something, but then Louis rolled off her and moments later was in the bathroom pissing loudly, so that was that. The second time was even worse—over in four minutes flat.

Tom Ashlock. Lenny Bergstrom. Arthur Blixt. Stephen Finn. By spring we were sluts, sirens, alarming to girls and boys alike as we scoured in vain for someone to satisfy us. When Moose came home at Christmas, Ellen abandoned me for his sacred compass; a brutal disappointment, since I'd counted on being included. For three lonely weeks I hardly saw her. Moose's departure left her listless, but soon the alchemy of our union was back at work, plotting our rescue from the crushing banality that surrounded us like those shrinking rooms full of water from which TV heroes must escape. The streets, the sky, the lousy moon. What was wrong with these boys?

Boys. We rolled onto our sides, staring at each other amidst the gravestones. The snow had melted, exposing a papier-mâché of last year's soggy leaves. A revelation was upon us: the problem was boys—too young, too inexperienced to make us feel what we longed and deserved to feel, whereas men, with their years of practice—men would know exactly what to do! And finding men wouldn't be so hard; Mr. Polhill, Ellen's driver's ed teacher, was constantly leaning over her desk and sniffing her hair, and as for me . . . how old did he have to be?

"Old," Ellen said. "Thirties."

There was a man I'd caught watching me by the country club pool the summer before. A foreign guy—French, I thought, who'd worn a tight little bathing suit like boys on our swim team wore. I'd found him creepy at the time, but now I revised my opinion: he was French, he was a man, he was perfect.

Mr. Polhill gallantly proffered the use of his personal car when Ellen asked him for extra driving practice after school, then suggested a small detour. That was all she would tell me. There was a blankness about her that I'd never seen before; I waited in the cemetery but she didn't come, and when I chased her down at school she refused to elaborate.

Meanwhile, through a friend of my mother's who knew Mrs. Lafant, the Rockford girl who was married to the Frenchman, I managed to procure a Friday night babysitting job at his house, where two brats drizzled ice cream down the front of the tight, low-cut dress I'd worn for Mr. Lafant's entertainment. Afterward, as he drove me home, I moved close to

15

him in the front seat. He went still, as if in disbelief. "You are a very lovely girl," he breathed carefully, in his marvelous accent. When I moved closer, he stroked my hair and I shut my eyes, opening them only when I noticed that Mr. Lafant had begun driving rather wildly. He screeched to a stop somewhere off Spring Creek Road, killed the engine and turned off the headlights. It took my eyes a few moments to adjust, and when finally they did, I discerned Mr. Lafant's erect penis groping from his pants like a mole emerging from a tunnel. His hands, which moments before had been delicately stroking my hair, now were guiding my head most assertively toward it. I was frightened. His obvious hurry made it worse; when I squirmed my resistance, he seized the back of my head and shoved me toward his groin while also (I noticed) glancing at his watch, no doubt calculating how much longer he had before his wife began to wonder. A wave of revulsion roiled through me. "No!" I shrieked, "No, no!" at which point my employer began to panic. "Shut up," he implored, shoving the inquiring penis out of sight. He drove me home in urgent silence, an angry muscle jumping in his face. I leapt from the car and he roared away without a word, his tires barking on our quiet street.

I would have sprinted straight to Ellen's house, but my mother had heard the car and padded onto the dewy lawn in her slippers and robe. "Well, that wasn't very nice," she remarked. "He could have waited until you went inside."

The next morning, Ellen met me at the back door of her big empty house and led me upstairs with the same indifferent look she'd worn all week. *I Love Lucy* was on in the TV room.

"So, did you do it?" she asked, her eyes not leaving the set.

"He didn't want to," I said. "He wanted me to suck it."

Ellen turned to me with interest.

"I couldn't," I confessed. "It was just too disgusting." Then I asked, instinctively, "Did Mr. Polhill . . . want that?"

Ellen began to cry. I had never seen her cry before, and I hovered near her, on the verge of hugging her as I would hug Grace when she cried, but hesitant. Ellen wasn't like Grace. "Did you do it?" I whispered.

"I tried," she said, "but after about three seconds, he—you know, he—"

"No! No!"

"In my mouth," she sobbed.

"Oh, my God!"

"And then I threw up. All over him and on the bed."

I was quiet, stilled by my horror at the scene she'd conjured, and at the same time tickled by some creeping mirth that seemed lodged within it. My mouth, of its own accord, twitched into a smile, at which point Ellen's crying swerved into laughter, outright hysterics, tears still dripping from her eyes. By now I was laughing, falling with Ellen into aching hilarity until I, too, burst into tears. "He must've died," I sobbed.

"He ran in the bathroom and locked the door," she said, and then we doubled over, both (as it turned out) helplessly wetting our pants.

Later, having showered and changed, stuffed our jeans and underwear in Ellen's washing machine, we put three Old Styles in a bag and carried them to the cemetery, along with a pack of Kools. "Forget the men," Ellen said. "They're perverted."

"The good ones wouldn't do it with us," I agreed. "They just want to do it with their wives."

We sipped the dry, cold beers. It was so warm, we no longer needed our jackets. We were fresh and clean, yet from somewhere within us— below us, it almost seemed, down among the dead Swedes—came a weight that was palpable. The weight of our boredom, our impatience.

"I have the answer," Ellen said, but without any of the jollity that had accompanied our prior inspirations.

"What?"

"Moose."

Moose. Who within the month, she informed me, would return from the University of Michigan for summer vacation, three friends in tow. Who would party and water-ski with these friends for a couple of weeks, relubricating the vast machine of his social life before he commenced a summer job at his father's factory. Whose friends would doubtless be the finest specimens the University of Michigan, or any university, had to offer. Not men, not boys. Experienced, but not perverted.

And yet, for all the epic allure of Ellen's brother and those within his hallowed ken, the very thought of another sexual undertaking exhausted me. I feared losing Ellen again after Moose's return, as I had at Christmas.

On his first Saturday home, we peeked down through the country club's chain-link fence at the river directly below, where Moose and his

17

friends—Marco, Amos, Todd—stuttered over the brownish water at intervals presaged by the roar of Moose's motorboat. Even at this distance, the sight of Ellen's brother was arresting: a taut, athletic-looking guy in neon-green swim trunks, the best water-skier of the four, by far. But he skied the least, preferring to egg on the others from the wheel of the boat.

"Which do you want?" Ellen asked.

"Including Moose?"

She looked at me oddly, then shook her head in adamant refusal. "Marco," I said, crestfallen.

"I'll take Todd," Ellen said, which mystified me; he was the palest of the three, angular in a way that reminded me of my father.

Moose's destination that night was a party in one of the vast houses on National Avenue, just north of downtown; our plan was to show up there, do it somewhere in the house with our respective choices, and afterwards meet back at the country club beside the swimming pool.

The party was disappointingly routine; Tom Petty straining some dad's stereo, a throng of drunk, roaring guys older than our classmates, but otherwise identical. At last I observed Moose again at close range—in the kitchen, where he and another guy were scrimmaging with sponge mops for a can of Tender Vittles on the sticky linoleum. A towering presence was Moose, big shoulders flicking under his white T-shirt like keys on a player piano as he wrested the cat food from his opponent with some fancy mop work, forearms buttery with tan, his appearance a winning amalgam of beauty, thuggishness and faint embarrassment. And something else: an awareness on the part of Moose and everyone else, a crowd of admirers thronging the room for a glimpse of his folly, that he was special. Famous.

At the sight of us—of Ellen—Moose abandoned the game. "Sis," he said, discarding his mop and slinging an arm around her shoulders. Thus encompassed, Ellen looked childlike, serene—bland in a way I couldn't have pictured. The crowd curled around her like a smile. I watched it all with jealous fascination.

Later, across a patio drenched in buggy light, Ellen and I tossed ourselves at Moose's friends with an abandon verging on carelessness. Moose cast acid looks in my direction, but as the party ground on, he lost track of us. Eventually Marco and I crept up a narrow flight of stairs to a third-floor guest room that reeked of mothballs. He peeled the clothes from my body and was just lowering himself on top of me like a crane setting an old car onto a pile of old cars when I recoiled. "No," I said. "Stop, wait!" stricken with the memory of Mr. Lafant. It was too soon, I didn't know this guy; I'd forgotten what I was supposed to do with him, and why. Marco, bewildered by this seizure of modesty after my slatternly behavior downstairs, went to take a piss.

I fled the room and bolted from the house, sprinting north along the river toward the country club, already revived by the thought of seeing Ellen and swapping our tales of woe, like always. Except, I thought, still running, what if hers was not a tale of woe? What if finally, after so long, she and Todd had found what we were looking for? The thought sickened me.

The club's iron gate was locked, a variable we hadn't foreseen. I stood outside, wondering whether to scale it. Finally I shimmied over the fence and dropped to the ground inside the club, intensely quiet under the bright moon and torn clouds. The warm golf course grass bounced under my feet. I ran down the concrete steps to the pool, whose turquoise bottom caught the light of the moon, and I saw something move in the water and it was Ellen. I felt such a shock of happiness that I called out her name and she hushed me, laughing, and I saw her clothes by the pool and flung off my own and dove into the wet, heavy silence. I felt the water move as Ellen swam past, her long hair fluttering over my skin. We burst into the air, giggling.

"So, what happened?" I asked softly.

"With what?"

I stared at her. "Todd!"

"Oh, he couldn't," Ellen said, with an indifference that overjoyed me. "Too drunk."

But we were grinning. There was no sense of failure; only this giddiness, as if we'd broken free—finally, somehow—from an onerous fate. We swam to the shallow end and looked at the sky. The air and water felt identical in temperature, two different versions of the same substance. It was strange and good to be naked in the pool where normally you had to wear a bathing cap. Clouds floated past the moon, milky, mysterious, and I heard a boat on the river below and thought, I'm happy. This is happiness—why was I looking for anything else? Ellen floated on her back, water pooling around her breasts, and no one had ever looked more beautiful to me. I reached for her. It was as if she had known I would, as if she'd reached for me, too. We stood in the water and kissed. Every sensation of desire I had ever known now amassed within me and fought, demanding release. I touched her underwater. She felt both familiar and strange—someone else, but like me. Ellen flinched and shut her eyes. For once, I had some idea of what to do. She clung to me tightly, then collapsed, trembling, her arms around my neck. When she laughed, I heard chattering teeth. We moved to the pool steps and sat, our bodies underwater, just our heads and necks above, and I took her hand and put it on me. She was tentative, afraid, but I kept my hand on hers until my heart snapped and my head hit the concrete behind me. We lay there, my head pounding, a lump forming on my scalp that would hurt for a week, and when the water made us shiver we got out of the pool and dried ourselves off with our clothes and spread them on the grass and lay on top of them and began again, more slowly now. Still, the intensity was punishing— we're killing each other, I thought. We're killing something. Afterward, we lay half-asleep, and finally Ellen said, "We could teach these assholes a thing or two," and we laughed and got dressed and walked back to Ellen's house, talking thoughtlessly, as if nothing had changed. We were best friends.

We slept naked in Ellen's single bed, pressed together with her hair everywhere, and again I had that sense, as when I'd first touched her, that she was less a separate person than a variant of myself—that together, we made one thing. I woke at dawn and had an impulse to leave, with it all still so nice. This was odd because it was Saturday, and normally we would have made Swedish pancakes and watched cartoons, probably spent the whole day together. But I left Ellen sleeping there and walked home in the May sunlight, and only as I approached my own house, the flat, unassuming yellow house bleached almost white by the bare morning sun, did what had happened with Ellen begin to seem pretty strange. I almost couldn't believe it. But when I remembered the feeling of it, the physical feeling, I felt that warmth in my stomach and all I wanted was to see her again, to have that again. Am I a lesbian? I wondered, incredulous. No other girl had ever attracted me.

I waited until that night to call her. Moose answered the phone (coldly, having surely been informed of my antics with Marco) and handed it to Ellen. I heard a guardedness in her voice that instantly provoked an equal guardedness in me, and our conversation had a weird, stilted feeling that was completely unlike us. It never went away. After that, seeing Ellen was like seeing one of the guys I'd done it with; she made me self-conscious, aware of the passing moments and the need to fill them with something. In the pauses I would wonder, Is she thinking about *it*? Does she want to do it again? But I didn't, anymore, because now Ellen seemed no different from a boy.

It was a horrible summer; I had no other friends. I saw Ellen only once, at the movies. "Wait," I gasped, yanking Grace into the shadows as Moose and his entourage spiraled from the theater into the carpeted lobby. The guys were sparring, tousling, and Moose leaned down and hoisted Ellen over his shoulder—so easily, as if she were a cat, and her clogs fell off but Moose wouldn't let her down, he ran with her through the glass doors and into the parking lot, where I heard the swells of her laughter. Someone collected the clogs and brought them to her. I watched, incredulous. To be coddled, protected that way—what must it feel like? To be at the absolute center, adored by the boy whom everyone loved, without trying. What could compete with it?

That fall, I saw Ellen walking home from school ahead of me. She was alone, sadness closing back around her now that Moose was gone. I forced myself into a trot and caught up. "I feel so weird around you now," I said.

"Me, too," she said.

"We have to forget about that. We have to go back to how it was before."

"We have to!" she agreed.

Then silence. I couldn't think of anything else to say, and we pushed terse, empty comments back and forth as I counted the minutes to my house. When finally it came into sight, I pretended my mother was waiting for me and ran ahead, leaving Ellen by herself.

I had thought it would be hard to make new friends, but it turned out that Ellen and I were neutralized by our disunion to the same degree that we'd been empowered by our accord. Eventually we settled down with boyfriends and went to proms and even signed each other's yearbooks—*Good luck with everything!*—and except in the most abstract sense, I forgot about that night.

I did pay one last visit to Ellen's house. This time with Moose, who graduated from Michigan and returned to Rockford to work for his father. I picked him up my senior year at a state championship hockey game, where he was watching teenage boys scramble over the ice. By then Moose's aura of fame had shrunk; even the youngest siblings of the kids who had revered him were gone, and East High, where once he'd reigned, no longer knew of his existence. He was still living at home, and I followed him up the dark familiar stairs, past the master bedroom where his invalid mother spent her days, past Ellen's empty room (she was a year older than I, and had already left for college) to his own attic lair: faded sports posters loosening from the walls, dusty trophies lining shelves. There was a seriousness about Moose that I hadn't remembered. As we sank onto his bed, I noticed a series of ropes and pulleys connected to a box attached to the ceiling. I asked what they were. "Nothing," he told me. "Some old stuff I outgrew."

When it was over he faded into a doze. I stared at him, the bulky shoulders, the slightly purplish cast of his eyelids; this locus of so many years of cumulative envy and mystery, idolatry and myth, now prone, snoring lightly into a pillow.

His eyes opened. "What?" he said, groggy.

"You," I said.

He looked puzzled, and raised himself onto an elbow.

"Just . . . Moose," I said, shaking my head. "Moose. Moose Metcalf. I can't believe it."

He grinned, uneasy. He knew exactly what I meant. Wind filled the bedroom from his tiny window.

"Actually, my name is Edmund," he said.

I was not a nostalgic person. I didn't save Christmas cards, rarely took pictures, felt mostly indifferent to the snapshots people sent me. Until the accident, I had always thought my memory was bad, but in fact I'd thrown the past away, a ream of discarded events—so that I could move, unencumbered, into the future. Now, as I made my limping way among the tall bare trees toward Ellen Metcalf's house, it was not with the intention of losing myself in misty-eyed recollections of my old friend, but to see the house now. To learn what it, and if possible she, had become.

The Metcalf manse was a rambling Tudor style that has always been popular among the midwestern rich. The lawn still impressed me, wide and lush despite the scorching summer that had just passed. On the grass were sundry child-oriented items: a bat, a large plastic gun, a smallish fluorescent orange bike. What age child they denoted I had no idea. I touched my face, stuccoed with Mary Cunningham's thick, flower-scented pancake. I was still badly bruised; rather than fading, it seemed, my bruises simply changed color, like fireworks whose finale won't arrive. I felt darkly conspicuous; a dour visitor, a drug-ravaged starlet incognito.

The area behind the house had been re-landscaped; flower beds shaped like lima beans blossomed with wine-colored begonias. I stood on the flagstone patio and listened to the silence. I went to the screen door that led to the kitchen—the door Ellen and I had always used—and gently tapped. I rang the bell. When it was clear that no one was home, I opened the door and went in.

The difference shocked me; I remembered the kitchen as a dark room with greenish walls and high windows that made you feel you were straining to see the sky from the bottom of a well. Now the windows were wide and lower down, and the room had been opened up, cracked wide so you saw light and sky and green lawn spotted with piles of raked leaves. Very California, I thought, tapping my heels against the pizza-colored floor tiles, with an impressive array of beaten copper pots dangling above the stove.

And if someone comes home? I asked myself, ascending the front stairs after a glance at the living room, where modern art had commandeered the walls. But I wasn't afraid. I felt shielded—protected, somehow, by my dark glasses and mask of makeup, the silk headscarf tucked into the top of my trenchcoat to hide the bruises on my neck. This isn't me, I thought, rounding the stairs and emerging into the upstairs hallway, whose crisp walls and luminous floors effaced all traces of its former

23

dreariness. How could I be caught, when I didn't look like anyone? As a model, of course, I'd carried my face like a sign, holding it out a foot or so in front of me—not out of pride or vanity, God knew; those had been stamped out long ago, or at any rate, disjoined from my physical appearance. No, out of sheer practicality: here's what I am. Calling card, handshake, *précis*, call it what you like; it was what I had to offer to the world where I had spent my life.

I was heading for the master bedroom, a room I'd glimpsed only when Ellen would go in or out, a shadowy peek, a gust of scented air, her mother's hushed, plaintive voice. Now the door was open. I went in. The room was immense and spare, bars of sunset angling through wood blinds that looked custom-made. There were big ficus trees and a modern-looking bed with long delicate posts. The walls were yellow-white. In a plush adjacent dressing room I smelled one of the Chanels, but my damaged nose could not distinguish which. Long mirrors, walls covered with framed photographs. I went closer to look—I wasn't yet allowed to wear my contacts—curious about the family who lived here now. Instantly I recognized Ellen, aged by many years but still beautiful, the bones even stronger in her face. She was standing on a beach with a man at her side, her husband, presumably, who looked ten years older and had the tanned skin and white teeth of a German.

Ellen Metcalf. I was in Ellen Metcalf's dressing room.

Straining to focus my bleary eyes, I studied other pictures: Ellen lounging with her husband in some foreign clime; the squashed face of a newborn; some youthful photos of Ellen's parents done in the manner of Hollywood stills; a montage of two children, the older a girl who—poor thing—looked nothing like her mother. I wondered if she'd been adopted. Ellen and this daughter in matching bathing suits, lying beside the country club pool. As I surveyed the whirling narrative of Ellen's life, I began, for the first time, to feel anxiety at the thought of her coming home and finding me there. It wasn't my trespassing that concerned me; more a basic sense that I couldn't be seen this way.

I decided to go. But no sooner had I left Ellen's dressing room than I heard footsteps in the hallway outside the bedroom door. Appalled, I yanked my sunglasses over my monster-red eyes, shot back into the dressing room and hunched in a closet, gently coaxing the door shut behind me. I hid there, panting in a darkness full of filmy dresses scented with more of that mysterious Chanel, until it occurred to me that the humiliation of being caught inside a closet would surely exceed that of merely standing in a dressing room, and I flung open the closet door just as a girl of about thirteen, with earphones on her head, wandered in from the bedroom.

She jumped, then gaped at me, startled and guilty, as if she were the one who'd been caught. It was the girl from the pictures, a sadly average-looking girl with thin, drab hair and insect-like glasses on her face. She pulled off her earphones.

"Who are you?" she said.

"I'm an old friend of your mother's," I replied as casually as I could manage. "I was passing through town and thought I'd stop by. But I guess she's not home."

This flimsy pretext seemed, oddly, to satisfy her. I saw how unlike her mother she was; Ellen would have been all narrow-eyed suspicion. But this was an open, curious girl. Thank God.

"She won't be back for a while," she said.

"Darn," I said, and then, because it seemed only natural, "Where is she?"

"Chicago, at the hospital."

"Nothing wrong, I hope."

My ignorance clearly surprised her. "Ricky had leukemia? But now he's in remission."

"Oh, that's good," I said. "That's terrific. The house is beautiful. I haven't seen it since your grandparents lived here."

"I'll show you my room, if you want."

I followed her down the hall. She had a light, skipping step. Her room was Ellen's old room, painted blue now and a little dark; she was one of those girls who pulls the shades and burrows in bed with a book (not the sort I ever knew well). Indeed, there was a pile of books heaped by the bed and even on top of it. The covers were mussed, as if she'd been underneath, reading.

But the place where she led me out of pride or habit was a large rectangular fishtank. The water bubbled merrily. A chair was poised beside the tank, as if the girl spent time there, watching her fish. And they were beautiful fish, I had to admit, though I wasn't fish-inclined. The two smallest were a phosphorescent blue, like peacock feathers. "Those are damsels," she said, seeing me notice. "Blue damselfish."

"What's that?" I asked dutifully, pointing at a fish with sharp prongs curved around its tail like a comma.

"An angel flame," she said, then added proudly, "This is a saltwater tank."

Having no idea what difference that made, I kept quiet.

The girl stood across the tank from me, eying my face through the percolating water. "Why do you wear sunglasses inside?" she asked.

"I had an accident," I said. "A car accident."

"I thought something happened," she said. "Your face looks kind of strange. Does the light hurt your eyes, is that why you wear the glasses?"

"No," I said. "They just look bad."

"Can I see?"

"You don't want to," I said. "Really."

"Yes, I do."

She did. She wanted to see my eyes, this girl, and came back around the tank for that purpose, slim, wiry, her head about the height of my chest. I'd been wrong about her age: she was older than thirteen. She seemed almost like an adult. "Believe me," she said, "I can handle it."

I took off the glasses. The room wasn't nearly as dark as I'd thought. The girl looked evenly into my eyes: the gaze of someone who has already seen her share of pain, and knows what it looks like.

"How will you look after it heals?" she asked.

"Like I looked before, more or less. These doctors, you know, they're fantastic."

She nodded. I had the feeling she didn't believe me.

"What's your name?" I asked.

"Charlotte," she said.

I thought at first that I'd misheard her. I didn't ask again—just let the surprise ricochet through me once, then dissipate. "No kidding," I said. "Mine, too." Right away I saw my mistake; she would tell Ellen, and Ellen would know what had happened to me.

"That's incredible!" she said. "I don't know any other Charlottes. Only one Charlene."

"Charlotte is a better name."

"I think so, too," she said. "It's fancy."

There was a pause. To distract her, I asked, "And your uncle? Is he still called Moose?"

The girl smiled, blood rising to her cheeks. Same old Moose, I thought.

"You knew my uncle?" she asked, with excitement. "Before?"

"A little," I said noncommittally. "Before what?"

"Everything that happened," she said, and some memory grazed me, then, some disturbing thing I'd heard about Moose. I couldn't call it back. "He's still called Moose," was all she said.

I had been trying, in as relaxed a manner as possible, to steer us from her room in the direction of the front stairs. But just as I began my gimping descent, just as I was beginning to rejoice at having slithered from this potential debacle without having so much as roused the suspicions of my young hostess—just then, a shadow of prudence fell over her. "Don't you . . . want to leave a message? Or a note?" she asked, pattering down the stairs behind me.

"No, that's okay." I was struggling with the front door.

"But I—I thought you—" Even as she helped me open it, I felt the beat of worry in her, which provoked in me a corresponding guilt, as if I'd nabbed the family silver and were about to make a run for it.

"Tell your mom I'm sorry I missed—"

"What's your—"

But I was out the door, loping across the lawn—a freakish sight that must have been—away from her.

As I hurried back to Mary Cunningham's, I was gripped by jealousy so sharp and unexpected that it felt like sickness. I wanted that girl. She was mine, she should have been mine; even her name was mine. I wanted that house, that life; the kid with cancer—I wanted it. I wanted children, people around me. I wanted to send a young Charlotte into the world to live a different life from mine.

Such feelings of envy and remorse were so alien to me that I hardly knew how to respond. There was a voice that spoke to me at times of internal duress in exactly the way I spoke to Grace: briskly reassuring at first, and if that didn't work, brusque to the point of bullying. All my life

I had heard that voice, and when its scolding was not enough to still the fear in me, I took action—walked, danced, made phone calls—whatever was required to stop the whining. I despised whining, my own more than anyone's.

But now I was too tired to move. I collapsed onto the daybed Mary Cunningham kept in her front room, unable yet to attempt the stairs, and decided I would inquire that very evening about the precise contents of that swank liquor cabinet I'd noticed in her living room. In the Midwest you could usually count on a decent stock, even at an old lady's house. My face ached and throbbed; I'd stayed out too long. Upstairs, when I wiped off my pancake makeup with the special creams Dr. Fabermann had given me, my monstrous reflection looked more angry and swollen than it had in days. Like a newborn, I thought, exchanging looks with my frantic, scalded eyes—a newborn howling in pain and outrage.

I soaked a cotton pad in vitamin E oil and gently swabbed my face. I spoke to it in tones that were uncharacteristically soothing. "There, there, come on now," I said, "it's not so bad," dabbing the oil on my hot skin. Everything will be fine. This is the angry healing phase, that's all. It will end and then you'll have a new face—your old face but new again, like Ellen's house. This is your Charlotte, I thought, looking at myself in the mirror. This is your Charlotte, and you must take good care of her so she'll grow up to be a beautiful girl, and live an extraordinary life.

# Chapter Two

*It was almost* a new year, 199–, by the time I ceased malingering and returned to New York. There, Dr. Martin Miller, plastic surgeon-cum-society dinner guest, performed a second operation to "fine tune" my bone-grafted nose, my crooked eyelids, and my cheekbones: the tools of my trade, you might say. Dr. Miller, who was married to a model, normally devoted his reconstructive powers to making wealthy, attractive people look even more attractive—not scrapping with the "gross disfiguration" that follows cataclysmic trauma to the face. But he'd given nips and tucks and blasts of suction to enough of my friends that he took me on as a favor. He worked from photographs, which of course I had in bulk, and would do his best, he said, to make me look like myself.

"After such a trauma, Charlotte," he warned, "restoration will always fall short of perfection."

"I was never perfect," I said. "In fact, I'm expecting some improvements on the original."

Grace came back to New York with me in mid-December so I wouldn't have to face my empty apartment alone. I had lived for seven years on the twenty-fifth floor of a modern high-rise at the end of a cul de sac on East Fifty-second Street, so my view encompassed the East River, the bottom of Roosevelt Island and Long Island City. The apartment was in better shape than I'd feared; Anastasia, my alcoholic cleaning woman (as I had discovered when the vodka in my freezer turned to solid ice), had gone so far as to shampoo the wall-to-wall carpet, so the place looked better than usual. The doorman had been forwarding my mail and Grace had paid my mortgage and bills from my savings, so aside from the diminished balance in my account, no awful surprises awaited me. Grace stayed two weeks, nursing me through my second operation until the bandages came off and the ointment was out of my eyes. On the day before she left, we took a cab to Central Park and wandered in the aching cold, I wearing my now standard uniform of a head scarf (wool, for the change in season), dark glasses and pancake makeup, Grace in the black mink coat Frank had given her last Christmas.

"Watch out no one sprays that coat," I said.

"Sprays it?"

"With paint. You know, animal rights."

Grace laughed. "I thought you meant someone might pee on me."

"Jesus. Is that what you think goes on in New York?"

"Worse," she said sweetly.

A weird sequence of weather events had left a thin skin of ice around every tree and branch and twig. Each time the wind blew, a splintery groan issued from all directions at once.

"What will you do after I leave?" Grace asked.

"Finish getting better," I said, pulling the scarf tighter around my face. "Unleash myself on the world."

"And then what?"

"Isn't that something? Considering where I started?"

"I mean what will you do? How will you live?" Her face was sharp with worry.

"Stop," I said.

We stood in silence. Grace looked at the sky. She was one of those people who so overestimate their own subtlety that they end up divulging their worst fears in detail. I knew she thought my life was ruined.

"You can always come back," she said, "if you feel like it."

"After five months in Rockford! I'll have convulsions if I go back."

"Oh, please," Grace said, "spare me that act."

During my recovery from my second operation, I let my machine answer the phone, watched a lot of TV and became an unofficial monitor of East River boat traffic. It was far too cold to sit on my balcony, so I watched the slow parade from the soft white upholstery of my sectional couch:

bright red tugboats and blue-and-white police boats and long flats of garbage held down by nets. I smoked Merits into a giant zinc ashtray. When I called people, I pretended I was still in Rockford, and when sirens or honking horns from the FDR managed to vault the twenty-five floors to where I sat, I pressed the mute button.

Why didn't I urge my friends to bring me casseroles and groceries and lounge with me on my sectional couch? Because I was weak. Oh, yes, that *is* the time when you need people most, I assured myself as the silence thumped at my ears. But you have to resist. Because once they've seen you like this, once they've witnessed your dull, uneven hair and raspy voice, your hesitancy and cringing need for love, your smell—the smell of your weakness!—they'll never forget, and long after you've regained your vitality, after you yourself have forgotten these exhibits of your weakness, they'll look at you and *still see them*.

Late one afternoon, I heard the machine pick up as I watched the early darkness fall over Long Island City. It was Anthony Halliday, the detective. I'd forgotten him.

"You returned a call from me a couple of months ago," he said. "I've been leaving you messages since then."

I had a dim recollection of someone telling me this detective was in a mental hospital, but my memories of the Rockford convalescence were already so muted and strange that I couldn't be sure. He sounded sane enough. I waited a half hour and called him back.

"Anthony Halliday," he answered.

"Charlotte Swenson," I countered.

"Charlotte Swenson." He sounded pleased to hear from me. "Are you back in New York?"

"Not yet."

"I understand you had a serious car accident."

"Yes," I said, then faltered, unwilling to elaborate. "So what's this about?"

"A guy disappeared a few months ago," the detective said. "He went by the name of 'Z.' I understand you knew him."

"I knew who he was."

In the small and protean circle of nightclubs where for years I'd spent a portion of my time, Z had become something of a fixture in the months before my accident. He was one of those people whom it was impossible, and slightly unpleasant, to imagine in daylight.

"What does that mean?" I asked. "Disappeared."

"No one's seen him since August."

"Do they think something happened to him?"

" 'They' is me, at this point," he said. "The police aren't really involved."

"Why are you looking for him?"

"Hey," he said, and laughed. "I'm asking the questions."

"Well, that's not much fun for me."

Was I flirting with this detective, this Anthony Halliday? It had been so long, I wasn't even sure.

"I'd like to meet with you when you're back in New York," he said. "When will that be?"

"Couple of weeks."

"I'll call you in three," he said. "Meantime, take care. Get well."

"You, too," I said.

There was a startled pause. He hung up without saying good-bye.

It was not until late January that I finally made a lunch date with Oscar, my booker. By then my face had been healed, or "settled," as I thought of it, from the second operation, for almost a month. But I'd postponed its reckoning with the world for the simple reason that I still didn't know what I looked like. I'd spent as long as an hour staring through the ring of chalky light around my bathroom mirror; I'd held up old pictures of myself beside my reflection and tried to compare them. But my sole discovery was that in addition to not knowing what I looked like now, I had never known. The old pictures were no help; like all good pictures, they hid the truth. I had never kept a bad one—this was one of my cardinal rules, photographically speaking. One: never let someone take your picture until you're ready, or the result will almost certainly be awful. Two: never keep bad pictures of yourself for any reason, sentimental or otherwise. Bad pictures reveal you in exactly the light you wish never to be seen, and not only will they be found, if you keep them, but invariably by the single person in the world you least want to see you that way.

Now I'd made a new discovery: bad pictures were the only ones that could show you what you actually looked like. I would have killed for one.

Eventually I gave up, and made the date with Oscar.

We met at Raw Feed, a restaurant in the West Twenties whose front man was Jess DeSoto, a garrulous male model and my friend. I arrived early and stood outside for several minutes, touching my hair and face, leaping away from the glass doors each time people approached to go in or out. It felt like years, not months, since anyone had seen me.

Jess DeSoto was part of my generation of models. I'd worked with him countless times over the years, slept with him twice while waiting out a rainstorm in Barbados, attended his wedding, and bought a silver rattle at Barney's when Geo, his little boy, was born. Now he gave me one of those warm, flustered hellos you give to people you know you should know, but don't. I looked straight into his eyes and told him I was meeting Oscar, awaiting the crack of recognition, his embarrassed laughter and passionate hug of apology. Nothing. "This way," he said, and with his swaggering walk led me to a booth along the wall and set two menus down. "Enjoy," he said, and hurried off to greet another party.

I slid into the booth. My encounter with Jess affected me like a cuff to the head, leaving behind it a slightly blinkered calm. I watched the winter light pour through the plate-glass windows and waited for Oscar to come and set things right.

Other people I knew passed my table: Annette Blanque, my Paris agent; Sutie Wa, a model friend; Mitch and Hasam, club promoters-cum-Hollywood consultants on a remake of *Saturday Night Fever* that hovered perpetually on the verge of production. Each one of these people looked at me in the particular way people do inside the fashion world: a quick, ravenous glance that demands beauty or power as its immediate reward. And then they looked away, as if what they had seen were not just unfamiliar, but without possibility. I ordered a vodka martini and lit a cigarette. The waiter came and asked me not to smoke.

Oscar kissed me hello on both cheeks and slid into the booth, sitting at such an angle that we weren't facing each other directly. Oscar was the only black man I'd ever seen who truly looked as if he'd been raised by East Coast bluebloods. Anyone can wear J. Crew, of course; what set

Oscar apart was the disregard with which he wore far more expensive clothing—rumpled blazers, shoes without socks, cashmere slacks—all of which managed to suggest a lifetime of money. This was a triumph of pure self-invention. Oscar had begun his life as someone else, but who that was seemed impolite to ask, when Oscar had taken such pains to efface him. The only clues I had were two thick scars on his left forearm, a tinge of a Caribbean accent (audible when he was tired) and, of course, his shadow self: that caricature that clings to each of us, revealing itself in odd moments when we laugh or fall still, staring brazenly from certain bad photographs. After the accident, I had lost the power to see people's shadow selves, but as my vision improved, and as the fog burned off whichever cerebral lobe I required for this visual archeology, the shadows had slowly been returning. Oscar's was a portrait of sheer grief, a face so anguished it resembled a death's head. Not that Oscar himself looked anything like this; he had a lively, beautiful face and perfect white teeth (not a single cavity, he'd told me). It was only occasionally, when he dragged on a cigarette, that I glimpsed the other—a nagging, flickering presence. I had been studying people's shadow selves for many years, but Oscar's still had the power to shock me—so gaping was its contrast to his apparent self. Yet this was often the case in the fashion world, where beauty, the best disguise of all, was so commonplace.

"Well well well," Oscar said, glancing at me. "Well well."

"Well?"

"Better than I expected."

"Thanks," I said dryly. "Different, though."

"Oh, yes."

"Did you recognize me?"

Oscar snorted. His business, after all, was the business of sight, of recognizing what he'd never seen before. "Through the window," he said haughtily.

At this news, I relaxed. "Different how?"

His eyes moved over me in the appraising survey peculiar to my line of work, when someone takes in your face, your bones, your eyes, and calculates their worth. You hold very still for that look. "Uneven," he said, "for one thing."

"Oscar, you have to tell me. I need to know."

"Oh, Oscar will, darling," he said. "Just give him time."

Oscar had been my booker since I first came to New York at twenty-one, claiming to be nineteen, with a few Marshall Field's ads in my book. He'd masterminded my rise to almost-almost-stardom, then partnered me through my slow minuet down a gauntlet of catalogue jobs whose end, mercifully, I still had not reached. I'd known him fourteen years in all, during which I'd allowed myself to age at approximately two-year intervals, so that now, at thirty-five, I was allegedly twenty-eight. And as my career trajectory had flattened and begun to sink, Oscar's had risen steadily, and I'd followed him from agency to agency until now, at Femme, he booked mostly stars. But he'd never been a shit to me. We'd known each other too long.

I ordered escargot, and Oscar filled me in on rumors of drug addiction, plastic surgery and egregious behavior among "huge girls," as top models are admiringly known by their colleagues. Girl-girl affairs were the new fad, he told me; models shacking up together over the violent objections of their rich, powerful and occasionally gun-toting boyfriends.

"Have you ever done that?" Oscar asked. "Been with a girl?"

"Never," I said.

"Nor I," he said, and laughed.

My escargot arrived, and I let one slide down my throat, luxuriating in the taste of garlic. After the accident, my sense of taste had been dulled; then, in the past few weeks, flavors had begun rocketing across my palette.

"Business is good?" I asked.

"Strange," he said. "This mania for real people is becoming a full-fledged pain in the ass."

"You mean powerful women in pantyhose, that kind of thing?"

"That was unpleasant enough," Oscar said. "Now it's people in the news. You haven't heard?"

"Oscar," I said. "I've been in the Midwest."

A few months ago, he told me, a booker at Elite had spotted a beautiful, starving Hutu refugee in *Time*. Somehow, through Doctors Without Borders, this booker managed to track the refugee down and fly her and her eight children to New York, where "Hutu," as she was known (her name having been deemed unpronounceable) promptly shot covers for *Marie Claire* and Italian *Vogue* and garnered an avalanche of publicity for Elite. Not to be outdone, Laura, the CEO of *Femme*, noticed a beautiful North Korean girl in a story about famine.

"She says to me, 'Oscar, get me that girl,'" Oscar said, in a perfect imitation of Laura's heavy Czech accent. "So I embark on this mad goose chase, coming home from work and ordering dinner for my Korean translator, Victor, so the two of us can start calling North Korea, where it's already the next day, looking for the girl in the picture. After a week of this we track down her father, and Victor tries to explain that we want to fly the girl in the *New York Times* picture to New York, her father thinks we're threatening to kidnap her, he's begging us, No, please, I have no money . . . Lord give me strength to go on! Anyhow, she's living in my guest room as we speak. Five-foot-one."

"How weird," I said.

"Oscar is in complete accord."

"Is she working?"

"*Mademoiselle* did something, *Allure*. We'll see what happens. Meanwhile, Laura has me chasing these two Ukrainian studs she saw on CNN working on an oil rig that capsized. My fervent hope is that these two can inherit my guest room from Miss Korea. But I'm not sure I'll have the heart to move her—she sobs in there every night, poor angel. She bought this enormous Sunkist orange that she keeps on the windowsill, and I keep telling her, 'Eat it, darling. There are hundreds of thousands of these in New York City. Eat the frigging orange, already!' But she just holds it in her hands and looks at it."

"Why don't you send her home?"

Oscar shrugged. "She's desperate for money," he said. "Her family sells kim chi, for pity's sake."

"But how long can it last, this reality thing?" I said. "I mean, let's face it: most people just don't look that great."

Oscar shook his head. "It would appear there's a new layer."

"The bullshit layer."

"Yet it exists," Oscar said, with a sigh, "and we must contend with it."

The lunchtime crowd at Raw Feed was beginning to thin. Now and then I noticed tourists peeking in from outside, cupping their hands around their eyes and squinting through the glass.

"What kind of work do you think I'll be able to get?" I said this nonchalantly.

Oscar was lighting a cigarette. The waiter, I noted, did not intervene this time. "I've been watching you," he said, "asking myself if it's possible."

"I love it! You're booking five-foot-one Koreans and you have to ask yourself if you can book me."

"Two different matters entirely," Oscar said mildly. "She's a fad."

"And me?"

"You're an old dog," he said, with affection.

"I have a crazy idea. Want to hear it?"

"Always, darling."

"Relaunch me," I said. "Pretend I'm a new girl. Because Oscar, *no one recognizes me.*"

This revelation did not appear to shock him, as I'd thought it would. "You're too old for a new girl," he said.

"I don't have a single line on my face! It's like I've had a facelift—I could be twenty-three." I was leaning forward, raising my voice, thus violating one of my cardinal rules: never let people see what you want.

"Twenty-three is too old," Oscar said, exhaling smoke. "And you don't look twenty-three, dear, much as Oscar loves you."

A wave of exhaustion felled me; if I'd closed my eyes, I think I could have slept. "Will you think about it, please?" I asked, as he paid the bill.

"Certainly," he said. "But you should think about your alternatives. As I imagine you were already doing, before your accident."

"What makes you say that?"

"You're a reasonable person," Oscar replied.

Outside the restaurant, he pulled the lapels of his beautiful coat tight around him. He wasn't wearing a scarf, and the skin on his neck looked chalky and dry. As his breath appeared in white plumes, the death's head blinked at me, a tattered ghost escaping from its rictus mouth and melting into the atmosphere. "Where are you headed?" he asked.

"To the dogs, apparently," I said.

I walked Oscar west, in the direction of Femme, along streets that might as well have photographed in black-and-white, so empty were they of color. Car alarms went off in whooping succession, birdcalls in a strange mechanical forest.

"Have you considered seeing a shrink?" Oscar asked me.

"Oh, that's great," I said, turning to him. "You can't figure out how to relaunch me, so I should see a shrink."

"No." He sighed heavily. "Because you're in la-la land."

We circled the block where the agency was, yet avoided walking past it. I sensed Oscar's reluctance to go. "You've been through something terrible," he said. "That's why people go to shrinks."

"Do you? Go to a shrink?"

Oscar beamed his white smile at me, but the anguished shadow face was right there, peering out from behind it. "Nothing bad has ever happened to me," he said. "My life has been one enormous bottle of Karo syrup."

"Poor you," I said, and laughed, my head back, so that suddenly I was looking above the buildings, up at the winter sky. And then I saw the sign. It snagged my gaze and held it, an old advertisement painted on the side of a brick building. Griffin's Shears, it read. The paint was faded but still legible, a faint chalky blue, and beside the words I made out the silhouette of a pair of scissors. Without realizing it, I had stopped walking. We were on Seventh Avenue at Twenty-second Street.

"What?" Oscar said.

I didn't answer. I didn't know. "Look at that," I said.

Oscar looked up and down, then swiveled his head. "What?"

"That old ad! Griffin's Shears."

Oscar looked at me.

"It's like a ghost," I said.

We stood there, looking at the ad. I felt moved by it in some way I couldn't explain. It reminded me of Rockford, of its factories and smokestacks and industry. A glimpse of New York's shadow face.

"I have eighty titanium screws inside my head," I said, still watching the sign.

"Don't say such things," Oscar murmured.

"The bones were all crushed."

Now he turned to me, with surprise, admiration, maybe, and something else: love, I guess. We'd been close for so many years, that confluence of work and social life that makes for a certain kind of friendship. But I knew, as Oscar did, I think, that we wouldn't go on as we had.

"If you give up," he said, "I'll lose my faith in everything."

"I never give up," I told him.

I hadn't brought a man home with me since before the accident, but no sooner had I hugged Oscar good-bye that afternoon than I sensed my months of abstention coming to an end. A knot of desire had formed in my belly, tightening as day went on so that by evening I'd forgotten everything but the need to cut it. I was not like most women. For me, the sexual act had nothing to do with love, or rarely. On the contrary, the less I cared for or even knew a man, the more easily I lost myself in his physical company. I didn't mind awkwardness—I was good at asking for what I wanted and making sure I got it. I liked not knowing what he would do or want, and I didn't worry much about my own performance; as I saw it, any man who succeeded at picking me up with so little effort, with no strings attached and without having to pay for it, should consider himself to be having an extremely good day. I'd been a safe-sex practitioner since before the phrase existed, not for health reasons so much as a basic squeamishness at the idea of mingling cells. Embracing, kissing—even the grittier exchanges I had no problem with, but the things I couldn't see, the molecules and atoms—those should stay apart, I felt. The onslaught of AIDS had made this qualm easier to justify; men had finally stopped bitching about the condoms.

There are lots of ways to find casual sex, but I had a favorite routine. It began with dining alone at one of several East Side restaurants near my apartment, places frequented by businessmen and diplomats with some connection to the United Nations. I would order a salad and wait for a glass of wine to arrive at my table. Then I'd either wave my thanks, or, if I found the man attractive, make my greeting slightly warmer, so that he knew he was welcome at my table. I kept conversation to a minimum; if I let it go on long, I'd found, the man ceased to be attractive no matter what he looked like.

Tonight I was relieved to discover that even with my new, indeterminate face, the ritual took no longer than usual to complete. His name was

Paul Shepherd. He had a pale blond beard and hair just a shade or two darker, like sand. He worked for the World Bank in Hong Kong but was originally from Minnesota. Despite his courtly, diffident manner, it was obvious he was a regular cheater. So many were. I felt glad to be the treat, rather than the one they slunk home to.

Inside my apartment, I poured us each a glass of scotch. Paul Shepherd wandered to the living room, stood at the sliding-glass door to the balcony and looked outside at my (I must say) spectacular view. The balconies in my building were staggered, which made for a jumbled exterior but gave the impression, from inside, that you were the only one with a balcony, that there was nothing above you.

"You're midwestern," Paul Shepherd surprised me by saying.

"What makes you think that?"

"This apartment, the feel. I don't know. Am I right?"

"I'm from Chicago."

Like all men in my experience, Paul Shepherd vastly enjoyed being right. "Oh, yeah? What part?"

"Actually, not Chicago," I said, to my own surprise. "Rockford, Illinois."

"Never been."

"It's hell on earth."

His brows rose. "Bad luck, talking that way about your hometown."

I laughed. "That may explain the last five months of my life."

Paul Shepherd said nothing. We looked at the view, Queensborough Bridge to the north, Long Island City's broken industrial silhouette to the south. I thought of the few things I'd brought with me when I first drove to New York in my battered green Fiat: my grandfather's gold watch, packed in a suitcase that was stolen while I stopped at a Denny's on my way; my grandparents' letters to each other from the summer my grandmother spent in New York before they married, letters full of wit and play, her confidence in the safety of writing by lamplight at 135th and Riverside. But I'd lost them during one move or another, and now all I remembered was the sepia tone of their ink and my grandmother's neat, ruled penmanship. I felt a thud of regret. Oh, for God's sake, I chided myself, how often do you think about your grandparents—once a year? Would you look at those letters if you had them? Weren't keepsakes just a wee bit quaint in a world where you could travel anywhere in a matter of hours; where you could call Bangladesh from a pay phone on the beach? I'd had a diamond necklace ripped from my throat years before, a present from Hansen, my fiancé. After that, I gave everything I had of value to Grace. Let her keep it, I'd thought—in Rockford, land of small objects, where my valuables would be safe, at least, if not really mine.

"Penny for your thoughts," Paul Shepherd said, and I jumped. I was lapsing into reveries without knowing it—a form of mental incontinence I associated with spending too much time alone. He was sitting on my couch, and I sat beside him, now, tucking my legs under me. I hadn't seen his shadow self. Often I found it by asking myself what the person's opposite would be; what he was working against, compensating for. But so far Paul Shepherd was a nice man with a sandy beard and a wife and several children he hadn't mentioned. I could always tell. Divorced men spoke up instantly, proclaiming their status. The rotten ones (and I could usually spot these, too) implied or even said they were divorced, but were actually married. I'd occasionally had the urge to track down one of their wives and give her a call, for her own protection. "Your husband doesn't love you," I imagined saying. "I suggest you get rid of him."

I leaned close to Paul Shepherd. This was always interesting: the moment when the surface first peeled away and what was underneath— desire, perversion, whatever it might be—moved into the light. The truth. I wanted to see it. Everyone was a liar, blah-blahing their way through life, pretending to be good and constant, to have and to hold and all that. Everyone was a politician, wearing a pious face until the last possible moment when the press unearthed a taste for child amputees or a beheaded mistress chained to a radiator. And I'd been pious, too, at first—I'd believed my own act until the pressure of sustaining it became too much. Since then, I'd sought out the opposite: I wanted to be the child amputee or the mistress, to make my domain the dark corners where I could see the things people took such pains to hide from everyone else. I put my hands on Paul Shepherd's chest and kissed his neck. He groaned and leaned back. We were strangers, with nothing to hide from each other.

We adjourned to the bedroom. I was in something of a lather, having been deprived for so long of not just sex, but any sort of physical contact. I felt clumsy, irrationally afraid that my face would be damaged. Paul

41

seemed pretty starved himself, and the whole thing was over quickly. We lay there awhile and I thought we might begin again, but he stood up to go, murmuring something about an early meeting.

And it was only as he rose from the bed, his body illuminated by the colored lights of the city, that I caught the glint of calculation behind his eyes, a cold, blank set to his face. His shadow self, and not a nice one.

When all else failed, I found it by looking at people when they thought they couldn't be seen—when they hadn't arranged themselves for anyone.

He dressed, used the bathroom, then joined me in the living room, where I sat in my silk kimono, smoking. He leaned down from behind me and put his arms around my neck, and in the bright light he was kindly again. But I'd seen it.

"I have to go," he said, retrieving his coat and scarf and briefcase. It was ten forty-five. I was grateful not to be the one heading back out into dark New York. At the door, he handed me his card. "Give me a call if you're ever in Hong Kong."

As he stepped from my apartment into the hall, I said, "Just a minute."

He stopped. I sensed impatience, the cool mathematician prowling behind his sandy face. "Yes?"

"How do I look?" I asked.

"What do you mean?"

"Look at me," I said, and he did. "If you were going to describe me, what would you say?"

He took a long look. The light in the hall was warm and flattering. I found myself holding my breath.

"You look tired," he said, and the two halves of him fused in a moment of humanity. It wasn't what I'd hoped for, yet I felt relieved.

"Good night, Paul Shepherd," I said.

# Chapter Three

*Toward the end* of her bicycle ride, Ellen's daughter, Charlotte, paused in Shorewood Park to watch the water-skiers from beside the spindly bleachers arranged on the riverbank for the Wednesday and Friday night water shows. One wore a red bathing suit. He buzzed in Charlotte's direction, hewing the river in two until she hid her face. But it wasn't Scott Hess. All summer long he had haunted her, and she hadn't seen him yet.

Unsure of the time, she resumed pedaling toward home. They were having dinner tonight with Uncle Moose, a biannual ritual that always roused in Charlotte an anticipatory flutter, some peculiar alloy of expectation and dread. She found herself rushing, now, streaking past the restored portion of Rockford's original marshland—brackish water, broken sticks—past modest houses and raw-throated dogs and lawns that smelled of the river. She skimmed under the Spring Creek Bridge and ploughed the paved jogging path beside the old railroad tracks, tame and manicured now, surrounded by grass.

Near the YMCA she stopped to cool off. A man in a yellow shirt sat cross-legged on the Rock River's grassy bank, one arm in a sling. Charlotte leaned her bike against a picnic table and moved closer to him. She took off her glasses, letting the lush greens mingle with the river's muddy brown. Rockford was a nineteenth-century town, bisected north to south by the Rock River. On the west side, across the water from where Charlotte stood, were a smattering of brick factory buildings and a neglected downtown; north of these were the industrialists' old riverside homes, still cushioned by dense trees and thick, fragrant lawns. A fatigue seemed to hang over these original parts of the city, as if their exertions of a hundred years ago had drained them beyond recovery. Nowadays, the action lay on the river's east side, where Charlotte lived, whose vital artery was not the river at all but State Street, running west to east, accruing strip malls and superstores and condominium spuds as it moved farther from the old city center until, by the time it reached the interstate, five miles out, it encompassed six lanes of traffic.

The last time Charlotte had seen Uncle Moose, she'd been seated beside him at the country club. He was a history professor at Winnebago College: a handsome, erratic man whose attention she could never fully capture. When he'd opened his wallet to pay for dinner (insisting, despite her father's protestations), she had glimpsed inside it a picture she'd noticed before. Of water. The only picture he carried.

"What's that?" she'd asked, but Moose seemed not to hear. "That picture," she said, more softly. "What is it?"

Moose slid the picture from its cheap plastic sleeve and handed it over. It was a photograph of a river, ancient, sepia-toned, its whites bleached to snow. It had the beloved, handled look of pictures of people's children. But it was a *river*. At the bottom, someone had scratched into the negative "Rock River, 1904."

The strangeness of this had affronted Charlotte. "What's the point of it?" she asked.

Moose glanced at her with dark, skittish eyes. Charlotte sensed that she'd disappointed him. "Evidence," was all he said.

It surprised her, how many times she'd thought of that photograph in the intervening months. *Rock River, 1904.* A domed building—or had she invented it? A riverboat. Church steeples. *Evidence,* he'd said. Evidence of what?

The man on the grass had turned and was looking up at her. "Good evening," he said, with odd formality. Even without her glasses, Charlotte knew she had never seen him before. He had a long gash down one side of his face. Inside his sling she saw an arm in a cast.

"The girl in perpetual motion," he said. "Every day, on that bicycle."

A weirdo, Charlotte thought, and her interest sharpened. The man rose to his feet, as if it bothered him to sit while she was standing. He wore old khakis and had a tired adulthood about him, a relief from the evil cuteness of boys her age. He moved with a limp. Charlotte wondered what had happened to him.

"Rockford, Illinois," he said, and the curl of his accent, which she'd barely noticed, bent against her city's name. "So very ugly."

"Go back where you came from, if you don't like it," she said.

He smiled. White teeth. "That's not possible."

"Then don't call it ugly."

He studied her. "How old are you, if I may ask?"

"Sixteen."

"You're pretty."

She narrowed her eyes. "I'm not."

"Unusual."

"That's not the same."

"It lasts longer."

Liar, Charlotte thought, but she was flattered. Her build was slight but very strong; "wiry" was a word people used to describe her, though in her own view, she was distinguished by a near-total absence of breasts. She had waited, hoping they would arrive, erupt, emerge—rise from the bony tray of her chest like two lovely cakes. Last year, she had ordered a pressure device from the back pages of a magazine (it arrived in plain brown paper) and squeezed it between her palms each morning and night; at a later, more desperate juncture, she had swallowed fifty green pills of dubious provenance on successive nights, pills that made her urine smell like lavender.

"Boys don't like me," she told the man, emboldened by the very fact that he was a stranger.

"They'll grow up," he said, "and admire your eyes."

"I wear glasses." She was holding them in her hand.

He scanned her face as if trying to imagine it. Charlotte resisted the urge to put her glasses on. "Contacts hurt," she explained.

"Glasses are normal," he said.

Across the river, the sun had vanished behind downtown like a coin in a slot. Charlotte wondered how long she'd been standing there. She straddled her bike. "Well. *Adios*."

The man raised a hand to his injured face. An indeterminate gesture, part salute, part wave.

Charlotte sailed the short distance to the Y, then peeled around it to the expressway. She felt jittery, breathless. In life she was secretive: a hoarder of thoughts and fears and weaknesses—most of all her hopes, lest they be diminished. Yet in the presence of strangers, confidences forced themselves from Charlotte almost indiscriminately, drummed out by some pressure she was not even aware of. Later, she would reassure herself that no one would ever find out—the people didn't know her name! That was the beauty of it.

She scampered her bike across the expressway, pavement hot under her tennis shoes, white lights of distant cars pulsing toward her in the dusty sunset. Her own street dead-ended against the expressway's opposite side; she pedaled up the long driveway and left her bike in the shed. Her mother watched from the kitchen window as Charlotte ran across the lawn. Ellen was dressed for dinner, her hair in a clip.

"Where have you been?" she cried. "We're leaving in ten minutes!"

"Don't worry."

"Go. Go. You're all sweaty."

"I'm going!"

In her bedroom, Charlotte paused to check on her fish, veiled, mysterious creatures suspended in saltwater. They had an air of great knowing, as if this room, this house, this life of hers could be understood by the fish in silent, watery reverse. Charlotte had worked for nearly a year at Fish World, where she had a discount.

She showered quickly and returned to the kitchen, where Ricky and her father were beginning a game of chess. Harris had taught him in the hospital; their matches could straddle days.

"How was your ride?" her father asked.

"Good. Hot."

She stood at the refrigerator pouring a glass of juice, her father's gaze jabbing her between the shoulder blades. "You thought any more about this school thing?" he said at last, with strained nonchalance.

She drained the glass. "Nope." She was thinking of the man by the river, feeling the beat of residual excitement.

Her mother hurried into the kitchen, high heels clipping the tiles. "Come on, come on," she said. "We're late."

"Ding-ding, Mom," Ricky said. "We've been waiting for you."

They took Ellen's new Lexus, gliding over the expressway in the silky beginnings of dusk, Ricky flopped against Charlotte in the backseat as if she were an element of the upholstery. In the rearview mirror, Harris observed this physical ease between his kids with a kind of wonderment; when he tried to hold Ricky—even touch him, sometimes—his son flinched away like a deer. Ricky's hair had grown back fine and dark; he was beautiful, this boy of thirteen, beautiful in a way that unnerved people, made them gape at him in the supermarket, the hospital. Harris was embarrassed by this beauty of his son's, as if it bespoke some indulgence or folly of his own. But it was all Ellen's: the olive skin, the long black eyes.

As they crossed the river on the Spring Creek Bridge, Charlotte glanced north and saw the water-skiers still there. It wasn't Scott Hess, but she sank into the memory nevertheless: a party last fall, the beginning of sophomore year, when she'd smoked pot and gotten stoned, her first time. Skidding, uncontrollable laughter, dipping French fries into mustard, then dabbing them in Equal, which was all the party giver's diet-conscious mother had around. Everyone swarming into a purple Jeep with Scott Hess: athlete, star, junior, a boy to whom Charlotte never had spoken directly. Squashed against him in front, she'd grown less aware of the wriggling kids around her, less aware of R.E.M. on the stereo, and more aware of the heat issuing from Scott Hess's upper arm. A sick, painful longing came loose in her. Each time Scott turned the wheel, Charlotte pressed harder against him as if by accident, and he groaned, nursing football injuries.

As it happened, Charlotte lived nearest to Scott, so after he'd dropped everyone off it was just the two of them in the purple Jeep, making polite chat about the game and Scott's bruised knee and dislocated shoulder, not to mention the black eye he'd sustained in a locker room fight two weeks ago. "And then there's the stuff you don't see," he said. "My back's shot— I'm on painkillers half the time, and what about this?" He brandished aloft his left thumb. "I can't even straighten it all the way!" Charlotte only half-listened. She felt like an old radio issuing weird, splintering frequencies; she would perish if she couldn't touch Scott Hess, or make him touch her.

Two blocks from her house, she said, "Hey, stop the car a sec." Quizzically, Scott pulled over and Charlotte shimmied close and kissed him on the lips, actually took his face in her hands ("Where did you get the guts?" her friends asked later, but it had taken no guts at all), and Scott, though initially startled, responded to her ministrations with rising enthusiasm. Soon he was driving again—toward an old orchard, it turned out, wizened trees contorted against the cloudy night.

"What kind of trees are those?" Charlotte asked, making conversation as Scott fought with the knobs controlling her seat.

"Pear I think." He'd pushed her seat back to a horizontal position and was yanking open her jeans. "You know, from back in the day." Then he climbed on top of her (supporting himself with his un-dislocated arm), and with one or two grunts of pain from his wounds dispensed with her virginity and collapsed on top of her in an apparent faint. It hurt. Charlotte pressed her eyes shut, amazed at how much it hurt, yet beneath the pain she felt the hunger still, completely unslaked. Scott's head lay on her chest like a meteorite. Charlotte opened her eyes and watched pear trees drop their clenched leaves on the windshield. Finally, maneuvering her mouth close to Scott's ear, she whispered, "Can you, like, do something else?"

No response. Then, at last, some intimation of consciousness bestirred Scott's bulk, and he lifted his head and muttered, "I look like Superman to you?" which Charlotte took to be a joke, an ironic commentary on his paltry efforts thus far, until Scott hauled himself from her, groaning like an old ship being lifted from the sea to have its barnacles scraped, looked down into her face with his small, blank eyes and said, "I don't even know you."

An instant later, it seemed, he was driving toward Charlotte's house while she yanked up her underwear, barely managing to zip her jeans before she found herself standing at the mouth of her driveway. "Thanks," she said, not entirely managing to purge her voice of sarcasm. Scott Hess looked straight ahead and said nothing.

Charlotte had assumed he would keep quiet about what had happened—what was there to brag about? But by Monday morning everyone in her small class had been alerted to the fact that Charlotte was a mad slut who'd thrown herself at Scott and begged him for it doggie style, that she'd given him five blow jobs and still wanted more—that she was a nympho animal who couldn't get enough. Walking through school that Monday had been like finding herself abruptly radioactive, or the locus of a reverse magnetic force field; no one could seem to come near her. Boys sniggered uneasily at the sight of her; girls folded into groups from which her three best friends gazed at her helplessly, passengers through the windows of a train she had missed by one minute. No one else would look at her, but never had they been so aware, so keenly aware of her presence—it sent a tremor through their ranks that Charlotte could practically hear. But what had she done? She asked herself that question throughout the day, and after school, when her toxicity had abated to a point where her three best friends could approach, she'd told them what happened and put the question to them: what had she done wrong? Two of them were sleeping with their boyfriends—how was this different? No one seemed to know.

"Next time, don't do it unless you're in love," said Laurel, now the sole remaining virgin in their quartet.

"I was in love," Charlotte said.

After that, Scott laughed when she passed him in the hall—limping from his wounds, on crutches for two weeks with an Ace bandage around his foot until torn knee ligaments sidelined him for good. As long as he was with other boys, he laughed, but if it was just the two of them in the hall, he turned his face away. He was afraid of her, Charlotte saw this clearly.

Later, she came to understand that her mistake had been largely one of timing. By the end of sophomore year, she regularly heard girls talk of jumping the bones of boys they liked with no mention of love. And yet a taint still clung to Charlotte. She was seen as odd, perverse. Of course, had she been pretty—had she looked like her mother, for instance—the situation would have been different. Charlotte understood this with a deep, angry ache: There were two worlds, and in one of them, everything was harder. No one came to you, and if you went to them, you were likely to be punished for it.

Of course she was changing schools. To escape from the people who knew her. To vacate a world where the slot she'd been allotted felt minuscule.

Now, in the car, she said, "Mom, I think I'm going to add a new fish."

"What kind?" her mother asked, but Charlotte heard her distraction—they were late to meet Moose—and didn't bother answering.

Moose and his second wife, Priscilla, were already seated in the vast carpeted dining room at a corner table overlooking the Rock River. The Rockford Country Club was poised on a bluff directly across from Shorewood Park, where Charlotte had stopped to watch the water-skiers this afternoon. The bleachers and water-ski jump were still visible just beyond Moose's shoulder in the blue twilight. As always, Moose sat sideways, disliking to face the room head-on but disliking equally the vulnerability of having his back to it.

"Moose!" Harris shouted, offering his hand and then stepping back quickly as Moose rose from his chair. "What're you drinking there? Martini? Why not? Darling, what can I get you? Kids?" He barked the drink orders at the waitress, a college girl home for summer vacation, then heard himself and sat down, abashed. Moose awakened in Harris a manic desire to seize control, as if he were trying desperately to stave off some communal embarrassment.

"How's work, Harris?" Moose asked in his curious monotone, when everyone was seated.

"Can't complain. You?"

"Good," Moose affirmed, nodding slowly. "Very good."

Harris noted, with some satisfaction, that his brother-in-law looked like hell. Still handsome, yes (he grudgingly allowed), in a heavy-browed, almost adolescent way that invoked his mythological past, which Ellen still cherished. But Moose's eyes were dull, as if he were asleep behind them. His shirt was wrinkled, his hair a mess, and he managed the unlikely feat of looking bloated and deflated simultaneously. Yet for all that, he retained a certain kingliness, an orb of superiority that girded him even now, in his disgrace. Harris found this exasperating.

"What happened with the Kool-Aid wine coolers?" Priscilla asked Harris. She was a nurse at Rockford Memorial, a slender woman whose cropped hair and delicate face would have counted as gamine in New York or Paris, but in Rockford were thought to be tomboyish, odd.

"Tested badly," Harris said. "People thought it was trying to sell booze to kids."

"Imagine!" Priscilla said, with an impish widening of eyes.

"We get paid either way." Harris spoke this wearily. He'd given up trying to explain that he had no vested interest in the products his firm, Demographics in America, tested on Rockford's consummately American population. No one believed him.

"Dad, tell about the cereal," Charlotte said.

"That's a strange one," Harris said, forcing a laugh. "Turns out breakfast cereal treated with trace amounts of radioactivity—completely harmless, apparently—has the property of glowing just slightly." He noticed Ellen wasn't listening, and finished quickly. "They want to find out if the stigma of radioactivity is too much, or if parents will let their kids eat the stuff."

"Would you?" Priscilla asked.

"Of course not," Harris said, and glanced at Ricky, who was busy connecting many cocktail straws to make one gigantically long straw originating from his front tooth. "But they're not asking me. They're asking—well, you know." His wife was gazing across the room as if in search of someone. Who? Harris wondered.

"America," Priscilla finished.

"Right," Harris said gloomily. Forget the odd tidbits he'd saved for their collective amusement: the fiber supplements made from kudzu leaves; the permanent sunscreen. He remained in a state of perpetual astonishment at how efficiently the combined presence of his wife and her brother could transform a business he'd spent the better part of his life creating—a business whose success had attracted pollsters and politicians from every major party; that had bankrolled hand-painted Italian tiles, private schools, Ellen's new olive-green Lexus and the gargantuan mortgage payments on the house occasioned by Moose's legal debts—into a lousy, grubby way to make a buck. What are they doing that's any better? he protested silently.

"If you bring the cereal home, I'll try it," Charlotte said. But her father seemed not to hear.

They picked at black olives the size of goose eggs, carrot sticks, pairs of bread sticks sealed in plastic. The waitress brought a second round of drinks, and Moose and Harris gulped their martinis with fervor. "Fried chicken for everyone?" Harris bellowed at the group. Then to the waitress: "Fried chicken for everyone." Thursday was Fried Chicken Night.

Janey and Jessica Stevenson made a tentative essay from their parents' table and fluttered to a pause several feet behind Ricky's chair. At a smile from Harris, they ventured forward, spidery girls who looked older than Ricky, though in fact both were younger.

"I think you've got company, son," Harris said.

"Dire! You guys made it!" Ricky cried, and leapt from his chair. "Mom, I'm going outside until dinner," he said, with the slurry speed of an auctioneer.

"Mom, *may I please* go outside until dinner?" Ellen rephrased, and Ricky flung the words back at her over his shoulder as he fled the table. All of the adults, except Moose, burst into laughter. This was a new development since Ricky's illness: the more obnoxiously he behaved, the greater the hilarity he induced—loud, disproportionate laughter that Charlotte found dispiriting, like laugh tracks on sitcoms.

"He looks wonderful," Priscilla said.

"Fingers crossed," Ellen said, a zigzag of worry unsettling her face. Ricky had finished his three years of chemo last spring, and now she drove him to Chicago at the end of each month to be tested. She found it even more harrowing, this fledgling state of health—so easily crushed. After a year, his chances would improve dramatically, but the year felt endless.

"I think he's licked it," Harris said. "I think it's a thing of the past."

Charlotte said nothing. She believed her brother would be well, had believed it from the start, when he was bald and sick and petrified. Perhaps Moose believed it, too, for he was looking out the window at a last water-skier wafting in near darkness from the end of a string. Or perhaps he was too preoccupied to care. Two years out of college, Moose had been living at home and working for his father—he'd had two patents pending on small inventions he'd made involving the manufacture of fertilizer. On weekends, he applied his engineering skills to less rigorous tasks; there was a famous device he'd operated from bed with a big toe, which made a can of beer roll from a chute into his outstretched hand; he'd rigged his parents' icemaker so it coughed out red, tequila-laced cubes for his margarita parties. A consummate host was Moose, greeting his guests in outrageous paisley shirts; a fomenter of egregious acts who remained curiously detached in their midst, enjoying the revelry around him—the riotous dancing and drunken intrigue, the vomiting into planters, or (once, in winter) the burning of someone's clothing in a fireplace—from a slight but unmistakable distance.

Then, without warning, the parties stopped. Moose began to read, grinding his unpracticed eyes against page after page, groaning his way through books with an exertion that made him sweat (he'd read so little in his life), and gradually more ease, reading through the night, returning books to the Rockford Public Library in secretive piles. His fixation was the evolution of technology, wheels and gunpowder and smelting, the ramp device the Romans used to board the Carthaginian fleets, the history of clockmaking, the printing press, the chronometer, longitude. And glass—glass he returned to repeatedly, that magically liquid solid that had made possible eyeglasses, telescopes, microscopes, all manner of visual discovery; glass that in myth had surrounded Alexander the Great in the form of a bubble, allowing him to visit the bottom of the sea. For Moose had sensed that a terrible reversal was in progress, a technological disaster whereby the genius of the Industrial Revolution would be turned on people themselves; whereby human beings would be assembled from parts just as guns and boots and bicycles had been once.

This had come to him in a single afternoon, sitting beside the interstate, where he'd pulled over on his way home from a party in Wisconsin. He had not described the experience to anyone.

Nor did he share the news that he was applying to master's programs in history until he was accepted at Southern Illinois University at Carbondale, at which point he packed up and left—never to return, it had seemed to Ellen—to everyone who had known him before he became this new man. Within six blazing years, Moose transferred to a Ph.D. program at the University of Pennsylvania on the strength of his master's thesis, which he expanded into a prize-winning dissertation (*Bathe the World in Light: How the Dissemination of Clear Glass Altered Human Perception*; Oxford University Press, 1987), accepted a tenure-track job at Yale, and married his first wife, Natalia, an Argentinean completing her Film Studies dissertation (*Man Alive: Rupture and Redemption in the Films of John Cassavetes*; Soho Press, 1988). For more than a year, the couple dwelled inside a humming sphere of good fortune; Moose brought to his teaching the full arsenal of his charisma, and the students revered him.

It was not clear to anyone exactly when, during Moose's second year of teaching, Transformation Number One began giving way to Transformation Number Two. His physical appearance slipped, but then a certain slovenliness was tolerated because of his engineering background, the fact that he was still an inventor of sorts, still a presence in the labs, where unkempt hair and mustard stains on one's sweater were the norm. Then commenced what the lawyers would term, in the thousands of pages of documents generated by the criminal and civil suits filed against Moose, his "Reckless Acts in the Guise of Pedagogical Tools." In one case, he'd placed a single bullet in the chamber of a Smith & Wesson revolver during class, spun the barrel, held the gun to his own head and fired. The students were stunned, and several broke down and rushed from the classroom, until later it was agreed that Moose had removed the bullet from the gun through sleight of hand.

Several weeks later, he announced to a different class that they were embarking together on a "thought experiment": the classroom was rigged with enough explosives to blow it, and everyone inside it, to high heaven, presuming there was such a place. The explosives were controlled by a detonating device, which Moose entrusted to a group of eight randomly selected students whom he sent from the room to rove the campus and debate whether to use the devastating power in their grasp. He and the remaining students, meanwhile, would pass the time discussing humankind's ability to resist the lure of destructive technology. This dialogue began jovially enough, with a clear consensus that the "bomb" was imaginary, the "detonator" a prop—though the students did hope it would activate bells, at least, or flashing lights. But by the time they had hashed their way through cannons, rifles, machine guns, pesticides, chemical and biological weaponry, cloning, genetic manipulation, autonomous robots capable of thought, and the various bombs, to which they returned repeatedly, the class was afflicted by a collective shortness of breath.

Among those tending the detonator, a similarly jovial mood had prevailed at first—they'd been liberated from "Technology and the Human Soul" in the midafternoon. They went straight to Durfee's Sweet Shop for coffee and warm cookies, and only as they sauntered down the block sucking chocolate from under their fingernails did they realize that they'd left the detonator by the cash register—*oh, shit*—and run back for it. Then they gathered around, staring at the nondescript wedge and imagining it was real, that so much power was actually theirs, the power to destroy buildings—end lives—and a twisting, stomachy feeling overcame them. Two students began to argue for whanging the thing just to see what kind of floor show Professor Metcalf had rigged for their entertainment, while the more cautious made the point that this was a morality test, so if they chose wrong (even on purpose), their grades might suffer. As the group returned to campus, one of the gung-hos tried to snatch the detonator away from the pacifist who was guarding it, which led to a scuffle upon the floor, students hurling themselves after the detonator until a pacifist nabbed it and sprinted with it straight to the History Department office, where it was puzzled over without much seriousness until the police arrived. At that point matters turned grave, however, and a chain reaction of clanging alarms, the evacuation of a four-block radius, and a bristling accretion of helicopters, ambulances and fire trucks, climaxed in the arrival of an FBI bomb squad whose members wore bulking suits made partially of lead. Not that they planned to go inside the building; they sent a robot guided by remote control, a "small spider" who tiptoed down hallways and up stairwells on six dainty legs until it reached Moose's classroom, where it tapped through the door and informed him, in a strange robotic voice, that he was under arrest. But Moose didn't hear the spider at first; he was asleep, head on desk, inside whose middle drawer lay the bomb, directly beneath his ear. With Moose's cooperation, the FBI ferried the bomb to its special bomb-diffusing truck, a truck that would force any blast to occur vertically (thus protecting the populace), where, in the course of dismantling it, the FBI discovered that a signaling flaw had rendered the detonator useless, an error psychologists for the defense would maintain was a subliminal desire on the part of their good-hearted but mentally unbalanced client to protect his students from himself.

Moose was arrested and placed in a psychiatric unit, where an in-patient evaluation deemed him psychotic. Ultimately he pled guilty to a charge of possessing explosives in exchange for the government dropping its twenty-four counts of attempted first-degree murder, the flawed detonator having thrown an insurmountable wrench into its case. Yale accepted a large settlement from Moose's family in its civil suit against him, eager to stem the hemorrhage of scathing publicity the incident had already unleashed.

Moose was released from federal prison on time served—a full year, by then—and transferred his four-year probation to Illinois. He returned to Rockford and moved back into his old bedroom, the toe-activated beer dispenser yawning empty, ghostly above his head. His father had been felled by a stroke during the crisis, and Moose wheeled him around in a chair until a second, more devastating stroke drove him into a coma. At first, Moose himself had been virtually comatose, buried under a landslide of failure and despair, the knowledge that people who once had admired him now feared and avoided him, that his mammoth legal bills and settlement had bled his wealthy family into debt. Yet even now, a restless scurrying persisted within his brain, the beams of his technological convictions probing agitatedly for some topic on which to affix, now that he was so far away from everything. And one day, as he pushed his father's wheelchair alongside the river, this quiet, steady man Moose loved with a pain at the core of his chest, whose catcher's mitt hands now hung at his sides, insensate as loaves of bread, Moose looked across the river and felt the past unroll suddenly from behind the present panorama of dead chrome and glass and riverfront homes as if a phony backdrop had toppled, exposing a labyrinth. "It's all here," he murmured wonderingly, and experienced a lifting within himself. "Everything is here."

He leaned forward and spoke urgently into his father's slack face, "Pop, everything is here!" and it seemed to Moose that some response or approval had waved to him from the cloudy reaches of his father's eyes.

And the joy of that discovery had rescued Moose, had given him hope:

the Industrial Revolution had happened right here in a form that was exquisitely compressed; everything he needed to know was right under his feet! He began stockpiling facts about Rockford's history until the mention of any single year could prompt a detailed recitation of which buildings were under construction and which businesses at their zeniths, the mayor's name, a rundown of the influential families, a recipe for a certain raisin pudding. A friend of his father's on the board of Winnebago College was able to procure for Moose a part-time teaching position, whose small salary sustained him while he worked feverishly on a multivolumed history of his hometown whose explicit purpose was etiological: to discover *what had gone wrong* between its founding in 1834 and the present day—what, precisely, had been lost in the ineluctable transformation from industry to information.

"It's so sad," Charlotte had heard her father say. "What he's trying to figure out is why he cracked up. Like a hundred and fifty years of trivia is going to answer that question."

But to Charlotte, her uncle's exile was more intriguing than that. At night, the house thick with sleep, she would peer out her bedroom window at the trees and sky and feel the presence of a mystery. Some possibility that included her—separate from her present life and without its limitations. A secret. Riding in the car with her father, she would look out at other cars full of people she'd never seen, any one of whom she might someday meet and love, and would feel the world holding her, making its secret plans. She was an exile, too.

The waitress arrived with a giant round tray, which she set on a stand near their table.

"Char, go get Ricky, would you, honey?" Ellen asked.

The instant Charlotte was gone, Harris spoke urgently to Moose and Priscilla, though only Priscilla returned his gaze. "You could do me a hell of a favor," he said, "if you'd ask Charlotte why she's switching schools."

"She's leaving Baxter?" Priscilla said.

"We didn't find out until a few weeks ago. She says she's going to East." The idea made Harris frantic. East was public, blue-collar, a bunch of machinists' kids! In general he marveled at his daughter's equanimity— the Lord, in His mystery, had apportioned his son the beauty and his daughter the strength. But at times he was overcome by an urge to break Charlotte, make her see how resolutely the deck was stacked in her disfavor. As if knowing this would protect her from something worse. Harris wanted to save her.

"Have you asked her why?" Priscilla said.

Harris flung up his hands. "Have I asked!"

"She's completely closed," Ellen said. "She won't talk to either one of us." She was craving a cigarette. Lately she'd begun sneaking them at home: Kools, which made her feel like a teenager.

"Of course I'll try," Priscilla said, "but if she won't talk to you . . ."

Ellen glanced at Moose and found him watching her, but when their eyes met, he looked away. She understood. Looking into her brother's eyes seemed to confirm an unbearable truth that only the two of them recognized. Of all her many regrets: not getting out of Rockford and seeing the world when she was young and unencumbered; marrying too early; not taking Ricky to the doctor the moment she'd first spotted those fingery bruises on his legs—her mind spasmed late at night in a frenzy of terror and regret when she measured the chasm between the life she'd imagined for herself and the one she was living—of all those regrets, her brother's transfiguration still felt like the most shocking, most inexplicable loss.

When Charlotte and Ricky returned to the table, the adults were becalmed in a silence that could only mean they had been discussing Ricky's illness. Exchanging an eye roll, the children resumed their seats.

"Charlotte," Aunt Priscilla interjected awkwardly into the stillness. "Your father mentioned you're switching schools."

"Yeah," Charlotte said warily, nibbling a wing. "I decided to go to East."

"Any special reason?"

"It's much bigger. Lots of kids I don't know."

"That must take some courage," Priscilla said.

Oh, terrific, Harris thought: go ahead and congratulate her.

"I'm already pretty out of things at Baxter," Charlotte said.

"Really," Priscilla said. "When did that start?"

"Last year. At the very beginning."

Ellen listened greedily. She had given up even trying to talk seriously with Charlotte about her situation; whenever she dared to, her daughter would turn those flat, cold eyes on her as if to demand, How on earth can you possibly help me? "You were always so popular," she blurted, unable to stop herself.

Charlotte looked at her mother—her sad, beautiful mother. How could anyone so beautiful be so sad? "It has nothing to do with popularity," she said.

"It sounds like it has to do with a sense of belonging," Priscilla said.

There it was, that warm—what?—sympathy. A luxuriant sleepiness overcame Charlotte. "I think so," she said.

"What's the difference," Ellen asked, hurt, "between that and being popular?"

Charlotte didn't answer. Her aunt had opened a perfumed chamber to her, a grotto of tenderness.

Harris could contain himself no longer. "I'm concerned about your education!" he cried. "I'm concerned about your getting into a decent college and having the opportunity to make something of your life!" Because looking like you do, he thought helplessly, the world isn't going to cut you many breaks. "Does that mean anything at all to you?"

"Yes," Charlotte said. She felt tired. How had she been dragged into a discussion about school with her father—the very thing she'd managed to avoid all summer?

"Look, Charlotte," Harris said, more gently. "The fact is, running away from your problems isn't going to solve them."

"Who says I have problems?"

"Well, obviously you do, or you wouldn't be switching schools."

"That's circular logic." Moose.

He'd been silent so long that the sound of his voice jolted everyone. Harris gawked at him. "You said she can't solve her problems by switching schools," Moose explained. "And then you said the fact that she's switching schools proves that she has—"

"What the hell does that have to do with the price of rice in China?" Harris broke in.

Moose went silent. As they all waited for him to resume, a slight dread overtook the table—even Harris felt it—a fear that this rarest of conversational efforts had been snuffed. "I'm sorry," he forced himself to say. "I interrupted you."

Moose faltered, then began again. "Maybe she doesn't want to be like every other kid in Rockford," he said in a clumsy rush.

"I don't want that, either," Harris said. "That's exactly what I want to avoid. By giving her a decent education!"

Charlotte, a little bewildered by the tempest forming around her, said, "Dad, I'm constantly learning things."

"I'm not talking about tropical fish!"

"Oh, but there's where you're wrong," Moose said, and in an unprecedented spate of enthusiasm he rose suddenly to his feet, knocking his chair backward so that it crashed into the wall and sent a shiver through the plate glass windows. A hush befell the dining room. "I'm sorry, but I have to say this," Moose told Priscilla, who had hastily righted his chair and was tugging his hand, urging him back down. "She can learn the things that matter by studying almost anything," Moose said loudly, addressing Harris. "We teach our children blindness! Not to see, not to think—that's what they learn in our schools. And the world is being robbed by it!"

Moose had commandeered the room; ungainly, unkempt, yet somehow dashing, the detritus of an old charisma still alive in him. Charlotte listened in awe as her uncle silenced her father, pinioning him to his chair. "What matters is that she think for herself," Moose declaimed, slicing the air with his hands, "that she question authority! That's what will make her exceptional!"

"I gather you hold yourself up as a shining example," Harris said.

"Oh, Harris," Ellen said bitterly.

"No," Moose said, the very word an expiration. He dropped back into his seat. "I don't hold myself up as anything."

Harris was fuming. How dare Moose embarrass him—embarrass all of them in the country club dining room!

"I agree with you, Uncle Moose," Charlotte said passionately. "I agree with everything you said."

"You can agree with him until the cows come home," Harris said, forcing himself to speak softly. "The question remains: What. About. Your education?"

"I can study with Uncle Moose."

Everyone looked at Charlotte except her uncle, who was gazing into his lap. She wondered if he'd heard. "Mom has your book about glass," she told him, "and I read the introduction, about how glass windows let in all the light in medieval times and suddenly everyone could see more clearly and it changed the way they dressed and how clean their houses were, and then they got glasses and mirrors so they could see what they looked like for the very first time, and how it—"

"Charlotte?" Harris announced, in an oddly congratulatory tone. "That's the worst idea I've ever heard in my life."

But Charlotte was watching her uncle, in whose averted face a scarlet blush was proceeding toward his neck. Slowly he lifted his head. His eyes met hers for a moment, then skidded away. "Why would you want to study with me?" he asked.

"I don't know." She struggled to find words for the feeling she'd had, watching her uncle silence her father just now. Charlotte felt a sudden, urgent need to be closer to Moose, to have him look at her as he'd done a few minutes ago, with recognition. "There's something I want to find out," she said.

Moose nodded. Then he said, "All right."

No one spoke. Even Harris found himself mute. Somehow, he knew it was too late to undo this thing—worse, that he'd brought it on himself. His eyes grazed his wife's, expecting accusation, but he was relieved instead to find softness there. "Well, I'm glad I made my point," he finally said, then laughed—a helpless giggle that caught in him and persisted. Everyone looked at him oddly—except Moose, who began laughing, too, a big chesty laugh that seemed to throw its arms around Harris's like two drunks, their commingled mirth hushing the dining room a second time. Harris dabbed at his eyes. His plan had backfired—completely, unequivocally. What could you do but laugh?

Ellen smiled at her husband. It pleased her to think of Charlotte studying with her brother, as if having them in each other's company would somehow bring them both closer to herself. Then her eyes fell on Ricky's empty chair, and she flinched. "Where is he?"

"He went outside," Charlotte said, and turned on Ellen her cool, unreadable eyes.

"Go get him, Char, if you don't mind," Harris said. "We should think about heading home."

Charlotte grabbed a handful of chalky after-dinner mints from the crystal bowl near the door and went out. The darkness was sultry, the warm air delicious on her bare arms. She took off her glasses and let the night run together around her. "Ricky!" she called softly into the darkness. She skipped down the concrete steps to the pool, which gleamed a sharp, luminous turquoise. It was empty. "Ricky," she called again.

She returned to the golf course, pausing to take off her sandals, which she held in one hand. The grass was fat and cool, prickly under her feet. At some distance she saw flickering shapes, and put her glasses back on. They were in a sand trap, three pairs of shoes lined up along its edge.

A hard moon poured cold blue light over the golf course. The sand in the trap was damp from the sprinklers, which must have just been turned off. Charlotte reached the edge of the trap and saw an enormous sandcastle splayed in the moonlight. Surprisingly delicate, its turrets accented with little pinecones. The girls were digging a moat.

"Wow," she said. "The morning golfers will freak."

Ricky lay on his back in the sand, looking up at the stars. "We're leaving," Charlotte told him.

He raised a hand, and she pulled him to his feet.

The clubhouse gleamed through the dark. Charlotte carried Ricky on her back, his arms around her neck like a possum. She'd given him her sandals to hold, and they bumped against her collarbone. He was even lighter than he looked. "You okay?" she said.

"Tired."

"You've been running around."

"Remember before?" Ricky said, after a pause. "How tired I was?"

"Yes," she said. "But this isn't like that."

He could say or do anything he liked, but people looked at Ricky and imagined him dead. He must feel it constantly, Charlotte thought, must see it everywhere he looked.

"Am I well?" Ricky asked drowsily, into her hair.

"You're well," she told him.

Under the portico, the adults were congregating outside the clubhouse doors. Uncle Moose and her father walked together toward the parking lot to bring the cars around.

"Down," Ricky said. Charlotte set him on the grass and took back her sandals. As she paused to put them on, Ricky stampeded toward the grown-ups, yelling something, pitching a pinecone at Jessica, who was walking a little ahead with her sister. It hit the back of her skull, and she shrieked. And now came the inevitable laughter, twirling like ribbons into the warm night. Charlotte looked at the sky, its cryptic, heedless promises filling her with delight. It was already August. In that old orchard where Scott Hess had driven her, the pears must be fully ripe, if not already gone.

# Chapter Four

*As the days* after my lunch with Oscar multiplied without a call from him, I turned to wholesale afternoon drinking. A week had passed, I'd left him three messages he hadn't returned, I'd seen friends in the evenings and found it eerily awkward, as if there were something everyone wanted to tell me, but was afraid to.

When I had first broached the topic of an alcoholic beverage with Mary Cunningham last October, she bustled about her impressive wet bar and emerged with her favorite cocktail, a daiquiri sweet: an icy, pale green elixir that infused my head with a melting sensation of peace. I had sought out that peace thereafter in further ladylike daiquiris with Mrs. Cunningham and occasional swigs from the wet bar when she was away at the hairdresser. But it was back in New York that my drinking, as readers of charts like to say, spiked; it spiked the warm milk I drank before bed, and gradually my early evenings, when I sipped vodka tonics on my sectional couch and studied the faux-Gothic ruin on the southern tip of Roosevelt Island. One morning I found myself looking for booze at nine-forty-five. There was none left.

I called Oscar again. He was in a meeting (that great modern euphemism), but I left word that it was urgent, then opened the new *Vogue* to distract myself. The model/hooker/junkie thing was back in play, girls propped like broken puppets against graffiti-scarred walls, snail trails of mascara etched on their million-dollar faces. I never lost interest in which younger girls were getting work, girls with the faces of tree frogs, bison and antelopes. Yet the pictures shimmered with a pollen of newness that

I still could not resist; it made me turn the pages in a kind of trance until I had seen every one, at which point the pollen would have vanished as irrevocably as the fabled dust on butterfly wings, replaced by a familiarity that was almost crushing.

In the kitchen, I managed to unearth an ancient brandy bottle, and poured myself a glass. Hansen, my fiancé, had been partial to brandy, so I kept a bottle around in the assumption that it was one of those things men liked. For all the men who had drunk my brandy since Hansen, it was his memory I still consulted when I wanted to know something about men generally. No one would have been more shocked by his archetypal status in my thoughts than Hansen himself. We hadn't spoken in more than a decade.

I drank, staring at the phone in a rising state of outrage. Finally, emboldened by the drenching heat in my chest, I called Oscar again, this time identifying myself as Sasha Lewis of the *New York Post*. He was on the line in three seconds—I counted.

"Fuck you," I greeted him.

*"Pardonnez-moi?"*

"You're taking calls from the *New York Post*, but when it's your oldest client you're in a meeting?"

"That was beneath you, Charlotte."

"What the hell is happening over there? I haven't heard a—" My drunken belligerence surprised even me.

"If you wish to have a business conversation," Oscar said coldly, "call me in a businesslike fashion."

"I have called—and what about?—I told you—"

"Beep," he cut me off. "That was my aggravation meter. You're entering a danger zone."

I slammed down the phone, then sat limply on the couch, shocked by my vivid display of desperation.

I opened my address book and searched for someone to call. I went through it page by page: other models, rich men in various parts of the world; clients I'd worked for regularly over the years. But their calls to me had begun tapering off, and the energy it would require to reel them back into my life felt herculean. Hansen was still under "H"; I'd transferred him from book to book over the years so he always looked current, though surely by now the information was obsolete. Or maybe not; maybe you didn't move, once you'd settled with a wife and children in a house outside Seattle you'd designed yourself. Why would you?

My eye fell on a tiny Post-it that I'd added to the H's: the detective, Anthony Halliday. He had called me again, exactly when he'd promised, but I had avoided calling him back. I wanted no part of his search for Z. Yet the allure of calling a person who actively wished to speak with me was too potent to resist.

"It's Charlotte Swenson," I said, when he answered. "I'm back in New York."

He sounded pleased, and suggested paying me a visit. I imagined this: a private detective inside my apartment, looking at my things. "I'd rather come to you," I said.

"When?" he asked. "Now? Today?" And the eagerness in his voice was so welcome to my drunken ear, so sweetly beckoning, that it jumped the wall of my resistance, and I agreed to come immediately.

Before leaving, I had another large glass of brandy and two Pop-Tarts, which I kept around in large numbers because they were easier to make than pie and I considered them dietetic. I wrapped myself in my long alpaca coat and rode down in the elevator. It was 10:30 A.M. and I was hugely drunk, full of joy and purpose and mischief. My only regret was over all the days of my life I'd spent sober. Why, when drinking wasn't illegal? Why had I deprived myself?

Outside, the temperature was below zero and tiny splinters of ice swarmed the air and lodged in my poor face, which was still tight and a little tingly from its second operation. I hailed a cab and instructed the driver, an elderly Sikh playing Gilbert and Sullivan tunes on a tape deck, to take me to Fourteenth Street, where I made him idle at the curb before a store that sold bins of winter clothing. I chose a black face mask that covered the whole of my head and neck, and pulled it on. When I returned to my cab, the Sikh promptly locked the doors, refusing to let me inside until I removed the mask. As he drove, I slipped it back on, looked in his rearview mirror and let out a whoop of laughter. The Sikh shook his head.

The detective's office was on Seventh Avenue just south of Twenty-fifth Street, inside a seedy brick building whose elevator lurched skyward with an ominous rattling of chains. It released me into an empty corridor lined with doors containing panes of frosted glass where the names of businesses were stenciled: Nelson Watch Repairs; Dr. A. A. Street, Dentistry; Hummingbird Travel Services. None of them showed any visible signs of human occupancy. My steps slapped against the walls. Finally I reached a door that read "Anthony M. Halliday, Esq. Private Investigator."

A young girl in stone-washed jeans led me through a cramped reception area to the detective's office, a small disheveled room crammed with hundreds of loose-leaf files, many disgorging their contents onto the floor.

"Petit, don't make it so complicated," said the man behind the desk—Mr. Halliday, I presumed—into the blue cordless phone wedged between his ear and shoulder. He raised a finger in apology and motioned for me to sit, which I was able to do only by removing a pile of files from the single extra chair.

"The guy's a sleazeball, his story's bullshit, there's no mystery here," the detective was saying. "Agatha Christie wouldn't touch it."

He looked forty or thereabouts, with a pale, diamond-shaped face and a head of unruly dark hair shot with gray, though its unruliness seemed less a matter of style than the lack of a recent haircut. Dark circles under his eyes: an insomniac. Hard living showed somewhere in his face, though precisely where I couldn't say. He wore a crisp white shirt straight from the cleaners and a tweed jacket that had spent the past several days tossed over the arm of a chair, or possibly on the floor. I guessed he must be single; a woman would have hung the jacket up.

"Remember, easy on the notes," he said. "No, writing doesn't help you think, it's the other way around . . . if that notebook gets subpoenaed and you end up frying our guy, I'm gonna be a very unhappy camper . . ." I stared at him, looking for a shadow self. I'd had glints, nothing clear.

"Okay, *hasta*," he said, and hung up. Then he looked at me and smiled. "Charlotte Swenson," he said. "We meet at last."

"Mr. Halliday."

"How are you feeling?"

"Better," I said. "Thanks."

"You look well." I sensed his eyes moving over my face, detective eyes, trying to read it. This was not a feeling I enjoyed.

"It helps that you've never seen me before," I said, and discharged a voluble laugh. Uneasiness—distaste, even—strained the detective's expression, and I smelled my hot, brandy breath and realized he must have, too, in the small room.

"Thanks for coming in," he said. "I appreciate it."

"Still haven't found him?"

He shook his head.

"Any leads?"

He glanced at me. "A few."

"Such as . . . ?"

"Hey," he said. "This happens every time we talk."

"What happens?" I was stalling, waiting for his shadow self to appear. I saw pain around his eyes, but that wasn't it. That was right on the surface.

"You start interrogating me."

"Do you think he's dead?" I asked.

"No, I don't," he said. "Do you?"

"How would I know?"

He left the desk and shut the door to his office. Six foot two, I guessed. Brown slacks, scuffed black shoes. A long, awkward stride, as if he were used to larger spaces. "I have a few questions," he said, resuming his seat and pulling something from a drawer. "And I'd like to tape us, if that's okay."

I smiled to conceal my dismay. "Why not?"

He turned on the machine, a small, deadly looking thing that he nudged to the edge of his desk in my direction. "You know when he disappeared," he began.

"Not really."

"The first week in August," he said. "Which is . . . exactly when you had your accident. Correct?"

"Yes," I said, and forced myself to meet his gaze. The silence between us felt endless, multigenerational, a silence in which I was fully aware of the earth turning slowly on its spit.

"Coincidence," he remarked at last.

"The world is full of them," I replied. I was regretting the brandy. Or perhaps I should have drunk more of it.

Mercifully, there was a knock on the door, and the girl in stone-washed jeans pushed it open. "Tony, I'm so sorry," she said, "but Leland's here. He just, like, showed up."

Halliday looked at the girl, then at me. He seemed briefly immobilized. Then he shut off the recorder, hove a sigh and stood. And as he walked past me from his office, eyes set in the direction of his unheralded guest, I saw it: the enraged shadow. A contortion of anger, like a scream.

Then I relaxed.

Halliday must have taken his guest into the hall, because I never saw the mysterious Leland and heard not a word of their interaction. I waited, listening to a pale bleat of sirens from Seventh Avenue, sounds that seemed filtered through the linty gray light that fell through Halliday's lone window. I grappled with the urge to leave, to breeze past the detective, "Sorry Tony, had to run!" knowing he wouldn't be able to stop me. But the gesture seemed craven, overdramatic; an admission. Most of all, I didn't want to be alone. I wanted to sit a while with this detective, even if it meant answering questions.

I would lie, of course. I lied a lot, and with good reason: to protect the truth—safeguard it, like wearing fake gems to keep the real ones from getting stolen, or cheapened by overuse. I guarded what truths I possessed because information was not a thing—it was colorless, odorless, shapeless, and therefore indestructible. There was no way to retrieve or void it, no way to halt its proliferation. Telling someone a secret was like storing plutonium inside a sandwich bag; the information would inevitably outlive the friendship or love or trust in which you'd placed it. And then you would have given it away.

The detective returned to his office a different man: fretful, preoccupied and possibly afraid, all of which he concealed behind a careless smile. The conversation had been personal, I thought, not business. Who was Leland? Halliday sat back down and turned on the recorder. "Now," he said. "Where were we?"

I told him that Z was a Greek, from Santorini, he'd said. Silver wedding band on his left hand. He was one of those people whose physical description required liberal use of the word "medium": height, build, hair, tan. The overall effect was of a decent-looking European playboy. His one intriguing feature had been his eyes: wide and dark and watchful but also sardonic, as if everything fascinated him and everything, his own fascination included, was somehow ridiculous.

I'd noticed him for the first time at Pollen, a restaurant on the Bowery where the mystical collision of fashion and celebrity had erupted briefly the previous spring. And in a matter of weeks, with a sudden ubiquity that was possible only in a world without memory, Z had become a fixture. He had money, the universal calling card, which he began putting into evenings at certain clubs. He gravitated inevitably toward Mitch and Hassam, the promoters, and soon the three of them were partners in something new, bigger than anything New York had seen in years, or so the rumors went.

"Did you talk to him?" the detective asked.

"He was not a big talker," I said.

"You had no idea what he was doing there."

I shrugged. "He was a playboy."

"But beyond that."

"I don't mean to shock you," I said, "but to some men, the pursuit of women is an end in itself."

The detective leaned back and smiled. I wondered if the brandy was making me witty, or if this was going to be God's way of compensating me for the loss of my face.

"You should talk to Mitch and Hassam," I told him.

"They hired me," he said. "He walked away with a nice chunk of their change."

"How much?"

"Twenty-five. The perfect amount, really—enough to make a difference, but not worth chasing after for too long."

"Then why are you chasing him?"

Instead of answering, Halliday turned to the window. I noticed a silver picture frame aslant among the clutter of his desk. I wished I could see who was in it.

"Thank you very much," he said, startling me. I sensed his frustration, as if he'd counted on me for something and I had disappointed him. I was sorry.

He came around the desk and saw me to the door. Standing, I revised my estimate: six-one, three inches taller than myself. I hesitated, swaying a little (the brandy), while the cold, empty day barked at me from beyond the walls. "That's it?" I asked, moving slightly closer to him. "There's nothing else?"

"You tell me."

"I could start making things up."

"Thanks," he said. "I save my fiction for bedtime."

"Call me then," I said shamelessly. "I tell excellent stories."

"Somehow I knew that."

We shook hands. I sensed him waiting for me to go, and yet I lingered, absurdly. Desperation upon desperation, I thought, but was too drunk to care.

Back on Seventh Avenue, I pulled the mask over my face and decided to let it be a lost day. I wandered north, my head down, but the wind clobbered me and the lower part of the ski mask grew soggy and cold with my condensed breath. At Twenty-eighth Street, I turned east, so the wind was behind me. I raised my head in search of some flag of color, some blink of relief from the gray-brown vista of tottering trucks and greasy brick.

And then, as if my eyes had suddenly refocused, I spotted an old painted sign like the one I'd seen a week ago, with Oscar—a series of ads directly across Sixth Avenue, stacked one atop the other in a column on the exposed side of a weary building. "FURS & WAISTS," I made out in giant letters near the top, and at the bottom, "Hollander Ladies Underwear," with many illegible others in between. It's a sign, I thought, the wind gulping my laughter. A sign in the form of a sign.

At the corner of Sixth Avenue and Twenty-eighth Street I stopped and turned slowly around. They were everywhere—signs and the possibility of signs, many faded to translucence, as if I'd gained some new power that allowed me, finally, to see them. "Harris Suspenders Garters Belts." "Maid-Rite Dress Co."; mementos of the gritty industrialism I'd come to New York to escape. But today the signs looked honest, legible in a way that the negligéed models I'd seen this morning in *Vogue*, prone in a parking lot surrounded by broken glass, would never be.

East, then south in search of more signs ("Harnesses," I saw. "Stables."). Finally, shaking spastically from the cold, I peeled the ski mask from my head and ducked inside one of those bars invisible to all but those seeking alcohol at midday, bars whose stools are sparsely occupied by men with hypertrophied noses and timid, watery eyes. My entrance caused a minor stir that subsided the moment I myself claimed a stool and ordered a drink—a brandy. Brandy was the order of the day. A fish tank gurgled in the window, overwhelmed with algae to the point where the presence of fish inside was anyone's guess.

Beside the tank was a pay phone. When I'd finished my brandy, I called my voice mail for messages, skipping past Grace (who left one each day to cheer me up), hoping, irrationally, for a call from Anthony Halliday. No such luck. But there was a message from Oscar, left only minutes before. "Call me immediately," he said. "I have extraordinary news."

"Extraordinary," I said, when he came on the line after a mere five seconds (I counted). "Not a word I've been hearing too often these days."

"Lady Luck has arrived and we are in her debt," Oscar informed me.

Within the last hour, he said, a reporter from the *New York Post* (a real one this time, though at first he'd thought it was me bluffing again) had called the agency. Like every other publication in America, the *Post* was doing a feature on models, but with a twist: they wanted a model whose appearance had changed radically in the very recent past.

"They probably mean a new haircut," I said, to withering silence. Then I added, meekly, "But I'm sure you already thought of that."

"Thank you," Oscar said. "They most assuredly do not mean a haircut; they mean a radical transformation like what's-her-name in the eighties with the scars. It's truly uncanny; if you didn't exist they would have to invent you."

It was, indeed, uncanny. And it was a measure of my own desperation, and Oscar's on my behalf, that we never questioned this uncanniness, nor considered the unlikelihood of such a coincidence actually taking place.

"But Oscar," I said. "If we tell people I've had this accident and I look completely different, won't it be harder for me to get work?"

"No, dear," Oscar said, almost pityingly. "Because if this article flies, you'll be a Real Person, a person in the news. From there I can wangle you some TV, maybe a longer feature—a cover, ideally. And that's your relaunch, sweet. There it is. I have goose bumps, God's truth."

I had goose bumps, too.

"Now listen," he said, "call this girl. Meet her as soon as possible—

today, if you can. Her name is Irene Maitlock. I'm warning you right now, she sounds a teeny bit drippy—writers usually do. Be nice, Charlotte. Nice nice nice."

"Irene," I drawled. "What a name."

"It's the name of an angel who's descended from heaven to save your ass," Oscar replied.

Irene Maitlock was one of those women I found difficult to look at without imagining how much they would profit by dropping just a few pounds, wearing a less pointy bra, a minimum of makeup, and clothing that had, if not personality, at least some semblance of an identity. Because the raw material was there! She had thick light brown hair that begged for highlights, a decent figure, lovely blue eyes. She also wore a wedding band, and so, I gathered, was not exactly desperate for my help. But I was less troubled by Irene's physical shortcomings than the annihilating side of my own personality that raged in the presence of women who invited the descriptive "mousy." Fortunately, I'd had time to stop at Ardville Wines and Spirits on my way home.

But Irene Maitlock refused my offer of Pouilly Fuissé—five demerits right there—and sat tentatively on my sectional couch. Mousy women felt an instinctive terror in my presence that had the unfortunate consequence of exacerbating their mousiness. Snip snip snip, I thought, watching her. Now you have bangs.

"So, you're a journalist," I said. "What do you write about?"

"Oh, all kinds of things. Drugs, cops, the Mafia. I'm fascinated by crime. And law enforcement."

"Where do I fit in?"

She smiled nervously. "Well, this story is sort of a departure. To tell you the truth, it was given to me. Not that I'm not interested—"

"Obviously you're not."

That surprised her. "What do you mean?"

"Obviously you're not interested in fashion."

She laughed, and I gave her ten points for sportsmanship. "No," she said, "I'm definitely not interested in fashion. But this story isn't about fashion. It's about identity."

"Oh?"

"I'm interested in the relationship between interior and exterior," she said, "how the world's perceptions of women affect our perceptions of ourselves. A model whose appearance has changed drastically is a perfect vehicle, I think, for examining the relationship among image, perception and identity, because a model's position as a purely physical object—a media object, if you will"—she'd risen out of her slouch and was sitting up straight, a spot of red on both her cheeks, discharging words in a cannonade—"is in a sense just a more exaggerated version of everyone's position in a visually based, media-driven culture, and so watching a model renegotiate a drastic change in her image could provide a perfect lens for looking at some of these larger—"

"Beep!" I said loudly, cutting her off.

"Excuse me?"

"That was my boredom meter," I said, although in truth it was my utter bewilderment, rather than boredom, that had caused her speech to grate on me. "You were nearing a danger point."

"Oh." She looked mortified. "I'm sorry."

Now I was sorry, too. Would it have been such a hardship to let her finish? Why should the fact that she'd flouted an opportunity for natural-looking blondness so offend me?

"So, let's see . . ." She was halting, diffident once again. Nice work, I told myself.

"Well, this is my face," I said briskly, framing it with my hands. "I'll take off my makeup if you want to see what it really looks like."

"Okay, or we could—"

"You're the boss," I said. "Tell me what you want to do."

"I thought I'd start by asking you a few questions."

"Oh," I said, and was overcome by an abject sensation of dread. "Will it take long?"

"Do you have to be somewhere?"

"No. I just—I hate talking about myself."

"Me, too," she said, and smiled. "Luckily, I don't have to."

"Let's be quiet a minute," I said. "I want to look at you."

"At me?" She seemed alarmed. I took a long drag on my cigarette and gazed at her intensely. "What do you see?" she asked.

"Stop talking, and I'll tell you."

She did, and I looked again, and immediately I saw a light, laughing presence. I saw her leaning against someone, putting her arms around him, kissing his neck.

"You love your husband," I said.

She looked astonished, then relieved. For a moment the laughing presence eclipsed the hesitant drip who'd occupied my couch thus far, and she looked—I never would have thought it possible—she looked beautiful. "Yes," she said. "Very much."

"Okay," I said, calmer now that I'd seen her shadow self and taken a liking to it. "Fire away." To prepare myself, I lay flat on my back on the couch, cigarette jutting from my mouth at a right angle. I shut my eyes.

"Tell me how you came to be a model."

"Oh, God," I said. It seemed so complicated, such a long reach into the past. "Can we come back to that one?"

"Ah . . . how large a role would you say your appearance has played in your identity?" She was reading the questions from a notebook.

"How can I answer that?" I asked. I opened an eye to look at her. "Can you answer that?"

"Have you ever been married?"

Ten points for not rising to the bait. "Almost. Once."

"How long ago?"

"Many years."

She waited, obviously hoping I would go on. Then she asked, "Do you think your appearance has played a major role in your relationships with men?"

"Not at all," I said. "The determining factor has always been my intellect."

No reaction. "How old are you?"

"Twenty-eight."

"Me, too," she said, with surprise. "We're the same age!"

More or less.

"Did becoming a professional model change your feelings about your appearance?"

"I think so," I said. "It must have." I strained to recall, but my memory smirked and refused to budge. It was a lazy creature, that memory of mine, and, since its exertions during my Rockford convalescence, more phlegmatic than ever. "Let's come back to that one."

I heard her sigh, and peeked to find her rubbing her temples. "Have you participated in the fashion-world nightlife here in New York?"

Trick question, for sure. "Yes . . ."

"You've gone to nightclubs, that sort of thing?"

"Yes . . . ?"

"And what role do you play? In that nightlife."

"There's only one," I said. "I'm a girl."

"At twenty-eight you're a girl?"

Oh, spare me, I thought. "It's just an expression."

"Do you feel like a girl?"

"I feel like an old dog," I told her.

"What kinds of people do you meet in these nightclubs?"

"All sorts," I said. "Literally, every kind you can imagine." I looked at her again. "What do nightclubs have to do with it?"

"This almost-marriage you had. Did it begin after you started modeling?"

"I'd rather not talk about that."

"Why do you dislike talking about yourself?"

At last, a question I could answer. A topic I was itching to address. "I'll tell you why," I said, swinging around and planting my feet on the rug so I could look at her directly. "Because everyone is a liar. Including me."

"I beg your pardon?"

"We lie," I said. "That's what we do. You're selling me a line of bullshit and you want me to sell you a line of bullshit back so you can write a major line of bullshit and be paid for it." I said this with utmost collegiality.

"What makes you such a purist?"

"I'm not!" I cried. "That's the irony—I'm the biggest liar of them all! But I don't pretend to be anything else."

"What, you tell people you're lying and then lie to them?"

I laughed. I was starting to like her better. "I avoid pseudo-earnestness. How did you start modeling? How do you feel about your appearance? Blah blah, here's my sad story, now get out the violins—I can't bear it."

"In other words, you're afraid of serious conversation."

"Afraid." I shook my head. "Afraid?"

"Sounds to me like a pretty standard defense mechanism."

"Irene," I said quietly, and leaned very close to her. "Can you look at me and swear that everything you've said is absolutely true, that none of it is bullshit? There's no agenda hidden underneath, no ulterior motives—everything is exactly the way you've described it? Can you swear to that, say, on your husband's life?"

She blanched, averting her eyes. There it was: comprehension.

I lay back down, satisfied. I was ready for the next question, but the reporter was on her feet. "I think I'd better go," she said, slipping her notepad into her bag.

I didn't move. "Why?"

"Because you're right. This makes no sense."

"So you're giving up journalism?" Languidly, I rose to a sitting position.

"No," she said. "This."

"Jesus. You've written about cops and muggers and Mafiosi and you're running away from me?" I was beginning to sweat.

"I'm not running."

She wasn't running, but she was definitely on the move. "Thanks for your time," she called from the door.

I moseyed after her, careful not to look flustered. The locks on my door were many and complex; she wouldn't get out on her own. I was fighting the sense that I'd fucked up something major, that Oscar would never forgive me. But what exactly had I done?

"Good luck finding another model who's had eighty titanium screws implanted in her face," I said, unlocking the door and pushing it open.

She looked impressed.

"Eight-*oh*. Write that down," I said.

She brushed past me into the hallway.

It was seven o'clock, but it might as well have been midnight. The sky and river were black. To hell with the diet—I ordered a pizza and ate it. I finished the bottle of Pouilly-Fuissé. Sometime later, I opened another bottle and began watching *The Making of the Making of*, a documentary about how documentaries were made about the making of Hollywood features. Against a backdrop of camera crews shooting camera crews, an announcer in pancake makeup intoned his gravelly stand-up. "As movies about how movies are made become more popular, experts speculate that some day, every movie will bring with it a brother, or sister movie: the unique story of its own creation. But how are *these* stories made? What are the technical challenges, the dangers? What are the rewards? In the next hour, we'll take you behind the scenes . . . into the studios . . . onto the locations . . . where directors face the challenge of filming other directors . . . making films!"

I stared at the set. I wondered seriously if I might be hallucinating, a relapse into double vision induced by too much brandy in one day.

I muted the TV and called Grace, hoping she could elucidate the meaning of the program. Frank answered and informed me that she was in bed.

"At nine o clock?" I was skeptical.

"She's still recovering from her visit to New York."

"Or avoiding you—and who could blame her?" I bellowed, then rushed to slam the phone down before he did. It was sort of a contest between us: who could hang up first.

I was feeling very antsy. Before the accident, such a mood would have propelled me outside to a club, then more clubs. But I no longer had the energy. The city looked dark and corrupt and I was glad to be in my silk kimono and fuzzy blue slippers with the heat on full blast. Central heating was a must, I thought, as I padded around the apartment turning on lights. And plenty of good strong electrical outlets!

I lay on my bed with the lights on, Jacques Brel serenading me from the CD player. The TV was still on; *Unsolved Mysteries,* one of those shows you could watch without watching it, as if it were one story looping around and around. "Penny was fifteen when she rode into these woods and disappeared . . ." A shot of a blond girl riding a bicycle, pink-tasseled handlebars. I closed my eyes. When I opened them, a psychic was leading the police to young Penny's remains, a raccoon-eyed woman in a head scarf, humming as she stepped through crackling underbrush.

That night I dreamed about Hansen. I felt his arms and smelled him, and we were together in some familiar, beautiful place, possibly one of the towns on the Jersey shore where we used to go on weekends. Was the Jersey shore actually beautiful? I didn't know. I had made a point of never going back.

On the few occasions when I recalled myself with Hansen, I saw a girl whose energies and affections were trained entirely on one human being, but I credited my devotion less to Hansen himself than to the fact that we'd fallen in love before I discovered who I was—or was not. He represented the last time I had believed in something that I no longer believed in.

There was no denying that Hansen was terrific. Smart, great in bed, a landscape architect and fanatical gardener who knew everything a person could know about soil and plants. Even now, resting my eyes on a dusty vase at the dry cleaners or walking past the public library in the flush of spring, names of plants and flowers would startle me like someone whispering into my ear: coleus, baby tears, dahlias, jasmine. We met a few weeks after I came to New York, at the Metropolitan Museum. I would wander through the rooms of European paintings and stare at the canvases until my head ached, waiting for them to reveal themselves to me. Hansen introduced himself by murmuring, as I gaped at some frigid Poussin, "Are you trying to make it combust?" He took me to lunch in the cafeteria. He was twenty-five, a year out of graduate school. I was twenty-two, posing as twenty, but I told him twenty. Even after we were engaged, I never corrected myself.

There was no denying that Hansen and I were happy. We were perilously happy. We lived in a ground-floor apartment on Bank Street, two blocks from the Hudson. Our street had cobblestones. Hansen grew roses in the backyard, blah blah blah. The picture was coercive in its perfection. Pasta in the evenings, weekends tooling around in Hansen's baby-blue vintage Oldsmobile. Endless discussions of our love; its quality, its texture, its indestructibility. Fights, tears, jealousy over feeling ignored by the other at a party, followed by reconciliatory lovemaking. Presentation to one another's parents, who nodded sagely as they noted our clutched hands under the tablecloth. It was someone else. When I thought of it now, I was filled with a sense that it couldn't have been me.

At that time, a sojourn to Paris, usually for a year, was a critical part of every model's development. I put it off for many months so as not to be parted from Hansen. Finally Oscar set a date and announced that I was leaving.

On my last weekend in New York, Hansen and I drove to the Jersey shore. It was a rainy spring, and we holed up in our bed and breakfast room for two days, crying, screwing, staring morosely out our small round window at the sea. Hansen proposed to me in the dining room of a nineteenth-century beachside hotel, striped awnings on the windows. By the world's account, I was twenty-one. That night, while Hansen slept, I lay awake and listened to the sea's fitful breath. My life felt absolutely pure. Can it really be this easy? I wondered—you met someone, you fell in love . . . like an old story? It seemed too lucky, and for that reason, or some other reason, it provoked in me a tiny beat of disappointment. I had always believed my life would unfold in some more angular fashion. Instead, I'd virtually stepped from my childhood into this happiness.

In Paris, I shared a minuscule apartment with a model named Ruby, who had a cocaine problem and almost never slept. I put a sock over each of my ears, trying to repel her nocturnal phone chatter, her giggles and rages and tears as she shifted west with the hours, seeking out time zones where men she knew were still awake: New York, Aspen, Los Angeles, Honolulu, finally Tokyo, which she reached at dawn. But Ruby played only a bit part in the pageant of my lovesickness. I went to castings, I landed little jobs with *Elle* and *Marie Claire*, I walked beside the Seine, and invariably I was miserable. The unfamiliar sights hurt my eyes, the words I couldn't understand—I felt exiled, with no way to connect. In occasional lucid flashes, I was dumbfounded to find myself in such a state. Here I was in Paris, after all! Paris, where French people lived! And yet the fulcrum of my existence was the hour, usually around seven, when Hansen would call at lunchtime from his architectural firm. Hanging up was like being lopped from him physically. "I can't stand this," I told myself repeatedly throughout each day. I felt like I was dying, like the blood was being drained from me slowly. Clients complained about my listlessness, and there was talk of sending me home. Oscar begged me to stick it out. He offered to advance Hansen a plane ticket, but Hansen was designing his first project, a small park in Queens, and couldn't get away until July.

One Saturday, while I was walking by the Seine in my usual morose haze, I saw a man standing at an easel. When I stopped to watch him paint, he barely acknowledged me. I'd been hounded by men since the moment of my arrival, the usual rich compulsives whose particular drug (or one of them) was the presence of teenage girls in large quantities. But the lone painter's oblivion made it feel safe to stand beside him. Even I could see he had no talent. "You like?" he asked, turning to me suddenly.

I shrugged, which made him laugh. He was attractive in a muscular, straightforward way, and spoke no English. He pulled a ham sandwich from his shoulder bag and offered me half. We ate side by side on the river's edge, our feet dangling over the water. He opened a bottle of red wine, which we drank in swigs. He seemed perfectly indifferent to me, as if his day were unfolding exactly as it would have without me. Eventually he took out a book and began to read. I looked at the river, feeling a tentative contentment. It was June, sunlight lapping at my face and arms. The ratio of red wine to ham sandwich had left me not drunk, exactly, but dreamy. I leaned back, tipped my face to the sky, and shut my eyes. Then he kissed me. I yelped, my eyes popped open, and except for a lingering essence of red wine and tobacco on my lips, it seemed possible that nothing had happened. The Frenchman watched me, testing my reaction, then seized my face in his hands and kissed me again. Something awful stirred in me. He pushed me gently backward against the concrete and leaned over me, kissing my mouth and neck, whispering into my ears until my mind emptied of everything but a drugged sense that we must get to a place where we could undress. Clearly the Frenchman's thoughts were following this same itinerary; he pulled me to my feet, packed up his paints with alacrity and led me up to the street, where his miniature orange Citroën was parked. We got in, and as he twisted and wove among the Paris streets I tried to think of Hansen, but it was as if one version of me were still by the Seine in a zombie state of missing him, and now a second version had broken off and hijacked me into this stranger's car, where I was counting the moments until we could have sex.

Eventually we reached a run-down apartment house. The Frenchman led me inside by the hand, and we climbed what seemed an infinite number of steps, flight after flight, the stairwell echoing with cries of dogs and infants until, when we reached the seventh floor, I was only nominally clothed. I hardly saw the man's apartment, except to note that it was small and clean. We stayed there until evening, and then he drove me back to the apartment I shared with Ruby. His name was Henri. The next day I returned to the Seine to look for him, but it wasn't until the following Saturday, one week later, that he was back at his easel. When he saw me, he began packing up his paints, and the day proceeded similarly. After that, I learned how to get to his apartment by Metro and met him there. I had no idea what the rest of his life consisted of, nor he mine. We couldn't speak.

But the happiness! The cheesiest metaphors could not exaggerate the immensity of my relief; a spell had broken, a weight had been lifted from my shoulders, a large black cloud dispelled from the atmosphere. I'd wakened from the dead to find myself in Paris. I was free! Not from Hansen—I never thought of it that way—but from my misery. I wanted to skip and yell and sing. "You sound so much happier!" Hansen marveled when we spoke, and only then did I realize what a burden my desolation had been for him. I made a better impression at castings, and work began picking up. Of course I was aware that something was wrong with all this, but I tried not to think about it. It was a stopgap measure, I told myself, a drastic coping device until Hansen and I would be reunited. I felt like a part of myself was still with him in New York, holding my place among the hosta and clematis, while another entirely separate part was meeting Henri each Saturday for hours and hours of anonymous sex. I never took off my engagement ring.

As July and Hansen's visit approached, I was hobbled by dread. What would happen? Would he guess? Would I feel differently? But when he arrived, the love I felt for Hansen seemed, if anything, more intense. I didn't show up at Henri's that Saturday, and he must have known better than to come looking for me. I never saw him again. Hansen and I spent whole days at the Louvre and watched sunset from the Eiffel Tower. We chose a wedding date for one year later, in Paris. As we made love, I would sometimes be stricken by the knowledge that I had done these same things (and other things, too—things I hadn't done with Hansen) with a literal stranger, and so recently, and I would feel a kind of shock—not on my own behalf, but on Hansen's. He doesn't know who he's making love to, I would think, and panic would slash through me until I reminded myself that it was over now, a freakish aberration not to be repeated.

It was Hansen who first made me aware of shadow selves. He would lie in bed watching me for whole minutes, and I would look back into his eyes and wonder, What does he see? How can he not see the truth? Where is it hidden? It made me ask, when I looked at other people, what possible selves they were hiding behind the strange rubber masks of their faces. I could nearly always find one, if I watched for long enough. It became the only one I was interested in seeing.

Hansen stayed three weeks, and after he left, I experienced a modified version of my prior despair. I missed him bitterly, but with each day the bitterness abated and another set of possibilities began to assert itself, like shifting my weight from one foot to the other. A week after he left, I had dinner with a young playboy, dark-haired and light-skinned like the Carravagian boys Hansen and I had observed so recently. Again, as with Henri, the desire that I felt for this man was like a blanket tossed over my head. We went back to his house, a house in the middle of Paris with tall shuttered windows, and I spent the night without making love all the way, but the next morning I relented, and we began an affair. I felt exactly two opposite ways: gripped by the feverish eroticism of my new circumstances, and devoted to Hansen in a way that made the other feeling outrageous, inconceivable. In moments, I clutched at the notion of some larger "me" that could contain and justify my contradictory behavior, but more often I simply felt like the scene of two irreconcilable visions, two different people, one unerringly loyal and faithful, the other treacherous and greedy. My affair with Henri had pushed something open in me, and now I felt ravenous, in constant danger of going hungry. Hansen alone would never be enough.

As the weeks progressed, I developed a morbid fascination with the enormity of all he didn't know. I reminded myself incessantly that the happiness I heard in his voice when we spoke each night was predicated upon a trust and faith and mutual understanding that I had already betrayed countless times in countless different ways, ways that would make him scream, were he to glimpse them. The thought tortured me. I felt like a poisoner sprinkling arsenic on Hansen's food while he wasn't looking, watching him eat it bite by bite. I wished he would guess, but I did everything in my power to keep him from guessing, and it was easy. I sounded the same! He had no reason to doubt me! He believed that I loved him, and he was right! I was made for this treachery! Each night, as I reported to him the jobs I was on hold for, the church I'd wandered into, the croque monsieur I'd had for lunch, I would imagine rescuing him from his ignorance and my duplicity by telling him everything. This fantasy of absolution so enthralled me that at times I completely lost track of our conversation. To say it and have him know, to close the gap between us. I couldn't do it. And yet I knew that it couldn't go on this way, either, that sooner or later I would have to choose between Hansen and everyone else. A lifetime of deceiving a good man was more than even I could stomach.

So I left.

I flew back to New York to tell him. And in the moments after I did (because it was near his birthday, he thought I'd come to celebrate and had filled the apartment with flowers), after I told him everything, after he'd turned in confusion to look at the garden, flooded with sunset (asters, gladiolus, anemones, phlox), after he'd finished his glass of brandy in one shaking gulp, his first impulse, strangely, was to cleave to me, the person he trusted, the person he loved, and for a tiny pocket of time we held each other and the small life we had made, and I felt the sweetness of that life as I never had before. No! I thought, we can keep this, it doesn't have to end! But my words were already moving through Hansen, seeping through his veins toward his heart. I felt it happening, felt him beginning to seize up in my arms and realized with a kind of horror that I hadn't poisoned him before, as I'd thought; I'd done it now, here, all at once, and my punishment was to sit by and watch it work. I hadn't protected him from anything. As the revulsion overcame him, the disgust and rage, he shoved me, knocking me onto the bricks, and hit my face, and I watched the innocence leave him like a spirit leaving a corpse.

But what had killed that innocence—my betrayal, or the telling? Which was the poison? Ah, philosophy.

After Hansen, I was careful to limit my promises. If I cared about someone, I did my best to mean what I said as I said it. But I'd given up on the whole truth, much less my ability to tell it. Most of the time, I didn't even try. My philosophy, if you will, was eerily suited to what became my life; different cities week to week, a constant flow of settings and people; as my surroundings dissolved and reconstituted themselves, it seemed only natural that I do the same. I avoided the sorts of places where I'd been with Hansen—museums, for example. Or perhaps I simply lost interest.

Still, I had wondered many times, in the years since leaving Hansen, years during which I had promised almost nothing to a great, great many, whether we might both have been better off if I'd sealed my lips and led a double life, like everyone else.

# Chapter Five

*East High School* was vast, just as Charlotte had wished, corridors lined with hundreds of red lockers, corridors so long she could barely see to the end of one, even with her glasses on. Everyone was a stranger, and this infused the air with a glittering sense of promise. Charlotte knew better than to try to sit with the preppy kids in the lunchroom, but she could walk by and smile, and they would smile back.

She met Uncle Moose for one or two hours on alternate weeks at his office at Winnebago College on East State Street, a ten-minute bike ride from her high school. After the crescendo with which their accord had been reached, a certain letdown was inevitable. Her uncle remained awkward, aloof, rarely meeting Charlotte's eyes. Alone with him she felt a spooky kind of banishment, as if she might leave his office, which reeked of tomato sauce and stale Chinese takeout cartons mashed in the garbage, to find that the world as she knew it had ceased to exist. History meant little to Charlotte: facts about dead people. And Moose, deeply attuned to the apathy most people felt toward the pursuits he held most dear, achingly conscious of the erasure of history from this land without context, perceived his niece's indifference and was bewildered; what was she doing here?

Sometimes they met at Moose and Priscilla's apartment in a complex called Versailles, a half mile east of Winnebago College. They sat on Moose's tiny second-floor balcony, just big enough for two chairs and a small glass-topped table. Below, a boy rode a tractor-mower over the undulating grass around Versailles, and Charlotte blamed this mower for the many occasions when she and Moose began speaking at once and then stopped—then started—then stopped. But on her next visit the lawn boy was gone and a disastrous silence remained, an enormous stretch of nothing in which she and Moose foundered gloomily, solitarily. No more, Charlotte thought, mounting her bicycle with relief at finding herself back among the wind and cars and trees turning gold. I'm not going back, it's too strange.

At home, she felt the push of her mother's curiosity. Ellen had never been inside Moose and Priscilla's apartment. Were there many pictures on the walls? Did the phone ring often? Was the refrigerator full? Her mother's hunger for news of her brother exposed itself helplessly to Charlotte, and she felt her privilege at being allowed inside her uncle's life. Blue round soaps in the bathroom. Towels smelling faintly of flowers. Once, Aunt Priscilla left a banana bread in the kitchen, and her uncle, barefoot, had cut himself and Charlotte each a slice. She told her mother almost nothing.

In an album by her mother's desk, a younger version of Moose stared mockingly at Charlotte from old photographs. One in particular: her uncle standing in water to his thighs wearing neon-green swim trunks, torso broadening toward the shoulders like the flare of a cobra's head. The picture fascinated her. She'd pried it from the album and brought it to her room, where she kept it hidden between the layers of her blotter.

Late in September, she began writing short conversational essays on the reading Moose had assigned her, and these helped to alleviate their mutual shyness. Her uncle spoke to the essays and scrawled corrections upon them, waved them in the air and once was robbed of a page by a gust of wind. Moose leapt from his chair and sprinted from the apartment, and Charlotte seized upon his absence to push open the door to the bedroom, which she'd never seen. A bed with a green silken spread, a pair of giant fur-lined slippers poised beside it. A forest of prescription bottles on one bedside table. She peeked in Moose's closet: five worn tweed jackets, three pairs of black shoes. Soft plaid work shirts.

By October, they were able to engage in normal conversation.

"How's the family?" Moose asked with an ironic lilt, as if both asking the question and posing as someone asking the question. And Charlotte told him how the tension in their house rose each month before

Ricky's tests, which were later that week. "Your folks must be scared," Moose said.

"It's all they think about."

"And you?"

"It's weird," she said. "I know he'll be okay."

Moose cleared his throat. "I meant: How are you?" he asked, rather stiffly.

Charlotte glanced at him, but her uncle was looking over the balcony, where the lawn boy had raked piles of leaves into orange plastic bags that looked like jack-o'-lanterns. It was the first time Moose had asked a question about herself, personally. Charlotte waited, wanting to take full advantage of this pulse of interest, to answer him with absolute precision.

"I'm waiting for something to happen," she said.

### Two Men Take a Gamble

In the 1830s, when this part of the world was still untouched, the first speculator came to Rockford: Germanicus Kent. In 1834 he and his partner founded a town on the west side of the Rock River next to Kent Creek, where our downtown is now. They built a sawmill, which was one of the three things you needed for a town (the others were: a saloon and a blacksmith shop). Meanwhile, another speculator, Daniel Haight, settled on the east side of the river that very same year.

So Rockford started out as Kentville and Haightville, two almost invisible towns glaring at each other across the river and getting competitive before they practically existed. . . .

Pedaling home from Versailles, Charlotte wove among the Cadillacs on State Street, cruising the slight downhills standing up, the fall wind boxing her body, stinging her ears. She imagined herself at the opening of a tunnel, tipped forward on its downward slope. Something moved in her: a slow, sweet unraveling of anticipation.

After they combined their towns into Rockford, Germanicus Kent and Daniel Haight were like actors in a play with twenty-

five different parts: Haight was the first sheriff, first post-
master, first commissioner to decide where the State Road
(which is State Street today) should go. Kent was the first
election judge, first representative in the Illinois General
Assembly, and first ferrymaster across the river. . . .

On the day of Ricky's tests, Charlotte met a strange woman in her
mother's dressing room. She'd been listening to Alanis on her Walkman
and reading about Rockford's first bridge, a graduate student's paper so
old it had been typed on a typewriter. Headphones still on, she wandered
into her mother's bathroom to look for the lotion she'd brought back from
Florida last spring. White, pearlized lotion that smelled of the beach, of
coconuts. And there Charlotte found the woman: a stranger in scarf and
sunglasses. "I'm an old friend of your mother's," she said.

Looking back, Charlotte was mortified by the many suspicious details
of this "old friend" she had somehow failed to notice: the woman knew
nothing of Ricky's illness; hadn't called before arriving or rung the bell;
had walked around the house alone; then rushed away (limping!) without
leaving any message for Charlotte's mother, whose "old friend" she supposedly was. A thief—what else could she be? And Charlotte had stood
there, making conversation. Had shown the thief her fish!

She'd been absorbed by the question of what was wrong with her. The
woman wasn't old. She was very tall, but seemed narrow inside her heavy
coat. Her voice was raw. A car accident, she finally said. Last August. Then
she took off her glasses, baring to Charlotte her broken, vermilion eyes.

Later, as Ellen was getting dressed for a wedding reception at the
country club (an ordeal she dreaded), Charlotte moseyed into her dressing
room and loitered there. This was unusual, but Ellen paved over her surprise. Displays of eagerness tended to drive Charlotte away.

"Your jewelry is in this room, right?" Charlotte asked.

"In that drawer," Ellen said, pointing. "Would you like to borrow
something?"

"Is it valuable?"

Ellen turned to her, trying to read her shuttered, tricky face. "The
really valuable things are at the bank," she said. "Why?"

Without answering, Charlotte went in the bathroom and stood by her mother's sink, scanning the miniature skyline of bottles and lotions and creams and sprays and different kinds of makeup. In their midst she spied the pearlized lotion from Florida. Charlotte opened the bottle, poured some into her palm and rubbed it on her arm. She closed her eyes and lifted the smell to her face.

"Why don't you keep that, honey? I almost never use it."

Charlotte cracked her eyes, glimpsed her mother beside her in the mirror and moved quickly away. The image of herself and her mother together—in a mirror, a window, a photograph—flattened her with a blunt hopelessness, a sense that she might as well be dead. Her mother was beautiful and Charlotte was not; she knew this always, of course, and yet a defiant optimism hummed within her, a faith that she had forfeited beauty for some extraordinary compensation. Seeing her mother beside her annihilated that hope, leaving Charlotte to wonder whether someone so unbeautiful as herself would be allowed to go on, to have anything. Wouldn't someone more beautiful get it, whatever it was?

Stung, Ellen ran a brush through her hair. She was used to Charlotte's rebuffs, but now, after a whole afternoon at the hospital with Ricky, her eyes filled with tears.

"You don't worry about someone stealing the jewelry that's in here?"

Christ, why was she harping on the jewelry? Ellen looped her hair around and pinned it onto her head, waiting for her eyes to clear before she answered. "Not really. I mean, we've got the burglar alarm."

Still, after finishing her hair, she slid open the jewelry drawer and looked at the tray of velvet cups, Charlotte lurking nearby while she checked her favorites: the Elsa Peretti bracelet, the jade lozenge Harris had brought from Singapore, the tiny yellow diamond cuffs. The amethyst pin, a gift from Moose years ago. She wore it for luck when Ricky was tested each month. "The important stuff is all there," she said. "Why?"

Charlotte gave a disinterested shrug and left the room, as if Ellen were the one dwelling on the topic.

Harris stood at his dresser, assembling the oblong gold studs and cufflinks engraved with his initials that he wore to dressy events. Charlotte watched his meticulous toilette from her parents' bed, thrilling at each gust of irritation her father provoked in her. His shirt was flawlessly pressed, sections of fine, translucent netting in the arms. Had he ever worn a soft flannel shirt, even once? Did he even eat banana bread?

"No plans!" Harris exclaimed, as if this were out of the ordinary. "No friends coming over, nothing?"

"I have plans with Ricky. When he's done skateboarding."

Her father looked disappointed, as if this were a feeble excuse for nothing.

"Plus I've got tons of reading for Uncle Moose," Charlotte threw in, purely to annoy him.

Her father frowned, and installed his cufflinks in silence.


Driving to the club through the azure dusk, Harris thought of his daughter alone before the TV set and felt a twist of anxiety. "She doesn't seem to be making many friends at East," he said.

"No," Ellen said. "She doesn't."

"I worry she's gotten lost in the shuffle," he said, turning to his wife. "This whole Ricky saga."

Ellen sighed. "I can only worry about one kid at a time."

"How was today?"

"Fine," she said. "Afterwards he ran out the door with that skateboard."

Harris whistled. "Busy life."

Since the beginning of school, Ricky had assumed a new identity as a skateboarder, an identity whose component parts were baggy pants worn so low that Harris expected to see his son's bare ass any minute, and a partially shaved head, a thin sheet of hair dangling over baldness. "Kid's hair finally grows back," he said, "and he shaves it."

Ellen shook her head. She hated the hospital; even now the smell of illness, of hospital food, made her almost gag. From the moment she and Ricky walked through those glass doors, her brain objected to every sight they passed: The veal-complexioned people in their paper outfits—no. People crumpled in wheelchairs or walking feebly, dragging IVs alongside them on wheels. No! No! They stared at Ricky ravenously, these failing creatures, as if he were a gatekeeper jingling the keys to their release. Ellen's son had never looked more beautiful than shuffling beside her over the hospital linoleum; she imagined these sad, broken figures grasping for his narrow eyes and lingering summer tan—

"Let go, Mom!" Ricky barked, shaking free of her grasp and pounding ahead down the hall in his oversized skateboarding shoes. Ellen understood, from her sessions with Dr. Alwyn, that her feelings about the hospital were freighted with memories of her mother, who had taken to bed for whole years, swaddled in her mysterious illness, ringing a little bell—deceptively tiny, for it had made a sound like breaking glass that filled the house—asking for cranberry juice. And Ellen would bring it, climbing the stairs with the small silver tray to her mother's room, which was always dark. No matter how bright or pretty a day might be—soccer games, damp summer grass, diving lessons at the country club—Ellen always felt inside her the weight of that dark room; only Moose had the power to dispel it. Yet she couldn't bring herself to sell the house! Now, with Dr. Alwyn's help, she had come to see that her reluctance was not so very strange—that the urge to return to the scene of unhappiness with the hope of undoing it was natural, if not necessarily good. "Bigger windows!" she'd exhorted the architect. But your furniture will fade. Screw the furniture, Ellen had parried, taking a certain delight in shocking the man. She wanted light, light. Fresh air to wash away the smell of her mother's illness—her mother, now hale and robust at seventy-two, living in Palm Beach with a Cuban immigration lawyer. Who took lessons in the tango, the mambo, the hustle, and had wallpapered a bathroom by herself. Who, it now appeared, had never really been ill in the first place.

"Penny for your thoughts," Harris said. He'd been hoping she would ask about his golf—he'd played under par and won a client, Matthew Krane, a consultant to the Radisson Hotel chain. But nowadays she rarely asked.

"I hope Ricky comes home on time," Ellen said. "So Charlotte doesn't worry."

"Charlotte never worries," Harris said.

### Grass

Okay, the land. Well, it was totally different from now. (First of all, where IS the land now?) It was mostly prairie, and prairie in those days did not mean dried-out grass up to your knees with some flowers mixed in. Prairie meant a mixture of many grasses—Indian Grass, bluestem, side oats grama—that were extremely tall, taller than a person's head! With long tangled roots that reached way down deep into the earth. Prairie soil was incredibly rich and good for planting, but all the grass and roots were very hard to break through and turn over, which you had to do before you could plant anything. It could take a whole year to make prairie ready for farming. "Breaking the prairie" was the name for that process, and there were professional Prairie Breakers who were experts at it. But eventually the whole prairie got broken up and planted into crops, and the real original prairie hasn't been around for many, many generations. What we call "prairie" now is just grass.

Eight o'clock, no Ricky. Charlotte went to the window and looked at the sky, but it offered her nothing tonight: a starless darkness. In the kitchen, she slipped a mini pizza into the microwave. She went online to see if any of her three best friends were logged on, but they weren't—out somewhere, probably together, these girls she had known since third grade, sharing sprees of candlemaking, ant farms, weaving, papier-mâché; Halloween costumes in which each was a different colored M&M. The summer after freshman year, the other three had gotten boyfriends, and a gap had fallen open between them and Charlotte. Even as her friends schemed on her behalf, begging to know which boys she desired and promising, through espionage and subterfuge, through brainwashing, hypnosis and possibly witchcraft, to make at least one reciprocate; even as they urged makeup upon her, a padded bra with the future option of implants, colored contact lenses (violet being their top choice), an alternative haircut and some more intriguing mode of dress—*The thing is, Chari, you aren't really making an effort*—even as a machine of rehabilitation churned around Charlotte, she'd been seized by a deep new resistance in herself, an aloofness from her friends' earnest confabs on her behalf. It was true, she wasn't making an effort. It seemed phony—dangerous, too, as if she might lose something in the process. A last hope.

She sent an e-mail to all three: "What's up? Hey, I miss u guys :-)"

93

At eight-forty-five she started watching *Murder on the Nile*—part of an ongoing project she and Ricky had undertaken to watch every Agatha Christie movie ever made. It was half over by the time she heard her brother downstairs and paused the tape. He gasped when she walked in the kitchen. "You're stoned," she said, looking at his boggled eyes.

He didn't answer. He was prying open a box of Pop-Tarts.

"It's nine-forty," she said.

"Ding ding ding."

"Where were you?"

"Skating. I nailed a dire trick." He dropped a Pop-Tart into the toaster. "A Switchdance one-eighty."

Charlotte had no idea what this meant. "Who with?"

"Seniors." He could not suppress a grin.

"You're kidding. From Baxter?"

"No. From Saturn."

The Pop-Tart jumped, and Ricky caught it between two fingers, blew on it a while and took a bite. The flavor shot through his head, a crazy infusion of berries. Charlotte just stood there. At the Pit, where he'd been skating, he'd heard someone say his sister's name but thought at first he'd imagined it; he was stoned, which made everything loop around and curlicue until he was skating through time—kings, knights on horseback waving lances, then ollying back around to the steps, where he heard it again—"Charlotte Hauser"—and was so startled he lost his balance and the board blurted away. He listened. Two seniors. It seemed to Ricky they were using Charlotte's name as kind of a threat, like, If you fuck with me—Charlotte Hauser. Hearing his sister spoken of in this way so appalled him that he forgot it instantly, let it drop into the night and disappear. Paul Lofgren, a senior, had decided this year that he and Ricky were bros, a mysterious grace that had befallen him for reasons Ricky didn't analyze. And so he hung with these older kids now, Smashing Pumpkins on the boom box, the very air sweet and rare. Charlotte was folded into the night. When he nailed the Switchdance 180, everyone clapped.

"Who's the kid?" Someone to Paul Lofgren. And Paul, laughing: "Girl bait," which occasioned a bigger laugh (everyone laughed when Paul laughed), and although Ricky wasn't clear on how he could be girl bait when he hardly knew any girls, he liked it immeasurably better than being the kid who was sick.

Nibbling his Pop-Tart under Charlotte's solemn gaze, he felt a jerk of impatience. She was weak, a joke—his sister—without even knowing it! *Why don't you do something?* he wanted to shout, then wondered why he hadn't done something himself—or said something. Said anything. Opened his fucking mouth even once. He believed Charlotte had the power to determine the outcome of certain things. Did she sense his treachery (she could read his mind, he was sure), or was she sad for some other reason?

"I rented *Murder on the Nile*," she said.

"Subtle," he said. "Let's."

"Here, I'll make your pizza." She'd saved half her own to eat with him. Her thin brown hair fell around her face as she took a pizza from the freezer and carried it to the microwave. And in that moment, Ricky, like the pizza, seemed to travel some distance in his sister's hands, to arrive fully and decisively home, in this kitchen.

"I smoked pot," he said.

He spoke with a mix of conspiracy and challenge, longing for Charlotte's approval yet daring her to withhold it. She rarely did; Charlotte liked being Ricky's confessor, privy to all his evil deeds.

"Ding ding," she said.

She carried his pizza upstairs, trying to master the anxiety it gave her to picture her brother consorting with boys who despised her. It seemed possible they might turn Ricky against her, and this conjured an isolation more brutal than any Charlotte had imagined.

"I watched a little, but we can start over," she said as they collapsed onto the couch in the TV room.

"That's okay," Ricky said, penitent. He relied on his sister to be cheerful; her somberness tonight unnerved him. "I can watch tomorrow."

But Charlotte rewound the tape, as he'd known she would. They flopped together, chewing pizza, and as the movie began, Ricky felt comfort fold itself around him like a pair of wings. The skating, Paul Lofgren, it all just blew away. It was maybe even good, he considered, that the other kids didn't like Charlotte—it meant that whenever he came home, she was likely to be here.

"You're waiting for something to happen?" Moose asked. "Is that what you said?"

"Does it sound weird?"

He smiled. "There are those who would tell you I'm not the best judge of that."

Charlotte laughed. The air was full of leaves. Ten fat jack-o'-lantern bags squatted on the bright lawn around Versailles. "Do you think something will happen?" she asked, hesitant.

"Yes," Moose said. He was thoughtful now. Charlotte followed his gaze, but saw just the lawn, the jack-o'-lantern bags. What was he always looking at, this handsome, uneasy man her mother loved so much?

"Yes, I do," he said.

And then it did. Something happened. Something strange—stranger than finding the wounded lady thief inside their house. It happened several days after her last visit to Moose, when Charlotte borrowed her mother's Lexus and drove to Baxter to pick up her friends. She waited for them outside the school, a woodsy assemblage of A-frames built in the sixties. She waved to Mr. Childs, her old biology teacher.

"How goes it, Chas?" he asked. Mr. Childs was famous for conferring monikers upon his favorites; a nickname meant a B+ at least. "How's East?"

"Good so far," she said. "You dissecting yet?" Charlotte had loved dissection, especially larger animals like the baby shark and fetal pig.

"Worms, and you should hear the bellyaching. You're in chemistry now?"

"Chem II. But the labs aren't as nice."

A teacher Charlotte didn't know was crossing the lot in the canted sunlight. He looked familiar: dark eyes, an angular, expressive face that seemed just slightly to glower. "See you tomorrow," this stranger told Mr. Childs. His eyes skimmed Charlotte, braking on her just long enough for Charlotte to recognize him: the man she had met by the river last August.

"Have a good one, Mike," Mr. Childs said. And to Charlotte, who was staring after the stranger, "That's Michael West, teaches math. Tracy

Lapoint's husband got a last-minute transfer to Omaha, and Mike turned up out of the blue. All the right credentials."

"Where did he come from?"

"California, but I guess he's lived in Europe a good while. I've got to run get my kids out of day care. Nice to see you, Chas."

He crossed the parking lot to his car. Meanwhile, the man Charlotte had met by the river was backing out of a space. She bolted toward him without thought, shoes hammering the pavement. The man stopped his car and rolled down his window, squinting at her in the angled light.

"I met you last summer," Charlotte said, breathless. "Remember?"

"I do not."

"By the river. You said you were new in town. Remember?" But already she saw differences: this man had neatly trimmed hair, a smooth, tanned face, while the other had been scruffier. And injured, too—his arm? Charlotte stared at the man in front of her, red Lacoste shirt, tanned fingers tapping at the wheel. Both arms looked fine.

"I believe you are mistaken," he said, with a slight accent. Had the man by the river had one?

"No," she insisted. She wanted it to be true—to have this coincidence. "It was you."

He laughed, his teeth a white slash against his face. "We have hit an impasse," he said. "And I'm hurrying to go." He waited, looking up at her, and only then did Charlotte realize that her hands were on his car, he couldn't move. She lifted them.

"Good-bye," the teacher said. He raised one hand to his face in a farewell gesture, and Charlotte felt a deep, prickling shock. It was the same thing he'd done before, by the river: part salute, part wave. It was the same man. The strangeness and certainty of it fell against her.

"It was you!" she called after him as the car pulled away. "Why are you saying it wasn't?"

She stood in the lot, gazing after the car as kids shambled past her in groups. She felt stunned by the encounter, as if she'd brushed against a tiny corner of something vast and mysterious. But why? she asked herself. So he didn't remember. Or he did, but didn't feel like saying so.

"Chari," her friends called, cascading toward her through the parking lot. "Sorry, babe. My lock was like totally stuck," Roselyn said, enfolding Charlotte in her peppery embrace.

They piled into the Lexus. Charlotte had just gotten her license, and the others hadn't seen her drive. "Look how calm she is," said Sheila, in front. She could make the nicest thing sound mildly sarcastic.

"Chari, your brother is so egregiously cute," came Roselyn's gritty voice from the backseat. She had something known as "screamers" on her vocal chords, a diagnosis that had occasioned no end of hilarity among them, since Roselyn had a tendency to shout. Charlotte smelled her strawberry lip gloss.

"He's thirteen," she pointed out.

"Roz is stalking little boys," Sheila said, fiddling with the radio dial. "It's her new project."

"Yum yum," Roselyn said.

"What're the guys like at East?" Laurel asked. "Like, how evolved?"

"Meaning are they into ballet," Sheila said.

"Ha ha," Laurel said. Freshman year, she had joined the Rockford Dance Company, and now performed in one large ballet each season. Since then she'd taken to extending her legs at odd moments, casually gripping a thigh and easing it toward her head in a disorienting spectacle of limberness. To Sheila, who slouched and was bulimic, the sight of another human so giddy in her flesh was beyond endurance.

There was a pause, and Charlotte realized they were waiting for her to speak. "I guess they're mostly jocks," she said, forcing herself to concentrate. Her mind swerved to the math teacher, then to the man by the river. "Some are cute," she said. "But the girls are, too." She had an anxious sense of covering something up—as if she weren't actually a student at East, as if this were merely a pretext. "You should come visit."

"Let's," Laurel said. "Sisterhood."

"Rah rah," Sheila said acidly.

"You're not invited," Charlotte told her, which made Sheila grin. She liked being put in her place.

"Change it! Change it!" Roz shrieked from the backseat. She meant the song—Sarah McLachlan, whom she hated. "Change it before I scream."

"You *are* screaming," Charlotte said. "Right in my ear while I'm driving."

"No wonder," Sheila muttered.

"That's not why I have screamers," Roz said hotly. "The doctor says there's point zero zero connection."

No one answered. It was a fruitless argument.

"I saw that new math guy," Charlotte said casually. "Mr. West."

"Oh. My. God," Roselyn said, breathing hot strawberry fumes close to Charlotte's ear. "Is he not the most dire thing you ever saw?"

"I'm in his class," Laurel said, and Charlotte winced at the thought of the math teacher watching her point her feet into perfect commas.

"Is he nice?" she asked.

"Freaky," Laurel said. "Half the time when someone makes a joke, he doesn't even get it. He's like, formal?"

"Mucho curioso," Roz said, squeezing Charlotte's shoulder.

"I thought I saw him before," she said, then let it go. But her heart and stomach were alive with secret intelligence. She knew the math teacher in a different way; she'd spoken to him alone, by the river, when he was not a math teacher but someone else. That was how it felt—as if they had met first in a dream and now were meeting again in waking life.

At Cherryvale, the girls bought peanut butter logs and lemonheads at Mr. Bulky's and ate them furtively from small white bags while they clawed through the racks at Juxtapose, whose walls were emblazoned with posters proclaiming, "Back to cool," and "Enter the next level."

At Waldenbooks, they swarmed the magazine counter, sticky fingers snapping glossy pages as they riffled through them greedily, breathing each other's gum and candy and lip gloss as they spied on the slender girls moving about in their parallel universe. Girls squinting in deserts. Girls leaping in snowbanks. Girls fishing in waders past their thighs. Charlotte tried not to see them. There was no place for her in this parallel world; according to its dictates, she was worthless. Her friends didn't look like models either, but in some ineffable way they came closer, Sheila especially. And Laurel had her dancer's body and Roz, with her sultry voice and tangled hair, had been nicknamed "Luscious" since ninth grade.

Charlotte observed these facts without resentment; for her, there would have to be another way. She believed this.

At six-thirty, she drove everyone home, Roselyn last because she lived nearest. "I miss you, Chari," she said. "You're real."

"You, too," Charlotte said.

"I get sick of all the plastic people."

"It's an infestation."

"So you'll come, right?" Roselyn and her older sister were having a party that weekend. "Bring people from East."

"I'm not sure they're worthy."

"Then bring your brother," Roselyn said.

Charlotte was supposed to see her uncle the next afternoon, but she canceled the appointment, cut her last class, borrowed her mother's Lexus once again and drove to Baxter just before classes ended. She killed the engine and sat in the parking lot fiddling with the radio dial. When the first kids began coming out, she hunched down in her seat. They left the campus in waves.

Finally Mr. West appeared, walking with Abby Reece, Charlotte's eighth-grade English teacher. Ms. Reece was very pretty, and Charlotte felt a little queasy watching the two of them talk. Her heartbeat swished in her ears.

Finally he got in his rust-colored Oldsmobile Cutlass. It was three-fifty. Charlotte pulled out of the lot behind him and followed him south all the way to State Street, where he turned east and drove past the State Street Station, past Aunt Mary's and Alpine Road and Winnebago College and then Versailles, where Moose lived, then finally made a left into the parking lot at the Logli supermarket. The lot was vast and busy, and the math teacher grabbed a lone spot close to the entrance. "Shit!" Charlotte yelled, trying to memorize the place as she drove on. She saw him walking into the Logli and decided to idle near the exit doors. Nine Inch Nails was on the radio, a group she loathed, but she was too anxious about keeping her quarry in sight to bother switching stations. Every muscle in her body felt alert, primed for action. After thirty minutes, the math teacher emerged with a sack of groceries in each arm, and Charlotte floored the gas so her tires yelped and a pregnant lady glanced at her in fear. She sped to the exit nearest his parking space and waited there—not her most delicate bit of spying, it was true—but when he pulled out, she was right behind him. He drove west on State and took a left, then a right, then another left onto a street farther south, close to East High School and lined with smallish houses, some with weedy, overgrown lawns. He pulled into the driveway of one of the weedy ones.

Charlotte parked on the next block and sat there, Janet Jackson serenading her alongside the heckling voice in her own brain informing her that she could not do this thing—it would be a breach of normal conduct too egregious to recover from. Yet she felt she had no choice. She left the car and made her way on watery legs to the man's modest two-story house. White peeling paint, green window trim. She rang the bell and waited, and then the door opened and there he was, holding a can of Blue Ribbon. He regarded her coldly.

"It's me," Charlotte said. She clenched her jaws to keep her teeth from chattering.

"So I can see," he said.

"I met you yesterday. And before, by the river."

He didn't reply, and Charlotte glanced behind him into the house. It looked empty. "Did you just move in?" she asked, a bit desperately.

"Tell me what you want."

It felt impossible to explain. "Remember how you said Rockford was ugly and I said don't call it ugly? By the river, remember?" She watched him beseechingly, waiting for him to feel the link of fate connecting them.

Michael West cocked his head. Then, abruptly, he opened the door and stood aside to let her through. "Come here in the kitchen," he said, leading the way. It was small, a pale green linoleum floor. Two windows faced the driveway. The grocery bags sat on the counter, half unpacked. He gestured at one of the chairs.

"Beer?" he asked. "But then again, you're driving."

"How did you know?"

"I confess I am pessimistic about your career as a detective," he said, and laughed a little harshly.

"I don't want to be a detective," Charlotte countered. "I want to be a tropical fish dealer."

Michael West poured her a glass of orange juice, flipped a chair backwards and sat facing her across the table. "How old are you?"

You asked me that already, she almost said, by the river, but refrained. Allusions to the river did not seem to go over well. "Sixteen."

"The other sixteens are smoking pot and listening to Anthrax," he said. "Not following people in cars."

"I'm not like them."

"In what respect?"

She hesitated. The difference felt complex, difficult to name. "I don't have breasts," she finally said.

This made him laugh, more in surprise than anything. "Patience," he told her.

"No, they're done. But I don't have any."

"The name is 'small-breasted,' " he said. "Some men prefer it."

"Do you?"

"This is irrelevant."

"But do you?"

He rose to fetch a second beer and remained standing, looking out his windows. He opened the can and took a long swallow. "Do you often discuss your breasts with strangers?"

"No."

"Then why are you trusting me?"

"I don't," she told him, "trust you."

He laughed, perplexed, then resumed his seat and leaned toward her so that Charlotte smelled him: warm, bitter, tinged with something like cinnamon. His scowling look had finally disappeared. "You want something from me," he said. "What is it?"

"I want you to seduce me," she said, then waited in dread for him to laugh. He did not. He looked quite serious. "I think you're the right person," she said. It had come to her only seconds ago, when she'd smelled him.

"Are you a virgin?"

She considered. "Half and half."

Michael West looked bemused. After a moment he pushed back his chair and stood up.

"You said I had pretty eyes. By the river," she reminded him.

"Our mysterious chat by the river."

"You did."

"Well, they are," he said, not looking at her. "They're very dark."

Charlotte was aware of a tightening in the room, some emotion from him that she couldn't identify. Encouraged, she went on, "It would be easy! You know I would let you."

At last he looked at her. "You cannot talk a man into seducing you," he said. "He should feel a . . . a longing for you."

Charlotte shook her head. "No one does," she said, and to her own astonishment, tears filled her eyes. It had been years since she'd cried in front of anyone. She covered her face. "No one ever will."

She heard him moving behind her. He put his hand on her shoulder, a man's hand. Warm. But he didn't want her.

"You're learning something important," he said, rubbing her shoulder a little. She lifted her head. "The world is made of shit," he said, and Charlotte was startled by his look: empty, hopeless.

"What happened to you?" she asked.

For just a moment, he seemed on the verge of some disclosure. Then he smiled, his face resuming its harsh posture. "Nothing you could understand."

"You don't know that. You don't know one thing about me."

"You should go," said Michael West, more gently.

Charlotte stood, white kitchen light jumping against her eyeballs. It was almost dusk. Already the conversation felt unreal, like all her conversations with strangers. He walked her to the door. No one will ever know, she thought.

"*Adios,*" she said.

He didn't salute her this time.

She walked to her mother's car in the approaching dark, feeling ghostly, as if her real self were still back in Michael West's kitchen, and she were just an echo of it. She sat in the car for several minutes, waiting for the buzzing in her head to cease.

Finally she started the car and drove slowly past his house. The light was still on in the kitchen, but she didn't see him, and the rest of the house was dark. She drove idly, hardly conscious of where she was going until she found herself pulling into the parking lot at Versailles, where Moose lived, out of some misguided habit, some lingering sense of how she would otherwise have spent the afternoon. She didn't know why. She sat for several minutes, looking in the direction of her uncle's apartment while dead leaves dropped from the trees onto the hood. Then she turned the car around and headed home.

# Chapter Six

*Weather permitting, Moose* liked to walk the short distance from his apartment in Versailles to his office at Winnebago College, in part for the obvious benefits—fresh air and the like—although his concern for fresh air was mostly theoretical; he worried about it (or rather, the encroaching lack of it), enjoyed breathing it, but had long ago ceased to engage in the sorts of activities that celebrated its availability and freshness: hunting, camping, hiking, fishing. Athletics of all kinds.

No. It wasn't fresh air that impelled Moose's walks to work; it was the fact that in an era characterized by, among other ominous developments, the disappearance of the sidewalk, he offered up as a gesture of insurrection his own persistence in walking where a sidewalk should have been. I may look silly, his thinking went, as he rappelled over wedge-shaped hedges between parking lots and sashayed aside for heavy-breathing Chevy Suburbans, but not nearly as silly as a world without sidewalks—indeed, my apparent silliness is merely a fractional measure of an incalculable larger silliness whose foil I am. He didn't say these things aloud or even think them anymore, per se, but he walked with a certain burly pride, a saucy, righteous air that lasted precisely the one-half mile of State Street between Versailles and Winnebago College, at which point he turned onto a driveway that sloped down to the college grounds, and paranoia set in.

Following the road's insinuations, Moose gazed up into the frazzle of half-bare trees, postponing for as long as possible the intersection of his gaze with his two approaching colleagues: Janice Fine, with her needly little eyes and insect's hairdo, and Jim Rasmussen, who always looked like he was about to vomit. Together they had spearheaded a movement eight months ago to boot him off the faculty.

"*HEL*-lo," Moose greeted them at last, stressing the first syllable of the word. They nodded tepidly in return. Having passed them, Moose could not refrain from swiveling around to peer anxiously at the conspiratorial tilt of their heads, wondering if they were plotting his future unhappiness and unemployment. He forced himself to walk on. They were afraid of him, and jealous—yes, he believed they were—for despite his ignominious résumé, despite the fact that he was underpaid and cooped up in a small dark basement office where no other offices were to be found; despite these manifold indignities, which Moose endured with a stoicism made possible only by the imperative of a far more urgent project, he was a popular teacher. Students liked him; they eagerly descended to his subterranean lair to cajole their entrance to his overcrowded class and to request independent studies the college refused to pay him for. Why did a handful of undergraduates seek out a teacher who had a catastrophic problem with eye contact? Moose wasn't sure, exactly. Long ago, he had drawn people effortlessly to himself; for whole years he had hardly a memory of being alone. That time had passed, of course, and now Moose was alone a great deal. Yet his popularity among the students affected him like a last warm, lingering touch from that prior era.

Each semester, Moose selected two or three of the most eager kids and taught them independently, despite the acute discomfort it gave him to engage in one-on-one conversation, not to mention the lack of remuneration. These tutorials were critically important to Moose—his life's work: to bequeath the vision that had transformed him eighteen years ago, when he was twenty-three, to a handful of younger, abler others who might carry on the work when he no longer had the strength.

But how to make them see it? The question dogged, pursued and plagued him. Moose himself had had no teacher; he'd recognized the vision on his own, in a single moment—the way, when an ophthalmologist once pointed a bright light into his eyes, he'd borne witness to a bloodsoaked landscape, red earth riven with fissures like mud after a drought: his own blood vessels, the doctor had explained, and suggested that this sighting bespoke a higher-than-average intelligence.

"Bullshit!" Moose objected aloud, then sucked back the word because he was pushing open the door to Meeker Hall, the history building. The departmental receptionists, Amity and Felicity (they of the misleading names), eyed him with bristling wariness as he scooped the mail from his cubbyhole. "*HEL*-lo," Moose said, tossing the greeting at both women, then departing their domain with relief.

No, intelligence was not required for the kind of sight Moose wished upon his students—he was traversing the hallway, being careful not to glance toward his colleagues' offices lest he catch an eye and be faced with a choice between making conversation or stomping rudely past—for the vision was not intellectual but instinctive. A faint intimation, then knowledge, like the fall of an ax. He descended a flight of damp concrete steps to the basement level of Meeker Hall and slid his key into his office door. Only to find it . . . already unlocked!

His heart released a spate of frantic beats. He pushed the door open gently, gently, then stepped into his office alert to signs of burglary or surveillance, but the premises looked undisturbed except for the wastepaper basket—empty, for once—which meant that Jeremy Toms, the sweet boy with Down's syndrome whose job it was to clean his office (mysteriously excluded from the regular cleaning staff's route) had forgotten to lock the door when he finished.

Moose collapsed into his chair, drained. His office was simple to the point of cruelty: a square concrete room; standard-issue desk; two orange plastic cafeteria chairs and a beige metal file cabinet. But these blunt rudiments were all he required, Moose would remind himself on days when the poverty of his surroundings robbed him of hope; these were the flint and stone and tinder he would use to make a conflagration! Locked inside that beige file cabinet lay the makings of his multivolumed history of Rockford, Illinois, a work that would be unprecedented in its scale and ambition (he hoped, on good days), seminal in its agile mingling of genres and flourishes of unexpected humor, and scathing in its prognostications for postindustrial America, more than a few of which had already come to pass.

Moose glanced through his mail, the usual memos and departmental effluvia along with three heavier, textured envelopes that made his heart twitch: missives from other academics. But he chose not to open or even examine these closely as yet; three letters meant at least one disappointment—a rebuff, a rebuke, a dismissal—and he needed time to replenish his strength after the rigors of entering Meeker Hall before he could absorb it.

He turned instead to the several letters he'd typed the previous day on his Smith-Corona electric. Moose didn't own a computer, had declined even to use one of those supplied—nay, required—by the history department (further jeopardizing his status) for the simple reason that he didn't want it near him. Since the incident at Yale he'd come to distrust computers; they were too ineffable, too seductive, their connections too difficult to sever once they had formed. And so Moose had typed, two-fingered, all of the letters arrayed before him now. He was a zealous initiator of correspondence, hungered for the sense of communion it gave him, and launched hopeful epistolary forays into such unlikely realms as artificial intelligence, optics, physics and French ballet, disciplines where it was just possible no one had heard of his misdeeds, but (alas) equally likely that a query from an Adjunct Assistant Adjunct Professor of History (a nonexistent title invented to capture the vivid tenuousness of Moose's status) at Winnebago College was not sufficiently prestigious to provoke a reply.

Moose had a rule he observed rigorously: he waited twenty-four hours before mailing anything he wrote. At times this delay caused him physical discomfort, like having to stop short of completing a baseball or golf swing (those barely remembered pleasures), but he knew from experience that the anguish of mailing something and later discovering that some aspect of its contents had been egregious or ill advised, offensive or silly, was incalculably worse. So he waited. And here was a letter written yesterday to Sara Herz of Tulane, a medievalist whose early research on the structure of fourteenth-century houses contained work on the architectural implications of glass windows, which Moose had cited in his first book. Sara knew about him, of course, which had discouraged Moose from contacting her in the intervening years (I realize it's been awhile, Sara, but your recent article on late medieval Netherlandish women's clothing led me to revisit your earlier work on glass and to wonder where the two might intersect; namely, did the introduction of daylight into indoor life via glass windows

It transfixed Moose to imagine those early years of quickening sight
made possible by the proliferation of clear glass (perfected in Murano,
circa 1300)—mirrors, spectacles, windows—light everywhere so suddenly, showing up the dirt and dust and crud that had gone unremarked
for centuries. But surely the most shocking revelation had been people's
own physicality, their outward selves blinking strangely back at them
from mirrors—*this is what I look like; this is what other people see when they
look at me*—Lacan's mirror phase wrought large upon whole villages,
whole cultures! And yet, as was the case with nearly every phenomenon
Moose observed (his own life foremost), a second transformation followed
the first and reversed nearly all of its gains, for now the world's blindness
exceeded that of medieval times before clear glass, except that the present
blindness came from *too much sight*, appearances disjoined from anything
real, afloat upon nothing, in the service of nothing, cut off from every
source of blood and life.

Moose read the letter to Sara once again, feeling somehow that it
lacked the tone of breezy indifference he'd meant to strike, betrayed a
whiff of overeagerness, and thus (he feared) his essential isolation. He put
the letter aside, slightly breathless with relief that it was still in his possession to be refined, filtered of the broad and lurching impulses that
moved him constantly without his knowing. Control, control. As long as
he maintained it, the nefarious efforts of Janice Fine and Jim Rasmussen
would come to nothing. As long as he maintained it, he had some hope of
accomplishing the rest.

The next letter was to an art historian at Fordham University
named Barbara Mundy, whose book, *The Mapping of New Spain,* had kept
Moose wide awake for three nights running. He had hopes of enlisting Professor Mundy's help in interpreting his own vast collection
of Rockford maps, but an obstacle loomed: according to her author's
note, the professor had obtained both her B.A. and her Ph.D. from none
other than *Yale University,* thus raising the specter—even likelihood—
that she had been a student there at or around the time of the Bomb
Episode.

No, that was wrong; agitation had no place in such a letter. Moose
scratched it out and wrote in by hand, **I hope for, and look forward
to, your response**. Too stilted? Well, better stilted than raving. The
point was to induce a reply, to make her respond; make her correspond
(*and you don't know that she won't,* said a small voice that occasionally piped
encouragement within him—his father's voice, Moose sometimes
thought).

He slipped a clean sheet of letterhead into his Smith-Corona and re-
typed the letter to Professor Barbara Mundy as corrected, feeling a spasm
of gratitude for his continued access to letterhead stationery, gratitude
that brought with it a corollary, clammy intimation of just what it might
be like to face the world without access to letterhead—a person alone,
with no affiliations.

He sealed the letter and left his desk, restless. He raised the blind covering his single window, which was half belowground and half above it.
The belowground half provided a cross section of dirt and roots and grass
that reminded Moose of the ant farm he'd owned as a child. He'd even
had the opportunity, if you could call it that, to watch worms mate
from his desk chair, then observe the resulting baby wormlets as they
writhed and ate. The aboveground portion of window admitted a com-

promised slab of daylight, and, because it faced a paved path, afforded Moose an unparalleled view of his colleagues' footwear, their worn heels and frayed soles, their strappy sandals and white gelatinous feet. This top portion was stuck shut (the bottom did open, as luck would have it, effusing muddy water during hard rains). Nonetheless Moose endeavored, now, as he did nearly every day, to yank open the window's top half, convinced that without warning, his years of cumulative effort would cause the window to slide open effortlessly, much as he hoped the vision he was trying to impart to his students would blazon forth with sudden clarity.

And when it did, it would be everywhere they looked, because *we are what we see*.

Moose spoke these words aloud to his empty office, whose girding of nonabsorbent concrete shoved them back against his ears: "We are what we see."

And because this was so—we are what we see—once a person had witnessed the vision, that person's life would be razed like a twig shack by its annihilating force (Moose knew, oh, yes), a juggernaut that was like a whale rearing up beneath a tiny raft and hurling its inhabitant, and the petty utensils he had foolishly believed could protect him, to the far corners of the earth. Or maybe not a whale, for sometimes the shadows cast by shapes overhead—clouds, for example—had a way of resembling gigantic things looming up from beneath the water's surface, so perhaps the devastation came from above . . . the idea interested Moose, and he made a note to consider later on: "Clouds, whale."

In short, the vision was impossible to recover from—that is, if one defined "recovery" as the resumption of one's prior existence. It heaped a crushing burden upon those who had glimpsed it; the few, the very few who did were almost certainly doomed to—

A sound punctured his thoughts. A noise. A knock at the door: his niece. In she came, wearing a bright blue sweater, her hair in a ponytail. Ellen's daughter. And now his student. Moose still was unsure exactly why she was his student—to annoy her father, he'd thought at first, and been happy to collude. But Charlotte's persistent attendance had begun to baffle him.

Rather than take a seat, as she usually did, Charlotte stood in the doorway, and Moose became aware of some change in her. She looked . . . unhappy? Happy? He was inexpert at guessing other people's states of mind; in his febrile, oversensitized state, he tended to assume that everyone around him was suffering. Charlotte had circles under her eyes. She seemed distracted—by some inner pain. God help him!

"How are you today?" Moose managed to ask.

"Fine," she said, and sat (heavily) on one of the orange plastic chairs facing his desk. She set her books—the many books he lent her, most of which she did not read—on the second chair.

"Is Ricky . . . ?"

"Oh, he's great," she said, with a bitter laugh. "He's hanging around kids my age."

Moose succumbed to his wish not to look at her. Normally he forced himself to look; a person who wouldn't look at other people was untrustworthy—so said the world. He had trained himself to glance at people in conversation, but kept his eyes unfocused so their images remained muffled, imprecise. Moose believed adamantly in regulating the imagery one allowed to penetrate oneself. And wasn't "penetrate" precisely the word? Did not the things we saw, literally and figuratively, enter us in a way that was at once forcible yet deeply intimate? Moose scribbled a note to himself: *"Seeing—sexual??"*

He was startled by the presence of his niece across the desk.

"Here," she said, smiling with what seemed a great effort and handing him two sheets of paper from a blue folder with "Uncle Moose" printed across the front. "This is what I wrote for the time I missed."

Moose glanced at the pages. Ah, yes, her essay on mechanics. "Why don't you read it aloud?" he suggested, eager to be relieved of conversation for several more minutes.

This duty seemed to rally Charlotte, and she lifted the page. **1852: A Huge Year.** Her title. There was always a title, a headline. Moose found it sweet.

**1852 was the year when Rockford really changed from a little town into the very beginnings of a city. . . .** On she went. The railroad, the arrival of Swedes . . . the spike in population. Moose nibbled at his fingernails.

Then in 1852 the Rockford Power Company was formed to build a new dam. Now this "power" had nothing to do with electricity, because there was no electricity yet! This was mechanical power. . . .

The dam, the race, paddle wheels turning shafts that ran along the factory ceilings; Moose was comforted, as always, by the thought of mechanical power—its clarity, its simplicity. This pushes that. How far from the vagaries of power today; what did "power" even mean?

. . . And once all this was up and running, many more businesses came to Rockford, and it became famous for its manufacturing.

Moose closed his eyes. She was a sweet girl, his niece, so eager, grabbing at each thing he said like a seal lunging for fish, but what did she do with it? Where did it go in her high school student's brain?

"The basis of mechanics, as I think we've discussed," he said, "is the conversion of force . . ."—he paused for emphasis—"into motion."

Charlotte hardly listened. Reading aloud to her uncle, she had at last begun to awaken from the drenching torpor that had befogged her from the moment she'd driven away from Michael West's house. Exactly seven days ago. Since then, ordinary life had become intolerable, a denial of her link to him in every detail: her blue room, her fish, the garden hose coiled on the patio, her parents across the dinner table—each of these was a stone added to the several she already carried on her head.

After school, she would ride her bike past his house. Once, she went around back and found a handkerchief-sized lawn, a locked shed, a peeling picnic table. She dragged the picnic table to a window (replacing it precisely afterward, fluffing up the grass she'd crushed), then climbed on top and peered inside the house. Shadows, streaks of sunlight. Almost no furniture. The strangeness of it moved her. Yet Michael West did not feel the bond between them; she was nothing to him. A girl who had cried in his kitchen.

But here in Moose's office, the distance between herself and the math teacher began to seem porous, negotiable. Some rhythm she'd felt in his presence was sensible here, too. Charlotte noticed her scalp tightening over her head as she forced herself to listen to her uncle, and then a single phrase—"conversion of force into motion"—latched in her brain. She sat up very straight. Force into motion! It was a matter of forcing Michael West into motion, making him love her as she loved him. The answer was *power*. Mechanics. Abruptly it made sense.

"Of course, certain kinds of mechanization had existed for centuries," Moose was saying. "Water wheels, for example, date to the first century B.C. . . ."

"Windmills," Charlotte muttered, tapping her feet.

"Very good!" he rejoined, gratified by even this slim show of participation. "And we've talked before about mining, one of the earliest industries . . ."

She was watching him in that odd, expectant way, and Moose was silenced, enervated by the multitude of steps (millions, too many to ascend, or perhaps he simply lacked the stamina) that gaped between Charlotte's tentative, familiar observations and even the first faint vibration that precedes sight—the first ghostly penumbra of the vision. *I'm waiting for something to happen,* she'd told him once, which had excited Moose for perhaps an hour, until he reminded himself that the phrase could mean almost anything.

"You know," he said, "my head is aching a little."

"I have some aspirin . . ."

"No. No thank you." He held his head and waited for Charlotte to suggest a deferral. This code functioned beautifully among his college students, the most seasoned of whom were so accustomed to Moose's "headaches" that they took to their feet sometimes at an inadvertent massaging of his brow. But Charlotte held her ground, and Moose sensed—God help him—that she was maintaining her orange plastic chair out of a desire to speak with him about some matter unrelated to the Rockford Water Power Company. And in light of her earlier symptoms of distraction, it seemed possible—nay, likely—that the matter Charlotte wished to discuss with him was personal. God help him! But she was his niece. And his pupil! If she wanted help, he had to help her!

"What I need," Moose said, "is a walk. How does that sound to you?"

He locked his office door and led the way from Meeker Hall into a small wood behind it, dense, deciduous, spiky with half-denuded trees— a mere soupçon of what Rockford (or "Forest City," as it had once been known) must have looked like in 1852. In the strong, rather bitter wind, shriveled gray leaves clattered from the trees. Moose wore a red scarf Ellen had given him last Christmas. Charlotte crunched behind him on a narrow path, working to assemble the courage to ask his advice.

At last her uncle paused, and Charlotte turned to him, raising her voice. "Uncle Moose, if a girl loves someone, a—a guy," she veered away from "man," at the last second, "how can she make him *feel a longing for her?*" She had reprised this phrase of Michael West's so many times that it came out lightly salted with his accent.

Moose laughed as if he'd been kicked—such generous, delighted laughter that Charlotte couldn't take offense. "No one's asked me a question like that in oh, Jesus . . . how long?" he said, with shining, joyful eyes. "A hundred years, I think."

They were standing beside a thicket of saplings, and Moose shoved his way into their midst, holding two trees aside so Charlotte could climb in after him. "Here," he said, mashing leaves under his black shoes. "Unless I'm wrong, there's a creek just past here."

Her uncle led the way, stamping through dry grass to the edge of— yes—a creek, where shallow water purled around rust-colored rocks and dropped into a dark, still pool. Moose went to the edge and leaned over, peering into the pool. Then he squatted beside it. "As a kid, I used to fish here," he said.

"What did you catch?"

"Minnows."

He closed his eyes. Remembering his youth was a vexed experience for Moose; he understood that as a boy he had lived in blindness, but he knew, too, that some pain, an ache that nowadays accompanied him through each minute of his life, was yet absent. When Moose imagined himself as a child, he pictured a boy watching him across a doorway, through a screen, and a bubble of sorrow would break in his chest, as if he were seeing someone who had died or vanished inexplicably, a milk carton child, as if some vital connection between himself and that boy had been lost. And despite all that Moose knew he was achieving now or trying to achieve, still he felt—inexplicably—that he had failed to fulfill the promise of that little boy, and was being visited by his unhappy ghost.

Ellen, he knew, shared his sense of the broken promise. It was one of many reasons Moose avoided his sister. If two people saw it, did that not make it true, in some sense?

"Uncle Moose?" Charlotte said. For long minutes he had squatted by the pond watching speckled brown fish jaw the surface, during which she had gone from hoping he was marshaling his thoughts to answer her question, to believing he'd forgotten it, and her, altogether.

"Yes!" Moose turned, looking up at her with bright, wet eyes. What had they been talking about? He was disconcerted, lost in the pitch and roll of his thoughts . . . she wanted something, but oh, God, what was it she had asked him? And in his eagerness to know, his guilt over having forgotten, Moose looked carefully at his niece in a way he almost never looked at anyone, searched her face with eyes keenly focused. He saw her: a worried, hopeful girl who looked younger than her real age, breaking a leaf into sections. And for a moment it was Charlotte, not Moose-the-boy, who gazed at him across the threshold of that imaginary door.

"Follow your desire," he said, with a force that startled even himself. Surely this would answer whatever it was she had asked; it was the credo of innocence, of blindness—of boyhood happiness without the ache. Moose wanted that happiness for Charlotte. To set her free, he wanted that. To release her into the blind, supple pleasures of ordinary life, a life he could hardly imagine anymore, much less remember. A life he scorned and envied. "You're young," he said. "Go enjoy yourself. Grab pleasure wherever you can find it."

"But what if people turn against me?" she said, standing very near him under the trees. "What if they laugh?"

"Then leave them behind," Moose said, rising to his feet. "Don't let them shame you; shame is the world trying to break you, and you have to resist! You have to resist!" His own words galvanized him, and he surged on. "Don't look at yourself through their eyes—don't. Or they will have won, because . . ." He paused, then lunged forward, vertiginously. ". . . Because we are what we see."

It was the first time Moose had spoken these words to another human being. He had imagined it happening differently, a grand pedagogical denouement. No matter. Here, too, they would serve.

He felt a sudden peace. *We are what we see.*

Charlotte was staring up at him. In her look Moose saw the faces of his students at rare times when a swell of emotion still took him in class, energy coursing from his fingers, the top of his head. He would feel their attention tighten around him and experience a whiff of euphoria, an old, half-forgotten pleasure from a time when he was someone else.

"Follow my desire," Charlotte said. "That's what you think?"

"Wherever it may lead."

Moose let her go, opening his hands in the cold fall air, releasing her into the world, the blind, peaceable world where he no longer seemed to have a place. "You have nothing to fear," he said, "nothing." Then added, "It's your only chance at happiness."

Michael West stood inside a house of white brick, a modern-looking house whose whiteness brought to mind whitewashed houses on a cliff. He closed his eyes and breathed the memory: white walls, a sea pale as milk, wind that left on the skin the finest layer of salt. He allowed himself one memory each day, and did not permit it to evolve beyond the immediate senses. He almost never remembered people. He believed he could make himself remember nothing, if he chose, but believed, too, that things suppressed entirely had the power, in some cases, to explode.

"Can I get you another drink?"

It was Mindy Anderson, mistress of this white house where the annual Parent-Teacher Cocktail was taking place. A thin woman with a long nose and wispy blond hair. She was terribly concerned about his happiness.

"Yes, please," Michael said. "Another beer would be great."

Since his arrival in Rockford, he had begun for the first time to drink alcohol, and he was blown away by the sheer pleasure of being slightly drunk. The floating sensation alcohol induced, the belief that one could do anything; how well matched these sensations were to his present gigantic surroundings—houses like ships, supermarkets bigger than the biggest mosques, vegetables, mailboxes, all enlarged beyond belief, to the point of comedy. Miles and miles of parking lot. You could build a city in the forgotten spaces between things. Being drunk made him feel more American.

A couple approached, the woman large in the way that couches and refrigerators were large, dressed in a loose floral pantsuit that hopped around her like a collection of eager pets. "Someone told me you're Mr. West," she said in a tone that made him long to say she was mistaken. "My daughter, Lori Haft, she's in your algebra class."

Now the husband pitched forward and introduced himself, a big man who wheezed a little when he breathed.

"Lori, yes," Michael said. A girl with golden hair and long thin legs like tusks. Could this truly be her mother?

"I'm concerned about her grades," she said, narrowing her eyes. Her hair was short, cut close to the head. Michael felt a pulse of anxiety. He knew this woman: the fool who sees everything. She had dogged him throughout his life, though more often she appeared as a man.

"Please. Tell me your concerns, Mrs. Haft."

"Well, she studies like mad, but she says you don't give her any idea what's important. She doesn't understand you." Her eyes crackled with suspicion.

Any threat, even a small one, like this, induced in Michael West a calm that was almost like sleep. "I feel that I'm being quite clear," he said. "But perhaps not enough."

"Perhaps," she said with faint mockery, as if the very word proved her point.

"If she will meet with me after class, I'll review with her what is important."

"Really? You'd really do that?" There, a relaxation. She was selfish, finally; selfish above all else. Nearly everyone was.

"If Lori takes the initiative, I will be available."

"Abby Reece says you're from California," said the woman. "But you sound foreign."

Mentally, he cursed her. His accent was so slight, as long as he avoided words he hadn't practiced. Soon it would be nonexistent. Of course, he hadn't yet developed an individual voice; his phrasing and diction were copied from TV and the people around him. His grammar was cautious, studied. But eventually a voice, too, would come. It always did.

"I've lived abroad for many years," he said.

"Where is it you're from exactly?"

"Smithton. It's near L.A.," he said, and then, as if she might not understand, "Los Angeles."

Of course, an evasion like this would be pointless elsewhere in the world; people identified one another by dialect, family, accent. But in America, there was always someplace else. And Michael West had a gift for languages and accents—more than a gift, he could not resist them. They acted upon him like magnetic fields, unmooring his speech from the landscape of his own past and reconfiguring it in the image of his immediate surroundings. Accents were history; an accent declared *I come from someplace else.* But for Michael West, the past was gone, pulverized into grains of memory too fine to decipher, or to leave him with any sense of loss.

"And where is it you spent all those years abroad? Mexico?"

He had a sensuous fantasy of seizing her proud, bloated head and pushing his gun into the loose underside of her chin, watching her expression collapse into fear so abject it looked like tenderness. "France," he told her, squashing the 'a' so flat that it broke in half and occupied most of the word. You want America, there it is, he was thinking.

Mercifully, another woman who was friendly with this one came along, and Michael was released. He went to the window and gazed outside at the odd arrangement of lawns: one of short green grass, a second of long dry brown grass. They met behind the house in a line. He closed his eyes, releasing himself to the exhaustion that had consumed him ever since his arrival in Rockford, Illinois. Each night, he anticipated sleep like a meal.

"We're thinking of doing the whole thing prairie." Mindy Anderson, at his side once again.

"Prairie?" It was not a word he knew.

"See, we did this patch as an experiment," she was gesturing at the brown half of the lawn. "I think George thought it would be too wild, but I love it. Of course, it's half-dead now."

"How does it work?" He asked the question tentatively, always reluctant to acknowledge the vast dark spaces in his knowledge. But instinct told him that this discussion concerned fashion, not substance, that not knowing was all right.

"Well, they have the basic mix of grasses. Then you pick one of the Wildflower Moods. I picked 'Rainbow,' you should've seen it in the spring and summer, it was every color you can imagine, but subtle, too, like—like real wildflowers in a field. Oh, shoot, people are leaving. Excuse me."

Good, he thought, people were going home. Soon he could sleep. Prairie. Prairie was grass, wild grass that was fashionable for lawns. "We're doing the whole thing prairie," she'd said. *Doing prairie.* Softly he murmured, "Have you ever thought about doing prairie?" But no, the stress was wrong, the grammar too formal. The sentence had to lean. "You ever thought about doing prairie? You ever thought of doing—"

"Don't talk to yourself. Talk to me."

It was Abby, smiling. Abby Reece, an English teacher whose wavy dark hair was faintly streaked with gray. Her eyes, too, were gray, wide and thoughtful and easily hurt. Four times, Michael West had taken her to dinner. The last was two nights ago, and they had seen a movie—his first in many years. He had gone to the theater the day before to observe the process: ticketing and concessions, restrooms, seats; the less he knew, the more conversancy he required to be at ease. And when he returned to the theater, with Abby, it had all been familiar, like second nature. The movie concerned a doctor who begins to think that his patients are animals. Pigs and sheep lay in hospital beds. Michael hardly knew what to say about it afterwards, but this seemed not to matter. "Yuck," Abby proclaimed, and they had returned to her house and lain on her metallic blue bedspread and had sex—his first time in some months—while her children slept. Afterward, while they drank tea in Abby's kitchen, the children had appeared, two of them, like little ghosts. Michael hadn't seen them before; Abby didn't want him to. They were very small. In their presence, he felt the stirring of a memory, which he snuffed. Abby hustled the children away. "I'm sorry," she'd said at the door, as he was leaving. "They almost always sleep through the night."

Abby Reece brought with her a life; her small house, her two children and slender gray cat, her collection of antique dolls with china heads. It could become Michael's life, too—overnight, the way restaurants appeared on State Street fully formed, assembled from plastic parts that arrived in long boxes stacked on trucks. He had driven to these building sites in the middle of the night and watched the crews at work. Each part was numbered. Even banks could be built in this way. The indoor music, he'd learned, was beamed down by satellite to all incarnations of a particular store or restaurant, so that in New York and Atlanta or Los Angeles, the same song would always be playing.

"I say we blow this pop stand," Abby said.

"Sure," he said, dissatisfied by the way the word caught on his teeth. *Sure.*

Good-bye, good-bye. So very nice. He shook hands with the host, a rich jowly man whose five children were either students at Baxter now or had been once. "Such beautiful art," Michael said, eyeing the smears upon the walls that looked like shit, or snot.

"We're glad you're here and we hope you'll stay," the host said jovially.

"Thank you," Michael said.

In the car he took Abby's hand. Her hands were strong, a mother's hands. At night he imagined them touching him.

"I've got to let the sitter go," she said, "but you could stay for dinner." Perhaps because he had already seen her children.

"I think not," he said. "I'm so tired."

She smiled through her disappointment. She was a good, trusting person. He had given her the impression that a tragedy had befallen him, a dead child, a dead wife. He had not been specific, and she was too polite, too respectful to ask what exactly it was that had caused him to abandon one life and begin another. Like most people, Abby assumed that only a catastrophe could cause a person to do such a thing, but Michael West had done it more than once. There was a freshness in leaving behind one life for the next, a raw, tingling sensation that was one step short of pain. An imperative of the mind and spirit had reshaped the facts of his life like tides rearranging a shore. And in each new life there was Abby, awaiting his arrival—more than one Abby, sometimes—people with empty places beside them where Michael could stand and look as if he belonged.

They passed two McDonald's, but he had trained himself not to look at them in the presence of other people. He had never been inside one.

Michael pulled into the driveway of Abby's house, a small one-story made of yellowish brick, indistinguishable from thousands of other houses in Rockford. "You want to come in for a minute?" she asked, from politeness this time. Expecting him to refuse.

"Sure," he said, testing his pronunciation once again. He wanted to prolong the presence of people around him another few minutes, to put off his solitude. With solitude came exhaustion, sleep, but underneath that sleep, running through it in the form of urgent and disturbing dreams, were the questions he would have to answer as soon as he was rested: What was he doing in Rockford, Illinois? And where was the conspiracy he had come to America to destroy?

Abby looked surprised, pleased that he would come in. Her husband, Darden, had bolted to California two years ago with a young woman in possession of a false nose, a false chin and two false breasts. Except for occasional grudging payments, he'd had no contact with Abby or his children since that time. Michael had to forcibly curb his curiosity about this man, Darden Reece. What had he hoped to find in California, and had he found it?

Abby opened the front door and the two children, Colleen and Gavin, tumbled toward her across the room. Michael glimpsed the babysitter quickly hang up the telephone, and winked so she would know he'd caught her. She had long orange fingernails and was chewing a massive wad of gum that bulged in her cheek. Her age—sixteen, he guessed—reminded him of the other girl, the one who had followed him to his house.

Without thinking, Michael lifted Colleen into his arms, a mouse of a girl, feet sticky with something from the floor. Abby, who was paying the sitter, looked up startled, but glad, too—glad he'd wanted to lift her daughter. Michael held the wriggling four-year-old girl and felt how easily she could become his own. People were vines awaiting the chance to cling—Colleen's sticky feet on his shirt, her small arms around his neck, her mother standing nearby, watching them with anxiety and hope.

So easily, one could slip inside of other people's lives. Gavin, the two-year-old, clung to Michael's leg, and Michael lifted him, too, so both children squirmed in his arms, and he felt a pull deep as gravity, an exhausted longing to relax, to lie down here with this woman and her warm, squirming children and never leave. Then he extinguished the thought. It wouldn't work; his soul was too small. Most peoples' were large and soft, engorged with sensations and needs that would have made life unbearable for Michael West, like trying to function with his stomach cut open, holding in guts with both fists. His own soul was tight and hard, white as a diamond. People saw in it whatever they chose. That was his gift: to be blessed with a soul that promised whatever people wished, and yielded nothing.

He knew what would come of "settling down," how welcome it would feel at first. But if he were to marry Abby Reece and move into her house and go to church on Sunday mornings with her children, if he were to "barbecue" and feed the cat and take up golf, all the while, his hard white soul would be burning slowly through the soft tissues of this new life until finally it would pierce the last layer and he would find himself outside it. No matter how many layers a life contained, his soul would eventually work its way through the outermost one, and take him with it.

Abby had gone to the kitchen to start dinner. Still holding the children, Michael leaned in and told her he was leaving. "No!" Colleen cried, and Gavin imitated her without understanding, "NO. NO!" They clung to his neck like frantic monkeys when he tried to release them.

"Kids," Abby said sharply, and they let go in a single motion. When he set them down they stood quite still.

She had poured a package of microwave fettuccine into a glass bowl—powder, noodles—and was adding water. "Sure you don't want to stay?" she asked lightly.

At the door, Colleen hugged Michael's legs and kissed both his knees. He did not lift her again.

He drove quickly to his house, a tiny two-story which was the precise opposite in atmosphere of the one he had just left. Abby had never seen his house, and she would be shocked, he thought, by its emptiness. Right now, the house suited him perfectly.

*Tired. Exhausted. Bushed. Beat.* Colloquial English lacked sufficient vocabulary to express the enormity of what he felt, had felt for months, ever since his arrival in this place. He reached for a beer, then changed his mind and poured a glass of milk, which he took to his room. There was a bed, a dresser and of course a TV set, that American treasure chest. He watched the programs that everyone watched, and when he wasn't watching, he listened—for accents, facts, common knowledge. Sometimes he had trouble distinguishing between TV events and real ones; certain things on TV could not happen in life, even in America. He showered down the hall, listening to shreds of TV sound through the running water, and with his hair and body still damp, he lay down on the bed and glanced at his book of Japanese erotica, then decided against it. Too tired. He felt a moment of regret for not having stayed with Abby; he longed for sex with a human being. But sex, not love; not *making love*. It was too much work.

In the middle of the night, the doorbell rang. Michael woke in a paroxysm of fear and leapt to his feet, which made pricks of light flood his head. For a moment, he felt close to passing out. But already the calm, reasoning part of him was restoring order: if his compatriots had tracked him down, then so be it. He had always known they might. Still, anxiety cracked through his limbs when the bell rang a second time.

He pulled on his jeans and pushed his Walther into the waistband, against his stomach, not that a gun would be any use if they had found him, but it made him feel stronger. He pulled a shirt from a hanger and buttoned a couple of buttons, enough to cover the Walther, then stepped nimbly into the empty room at the front of the house, the room from which he could glimpse whoever was standing at the door. Someone thin, female. In the moonlight, a red bicycle gleamed against the grass.

He descended the stairs and opened the front door. It was the girl, holding a bowl of fish.

He experienced a wave of relief so immense it made his eyes sting. He felt as if the girl had brought that relief, irrational though this was.

"Hello," he said, dizzy from the sudden calming of his heart.

"Hi," she said, and held out the fishbowl. There were three fish, smooth and brightly colored: crimson, vermilion. They looked like flowers. "These are for you."

"Thank you," he said, taking the bowl from her. He felt half-asleep, the exhaustion already flowing back around the shards of his panic, reclaiming him. He opened the door and led the way into the kitchen, where he set the fish on the table. When he turned on the light, he noticed how bad its color was, green almost. He would get a different bulb, or else a shade. Something to filter the light. The fish bumped very gently against the sides of the bowl.

"They're cold," the girl said.

She wore a jean jacket and a white shirt underneath, a man's shirt much like his own. Her hair was pulled back in a ponytail, and she wore glasses. Her cheeks were red. "You carried these fish on a bicycle?" he asked.

"I only need one hand to steer," she said. "You should keep them by your bed."

"And why is that?"

"If you watch them when you go to sleep, they'll give you good dreams."

This got his attention. Dreams were a problem—not only did they curdle his nights, but at times left a troubling residue that touched his days. He preferred not to dream at all.

"Maybe you would always have good dreams," he said. "Fish or no fish."

"I'm telling you," she said.

He leaned against the sink, watching her. There was some response between them; he felt it each time she was near. Michael respected the power of chance, of vibrations, all the things one couldn't see. Occasionally, those things were more powerful than all the rest—you either bowed to them, let them in, or their force would break you. But this vibration was nothing like that. This was one of hundreds you sensed between yourself and other people.

Obviously he must send her away yet again. But he delayed. She was reaching into the pocket of her jacket for a cylinder of fish food, explaining at what times and in what quantities the fish should be fed. Michael didn't listen. Sending her away would not be enough; he'd done that already, twice. This time, he would deliver the message more strongly. He must shake her, but not frighten her deeply enough that she would turn to someone for help. Although he doubted she would. She could absorb it on her own, this girl. He watched her pale face and neck.

"Let's take them where you sleep," she said.

"That isn't necessary."

She picked up the fish with a quiet insistence that angered him and aroused his curiosity. If there was a single impulse Michael West found hardest to curb in himself, it was the desire to know every fact about a situation before he acted—to wait, test his beliefs about human nature and psychology against the bracing force of reality. He had suffered for it—more than once—yet the impulse remained, perhaps had even strengthened over time. So often he knew more than the people around him, sometimes a great deal more, and yet some part of him still longed to have his own predictions confirmed, or, better yet—and this happened rarely—to be surprised. There was something engaging, now, about allowing this young American girl to believe she could trick him.

"Upstairs," he said.

She went first. He followed her into the sound of the TV, and noticed from this vantage point her ass and hips and her smell, a clean smell, like the sea. He felt a first intimation of something overtly physical toward the girl, and it was simply the thought that he would like to smell her again.

"Wait," he said at the top of the stairs. He was picturing his room. "It's not clean. Give me the fish."

"Turn off the light," she said, "and then I won't see."

"You'll fall down, and my lovely new fish will die."

"I can walk in the dark."

He paused, taking his own mental temperature once again. There was plenty of time to get rid of her. But curiosity stopped him, he was unwilling to end the story so soon. Who was this girl? He'd met her before, of course—there was no one in the world he hadn't met before, usually many times. And yet he found her difficult to place. She stood in the half-light, holding her bowl of fish, and a moment later, Michael found himself inside the room, switching off the light. On the window sill stood a little kumquat tree he'd bought, and it filled the room with a citrus smell much sweeter than the taste of kumquats. He snapped off the TV. A terrific hush settled over room and house, a sound of its own. He hadn't pulled the shades, and a bright, hard moon thrust its light between the clouds. "Okay," he said, opening the door. He found that he was nervous—it was eerie, somehow. The girl came in and shut the door behind her.

"Wait—," he said. But apparently, moonlight was enough, because she made her way to the window and set down the fish beside the kumquat tree. Moonlight filled the bowl, and the flowing, dreamy movement of the fish seemed to capture Michael's own state of mind, as if he were swimming among them, as if he himself were the bowl in which they swam. The girl sat on his bed and kicked off her sneakers. Her back was to the window. Except for a slim black silhouette, he couldn't see her.

"Come here," she said.

It was time to stop, to *draw the line*, he told himself (a TV phrase), yet it also felt too late. Too late: the story was unfurling like a scroll. "It's time for you to go," he said, his accent strong in a way that startled him.

"Just sit here for a minute."

He sat. And only then did he feel the Walther against his ribs and remember it there. "Wait," he said, standing again, moving to the dresser. He opened a drawer, slipped out the Walther, and put it where it had been, under his socks.

"What are you doing?" she asked, and he heard a guttering of fear in her voice, slight but distinct. She was alone in a stranger's house, a stranger holding a gun, and she'd brought with her nothing but a bowl of fish. Stupid, he thought, desperate, crazy—the words arced through his mind, but he was also thinking, brave. Strange. It moved him. She had placed herself entirely in his hands while pretending not to know it, pretending to think she was in charge. And he had believed her.

And at that moment he decided, or rather, accepted the decision that had been made without his knowing. He would set down this coordinate, though it conformed to no picture he could recognize. In an empty universe, everyone must choose a few coordinates, and Michael West—or Z, as he had been until last August, and before that another name, a series of other names—chose to sit beside this girl.

She was lying down, arms at her sides, staring at the ceiling. He lay beside her, not touching. He breathed her smell. Plums, he thought, plums that grew by the sea. "Is that perfume?" he asked.

"Lotion," she said. "From Florida." She was terrified; he felt the mattress trembling underneath her. She'd been afraid all along, but he hadn't known.

"I love it," he said, and took her hand, which was hot and shook in his, and she rolled on her side to face him and he held her. They held each other very tightly. He felt her strength, the pounding heart inside her small frame, and in that moment he recognized her at last: the innocent. He felt an impulse to protect her, shield her from some proximate and overwhelming danger. But there was only himself.

# Chapter Seven

*On the morning* after my abortive interview with Irene Maitlock, Oscar called and read me the phone numbers of two psychiatrists. In a show of devastating restraint, he made no mention of the fact that I had hounded a *New York Post* reporter from my home, thus dashing my last, best hope of resuming my former life. "We'll speak again when you've met with one of these excellent doctors," he told me. "Or both."

I had no intention of calling a shrink; in my present, incomeless state, I couldn't have justified seeing a shrink even if I'd thought it would do any good, which I did not. Was a shrink going to succeed where the combined expertise of Doctors Fabermann and Miller had fallen short—namely, in restoring me to my pre-accident state? No. A shrink was going to make me, or "help me," as Oscar so delicately put it, accept my present circumstances. And I could do that alone—I'd done it all my life. My problem was that I didn't yet know what those circumstances were, exactly.

I waited twenty-four hours before calling Oscar back. "I saw Mitzenkopf," I reported. "And you know what he told me, Oscar? He said getting a few jobs would do more for my peace of mind than a hundred hours of therapy. Can you believe the honesty of a shrink saying that?"

"Dr. Mitzenkopf is female," Oscar replied, and hung up without further comment.

After that exchange, which concluded at ten-thirty-five on a Friday morning, I did not speak to another human being for seventy-two hours.

A colossal silence broke open and spread around me, a silence whose dimensions felt global, seismic, planetary; a seeping quiet that was familiar, I supposed, to astronauts and Antarctic explorers, but not to me. I sat on my sectional couch looking out at a snowstorm, jillions of white dots hurling themselves against my sliding glass door in a subatomic frenzy.

By Monday morning snow lay piled along the East River, heaps of gold in the slanted morning sun. And then the phone rang. "I have two words for you," said Oscar, when I answered in a voice grown froggish from disuse. "Italian *Vogue*."

I must have screamed.

"Careful of your face," he said. "It has to last until tomorrow."

The blood was beating against my cheeks. I sat down, light-headed.

"There's just one tiny thing," he said. "They believe you're the subject of an upcoming feature story in the *Post*. Let us not enlighten them."

I let this go. "Who's the photographer?"

"Spiro. Who happens at the moment to be incandescent."

"Not paparazzo Spiro," I said, referring to a fairly desperate second stringer whose postage-stamp-sized photos had freckled the lower-tier gossip pages for years.

"The very same," Oscar said. "My, how things change in a few short months."

Spiro's fortunes had turned last fall, Oscar said, when he'd had a one-man show at Metro Pictures displaying work he'd been shooting on his own: an homage to Gordon Parks consisting of black-and-white photos of a sixteen-year-old gang leader called Honey B. Reviewers praised the show's gritty authenticity, its unblinking portraits of urban violence rendered in magisterial tableaux reminiscent of Goya. *Bazaar* immediately hired Spiro to reprise the series in "Girl Gang," a now-infamous fashion spread featuring models in Martine Sitbon and Helmut Lang posing as gang members. ("Execution," a shot of Kate Moss holding a sawed-off shotgun to the head of a blindfolded and kneeling Amber Valetta, had caused a particular frisson of outrage and commentary.) Since then, fashion assignments had been coursing into Spiro's life without interruption.

"Strong women, that's his thing," Oscar said. "No more of this I'm-a-fucked-up-junkie stuff."

"Should I bring my gun?" I kidded.

"You should praise Allah for this reprieve and give the man what he wants," Oscar said. "Do you hear me, Charlotte? Are you listening very carefully to Oscar?"

"I am."

"Make. This. Work."

I hung up and went straight to the mirror to prepare my aching, indeterminate face for its big day. I massaged it gently, imagining I could feel the sharp little screws under my skin. I swabbed it with vitamin E oil, then stood back and took in the rest of me. Height: 5'10", weight: +/–125, measurements: 35"-25"-36". Hair: short (always), thin and straight, but redeemed somewhat by a natural dark brown luster. Eyes: green. Facial features: delicate, somewhat pixie-ish, the sort of features that register, at first glance, as young. Neck: long. Breasts: unremarkable—not especially large—but compared with the breasts of women my age who'd had children (my sister's, for example) still relatively lively. Waist: narrow and fluid, with a corresponding propensity to accrete weight on the ass and hips. Hands: long-fingered, prone to redness. Legs: straight, a little gaunt in the calves, in recent years a bit veiny (too much tennis as a child?). Feet: pretty once, increasingly dry and callused with the years.

What these qualities meant, how they conjoined to form a human being who looked and moved a certain way, I had no idea. As a teenager, I first became aware of people's eyes catching on me as I walked down Michigan Avenue with my mother and Grace during shopping trips to Chicago. They glanced, then *looked*—each time, I felt a prick of sensation within me. I knew how transistors worked; my father had shown me a picture of the very first one, at Bell Labs, a crusty, inauspicious-looking rock that had performed the revolutionary feat of transmitting and amplifying electrical current. The jabs of interest I provoked in strangers struck me as an unharnessed energy source; somehow, I would convert them into power.

As children, Grace and I liked to pretend our life was a movie projected onto a giant screen before an audience who watched, rapt, as we ate our pork chops and finished our homework and went to sleep side by side in our twin beds, Grace rising to shut the closet door if I left it open. Gradually, mysteriously, that fantasy evolved into a vocation—I came to imagine my future not in terms of anything I might do or accomplish, but the notoriety that would follow. During my college years at the University of Illinois at Urbana-Champaign, I would venture into Chicago and gaze up at the glass towers lit into the night. Somewhere among those shimmering panes lay the mirrored room, a place I had never seen and knew little about—the famous people who lived there were not the sort you saw, or could talk to. To the extent that I had an academic bent, it was poetry, of all things, Pope and Keats in particular, who between them seemed to encompass the entire spectrum of sensuality and cynicism available to humankind. I managed to memorize half of "The Eve of St. Agnes," and would mutter stanzas to myself when I was bored, alone, or at aerobics class. But the pleasure I took in my poets was sharpened by a piquant air of doom; they would never deliver me to the mirrored room, those two—one gnomish and unsightly, the other racked by fits of coughing, both dead—and so I knew I would eventually spurn them for some less worthy partner.

I was discovered on a Sunday between my sophomore and junior years, a summer I spent in Chicago with two sorority sisters, Sasha and Vicky, all of us working as paralegals for Vicky's Uncle Dan. We were blinkered on dope, sacked out in Lincoln Park wolfing down marshmallow treats when a woman approached, looking frighteningly businesslike. "Can I talk to you girls a minute?" she asked, to which Vicky, prelaw and paranoid, pinched out our joint with her bare fingers and dropped it down the front of her dress.

"Uh . . . sure," we said, all retarded movements and red goggle eyes; I'd forgotten the Visine.

The woman turned to me. "I work for a modeling agency," she said. "Is that something you've thought about?"

"A little," I said.

"How old are you?"

"Eighteen."

Vicky, truthmonger, legalist, peered at me cartoonishly—my twentieth birthday was two weeks away. But to my good fortune, the still smoldering joint chose that moment to announce itself inside the waistband of her dress, and she yelped, swatting at her midriff. Sasha yanked her away.

"Just eighteen?" the woman asked. "Or closer to nineteen?"

"Um . . . almost eighteen?"

I was a natural.

The woman gave me her business card, and I rejoined Sasha and Vicky, who were piled on the dry, rubbery grass in weepy hysterics over the charred hole in Vicky's sundress. We tottered to the Farm in the Zoo and watched a patient cow get milked by a machine attached to her udders before an audience of gasping children. White milk shot through translucent plastic tubes. I've been discovered! I kept thinking. Someone had recognized me, singled me out. I saw nothing strange in the fact that *being* discovered, rather than discovering something myself, should prove the decisive event of my life. Being discovered felt like a discovery.

Can there be anyone left on earth who remains ignorant of the details of a fledgling model's career? Interview agency. Test shots. Absences from college for jobs. Photographers. "You've got it!" Cocaine in tiny spoons, in amber vials. Expensive dinners no one touched. The world in which I found myself afforded an unbroken vista of pure triviality, but it had a lazy, naughty appeal, the allure of skipping dinner and eating a gallon of ice cream instead, of losing a whole weekend prone before the TV set. I enjoyed the inconsequence of this new life even as I scorned it for being nothing; I enjoyed it *because* it was nothing. Chin down. Stop scrunching your hands. Don't stare, relax your eyes. Stop talking. It's harder to see you when your face is moving.

Being observed felt like an action, the central action—the only one worth taking. Anything else I might attempt seemed passive, futile by comparison.

Trivial, yes. But I was aiming for the mirrored room. There was nothing more essential in the world; nothing that failed, when placed beside it, to disappear completely.

I dropped out of college six months before graduation.

The weather was milder the next morning, the morning of my job for Italian *Vogue*, so I put my ski mask to rest and hailed a taxi outside my building.

Broome Street in the bald early light looked broken and gray, like old plumbing. Every gate was down. I trudged and skittered onto Crosby, where the studio was, nearly losing my footing in piles of snow already soused with grime, avoiding the miniature ice rinks that had formed across caved-in portions of the sidewalk.

An industrial elevator released me into an abundance of yellowy light that caught me by surprise, as if I had stepped outdoors, rather than inside. A loft: white floor, white walls, rows of windows along two sides. Dance music thumped softly; on a zinc countertop lay a spread of muffins and orange juice and coffee. I felt a small detonation near my heart. I was back at work.

Spiro greeted me as I poured my coffee. He was a man assembled of elbows, tendons and jaw, with heavy-lidded eyes that leaned a little from their sockets. "Charlotte, oh, my goodness," he said, kissing the air on both sides of my face as if we were old friends. "You look totally different, how intense! Who did your surgery?"

I told him, emphasizing Dr. Fabermann's contribution, and he narrowed his eyes with great interest. "Don't you think it would be so amazing for girls to get regular surgeries on their faces so they'd always look different?" he asked. "Like once a year, at least. I mean this changing the hair color every five months is so tired. Blond, black, blond, red—like oh, you're such a chameleon! I'm really into tissue, you know, the real human being."

"I'm not sure I would've done it voluntarily," I said. "But I'm learning to live with it."

"Change hurts, isn't that right?" Spiro said. "Tissue is where you feel pain, not in your hair, not in your nails, not in your eyelashes. That stuff is so easy."

"This is true," I said, although he sounded slightly mad.

"So look, Ellis is doing makeup. Do you know Ellis?" I did not know Ellis. "He's just finishing Daphne, then he'll do you. And the clothes are a riot, take a look." He gestured at a rack fat with velvet dresses, purple, green, red, gold, all with steep necklines and white ruffled collars.

"Very sixties," I said, but Spiro was already halfway up a ladder, conferring with his assistants about lights.

In the middle of the room sat a giant hollow cube of white plastic. I went to look at it, carrying my coffee, and I noticed a young Asian girl sitting crosslegged in one corner of the loft, smoking into a foil ashtray.

She looked too small to be a model—the stylist, maybe? As she smoked, she stared straight ahead as if entranced. Not the stylist, I thought; she was too inert. No one else seemed to notice her.

A door opened onto a roof deck, and I stepped outside into the cold and peered down at lower Manhattan shuddering slowly to life. Yellow cabs, white sky; a whooping succession of car alarms that seemed incited by the very act of listening. What was this feeling inside me? I wondered. Peace of mind, but without the drunkenness. Peace of mind, but with something added; energy, maybe. I thought it might be happiness.

The door opened and Lily Cabron, an old hairstylist friend of mine, came outside. "Oh, Charlotte," she said in her slight accent, and hugged me tightly. "You poor baby! You look great, though. Did it fuck up your hair?"

"It did," I said. "They say it's the anesthesia."

"Trauma upsets the hair," she said. "Hair wants everything the same. No changes ever."

"Like people," I said.

I hadn't worked with Lily in ages; I no longer got the kinds of jobs Lily worked on. And because she was married nowadays, with children, I no longer saw her at night. "How are the girls?" I asked.

"Big," she said. "Loud. Hungry. They're eating me alive. You'd be surprised, Charlotte," she added, "how very wonderful it is."

"I would be surprised," I said, and laughed.

Back inside, the music seemed louder, a nascent excitement already rousing the room. The Asian girl was still slouched on the floor, gazing at nothing. "Who is that?" I asked Lily, as we headed toward the makeup room.

"She's new," Lily said. "I think she . . . was in the newspaper or something. From Korea?"

Where had I heard about this? Somewhere recently; I groped the white empty corridors of my immediate past, and then I remembered: Oscar's North Korean girl. The one who wouldn't eat the orange.

"Wow," I said, and turned to look at her again; the girl was so oblivious that outright gaping seemed permissible. "So she's part of this shoot?"

"She's the backup."

"Backup what?"

"Model. You know, in case someone's not comfortable."

"Oh, is it nude?" I asked, surprised that Oscar wouldn't have mentioned this.

"Nude? No no!" Lily said, distracted by the rack of dresses. "Did you see? Here's my favorite." She pulled one off the rack and held it to her neck, a waterfall of crushed yellow velvet. "My girls would go ape-shit for this stuff."

In the makeup room I met Ellis, a buff Australian with a deep tan, fragile blue eyes and a beaten looking face. His long, dirty-blond hair was pulled back in a beaded leather thong. He'd just finished Daphne, a new girl whose face I'd been seeing everywhere: white-blond hair and a rotten, downturned mouth. I sat in the makeup chair, feeling a thrum of pleasure at each familiar detail: the hot bulbs around the mirror, smells of hairspray and powder and hair dryer exhaust. The big slovenly makeup box.

To my alarm, Ellis began swabbing off my base. "Do you have to do that?" I asked. Since the accident, no human outside the medical profession had seen me without it.

"Spiro wants to use this real hypoallergenic one," he said.

"Believe me," I said, "mine is hypoallergenic." But Ellis continued to work, pinching the dainty cotton pads between fingers that looked organic, like roots.

When my base was gone, Ellis drew himself back and looked at me. "Something happened to you," he said.

"I had a little accident." I was forcing myself to hold still.

He took my face in his hands, moving his eyes over it as if he were reading. His palms were warm, almost hot, and the feel of them on my skin had an instantly calming effect, like the touch of a magician. "Little?"

"Well, medium-sized."

"Brave girl." He let me go and began applying the other base, a lighter one, nudging it over my skin with a fresh latex sponge. "This covers really well," he said, I thought to reassure me. His touch felt so warm. It was hard to believe this was work.

In the adjoining room, Lily had spiraled Daphne's hair around scores of the tiniest curlers I had ever seen, and was blowing them dry. The girl's exposed ears were covered with crimson powder. "Freaky ears," I said to Ellis.

"Spiro's a freak," Ellis said.

"Hey, Charlotte," Lily called through the doorway, over the dryer. "After your article comes out, will you possibly write a book?"

Ah, yes. The article. "I don't even read books," I said.

"Who cares? An interesting thing happened to you."

"You'd think it would be interesting," I said, "but it's actually pretty boring."

"But you know—to look different all of a sudden, overnight," she said. "Everyone imagines that."

"Do they?" I flicked my eyes at Ellis, hoping he would proffer an opinion, but he was absorbed in his work on my face.

"Close," he said, and shadowed my eyes.

"You can tell us what it's like," Lily said. "What happens next."

"But if what happens next is that I write a book, won't I be writing a book about writing a book?"

Ellis was pinning up my hair. "Ears," he said, dipping a giant soft white brush into a tub of scarlet powder. "Don't get ticklish."

"I have this friend you should talk to," Lily said. "She's with a big firm. She knows exactly how all those things work, getting published, getting in the news."

"Sure." I was barely listening. Ellis was brushing the red powder onto my ears, an experience I found almost unbearably sensual. I shut my eyes and let the dance beat judder through me. I imagined Ellis kissing my mouth, a long deep kiss, his warm tongue. Then leaning forward, unzipping his black jeans. Blood rushed to my face and made it ache.

I sensed a commotion of nervous energy, and knew that Spiro was near. When I opened my eyes, he was examining Daphne's hair in the next room. Lily had removed the tiny rollers and now was spraying the resulting bubble bath of curls into a sharply defined mass that hugged the top of Daphne's head like a bonnet. "You did it!" Spiro breathed ecstatically. "Lily, you're a totally gifted supergenius, do you know that?"

Lily smiled. "Yes I know that."

Spiro nudged Daphne's curls. "Spray them really shiny," he instructed. "It should be exactly like marble, only it's hair. Look what a supergenius Lily is," he called through the doorway to Ellis and me.

"What's the story with that hair?" I asked.

"Flavian," Spiro said. "From ancient Rome." He was throwing off nervous energy like heat. "Wherever they have those Roman busts, like in museums?" he said. "You'll always see a few girls with this Flavian hair. I was in Naples last summer, and I went to the big archaeological museum there, and I looked at all that Flavian hair and I screamed! I mean it, I screamed out loud. I screamed, OH, MY GOD. OH, MY FUCKING GOD!!"

"The Catholics must have liked that very much," said Lily.

"Then? In this gallery on Madison Avenue? I found one of these busts, and I bought it. Didn't I, Lily?"

"Yes you did," Lily said.

"I showed it to Lily so she'd know exactly what I wanted. She told me something I didn't even know: she told me the Romans used drills to drill into the marble to make the middle part of each curl. I mean, obviously not electric drills, but . . . God, I wish I could show you," he said to no one in particular. "Shit, why didn't I bring that bust? Richard!" he called to an assistant. "Can we messenger for a Roman bust, or is it too risky?" He left the room to consult with Richard, but was back a moment later, plucking the Camel from Daphne's mouth. He took a long hit and replaced it. "The vibe in here is getting good," he said, dancing a little, popping smoke rings at the mirror. "Richard, can you turn up the sound? What about you folks? *Stai contenta,* Charlotte?"

"I'm happy," I said, moving to the music as much as possible while holding my face still for Ellis. And I was; happiness leaned against me from inside. I reached for my purse, took out two Merits and offered one to Ellis, who lit them both with a malachite lighter. Then he stood back and gazed at my face, smoking meditatively. I glanced at myself in the mirror, a stranger in beautiful makeup, and felt a twisting excitement I would forever associate with my first years back in New York after Paris, years during which an exquisite tension had gathered around me and begun to tighten, slowly lifting me up. When Oscar commenced to negotiate a three-year contract on my behalf with a major American designer, the tension reached its apogee, and I enjoyed the epistardom accorded those whom everyone believes will soon be stars. I was beloved. The air smelled like money. So close did I feel to the mirrored room that I experienced an anticipatory nostalgia for the sweet, small life I would soon cast off; its every detail felt precious. And much as I longed, now, to take credit for the failure of that tension to coalesce into something coherent, longed to be able to say, It was my fault, I blew it all with one massive and outrageous fuckup, vomiting on a designer's head, gamboling naked onto the runway—those horrors one dreams of half longingly, half in terror—I could never find a connection between any behavior of mine and the result, or lack thereof. The designer in question pulled out at the last minute and signed another girl whose grinning physiognomy was now a fixture on the wall calendar–exercise video circuit, and from that point on, my momentum began to ease, or drift. A subtle change at first, a calm that was almost welcome after the maelstrom that had surrounded me. But the spreading quiet soon assumed a creepy, menacing note—where had everyone gone? Like someone in an elevator whose cable has snapped, I began wildly pushing buttons, sounding alarms, but nothing could halt the sensation of rapid, involuntary descent. "Who took you to St. Barts?" I hollered at Oscar when he called to report my cancellation by a photographer whose support was mandatory for any model aspiring to the highest tier of success. "Who bought you a Claude Montana jacket with zebraskin lapels?"

And then, from one day to the next, I gave it up. It's gone, I thought, it didn't happen, not this time—not this way. Fuck them, I thought. And I meant it.

Did I need a shrink to help me then? No, I did not.

And that was basically that, although it took several more years before I was truly a catalogue girl with no prestige whatsoever. Just how many years I wasn't sure, exactly, because at that point, the point at which my acceleration began to reverse, time started running together—there was no more arc of ascension by which to measure it. The years began passing in clumps, so that one day I was twenty-three (to the world) standing at the threshold of the mirrored room, and the next, ten years had passed and I was twenty-eight and a professional beauty, by which I mean a person in possession of phone numbers of sumptuous homes around the world where she (or he) will be welcome, a person adept at packing on a half-hour's notice for a trip to Bali or a sailing cruise off Turkey's southern coast, a person who will never have to pay for her dinner as long as she doesn't expect to choose the company. Indeed, understanding how much she can reasonably expect is key to the professional beauty's continued circulation, and requires the use of an obscure algorithm involving the variables of how good she looks, how easy she is to be around, and what, exactly, she's willing to give in return. As the years go on and one's looks and novelty wear off, one had better start cultivating some other skills. Of course, the professional beauty's existence was generally an anteroom to some more permanent arrangement, and the ones with any sense married well as expeditiously as possible, while their stock was high. Such transactions weren't necessarily base or grotesque; there were plenty of stops on the road to trading looks for cash before you arrived at the old carp at the end of the line whose breathing was audible at dinner and whose daughters were nearer your mother's age than your own. In my case, marriage to money would certainly have been the prudent route, and yet I couldn't seem to do it. Having forgone a marriage of love, how could I promise those very same things out of mere practicality? It seemed dull and frightening. Try as I might to interest myself permanently in the real estate owners I met, owners of yachts and islands and seventeenth-century castles, of Bonnards and Picassos and Rothkos and vintage cars and zoo animals, private screening rooms and fleets of chestnut horses, my concentration always broke; my mind wandered, another man came along, and the prior one fell away or married someone else or simply vanished.

And at a certain point, after many years at this sort of life, I began to sense that my poor concentration wasn't really that. I'd compromised, God knew—I'd forfeited my hope for the mirrored room and settled instead for the chance to rub shoulders now and then with some of its inhabitants. But what made these compromises bearable was some last expectation I hadn't relinquished. I was waiting. Waiting and watching for a new discovery to refashion my life.

A signal. A mystery. Something deeper and more true than anything else. In nightclubs, those smoky boxes full of promise, and even on the street, I would find myself scanning faces, expecting one to stand out, to look back at me in a particular way, a way I would recognize only when I saw it. I wasn't desperate. I never doubted it would come, if I waited long enough.

Ellis brushed a last layer of rice powder onto my face, and I thought about waiting—how vulnerable it made you. Because eventually you got tired. You got tired and you made a choice, you picked someone—or worse, someone picked you—and you believed he was the person you'd been waiting for. And you gave him everything.

Spiro came in to look at me. "There's something new in your face, Charlotte," he said, approvingly.

"The whole face is new."

"No, but see, it's real now, you know?" he said. "It's like all that prettiness has burned off, and you're left with something deeper. Just the very bare essentials."

"Terrific," I said.

When I left the makeup chair (reluctantly, wishing I could prolong my tenancy there just another few minutes), I saw the Korean girl standing in the doorway, waiting to take my place. I'd forgotten her. I smiled, but her eyes looked unfocused, as if she couldn't see me. I went to the adjacent room and sat in the chair before Lily, who pinned three long brown hairpieces to my head and began setting them in the same tiny curlers she'd used on Daphne. Her fingers moved over my scalp with a ravenous life of their own.

"Close," I heard Ellis say to the girl, and then, "Your eyes, dear."

"She looks so unhappy," I murmured.

"I don't think she speaks any English," Lily said. "But she's getting some amazing work. Calvin Klein's started using her."

"What's her name?"

"Something complicated," she said. "Everyone just calls her Kim. Oh, before I forget!" She pulled a computerized address book from her bag and scrolled through it. "You have to call this friend of mine," she said, copying something onto the back of her business card. "Victoria Knight," I read.

"She does what again?" I asked.

"PR. Call her now, before your article comes out, so you can make the most out of it. Tell her I said to call—she can really help you, Charlotte."

My need of help was the one thing everyone seemed to agree on.

"How about some red ears?" I heard Ellis cajole the girl. "Everyone else has red ears . . ."

After a while, Lily pulled out the rollers, teased my hair, then used a pick to wind the curls into tight little coils, which she sprayed until they looked shellacked. Soon I was wearing my own strange bonnet of hair. From the set I could hear the flash, a light popping sound like the explosion of a bubble made of glass. I was dying to get out there.

A doorbell rang, and one of Spiro's assistants buzzed someone in. A moment later I heard the elevator, and then Spiro himself bounded into the room bearing aloft with shaking arms the marble bust of a woman's shoulders and head, about half the size of life. "I had to have it here, to remind myself," he said, cradling the bust in both hands and looking at it in the mirror. The marble woman wore a stack of curls very much like my own. Spiro held her up to my head and studied the two of us together in the mirror. "How's that for a little historical accuracy?" he asked.

But I wasn't looking at the statue's hair, I was looking at her face. It was oval-shaped, peaceful, distant, the eyes empty and flat as sky. She looked entirely absent—untouchable, as if she and this fashion shoot could not be made to overlap, despite Spiro's furious efforts. The centuries between us were simply too many. Her detachment lent an utmost dignity to the marble woman, even with Spiro's trembling hands at her throat. "History," he murmured softly. "You know? It all comes down to that."

Kendra, the stylist, brought in a couple of dresses and held the fabric to my skin. "Let's do purple," she said, and I left my chair and disrobed. Kendra helped me into the purple dress. The velvet felt cool and a little damp, like moss. The dance beat was rousing, insistent, a giant key winding the anticipation tighter and tighter in my chest. I popped a beer and had a sip, my first drink of the day.

On the set, Spiro's assistants were musing over a Polaroid of Daphne. I joined her inside the plastic cube, the two of us dancing together while the lights were adjusted. The cube was just high enough for us to stand in. At Spiro's prompting, we assumed tragic poses, fingers splayed, heads back. Our collective anticipation made a pressure in the room. I'd forgotten what this felt like; it had been so long since I'd had a job in which anyone cared about the pictures.

"Okay, Char, now sink down until your fingertips touch the floor," Spiro said. "Look at me, sort of cruel. Bitch goddess. There you go."

As he snapped the Polaroid, I noticed that the Korean girl had returned to the room, now fully made up and Flavified, draped in yellow crushed velvet and a foamy white collar. She was watching us dully from a chair—or not watching, for her eyes were as flat and empty as the marble Roman woman's eyes. I felt a jerk of anger. Girls spend their lives dreaming about being where you are, I wanted to say. Where's the fucking tragedy?

One of Spiro's assistants waved the Polaroid dry and pulled it open for him to study. "Oooh, look at Charlotte," Spiro said. The assistants, along with Ellis, Lily and Kendra, gathered around the Polaroid, then looked at me. I felt a rushing sensation inside as the old transistor kicked to life; I pictured sparks raining from my hair and eyes. I can do anything, I thought. I can recast the world in a different shape. I can make that camera burst into flame.

"You know," Spiro said, shaking his head as he looked at me, "Oscar told me about your accident and I was like, Book her. I didn't need to see a picture, I fucking knew."

I crouched demurely, waves or particles—which?—issuing from my skin.

"Ellis, can you shadow them a little more before you start?" Spiro said.

I closed my eyes and drew Ellis toward me, smelling his presence inside the cube, pressed powder, sweat, mint on his breath. As he shadowed my eyes, I felt myself controlling him from behind my face, guiding his hand irresistibly.

At an odd snapping noise, I opened my eyes. Ellis was pulling a pair of latex gloves over his gnarled hands. He crouched beside me, tore open a packet and removed a razor blade. My confusion amassed only gradually, so deep was my sense of control, my faith that my own lunar commands were moving everyone else. I watched Ellis, expecting him to snip a loose thread from my dress. Instead, he touched my face, exploring the skin gently with his latex-covered fingertips. The razor blade, in the other hand, hovered near me. "Hold it," I said, fighting my way to a standing position in the copious dress. "What's going on?"

143

Startled, Ellis turned to Spiro.

"He's going to cut you," Spiro said, as if this were self-evident.

"Cut me where?"

"Your face."

"Are you out of your fucking mind?" My hands flew involuntarily to my cheeks.

Spiro, Ellis and Lily exchanged looks of bafflement. "Did Oscar not tell you?" Spiro asked.

"No," I said. "He didn't."

"He cuts everyone," Daphne said.

I gaped at her. "And you don't mind?"

She shrugged, leaning against the side of the cube.

"I don't cut deep at all," Ellis said softly. "You'll hardly feel it."

"Does it bleed?"

"Well, of course it bleeds," Spiro said. "That's the whole point."

"This is insane," I said. Imploringly, I turned again to Daphne. "How do you expect to get work with cuts all over your face?"

"They don't leave scars," she said. "They usually take about a week to heal, as long as you don't pick them. Last time he cut me I worked twice that same week. People like, wanted the scabs on."

I stood in dumbfounded silence, wanting very much to be convinced. But it was my poor face, my abused, still-tender face with its hidden cargo of titanium. "Can't you use fake blood?" I pleaded. "I'll buy it myself!"

The word "fake" induced a collective flinch, as if I'd used a racial slur. "Fake is fake," Spiro said.

He handed his camera to Richard and came inside the cube to where Ellis and I were standing, so the three of us made a tight little triangle. "Charlotte, listen to me," Spiro said, with uncharacteristic calm. "I'm trying to get at some kind of truth here, in this phony, sick, ludicrous world. Something pure. Releasing blood is a sacrifice. It's the most real thing there is."

I nodded, waiting for it to seem true in the way he said, for comprehension to overwhelm my vision like the tilt of a kaleidoscope. I leaned on my reluctance and waited for it to die, to be extinguished by the enormity of this opportunity, the absolute necessity that I triumph.

"Everything is artifice," Spiro went on. "Everything is pretending.

You open a magazine, what is all that crap? Look how pretty I am, look how perfect my life is. But it's lies, nothing is really like that. And politicians, too, spin this, spin that, pulling something over on people—I'm sick of it. It literally makes me nauseous."

I listened with a teetering feeling inside me, as if I might sneeze. It makes sense, I thought. I agree. I wanted desperately to proceed, to reclaim the power I'd felt only minutes ago, with everyone looking at me. As if sensing he was close to persuading me, Spiro took my arms in each of his trembling hands and dropped his voice to a whisper. "I want to cut through that shit to what's real and fundamental," he said. "And I want you to be part of it, Charlotte, that's why I chose you. This isn't about fashion—we're way past fashion here. This is about finding a new way to live in the world."

I looked beyond Spiro's frantic jaws at the towering lights, the silver umbrella reflectors, the three assistants, the ladders and tripods and cameras and models in gushing velvet dresses and foaming collars and Kabuki makeup and Flavian hairdos. "It's too bad Oscar didn't call you when my face was mashed to a pulp last August," I heard myself say. "Every bone was crushed, you would've loved it."

Spiro released my arms. "She doesn't get it," he told Ellis, who jerked the rack of his shoulders as if to say, We tried.

My palms were still pressed to my face. For so long, the skin had been numb, too numb to feel anything. "This face has already been through so much," I said, in apology.

"Fair enough," Spiro said. He turned his back on me and signaled the North Korean girl. "Kim! Kimmy!" He waved his arms, and she jumped to attention as if she'd been slapped. "It's your lucky day, honey," Spiro called.

I vacated the plastic cube and the Korean girl stepped tentatively inside it. "Lily, can you touch up her hair?" Spiro said.

Without even glancing at me, Lily bustled into the cube with her pick and comb and can of spray and began elevating the girl's curls, which had drooped. I noticed that the girl was trembling, making the whorls of her lace collar shake. When Lily was done, Spiro eased the Korean into precisely the position I had occupied just moments ago. The atmosphere in the room was fragile, raw.

"Where?" Ellis asked.

"High on the cheek," Spiro said. "And a long one on the forehead."

I wanted to walk away, but I couldn't seem to do it.

Gently, Ellis lifted the blade to the girl's brown cheek, then dipped one corner under her skin like a swimmer testing the water with a toe. The girl flinched, but didn't make a sound. With delicacy and swiftness, Ellis pulled the blade through her skin. His shadow self appeared without my even looking for it: the gentle butcher, who massages his victims to loosen their flesh before putting in the knife. Blood dropped from the wound, and at the same time, tears rose in the girl's eyes and spilled from the corners. "Lily!" Spiro said. "Get those tears."

Lily darted over and dabbed at the girl's eyes with a tissue. Daphne moved close to her and put an arm around her shoulders. The Korean girl seemed not to notice. She looked straight ahead, enduring this assault with the incomprehension of one who accepted long ago that suffering has no purpose. I felt something in me collapse, a prickling around my eyes and nose. I turned and went to the makeup room, where I yanked the hairpieces off my head, twisted out of the dress and threw it all on the floor. I thought I would vomit—wanted to—but when I stood over the toilet, no release came. As I pulled on my clothes, I heard the dense click of the shutter, followed by Spiro's voice. "Beautiful, Kimmy! Ooh, look at that!"

I had left my coat on a barstool near the zinc countertop; I went there now with eyes averted and slipped it on, trying not to look at the set. But I had to look. The Korean girl was standing in the box, blood running from her cheek down her neck, soaking the white ruffles of her collar. A second cut on her forehead bled into one of her eyes and back out, down the side of her face. Daphne stood behind her, head flung back in a pose of ecstasy. There was a sweet, vulnerable feeling in the air, a postcoital tenderness.

"Okay, Daphne, straighten up," Spiro said. "That's it—now look at me. Kim, give me those eyes. Strong, both of you . . . feel your strength and your power. You're goddesses, all right? You rule the fucking world . . . good . . . good. Eyes, Kimmy . . . good."

All at once, for the very first time, the Korean girl looked at me directly. I felt the engagement of her sight physically, as if she'd grabbed me. While the shutter clicked, we stared at each other, our gazes interlocked, and something passed between us: a wordless acknowledgment of the depravity that surrounded us. It felt like a full minute before the girl blinked and moved her eyes, just slightly. Then they were blank, as before.

"I'm leaving now," I said in a normal speaking voice, but no one seemed to hear.

In the elevator, I noticed my face was wet. Red makeup came off on my hands when I wiped it, and I recoiled, thinking at first it was blood. I felt like I'd barely escaped with my life. And Oscar had known, of course. Had chosen not to tell me, hoping that when the moment came, I would find the pressure too great to resist. Had provided Kim, just in case. I couldn't blame him, really; before the accident, I might well have said yes.

Back on Broome Street, I walked without knowing where I went. I stared through boutique windows at couches, at vases of blown glass, letting the cold air clear my head. It's over, I told myself repeatedly, not knowing quite what this meant. I turned up West Broadway, a lunchtime murmur roiling behind the windows of restaurants. The models were out in force, their spindly doe's legs splayed beneath short winter coats. They looked so young—younger than I'd ever felt in my life. I noticed one with short, raven-colored hair who looked not unlike myself (we are interchangeable—the first lesson one learns as a professional beauty). She and I reached the corner of Houston at the same time, but I let her go ahead. From behind, I noticed people glance at her as she passed them crossing the street, their eyes holding her an extra moment, then reluctantly pulling away. The girl pretended not to see them, just as I used to do, but she felt the power I remembered feeling—I saw it in her walk, the way she held her head, a self-consciousness that made her every move look studied.

But was that really power? I wondered, following behind as she turned left, onto the north side of Houston. Or did it only feel like power? She made her way along, eyes straight ahead, the shape of her portfolio visible in her small backpack, and hovering around her, something only I could see: the nimbus of her faith that she had earned an extraordinary life, and would have one. No, I thought, it was wrong—there was no such thing as the power of beauty. Only the power to surround yourself with it.

The girl turned north, into the Village, but I continued west to Sixth

Avenue. I think I knew where I was going before I let myself admit it. People had flocked to the streets in their puffy coats. The snow was almost gone, sucked away by the gigantic furnace seething deep beneath the city's concrete. At West Fourth, I watched a basketball game through a chain-link fence; the sight of male bodies in motion, even bodies completely indifferent to my presence, cheered me somewhat.

Above Twenty-third Street, I was tantalized once again by the profusion of old painted signs; every building, it seemed, bore several faded tattoos, many superimposed and legible only faintly, only in parts. "5¢." "Hand." "Fish." I was in the flower district now, shop doors releasing humid, jungly currents into the cold, cats tangled behind steamy windows. I turned west and walked to Seventh Avenue.

Anthony Halliday's receptionist wasn't on duty, so I took the liberty of bypassing her desk and knocking directly on his door, which was closed. I opened it. The detective was leaning back in his chair, feet on his desk, reading a paperback. "Charlotte," he said, obviously taken aback by my unheralded arrival. He sat up and set the paperback aside. "This is a surprise."

He was looking at me oddly, and I remembered my red ears and pale, weird makeup. "What are you reading?" I asked.

"Something extracurricular." He seemed embarrassed.

I went around his desk and picked up the book. *The Long Goodbye,* by Raymond Chandler.

"Slow day," he said.

The office was a quiet, forgotten place, light streaking lazily through the window. From my vantage point beside the detective, I was able to see the contents of the photograph I'd noticed on his desk the last time: two redheaded girls who looked identical. Twins. Three years old? Five years old? I was terrible at guessing children's ages. They were laughing, sitting side by side on a swing.

"Why not write your own?" I asked.

"I'm trying," he said. "This guy"—he apparently meant Chandler— "is teaching me."

I went back around the desk and sat in the chair facing it. "Aren't you supposed to pull out a bottle of brandy and two snifters?" I asked. "Or is it whiskey."

He laughed. "In the old days, I would have," he said. "Although I might not have bothered with the snifters."

"The old days."

"I'm reformed." He rapped a knuckle twice against his desk.

"Shouldn't you keep some around for your less enlightened clients?"

"Not yet," he said. "Don't trust myself."

"But you seem so trustworthy." Shameless flirtation. I supposed he was getting used to it.

"What can I do for you, Charlotte," he asked, "on this winter afternoon?"

"Hire me."

His brows rose. "In what capacity?"

"Detective. Assistant detective, if you like. Apprentice."

He watched me another moment, then burst out laughing.

"I'm serious," I said, smiling at him.

"What are your qualifications?"

"What are yours?"

"I'm an ex-D.A. A lot of detectives are retired cops."

"I'm a retired model," I said.

"Looks like you were working today."

"It was my last job."

He shifted in his seat. "Doesn't having been a model make you a little . . . visible?"

"Not at all," I said. "Exactly the opposite. People who've known me for years stare at me like they've never seen me before." The smile was hurting my face. I had gone to the detective's office to cheer myself, to rest my eyes on his handsomeness and forget the rest of today. But for some reason, his presence made me more aware of how terrible I felt. It's over, I thought, and I knew what it meant: my life. My life before the accident. My life until this moment, and possibly including it.

"That sounds awful," he said quietly.

"I'm trying to view it as a unique opportunity to start over."

"Then do yourself a favor," he said. "Shoot higher than this."

For a moment, I thought he was kidding. Then I fumbled for an answer. "Then why don't you?" I asked. "Shoot higher."

"I did. But I landed here."

"What's wrong with it?"

"You spend your whole life watching other people," he said. "I have a feeling it eats away your soul."

"That's funny," I said. "I thought being photographed did that."

"Maybe both."

"In which case, hire me," I said, "since my soul's already shot."

He laughed, watching me. I sensed him weighing options, though what they were I couldn't guess. Then he surrendered, I saw it in his face. "How about this," he said. "It concerns our missing friend."

Z again. "Your friend," I said.

"I'd like to spend an evening going to the kinds of places he went. Not make a big deal of it, just sort of check out the scene. Is that something you could help me with?"

I narrowed my eyes, pretending to think. Halliday didn't need me for this; he was working for Mitch and Hassam. It was a date. The detective had asked me on a date. And yet I felt so sad, so hollowed out, that I couldn't seem to muster any triumph.

"Let's not call it a favor," I finally said. "Let's call it a free trial of my services, with an option to purchase."

He shook his head. "Call it whatever you want," he said.

# Chapter Eight

*After eight years* in the same one-bedroom apartment, I was suddenly finding it crowded beyond capacity. There was me. There was my unrecognizable face. And there was someone else. It was neither a child nor an animal. It was Despair.

Unlike the numerous other visitors I had entertained over the years, Despair lacked an outline, or, for that matter, any distinct shape. I couldn't even see it. But when I unlocked my door after returning from Halliday's office and stepped inside my quiet apartment, I felt it pull the life out of me.

I crumpled onto my couch, lit a cigarette and looked at the Pepsi-Cola sign mooning Manhattan from Long Island City. I waited for Despair to leave. But it didn't leave. It leaned against me, pushing at me from above and below with a drawling, mountainous weight. "When did you arrive?" I asked. "To what do I owe this unexpected pleasure? How long do you intend to stay?"

But Despair didn't have to answer to anyone.

When the phone rang, my new companion leaned on the receiver so that I hardly could lift it from its cradle. Oscar. I had meant to call him even as I dreaded calling him—I needed his advice on where to take the detective that evening.

"Charlotte, I'm sorry," Oscar began. His voice, shucked of its usual casing of irony, parody, hauteur and self-mockery, sounded like someone else. Someone sad. Or maybe that was what Oscar himself really sounded like. "I had to try," he said.

"I know."

"I did it for you."

"I know. I just—I couldn't go through with it."

"Of course not."

There was a long pause, a pause in which I felt as if Oscar and I were suspended underwater, watching each other through myriad fluttering tides, resisting their pull for yet another moment. Then another. I heard phones bleeping in the background, but Oscar stayed there with me. I'd never heard him so quiet.

"The Korean girl is in trouble," I said at last. "Kim."

He hove a long sigh. "She'll soon be out of my hands," he said. "I have two Ukrainians from the capsized oil rig arriving on my doorstep any day, as soon as their casts are removed. She'll go to one of the model apartments."

"Oscar, who'll take care of her?"

"She'll take care of herself. She's not a child—she's twenty, for pity's sake. You did it," he added. "I've got girls of fourteen living on their own."

I said nothing. I was gripped by an absolute conviction that the girl would die.

"Charlotte, the beast must be fed," Oscar said in that same sad voice. "We both know that."

I fell asleep on my couch. When I woke, at eleven-fifteen, I was pressed for time. I careened from my apartment at midnight, leaving behind a Daliesque assortment of clothing sliding from lamps and furniture, along with a skyline of empty bottles documenting my search for some bottle—any bottle—with even a finger or two of booze left in it.

Mercifully, my flask (a slender, ladylike cylinder) was still full of tequila. I shoved it in my purse and gulped a little in the elevator, distressed to find that Despair had followed me there and was planning to chaperone me through the evening—or perhaps the rest of my life. I arrived at a decision whose cruelty and senselessness shocked even me: if I was going to the bottom, I was taking the detective with me.

All I had to do was make him drink.

Anthony Halliday was waiting in my lobby. In his black jeans, dark blazer and slate gray shirt, he looked surprisingly good for someone whose business required little or no proximity to the mirrored room. My worries about how to secrete him past club doormen with doctoral degrees in the eradication of poor taste had been unnecessary. He kissed me hello on the cheek.

His cab was outside. I gave the driver the address of Jello, a nightclub on Gansevoort Street. The wheel of nightlife had turned again in my absence, and the desirable clubs were all new. Oscar had suggested two others, Pollen and the Ga Ga Lounge, Mitch and Hassam's new club, and I half relished the thought of Despair trying to make a place for itself inside these dens of nightlife, where mere unhappiness was about as welcome as an overweight cousin from New Jersey.

There was no one outside of Jello, and a lizard-faced bouncer admitted us without a wait. Medium-sized rectangular room. Black walls. Abundant black light staining every white surface purple, but not enough live bodies to create the churning, bearings-eliminating mass essential to nightclub felicity. I steered Halliday toward the bar, which radiated purple light from within its oval rim, underlighting the faces of everyone working behind it. Not ideal for the girl who took this bartending job in hopes of being spotted by a model agent, and there she was—there she always was—a blonde with a tangle of dry, electric-looking hair and weary circles under her eyes.

I ordered a double vodka tonic and drank it while we made our way to the VIP area. These regions varied from establishment to establishment, but two features were fairly unwavering: that the VIPs be kept separate from the hoi polloi, and that the hoi polloi be able to see them. Jello had met these requirements by erecting a large white cage, inside which the VIPs, few of whom I recognized, danced and yelled to each other over the music, while those outside, such as ourselves, peered at them through the bars. A sullen-faced gatekeeper was in charge of admitting and releasing VIPs from the cage.

"Is that where he would be?" Halliday asked, gesturing at the cage. It took me a moment to realize he meant Z.

"Probably," I said.

I sensed that Halliday wanted to go inside the cage but was hesitant to ask for fear of embarrassing me. And divested of my usual crowd, unfamiliar with this particular gatekeeper, I wasn't sure how to effect it. "Let's go," I said. "This isn't the place we want."

Back on the street, we hailed another cab. I directed the driver to the Ga Ga Lounge, in the West Twenties near the river.

"Tell me something about the mentality of the people in these clubs," Halliday said. "Why do they go? What do they get out of it?"

"That's hard to say."

"But you've done it for years."

Had I told him that? I was fairly certain I hadn't; perhaps he'd simply presumed it. "I used to," I said.

"It seems . . . superficial. Phony."

"I think that's the part I like," I said, and laughed. "Nobody pretends to tell the truth, they just go ahead and lie. It's a relief."

"Is that what you do? Just lie?"

I hesitated. What I loathed—what I'd always loathed—were the conversations people had tried to engage me in countless times over the years: you tell me how your father whipped you with a belt; I'll tell you how I was left to cry for hours alone in my room, how I wasn't allowed to play piano, how lonely and sad I felt as a child, and after that we'll be intimates, because each of us will know who broke the other. There was nothing phonier in the world. It was no one's business who'd broken me; maybe I'd never been broken.

"Who wants to hear the truth?" I asked. "It's usually dull."

"I disagree," he said. "Speaking as someone who listens to bullshit all day long. The truth is almost always more interesting."

"I guess you picked the right job," I said.

A clot of yellow cabs had formed, all oozing in a kind of agony toward a single destination. Halliday and I joined a restive mob outside a pair of warehouse doors presided over by two black doormen with the implacable look of Zen about their eyes. "Okay, nobody goes in until you calm down, people!" intoned one of these Zen masters, but the crowd's immediate response was to surge against the velvet ropes, anticipating its exclusion and objecting plaintively, vehemently. Just then, a rented limousine in less than tip-top condition halted outside the club and began disgorging its cargo: Gil Jamais, a middling promoter, followed by the troupe of young models he'd assembled that evening, girls who glistened with a dew of newness, their lovely youth catalyzed by the famished desire of everyone around them into an effervescence that allowed them to pour effortlessly among the panicky, paranoid crowd, past the bouncers (whose job it was to facilitate this pouring) and through the warehouse doors, decanting from car to club in a matter of seconds. There was no stopping them; such effervescence was too unstable a compound to remain among everyone else—its very nature required that it disappear instantly into memory. How clearly I saw this! And the fact that I saw it clearly imparted strange new information: I was not one of the effervescent; I was straining toward it, ogling its wall- and door-defying properties, just like everyone else.

Indeed, when Halliday and I tried to enter the thrusting, beseeching mob, it repelled us with rubbery impermeability. "People. Relax," the doormen chanted. Halliday glanced at me—we were nowhere near the door—and I sensed him resigning himself to the fact that there was nothing I could do. And at that point, strangely, Despair shed its adversarial role and came to my aid with a series of potent jabs to my back that sent me careening into the crowd, bobbing and weaving forcibly among petitioners (Halliday's hand in mine) while Despair admonished me, with a clammy pressure to my heart, that a feeling of extreme rottenness awaited me—the rottenness of a fizzled evening—should I fail to get us through the crowd and past the bouncers and into this fucking club. I blazed a trail all the way to one of the Zen masters, whose arm I went so far as to clasp (but not clutch) while imparting, in a calm, authoritative voice, the news that I was Irene Maitlock of the *New York Post*. "Feature story," "Mitch and Hassam," "Interview" and "Running out of patience" were some additional themes I touched on before handing him Irene's business card, which I'd saved from her abortive visit purely because it impressed me.

The doorman, doubtless a connoisseur of prevarication, looked at me with eyes that seemed transplanted from the Flavian statue I'd encountered earlier today. He glanced at Irene's card, handed it back to me and went inside without a word. He emerged a few moments later in the company of an Englishman I'd met before, a prep-school type in his mid-forties with chaotic teeth and soiled-looking eyes. The bouncer indicated me with a tip of his head, thus consummating his role as middleman without once invoking the use of his larynx.

"You're the reporter?" the Englishman said.

I shot out my hand in a manner that seemed reporter-like. "Irene Maitlock," I said, pressing the Englishman's amphibious flesh. "This is Anthony Halliday."

"Apologies," the Englishman said, with irony. "I'll get you upstairs."

After such a struggle, to have those doors swing open—for you—to fall through them as if they were suddenly, magically porous, as if you had assumed the power to sashay through walls, was an experience that sent a dart of pleasure through me even after so many years, and lent a certain rarefied magnificence to all that lay beyond. Halliday and I trailed the Englishman through the pounding darkness and press of bodies. On the dance floor, the throng moved as one elastic mass, like a school of fish.

Finally the Englishman delivered us to the foot of a curved flight of stairs manned by a bouncer whose Zen, if any, was the Zen of extreme boredom. "Mitch and Hassam should be up there," the Brit shouted over the music, and gave us an odd little salute when we thanked him. The bouncer pulled aside the velvet rope and let us pass.

This VIP area was elevated a half floor above the rest of the club. Fake palm trees and booths like big velvet commas girded the room, and to one side a small dance floor was lit from beneath by lozenges of winking colored light.

"Beautifully done," the detective hollered into my ear.

"I'm auditioning," I reminded him.

I led the way to the bar, ordered a second double vodka and sipped it. In my arms I held a light, spinning ball of excitement. Where did this come from? I wondered, then realized that I'd shaken my despair, or rather, in becoming Irene Maitlock, I had cast off Charlotte Swenson, upon whom Despair had thrust its unlovely self that evening. I waved to her, poor thing, buckling under the weight of her onerous, toxic date. And here I was, light, free, a lizard skittering away after relinquishing its tail to the sadist who was clutching it.

Halliday took in the room. The velvet booths were festooned with models draped across cushions and perched on the edges of tables like long-haired cats. Men bustled and fluttered around them, fetching drinks, whispering into their ears, touching their slender shoulders and ribbony arms in a manner that was both worshipful and proprietary. Though it was winter, the models wore thin dresses and carried no purses, like children. When they leaned over, their string-of-pearl spines showed through their dresses.

"How do they all know to come here?" he asked. "These girls."

"The promoters bring them," I said. "The younger girls probably have no idea where they are. A promoter will take fifteen girls out to dinner, then bring them here."

"What's in it for him?"

"Oh, money," I said. "The club pays him to bring the girls. And he gets a certain lifestyle—playboys let him use their limos, they invite him to the Hamptons in summer—they want access to girls. And restaurants usually comp a table full of models; they're good for business. A promoter can have almost nothing and live like a king."

"So he's basically a pimp," Halliday said.

"No," I said, startled. "The opposite. A promoter's job is to protect the models, make them feel safe. Otherwise he'll lose them, and then he's got nothing."

I felt the detective's disagreement, his disapproval, but I didn't care; I held my spinning ball of happiness and looked at the room, *Irene Maitlock, reporting on nightlife,* the models with their lanky adolescent bodies and lush breasts and faces like small enameled boxes, creatures who seemed the improbable hybrids of several exotic, even fantastical species. Of course people paid for their company.

"And Z?" the detective said. "Was he a promoter?"

"At a higher level," I said. "He wasn't hauling girls around; he was putting money into parties and clubs, with Mitch and Hassam."

"Speaking of the devil," Halliday said, for there was Hassam himself, edging toward us through the gluten of bodies, Hassam with his round face and wet dark eyes, shaking Halliday's hand. "This is a lovely surprise," he said, somehow maintaining a soft-spoken demeanor even as he shouted to be heard.

"Place looks beautiful," Halliday said. "You just opened?"

"Last week." Hassam was of indeterminate age, late thirties, probably; he claimed to be English and spoke with an English accent, but I'd heard a rumor that he was really from Afghanistan, that he'd fought the Communists and spent time in a Soviet prison. Since hearing that, I'd been scrutinizing his shadow self for traces of that violence, its pocks and ruts, but Hassam seemed peaceful to the point of sleep, or anesthesia. Only once, when some guy was hinting loudly over dinner that he'd been part of a terrorist cell in Argentina, did Hassam turn to me and say, "Listen to the crap"—just that, nothing else, but as he said it something happened in his eyes, or behind them, some disturbance butted out against them, and I began to wonder if those peaceful eyes weren't really Hassam's after all. He was married to a Swedish model and had two small children, Philippa and Nigel, whose pictures he carried in his wallet.

Mitch, alerted by whatever telepathic vectors had interlocked his destiny with Hassam's (whom he resembled in no discernible way) for years, now veered over to add his greetings. Mitch was the talker of the two, younger, with a brush haircut, a torso hotly contested by muscle and flab, a southern accent and the pushy, gee-whiz air of a collegiate sports star, which he may or may not have been. "Heya, Doctor," he said in his threadbare voice, pumping Halliday's hand. "What brings you to these parts?"

"Snooping around," the detective said. "As ever."

"Well, snoop away," Mitch said. "We had Mike Tyson in here earlier on, and Ethan Hawke—Annabella Sciarra's right over there." He jerked his chin in the direction of a shadowy corner. "Keep an eye out for Eddie Murphy . . . he's coming on the late side. Let's see, who else . . ." Sweeping the room, his gaze tripped over me.

"This is Irene Maitlock," Halliday said, with high amusement. "She's from the *New York Post*."

I'd known Mitch and Hassam for years and years; I'd been one of the girls they freighted from restaurant to club to Hampton compound back in their early days, and I'd slept with both of them, Mitch once, Hassam twice (long before the rumor about Afghanistan, or surely I would have learned the answer that way, sex being the realm in which the shadow self was most often driven from its lair). Now I shook their hands and looked into their eyes, Hassam's calm and bottomless, Mitch's blank and reflective as rearview mirrors, and pretended I was meeting them both for the very first time. The sensation was unexpectedly thrilling.

At the mention of the *New York Post*, Mitch's face underwent a succession of transformations: from indifference in the presence of a nonimportant nonmodel (namely, me) to greedy excitement in the presence of a member of the press (me) to a studied neutrality intended to mask his opportunism and create the impression that his ensuing solicitations (and I felt them coming like the prickling onset of a sneeze) were neither more nor less than he would have offered the nonimportant person he'd believed I was in the first place. "Can I buy you a drink? Can I show you around?" he asked me. "Is there anyone you'd like to meet? If we'd known you were coming, we could've like done something."

"I'm just fine," I said, trying not to laugh.

He secreted a business card into my palm with the furtive expertise of a seasoned briber of maître d's. "That's our office," he said. "When you want to come back, give me a call and we'll set you up, get you a table. Anything you want."

I was fascinated by the way he spoke to me: genderless, respectful, as if I were a man. So this was power, I thought. This was what it felt like.

"Any news of our former partner?" Hassam was asking Halliday.

"Some rumblings," Halliday said. "Nothing clear."

"I still kind of expect it to be a joke," Mitch said. "Like Z's gonna walk in here one night and be like, Hey, what about my blue? 'Cause he wanted to paint the whole place this intense, almost like purplish kind of blue . . ."

"Cerulean blue," Hassam said.

"Yeah, right, and he wanted to call it 'Eye,' you know, like eye of the storm kind of thing—which is not a bad idea, we still might do it someplace if he comes back—"

"He's gone," Hassam said, so quietly it was remarkable that we heard him at all, and we paused, waiting for him to elaborate, but by then the tide of petitioners and asskissers and models in search of free drinks tickets that had been pooling around us since first we'd formed our conversational knot, lapping at our edges with mounting pressure, finally breached the dam of our union, dousing Mitch and Hassam in air kisses and cabalistic handshakes and hyperbolic compliments on the new club and requests—requests above all, *I've got a friend who's stuck at the door. I'm looking for a little* (sniff sniff)—and although many of these petitioners were people I knew, though I might well have been among them before the accident, now I was invisible. They seemed almost to pass through myself and Halliday on their way to the promoters, and so I was able to train my new and unabashed curiosity directly upon them, the curiosity of a *New York Post* reporter. Only when Daphne came along, her face etched with three wet scabs on each cheek from the afternoon's blood-letting, did I turn away. "Look who worked for Spiro!" I heard Mitch bellow at her. He tried to touch one of her wounds, but she slapped his hand away.

"Let's walk around," I said, coaxing Halliday back to the bar, where I ignored his disapproving glance and ordered yet another double vodka.

We circled the room, Halliday staring at the booths. "In all those months, you never talked to him?" he asked, and it took me a moment to realize he meant Z. Though by now I should have known; he always meant Z.

"He was quiet," I said. "A lot of the time he seemed like he wasn't even listening, but I think he was. I think he heard everything."

"Why do you say that?"

"He was alert," I said. "He drank juice and tea—nothing else. If someone said his name he'd turn in a second."

"You watched him pretty carefully."

"I watch everyone," I said. "It's how I learn."

"I guess it's all you've got left," he said wryly, "if you don't believe what anyone says."

"Anthony," I said, and waited for him to look at me. "He was just some guy. He disappeared. What difference does it make?"

"People don't disappear," he said. "They go somewhere else." I sensed him debating whether to continue. Finally he said, in a kind of rush, "He wasn't Greek. He wasn't married. His name obviously wasn't Z. He wasn't in the import-export business, or even the drug business. He arrives out of nowhere, spends four months hanging around places like this, then disappears without a trace. What was he up to?"

"You could be talking about twenty different people," I said, but even as I spoke, I knew it was pointless; for some reason, Z had assumed a place in the detective's imagination. Maybe for no reason.

"In my opinion," Halliday said carefully, "you know a lot more about this guy than you're willing to say."

"You thought that before you met me," I said, and he didn't deny it. "Why?"

"Instinct."

I turned on Anthony Halliday what I hoped was a winsome, careless smile; I crouched behind it as if it were a sparkling bit of scenery. "I have pretty good instincts, too," I said.

"So why not share them with me, for a change?"

"You're angry about losing your daughters," I said, and knew the instant I heard it, even before surprise had rinsed Halliday's face of everything else, that I'd hit. "The redheads," I added, for good measure.

"How do you know I have daughters?"

I just smiled, watching him figure it out. He was a detective, after all. "The picture," he said, and grinned.

"They could have been your nieces."

He made a face. "Who keeps pictures of their nieces?"

"People without children."

After a pause, he said, "You're right. I miss my girls."

I hadn't said he missed them—I'd said that he was angry about losing them. But I let it go. "I need a drink," I said.

"That's the last thing you need."

I proceeded to the bar, ordered a double vodka and downed it. And in a single moment—the one during which I downed the drink—I traversed, with telescopic swiftness, the many gradations from mild tipsiness to staggering inebriation that I had savored at other points in my life, from fuzzy to toasted to totally gone—I swept through them all in one sip, one gulp (a gulp that encompassed a double vodka, it was true) and my arrival at the far end of that spectrum made me stagger. The room tipped on its side while my body strained to adjust to its new chemistry. Delicately, I rejoined Halliday at the balcony, where he was looking down at the boiling cauldron of non-VIPs. "Would you like to dance?" I asked, just managing to keep the words from smearing into one.

He took a moment to answer, watching me, assessing my drunkenness with the infallible radar of the newly reformed, or perhaps just weighing the question itself. Dancing in clubs was not for everyone.

"All right," he said.

By tacit consent, we bypassed the small VIP dance floor with its high-schoolish crowd of young models all dancing together, descended the curved staircase past the grim-faced VIP bouncer, then breaststroked our way onto the dance floor. To my surprise, Anthony Halliday could dance. He knew how to move, and, most important, he knew not to do too much. At first, I attributed this apparent skill to his detectivehood and the chameleon-like abilities it required, but it was more than that: he was a man who had danced a lot at some point in his life. I yelled this observation to him over the music, and he conceded its truth. "Not in a long time, though," he said.

"When?"

"As a teenager. Latin clubs."

The exchange of speech drew us closer, and Anthony rested his hands on my waist. I would submit that regardless of how many people one has touched in one's life, the very first time, whatever the occasion, is invariably interesting—to become creatures, rather than just voices and thoughts. In that moment, I released Irene Maitlock to the arms of her adoring husband and resumed my existence as Charlotte Swenson. Despair was left alone, without a partner.

"Why Latin clubs?"

"There were amazing dancers there," he said. "It was a whole world. I didn't care about the things I was supposed to be doing, and I got caught up in that."

We were touching from our chests to our knees. It having been several hundred years since I'd touched another person, I had to quell the riot of gasping relief this contact wrought inside me. "You probably have some policy about not getting involved with clients," I said, my mouth close to his ear.

"Actually, I do."

"I'm not a client," I reminded him.

I felt his chest move as he laughed. "Yeah, I know."

"Come on," I whispered, brushing his ear with my lips, "let's ruin each other's lives."

"I already did that," he said. "I'm trying to fix it."

"I can help!"

He laughed again. "Forgive me for doubting that."

"A teeny little relapse can be very cathartic."

"There's no such thing," he said. "I've tried it." We danced in silence, or rather, we danced in the roaring cacophony. I felt Anthony's chest rise and fall as he breathed. "Anyway," he said, "you won't miss very much."

"You're lousy in bed?" I felt him laughing. "Impotent?"

"Not until after the first bottle," he said. "Knock wood."

I drew back and eyed him skeptically—a shameless goad which (to his credit) he ignored. "I'll just have to live with your doubt," he said.

"The right partner is everything," I said. "Your wife obviously wasn't."

"She wasn't my partner. Johnnie Walker was my partner."

"Her loss."

"She might say so," he said. "Actually, I think it was my loss."

I lifted my face from his shoulder and kissed him, first lightly, a feathery lip-brushing baby kiss, then a kiss of deeper inquiry. Halliday didn't respond at first, beyond letting me do it. Then, as if a drawer inside him had fallen open, dislodging its contents, he suddenly kissed me back, pushing his tongue deep inside my mouth, running his hands down my back until he was holding my ass. A caul of desire dropped over my head, covering my eyes. I reached down and seized him through his jeans, but he took my hand, lacing our fingers together. "Not here," he said.

A line of taxis waited outside, and we tumbled into one. I gave the driver my address and the cab bolted east on Twenty-third Street. Anthony and I exchanged a long, tangled kiss, a kiss that involved passing through a series of doors to a series of rooms, so that withdrawing was difficult, tortuous. When I reached for his zipper, I saw him glance at the driver's mirror, where an alert pair of eyes flicked away. Anthony slid to one side of the cab, outside the driver's range of vision, braced his back against one of the doors and pulled me into his lap, kissing my neck, reaching inside my dress and holding my breasts. I stroked my ass against him. "Well, we've solved the impotence question," I said, and his laugh filled my ear with warm breath. He pinched both my nipples until the block of wax in my stomach, a block that had been solid ever since the accident—melted suddenly away. I felt for my purse, took out my flask and poured some tequila down my throat. Anthony stiffened behind me.

"Don't," he said. "No more."

"Okay," I said, and took one last, brimming, burning sip. Then I turned around, the tequila still in my mouth, rose onto my knees and kissed Anthony from above, letting the booze flow directly into his mouth. I saw the shock in his eyes. For a second or two, our lips were still touching, and then he choked and jerked away, gasping, and spat the tequila onto the floor. He stayed like that, face turned away, then slowly wiped his mouth with a hand. When he looked at me again, he was a stranger—pale, enraged. "What the fuck was that for?"

"I'm sorry," I said, trying to move near him. "I was just . . ."

*I was just what?*

He pushed me away, but I forced myself back toward him. I wanted us to kiss—just once more, so he would forget, so we could go on. "Stop!" he said. "Get away from me!" But I wouldn't stop or get away, and finally he hunched over, shielding himself from me so the only thing left to do was to climb on top of him, fighting to keep my balance in the bouncing cab which at this point was careering north on the FDR, my knees on Halliday's back like a child playing horsey. "Get off me!" he said in a muffled voice, but I ignored him, I draped my head alongside his and searched for his lips, which were sadly inaccessible—in fact the only means of ingress I could find was an ear, a white, lovely, vulnerable ear hidden like a seashell under his dark hair. I crammed my tongue inside it.

Halliday jolted as if I'd stuck him with an electric prod, then he reared up beneath me and flung me across the cab. The back of my head slammed against the window, and I saw stars, except they didn't look like stars, they looked like radioactive sperm.

"I've lost everything," he said, his voice hushed. "Everything I had in the world. But what the fuck do you care?"

My head throbbed and my eyes were full of water. I was afraid he would think it was tears.

"Stop the cab," he told the driver.

"Can't stop here," the cabbie said.

"Stop the fucking cab."

We pulled off the FDR and Halliday got out without a word. I didn't say anything, either. My ears were ringing so loudly, I couldn't hear the door slam, although the cab shook from the impact.

As the driver continued to my building, I relaxed into a dreamy numbness, a confusion about what had happened, exactly. But once I was back inside, taking my familiar steps past the sleepy-looking doorman, under the vast chandelier that looked like it had been filched from the nearest Hyatt, toward the bank of elevators, I felt my new paramour welcoming me home with a cold, seeping weight. I opened my flask and finished off the tequila in the elevator.

My apartment was just as I had left it, except that now the empty bottles and chaos of discarded outfits looked like the hopeful prelude to a ruined evening. I'd forgotten I had no booze. I stood in my living room, mulling this over for two or three seconds, then turned on my heel and headed back down to the lobby. It was 3:45 A.M., so my bar options were going to be limited. I turned down my doorman's offer of a taxi and tramped back into the freezing night. Three-fifty; I had ten minutes to find a bar. I proceeded calmly to First Avenue, heading for McFadden's, a tiny Irish pub I'd gone to once or twice before the accident, where the atmosphere of seedy die-hard drinking was offset by young couples swirling Irish coffees and eating lousy pie à la mode, but when I reached the place where McFadden's should have been, I found the space vacant, garbage piled behind its dusty windows and a "for rent" sign hanging askew. Three-fifty-seven.

Fine, I thought, no drink. I thought "fine" but I didn't feel fine—I felt extremely unpleasant, and the unpleasantness wasn't something I could put a name to; words like "bad," "sad," "sick," seemed mincing beside it. I surveyed my vital signs. Pulse: very fast, possibly around 120. Temperature: low. Hands shaking, heart racing a little . . . diagnosis? I was flipping out. Okay, I told myself, so it was a bad night, you made one bad call and it cost you a roll in the hay with a former drunk who has a violent streak—this is a tragedy? Go home, take a sleeping pill . . . tomorrow's another day, blah blah blah, but this rational part of me was oddly disenfranchised this evening, because the more I chastised myself, the more agitated I became, to the point where I actually screamed—doubled over and bellowed aloud in the empty street—a shriek of pain and helplessness that sounded like an animal's cry, even to me.

I began walking toward the East River. I had found that states of mental discomfort could be managed only through physical activity. *Don't think!* I can take this, I told myself. I'm strong, look what I've been through and survived. I wanted to get to the river, but it was hard to reach; a park blocked it off, and its gates were locked at sundown. But tonight, mercifully, mysteriously, the gate had been left open. I entered the park and crossed the FDR on an overpass. A frigid wind was holding court along the river, full of ice crystals and the smell of gasoline. I passed what I thought were bags of garbage, but they turned out to be people, human beings lying on the pavement and huddled under boxes—how could they survive this cold? Were they already dead? I walked faster, half hoping someone would leap out of nowhere and murder me, toss me into the freezing river—innocent me, cut down in my prime! Ah, tragedy.

The narrowing spit of concrete I was rushing along had winnowed away, and I'd reached the mouth of a tunnel. The wind crowded my ears, forcing a needle of pain deep inside each. I looked up at my apartment building looming overhead, its staggered balconies making the silhouette of a ziggurat against the pink, chemical sky. I turned and quickly began walking back.

The doorman looked befuddled at my return—I sensed him wondering if he had dreamed my previous homecoming. But this time I'd arrived with my new companion already on my arm, an evil lover who had crushed me in his embrace and inflicted upon me a venomous kiss, just as I had done to Halliday. In the elevator, I jumped to keep moving, and when the door opened, I bolted into the hallway.

I flicked on the lights, and my apartment ambushed me. *I can sell the apartment,* I thought. *I can sell the sectional couch.* I could sell the expensive necklaces and bracelets and earrings I'd been given over the years by rich, insolent playboys. I could sell my kitchen appliances. My towels, my makeup. My purses. My clothing! My Halstons and Chanels, my Gallianoses and Isaac Mizrahis. I could sell my stereo, my TV, though neither was state-of-the-art anymore. My furniture, the antiques I'd bought in Europe. I could sell my Japanese woodblock print of a snowy rural landscape.

And if I sold all of that, would I have enough?

*Enough for what?*

I slid open the door to my balcony and stood just outside it in the scouring wind. No, I thought, I don't want to sell those things. I was too drunk to sell anything.

It's over, I thought. It's finished. There's nothing left.

*Tragedy!*

The mirrored room was gone, I would never reach it—perhaps it didn't exist.

I turned my face straight into the wind. Jump. The thought floated through my mind like a streamer. I looked out at the soft pink darkness.

*Jump.*

I closed my eyes. The thought of leaping from my balcony into the snow-swollen night filled me with a lust even more potent than what I'd felt with Halliday—oh, the delicious thrill of giving myself to a single, violent act . . . I gritted my teeth, I swallowed it back . . . and felt something give in my knees.

My eyes still shut, I reached for the iron railing, curled my fingers around it and climbed over. Now I was balancing the narrow heels of my high-heeled shoes on maybe two inches of concrete still left to stand on. I gripped the railing behind me. The wind pummeled me, as if I were strapped to the prow of an icebreaking ship. Twenty-five stories of dazzling emptiness sucked at me from below. My head was spinning. Don't open your eyes. Chin down. Let them see you.

I let go of the railing and jumped.

It felt like an instant later that I hit concrete. I lay there, amazed to find myself conscious. Or was I dead? Certainly I was, had to be—how could I survive a fall of twenty-five stories? And yet I was conscious, or at least able to think. I lay in a heap, testing my crumpled limbs with tiny, fragile movements. When I opened my eyes, I saw double, as I had after the accident. I seemed to be looking at a pane of glass. Light spilled from behind it and there was noise, faint, intermittent noise . . . voices. A voice. I lay on the pavement, my eyes open, and listened, trying to understand, *Deberr . . . sister . . . chillrrn . . .* because the voice was familiar, it was the voice of a friend, an acquaintance or possibly a lover. No . . . no. It was the basso voice of Robert Stack, the iron-haired narrator of *Unsolved Mysteries.*

I was on someone else's balcony.

But how could that be? Still prone, I twisted my neck to look up, and sure enough, yes, now I understood; because of the staggering pattern that ensured sunlight and privacy to each and every balcony owner, this balcony, while directly below my own, jutted out three feet beyond it.

I began to laugh. It hurt, but I couldn't stop. I'm alive, I thought.

I staggered to my feet and tried to peer through the white curtain covering the window, but I couldn't see much of anything. I tapped lightly on the glass door, but the TV was on, *Deborah had taken no luggage and no extra clothing the night she disappeared,* and most likely, since it was—I checked my watch—4:45 A.M., whoever was inside was fast asleep.

Gently, I slid open the glass door and stepped inside the room. The layout of the apartment was the same as mine, but this occupant had apparently decided to make the more spacious living room into a bedroom, for there was the bed, to my left, with a lumpy shape beneath the covers that seemed—I glimpsed from the corner of my eye as I crept across the room—seemed to be moving, and moving in a way that was familiar. I stopped and turned. *She said she had a date, that's all she said, and when she didn't come back we started looking.* . . . A man's silvery head protruded from beneath a blanket, and beneath his head was a second head that emitted mews of pleasure as the man moved up and down. "Oh, God," said the second head, in a woman's voice. "Oh, God."

*Oh, God.*

On toes so pronged that my feet barely seemed in contact with the rug, I resumed my stealthy and now rather desperate attempt to flee the premises undetected. But my balance was off, my knee hurt, my toes were too pointed—hell, something went wrong and I tripped over the TV cord and lost my balance and crashed to the floor, knocking over a large copper lamp in the process and shattering both bulb and globe, which sent chunks of thick crusty glass into my hair.

An appalled scream, followed by commotion, all of it unfolding in sudden, ghastly silence—I'd unplugged the TV—and darkness, since the lamp was broken.

"Over there! There!" the woman shrieked in quite a different voice than the one she'd used a moment ago. I couldn't bear to lift my head. A second light went on. When finally I looked up, I found a heavyset man in a terrycloth bathrobe standing over me, wielding a blue aluminum baseball bat.

"I'm so sorry," I said, which, under the circumstances, sounded stunningly inadequate.

Clearly, I was not what the man had been expecting to see. He lowered the bat an inch or two. "What are you doing in our apartment?" he said.

I forced myself to stand. An older woman with lovely chestnut-colored hair was sitting up in bed, clutching sheets to her chest. "Mark, don't let him stand up!" she shrieked.

"It's not a him," he said. "It's a her."

"I'm your upstairs neighbor," I said. "From twenty-five. I fell off my balcony onto yours by mistake."

This explanation silenced them both for a moment. "What do you mean, fell off your balcony?" the man asked.

"I was doing . . . exercises," I said. "And I fell."

"What did he say?" the woman said.

"It's a she, Miriam," the man yelled back. "Says she was doing exercises and fell off her balcony."

"Exercises, my foot," the woman huffed. "Mark, get me my robe, honey."

"You relax, baby," Mark said. "It's under control."

"I'm drunk," I announced, in hopes of caulking up any remaining gaps in my story. The man eyed me, uncertain. "I'm blotto," I said. "Tipsy. Wasted. I had too much to drink and I fell off the balcony, okay?"

"I understand," he said, then shouted over his shoulder, "She was drunk."

". . . craziest thing I ever . . ."

Mark walked me to the door. I liked him, this man who loved his wife and desired her still, even with the two of them getting on in years. I was sorry I'd interrupted them.

"You know, we've got a nice gym right here in the building," he said. "On fourteen."

"I know," I said.

"You didn't hurt yourself, did you, dear?"

"No," I said. "I feel fine."

"Three aspirin," he said, winking. "Lots of water. Tomorrow, sleep in a little if you can."

"I will."

The door closed, and I was back in the hallway. But it was a different hallway. It was a different building. Why? I wondered as I padded over the soft carpeting to the elevator. Why? And then I knew: Despair had vanished. It had been too bulky, I supposed, grinning at myself in the elevator mirror, too gigantic and unwieldy to break its fall on that extra three feet of balcony. It had fallen the twenty-five stories and died.

I went back upstairs, but of course my door was locked. I returned to the lobby yet again, where I gamely explained my plight to the stupefied doorman, leaving out the part about falling off my balcony. He produced the spare key, and I went upstairs and let myself back inside.

# Chapter Nine

*After breakfast, Charlotte* stepped from the back door into the shimmer of her exhaustion. White sky, weird trees, her bike where she'd left it that morning, at three-forty-five, after coming back from Michael West's. Her sixth time. She recorded each visit on the pages of her calendar using a code she was still inventing: when exactly she left the house and when she returned; facts about the weather, recorded it all in entries like: N1T2″0412*//**KL1704 (November first; Thursday; raining; left at 12:04; returned at 4:17; with details of the visit sandwiched in between), so that later, when she was gripped by a fear that it might not be real—that it was nothing, had not even happened—she could look at her notes and be calmed.

She rode shakily through the raw, scraped-feeling morning, pulling the weight of her new life, its rich complications. November. Empty trees, dry old lawns, the cemetery. And underneath it all a quiver of excitement, invisible as electricity.

Charlotte recorded the things she and Michael had done together using letters (but avoiding X's), stars and slashes to denote the various acts, so she could remember what exactly had happened between them, and in what order. There had come a moment that first night (twenty-four days ago) when he had bent back her legs so her knees were by her ears, so she was bent in half, almost, clinging feebly to this stranger who had pushed himself inside her, when Charlotte had thought, "You're in trouble," the words distinct as if someone had whispered them into her ear. Fate, destiny—they dropped away, leaving only her fear: Who was this man? How had she gotten here?

Afterward she had ridden home slowly through a light mist (it was in her notes), feeling hurt inside, broken maybe, thinking, I'll never go back there, no one will ever know about it. But after two or three days her craving for him made her almost sick—to flee the tiny envelope of her life into the strange other world where he lived, to feel his hands on her. All of it.

"I have a boyfriend," she told herself, throwing back her head to look at the bare vectors of trees. "I'm dating someone. He loves me and I love him." That it be love was essential, beyond negotiation. Nothing less was enough to force their nocturnal encounters into a shape she could recognize. She tested his love in little ways; if he kisses me now, he loves me. If he smells my hair, he loves me. She rubbed the lotion from Florida onto her face and arms and stomach before going to see him, because he'd said he loved the smell—the first night, before they kissed. "I love it," he'd said, and then kissed her, his tongue strong and alive behind the stillness of his face. He had used the word "love," it was in her notes.

She nearly burst through a red light onto State Street, and the force of braking sent her halfway over her handlebars. The cold singed her nostrils. She was almost at school. She had to stop herself from riding into trees, into traffic, thinking of him. At dinner she sat stupefied until Ricky waved his arm in front of her eyes like a crossing guard. She drifted from her classes like a genie leaving a bottle, floated over the nothing houses until she found the one that signaled to her as she lay in her bed, a series of pulses sensible only to her fish, whose agitated motions registered the disturbance. And Charlotte would rise from her bed like a sleepwalker, pull on her clothes and carry her shoes in one hand down the back stairs to the kitchen door, not afraid of getting caught because by then she had left behind her life for a different one.

Last night, he had lifted her onto the kitchen counter and done it there, standing up! And so it had to be love, Charlotte decided, locking her bike to the long crowded rack outside of East. It had to be, for him to want her that much.

Melanie Trier's locker was open next to Charlotte's, a curiosity cabinet of miniature stuffed bears and other cute mammals brandishing tiny flags emblazoned with the school's insignia. Melanie's boyfriend, Tor, played football for East and had given her thousands of tiny gold bracelets that formed a chattering soundtrack to Melanie's existence, laughing on her wrists each time she breathed.

"Hey, Mel," Charlotte said.

"Heyryoucoming to the game?"

"I have a . . . an appointment." She was meeting Uncle Moose.

"Boo!" So fresh, genuine, this disappointment, as if Charlotte were a regular cheering presence at football games. She basked in Melanie's indiscriminate friendship, the amiable sense that there was no world but the one in which Melanie lived, so Charlotte must live there, too. "Positive thoughts," Melanie urged her, pensive now. "We need this win." She was on Pom Squad, flinging paper puffs and her own slender legs while Tor shouldered his way along the field.

"Positive thoughts," Charlotte promised. Then she paused, beset by an urge to mention Michael West, to say his name aloud. She wanted him to exist the way Tor existed. But no one could know. It was illegal, for one thing.

He had scars, one on his stomach that looked like the slash of a knife or some crude operation, smaller ones in his shoulder. He claimed not to know where they'd come from—one of countless things he couldn't remember. Lying close to his face, Charlotte found a faint pink line bisecting his right cheek. "That's from the cut you had by the river," she said, but he just laughed, not confirming or denying it. The river had become a joke between them.

His own curiosity was boundless: What kinds of tropical fish did Charlotte sell at work? What did her family eat for dinner? Which flowers grew behind her house? Ricky, his years of treatment—why was it longer for boys? What was the family support group like? And above all her father—how many products had Demographics in America tested? How were the focus groups arranged? Was it domestic or international? Gradually, when Charlotte's answers grew spare and tense, Michael said, "You don't like to speak about your father." And she told him, without thinking, "He hates me."

He wore a small amber bead around his neck on a leather string.

Charlotte adored the smell of that leather, sharp, dense; it smelled like far away, as far from Rockford as you could go. The other side of the world, wherever that was.

The jingle of Melanie's bracelets had ceased; she was gone, the halls were emptying, the bell was about to ring. For whole minutes, Charlotte had just been standing there, staring into her locker. Now she yanked out her books, promising herself, If I shut the door before the bell rings, then he loves me. She slammed the door a half-second ahead of the bell, and sprang down the hall to class.

After dropping Ricky at school, Ellen commenced her morning rounds, picking things up, straightening. Ricky's shoes—he must have five pairs of identical (to her eye) skateboarding shoes—crumpled socks by the front door. A red baseball cap. She lifted a T-shirt from the banister and inhaled his tart, childish sweat. And here came one of the telescopic moments, a moment when she glimpsed herself from some future point when her son would, or would not, still be alive. Yes or no? Preoccupied, Ellen sank onto the stairs. Silence. Crows. There was a phone call she wanted to make, but no.

She rose from the steps feeling slightly renewed, as if she'd sloughed off a layer of fear that would take time—hours, days—to replenish. In the master bedroom she made the bed and hung up wet towels and wiped the sinks, then traversed the hall, poking her head into the children's rooms, pleased to find their beds made. In Charlotte's room she raised the shades—her daughter liked darkness and artificial light, a difference between them (one of thousands). Ellen peered with apprehension into the fish tank. Saltwater was alive, Charlotte had explained; it could sustain only so much additional life, so the tank hung always in a precarious balance. Each time Ellen looked, she expected to find something dead, but she hadn't yet. Charlotte knew what she was doing. In this as in everything.

To justify her lingering presence, Ellen wiped the windowsills and opened Charlotte's closet, scanning the neat, paltry array of clothes. Her daughter would not be taken shopping. A teenage girl—who had ever heard of that? It made Ellen bitter; she had thirsted for such offers as a girl, but her mother was always too weak, too sick. Last time Ellen had managed to coax Charlotte into Saks, her daughter had made her wait far away from the dressing rooms, then handed her the clothes she wanted brusquely, without consultation. Ellen hadn't even told Harris; he would have been livid.

She slid open the drawers of Charlotte's desk, taking furtive glances at the sharpened pencils, the erasers shaped like fish, alert for clues to the inner life of her composed and opaque daughter, whom she half feared. By the computer, a stack of old books: *Winnipeg: A Social History of Urban Growth* (Christ, Ellen thought, why not just call it, "The Most Boring Book in the World"?). *Chicago: Growth of a Metropolis. American Locomotives: An Engineering History.* Was there some rule that every title had to have a colon in it? She opened Charlotte's dresser drawers. Sweaters, neatly folded. Socks. Nothing hidden underneath but the flats of cedar Ellen had given her to fend off moths. Stickers of frogs pasted to the phone. On the wall, a vast chart of weird-looking fish from Lake Victoria. Ellen had peeked into rooms of her friends' teenage daughters and been staggered by their riotous cargoes of heart-shaped metallic balloons and feathers and grinning fuzzy Polaroids and spangled hats and pressed corsages from school dances, the candied reek of perfume, posters of love objects always within kissing range; compost heaps of self-expression, self-absorption. But Charlotte's room was a mask, a surface picked clean of anything suggestive.

Yet even so, Ellen knew that something was happening to her daughter. She felt it when Charlotte was near and she felt it now, beneath the surface of this room. She knew. Something was happening.

She heard the distant dryer buzz and headed downstairs to welcome the laundry that gushed from that machine. Before Ricky's illness, she'd been finishing her B.A. at Winnebago College, spurred in part by the hope of seeing Moose, meeting him for lunch on the campus, though in a whole year they had done that only twice. Still, she'd loved being back in school. Her favorite course was "Enlightened Wanderers," where they'd read accounts by historic travelers, Marco Polo and the famous fifteenth-century Portuguese sailors, others she'd never heard of: Hsuan-Tsang, a Chinese Buddhist monk who spent sixteen years in India in the 600s.

Mary Kingsley, who'd fallen into an animal trap in West Africa and been buffered from nine impaling spikes by the Victorian thickness of her skirt. And Ellen had felt like one of them, an enlightened wanderer herself, embarked as she had been on her own exotic adventure.

But that was over. Long over, the affair that had injected her life with such promise, the affair that had included lovemaking in this very laundry room; Ellen turned now to look, as if some afterglow might cling to the place where she and Gordon had stood (stood!), some holographic trace. For months she had avoided washing the bra she'd worn on what had proved to be their last encounter, clawed through the laundry basket and pried it free to preserve some remnant of that smell—the smell of him, of them together. Now she climbed the stairs with her Matterhorn of folded whites and flicked off the light, both machines refilled and chomping. It had started at a dinner party in Gordon's house, a memory Ellen hoarded, allowing it to open only rarely, at special times, like a music box whose tune fades imperceptibly with each playing: herself standing by a windowsill crowded with African violets, looking out at the yard. Gordon touching the small of her back and saying very softly, close to her ear, "I think about you constantly."

Ellen had never repeated that phrase to Dr. Alwyn in therapy because she knew how cheap it would sound, and refused to hear it that way. At the time, the words had ricocheted through her like a box of marbles flung against a wall, had initiated nearly a year of surreal, pornographic encounters in locations that only rarely featured beds, and then only guestroom beds; she and Gordon were both too squeamish to offer up their connubial beds or the beds of their offspring for such purposes, though Gordon had once dropped to his knees and brought her to orgasm inside her bedroom closet. And yes, he had made her happy, or rather, the agony of guilt and eroticism he'd brought to her life had given it a new, exquisite focus. God, how she'd loved his ass, Dr. Gordon Weeks. Father of four.

In the kitchen, Ellen set the basket of laundry on the table and fished for the pack of Kools she kept deep inside a drawer among pencils and matchbooks so she could claim they were old, if Harris found them. She went outside the back door and smoked one standing up—it was too cold to sit on the patio chairs. November, these dark days. And then Ricky got sick and everything changed. She hadn't seen Gordon since then—or rather, she'd seen him innumerable times at school events, at club tournaments in which he and Harris both golfed, but during that fleck of time in which her life had reversed itself, sitting in a pale blue office in the hematology-oncology ward of Children's Memorial Hospital in Chicago, a new agony had commenced in which Ellen became convinced that her badness with Gordon—their badness together—had made Ricky sick. If she hadn't had the affair, her child would be well, not "well" in the way he was now, well-for-the-moment-and-you-should-thank-God-even-for-that; her child would be untouched. Ellen believed this.

She lit a second cigarette, narrowing her eyes at the lawn, the very same lawn where she'd played as a child. Here she was, at thirty-six; with the brutal efficiency of a Greek tragedy she'd been thrust into the very life she had sought to escape. Ellen had dragged Harris back to Rockford—true, true—when the children were young, Ricky just a baby. She'd done it for Moose, to be near him after his unspeakable disaster. But Moose, it soon became clear, didn't like to be near Ellen anymore. For years, she'd made regular detours in the course of her days to look for her brother's car, tracking his movements from the college to Versailles to the public library. It had relieved her, somehow, just to know where he was. But nowadays she rarely did that. Almost never.

Yet still she was shackled to Rockford. Harris refused to leave—couldn't, he said, his business was thriving and *Rockford is my business*. Harris wouldn't leave and Ellen couldn't leave Harris, not until Ricky was grown up and unquestionably healthy, or the stress could make him sick again. Paralysis: her punishment. Ellen half welcomed it.

She finished the cigarette, then brought both butts indoors and dropped them into the garbage disposal, grinding them until the faint smell of crushed nicotine had dispersed, then washed her hands with scented soap (Harris was a bloodhound), went to the kitchen phone and lifted the receiver once again.

For here was the diabolical thing: in the months since Ricky's chemo finally ended, Ellen had found herself longing again for Gordon, longing to begin it all again, to start from the beginning and feel that thrill, that childlike sense of escape. There was so much to escape from! There had never been a "breakup" per se; Gordon had understood implicitly when she'd said, "My son has," said it into the telephone, not even lowering her voice. Now she lifted the phone. Her heart clunked. She knew his numbers still, home, office, pager, knew his schedule by heart.

But she didn't call Gordon. She called Moose instead.

Holding her lunch tray, Charlotte threaded among the tables past Melanie Trier, who called out, "Hey, Chari, sit with us." It was the kind of girl she was. So Charlotte perched at a table lined with football players' girlfriends and the players themselves, some of whom needed two trays to hold the staggering quantities of food their bodies required (Charlotte counted nine glasses of milk on one). She joined in their prognostications about the game, how the other quarterback was a head case so it was just a matter of wigging him out, saying something weird (How about a riddle? Charlotte suggested), yeah, or like maybe a poem . . . she half listened, her mind on two tracks. Certain words emanated a new significance: "night," "teacher," "foreign," even "math," and Charlotte looked for ways to say these words because each utterance gave her a bowelly pinch of pleasure, like plucking a string.

Now the words "kitchen counter" were rising in her throat, demanding to be said. "We're having our *kitchen counters* redone," she blurted to Melanie, and knew, from her friend's blank response, that this had been a mistake. She was becoming a girl who muttered odd things in the lunchroom. Yet saying the words made her heart spin.

Tor turned his big, delicate face to Melanie and kissed her. The bracelets chattered on her wrists. And again the question rose in Charlotte: If this was love, did she have it too? Did you need to say "love" for it to be love? Michael hadn't said "love" except once, about her lotion. His gaze felt so empty; he seemed to rest his eyes on Charlotte but see something else, or see nothing. After they'd done it, she would turn to him and place a hand on his stomach (he was so thin, thinner than he looked in clothes), feeling the sheathe of muscle behind his skin, and try to guess his thoughts. She wanted to ask, Do you feel the link of fate that connects us? Do you think about me during the day, like I think about you? Do you wish I came to your house on nights when I don't come? Do you prefer small-breasted women, which you told me some men do? But instinct kept her from asking any of these things, lest his answers be wrong.

"I should go home," she would say instead, and pull on her clothes in the dark.

"Chari's coming to the game," Melanie told Tor, having apparently forgotten that she wasn't.

"Cool," Tor said, and Charlotte felt the adjustment of his gray eyes as he envisioned her beside the field, watching him.

"Positive thoughts," Melanie said.

"Positive thoughts," Charlotte agreed.

*Kitchen counters,* she was thinking.

Moose leapt from his living room couch, which was covered with maps of Rockford, and lunged for the telephone, anxious that it not wake Priscilla, who had worked the night before and was asleep in the bedroom.

"Ellen," he said, surprised; he and his sister rarely spoke. "Is everything all right?"

"Oh, fine," she said, sounding nervous. "I—I was calling to talk about Charlotte."

"Oh," Moose said. And then, very slowly, "What. About. Her?"

He spoke with utmost care, because the invocation of Charlotte caused a black umbrella of guilt to open inside him: guilt over the sense of obligation that dragged at him when he thought of his niece. Some weeks ago he had set her free in the woods behind Winnebago College, yet in no time at all she was back, essay in hand, and the surprise of her unwonted reappearance had spurred in Moose his first real irritation with Charlotte: How long did this have to go on? When would he be free of the obligation? What could—

"Moose?"

He was on the phone. Talking to his sister. About Charlotte.

". . . can't get a word out of her . . . ," Ellen was saying.

"Hmmm," Moose said, and closed his eyes, forcing himself to concentrate.

"It could be nothing, but I have this sense that . . ."

"Hmmm."

". . . she's in the grip of something."

This got his attention. Moose opened his eyes.

"And I thought you might, since you see her regularly, you might have . . ."

"Grip of what?" he asked.

"Well, I don't know."

Moose fixed his eyes on the sliding glass door, beyond which lay his small balcony, the autumnal grounds of Versailles, Rockford, Illinois, and the world, whose immensity the glass door thus synechdochally invoked. In his years of teaching, there had been five or six students who had seemed, if only briefly, only partially, to be edging toward something that might have been a first, glimmering suggestion of the vision he wished to impart. For Moose, the experience of their proximity had been a sweet agony whose nearest analog was love, a love more coiled and hopeful and desperate than any he had known in his amorous life. Male or female, it made no difference. Had Moose been told, at such a time, of such a student, that said student was *in the grip of something*, he would have experienced a catastrophic excitement. But Charlotte was not such a student, nor faintly reminiscent of one. Even those more promising kids had never really seen it; they had graduated from the college and drifted away into the service industries, and occasionally Moose would glimpse one hauling children through Media Play or buying soil at Home Depot, at which point he hid himself urgently, flailingly, ducking behind racks of lawn mowers, lunging around walls of frozen food, desperate to avoid the mundane and mortifying aftermath of his hope.

Still. *In the grip of something.* It intrigued him.

"I'll watch her, Ellen," Moose promised. "I'll look very carefully today, this afternoon. She's coming to my office at four."

"Thanks, Moose."

There was a pause. "And how are you?" he asked.

"Not bad."

Moose heard a falter in his sister's voice, and was moved to declare with feeling, "It's good to talk to you, Ellen," meaning it despite the labyrinth of discomfort that had interposed itself between them, a hangover from so much time spent together long ago, when he was someone else. He felt a deep, awful tenderness for his little sister.

"Thanks," she said shyly. "Same."

And Moose heard her happiness then—Oh, the joy that came of dispensing happiness to others, of entering happiness's interlocking circuitry! Yet even now Moose felt the persistence of whatever worry he'd heard in Ellen's voice *before* the happiness his remark had occasioned, and no sooner was the phone back in its cradle than he was felled by a crash of despair on his sister's behalf. We're all alone, he thought, crumpling back onto the fragment of living room couch that wasn't draped in maps of Rockford. We are all alone.

After several minutes of gloomy reverie, Moose was distracted by the sound of Priscilla turning over in bed, a sound that induced in him a twang of good luck at being married to someone who could sleep until— he glanced at his watch—ten-forty-five on her days off, who slept as if sleeping were a sport. He left the couch and went to look at his wife. She was dozing, her hand in a book, a trill of lavender visible above the bed-clothes, one of the silken undergarments that tangled around her in bed and around Moose, too, who slept in the nude. They smelled like flowers. Before Priscilla, he'd hated to sleep because of the nightmares—closing his eyes was like jumping off a cliff—but sleeping with her was like slipping into a warm sea and floating there, the nighties coiling like sea anemones around his wrists and ankles.

Priscilla opened her eyes, saw Moose in the doorway and held out her arms. He lay down beside her, mute while she kissed his face, his big strange face that appeared monstrous to him in the mirror sometimes, filled with hues a face should not have—green, purple, chartreuse—kissed him and said, "How's it going, silly?" and he said, "Okay," which seemed the most accurate summary he could muster of the gusts of happiness and unhappiness that had buffeted him so far that morning.

"Are you working?" she asked.

"Sort of."

"I'm reading *Moll Flanders*," she said, sleepily.

"So I saw," he teased. "With your eyes closed."

She smiled and rose from the bed, slender legs still brown under the short hem of her lavender chemise, though it had been months since she'd lain on the balcony in her bikini. Moose followed her into the kitchen.

"You were tired last night," he said.

"Ugh, it was craziness. Not to mention we were short-staffed—Andy took another sick day."

"The dolt," Moose muttered.

"Meanwhile, I'm starving," Priscilla said. She was adding milk and eggs to powdered pancake mix, blending it all with a large metal whisk. She always ate pancakes or waffles or French toast on her days off, yet she stayed thin—lissome, even. "Want to hand me that pan?"

"I've got it." Moose buttered the pan and placed it over the burner. Then he gathered Priscilla into his arms, enfolding his slender wife in his gigantic embrace, inhaling the light, peppery smell of her underarms.

This was the secret life. For most people, Moose assumed, the secret life was more terrible than anyone could imagine. These couples one saw barely speaking—their lives looked bad enough in public! And yet, would anyone guess at his? Of course, it was unlikely to last; Moose expected this. He had proceeded through the years along a massif of shifting plates, his steps growing more fearful, more tentative each time the ground buckled under him. But for now Priscilla was happy, remained happy, in part (Moose sensed) out of sheer relief at being emancipated from her marriage to Wes Victor, a local root-canal specialist who'd called her a lazy cow and demanded that she sell Amway products, who'd been disgusted by her failure, in three years, to produce even one child. Wes had remarried within months of their divorce, and now took evident relish in herding his copious progeny past Moose and Priscilla's table at the Cherryvale food court, where they went sometimes on a Saturday. Moose watched his wife's face very carefully during these encounters, attuned to the smallest flicker of regret or remorse as Priscilla saw her former and much more wealthy husband pass with his new wife, who tugged one kid by the hand, pushed a second in a stroller, carried a third in a drooping sack attached to her back and a fourth inside her womb, which led the way at a salute. But Moose saw only relief. "Look how he doesn't even help her," Priscilla said once, in the wondering, reverent tones of someone who, through a minor fluke of rescheduling, has avoided a plane crash.

Priscilla poured batter into four hissing pads. "Go. Work," she said, patting Moose out the kitchen door. "I've got my book."

In his living room, Moose was greeted by the major nineteenth-century surveyors' maps of Rockford—1858, '71, '76, '92—along with an array of twentieth-century maps extending to the present day. The Rock River spasmed identically through the middle of each, accentuating the changes around it: the gradual accretion of factories in the last century followed by their gradual dissolution in this one. Moose stared at the maps. It was all right there, the narrative of industrial America told in these glyphs: a tale that began with the rationalization of objects through standardization, abstraction and mass production, and concluded with the rationalization of human beings through marketing, public relations, image consulting and spin. Yet were Moose to invite a student to look at the maps (as he'd done many times), they would not be able to see this. He marveled and puzzled and raged at the awful gap between his vision and other people's, at his own consistent failure to bridge it. Yet what could he do but try? And keep trying, in hopes that someone, at last, would look back at him with recognition.

At the sound of the shower, Moose rose from the couch. Priscilla was in the bathroom, lifting the lavender nightie over her head, pink tooth-brush dangling lazily from her mouth. Steam floated up from behind the shower curtain, mingling with the smell of pancake syrup. Moose stood behind his wife at the sink and slipped his hand down that hard, slightly brown belly, kissing her neck. She laughed, rinsing suds from her teeth, then led him by the hand back into the bedroom, the bed still tussled and fragrant with her sleep, led him there and encircled him with her brown arms and legs. They made love quickly.

Afterward, Moose watched Priscilla's sleeping face while "Dancing in the Moonlight" played softly on her small transistor radio in the kitchen. At Cherryvale last year, he'd noticed her eyeing a poster for package tours to Hawaii: a couple thrashing through creamy surf, the man vigorous and young, unlike Moose, the woman slender and elastic, like Priscilla. "Would you like to go there?" he had asked, but she'd shrugged this off, knowing they couldn't afford it, knowing Moose hadn't boarded a plane since his return from New Haven twelve years ago. But Moose had resolved to take Priscilla there—to Hawaii, yes he would—and in the months since then he'd lain awake many nights, trying to acclimate himself: Fruit drinks. Coconuts. Saltwater. Happy people everywhere, people like Priscilla—Moose longed to be in their midst. But the trip frightened him, too, and he hadn't mentioned it.

Eventually he left the bed and headed back to his maps. Only then did he hear the shower still running in the bathroom and reach behind the plastic curtain to turn it off.

Charlotte rode to Winnebago College directly after school, her body alive with spidery anticipation. The twisty college road, the lunar quiet of the campus lulled her into a state not unlike what she experienced at night, sleepwalking from her bedroom to her bike. They were connected, Moose and Michael West, linked in a relationship of cause and effect that Charlotte could not have explained but felt deeply, instinctively. It had all begun with her uncle: first the sense of waiting, then seeing Michael West that second time. And Moose's advice—*follow your desire*—which had worked almost supernaturally.

She left her bike in the rack and made her way toward Meeker Hall, walking slowly because she was early. Wandering the curled paths, going in circles to make the extra minutes pass, she remembered last night, lying with him right after they had done it—not on the kitchen counter but again, upstairs (it was in her notes). "Where were you before you came to Rockford?" she asked, as he gazed at the ceiling.

"New York."

"And where before that?"

He glanced at her, moonlight spinning on his eye. "Overseas."

"Which sea?"

Rather than answer, he snapped a kumquat from his tree and broke the skin with his teeth. Its essence wafted over Charlotte: tart, bitter, sweet. Was it the smell of love? She waited for him to answer, but he sucked out the kumquat's insides and nudged the empty rind toward the open window.

As she was leaving, Charlotte paused in the back doorway, facing him, and forced herself to speak. "Maybe you could give me something."

"Give you something." He didn't understand.

"Anything."

She shouldn't have to ask. She had to ask for everything.

"Ah," he said at last. "A gift."

"It doesn't have to be new," Charlotte added quickly. "I mean, you don't have to buy it."

His eyes moved, he was thinking.

"It could be that," she said lightly, pointing at his chest. The bead of amber on its leather string was hidden beneath his T-shirt, but he knew what she meant. If he gives me that, then he loves me, Charlotte thought, and knew that it was true, that the other, smaller proofs had proved nothing. She looked into the mystery of his face—angles, corners, depths—the face of a stranger to whom she had given her heart.

"Or something else," she said casually.

"Something else," he agreed.

Charlotte arrived at her uncle's office to the odd sensation that he'd been awaiting her. "Come in, come in," he murmured, bustling uncharacteristically to usher her into her chair. She was surprised, encouraged.

When Moose was seated behind his desk, Charlotte took out her essay and read:

### How Two Machines Changed Everything About Grain

After the prairie got broken up, there were a lot of nutrients left in the soil, which they called "sod," and Rockford farmers in the 1830s and '40s started planting grains: wheat, corn, oats, barley, rye. They grew like crazy. After the harvest, each farmer poured his grain into cloth sacks with the name of the farm on them, which was how they were sold.

Normally her uncle sat hunched in his chair while she read, knuckles to forehead, eyes closed. But today, Charlotte felt his gaze trained on her face, as if something there had caught his attention.

But growing the grain was the easy part. The nightmare was getting those fat heavy sacks to a place where they could be sold. To get to Chicago, you had to load the sacks onto a cart pulled by a horse, praying to God the wheels didn't break or get stuck in the mud, because the roads were 100% dirt. That's what a road was: dirt!

She glanced at her uncle again, found him watching her still, and felt herself begin to blush.

To get to St. Louis, you loaded the sacks on a flatboat or a steamboat and floated them down the Rock River to the Mississippi River, but if the grain happened to get wet, then it was ruined. And the trip took so long by boat AND cart that when you got to market the price of grain was sometimes too low. How did these farmers survive, with so many hardships? You almost wonder.

As she read, Charlotte began to hear her essay in a slightly different way; imbued with whatever it was that had snared Moose's interest. She could feel the words in her mouth: "grain," "sacks," "dirt," "wet," each with its own soft weight.

Then in the 1850s came the railroad . . .

Moose was watching his niece as he'd promised Ellen he would. He noted her flushed cheeks, the skin pink all the way to her hairline, her bright dark eyes glancing at him shyly as she read. And again, half against his will, he heard Ellen's words, *in the grip of something,* and felt the stirring of a possibility.

A second invention, which became widely used in the 1850s, was the steam-powered grain elevator. Now, what is a "grain elevator?" Well, it's a building that can take in grain, weigh it, store it and release it.

Her uncle was staring at her in a peculiar way, and it came to Charlotte that he must notice the difference in her—he alone, of everyone she knew. And now Michael West seemed to float up between them, a sudden, spectral presence. Charlotte imagined she was reading the story

186

aloud to her uncle: *He carried me upstairs. The room was dark, but street light came in through the window. I saw the bones in his chest . . .*

A machine pulled the grain in buckets out of the railroad cars, a machine weighed the grain and a machine poured it into bins to be stored, which meant that no one had to haul those heavy sacks of grain around a dock anymore, because no one even put their grain in sacks anymore . . .

Moose felt a sharpening in the room, a quivering intensity that excited and confused him.

There were no more sacks of grain because now grain was sold by weight and poured like a liquid and mixed together with other grains from other farmers. Now it was not this farmer's grain and that farmer's grain, it was just Grain, capital G, everyone's grain mixed together, and this was a very big change.

"Oh-*ho*!" Moose cried, bolting from his chair. "Yes, it was! A very big change. Abstraction; standardization; the collapse of time and space . . . it was the beginning of modernity!"

He stood in a pose of astonishment. Not merely in response to Charlotte's words—perhaps not her words at all, but some feeling behind them, as if she were recounting a tale that mattered to her deeply, personally, in all the ways a thing can matter. The feeling half frightened him; what did it mean?

Her uncle had leapt to his feet and was regarding Charlotte in a way he never had before. And the prolonged surge of his attention roused a hungry, empty part of her that reached toward him helplessly, eagerly, craving more of his attention.

For the farmers (she read on, voice trembling) the combination of trains and grain elevators changed everything, really. Bigger amounts of grain could be bought and sold because you didn't need actual human beings to carry it around in sacks.

Grain wasn't separate things anymore; it was just one big thing called Grain, like water is one big thing called Water . . .

Moose lowered himself back onto his chair, allowing himself to imagine that Charlotte was on the verge, not of seeing—that would be reaching, that would be wishing—but of readying herself for the first faint intimations of sight. And he had a sudden impression of light, light everywhere, in the room and all around his niece, as if his office window opened not into the earth but to sky.

He was frightened to have Charlotte go on, afraid that whatever she said would destroy his hope.

Because of all these changes, the futures market got started, which meant that people began buying and selling the idea of grain without ever actually giving each other any grain or even touching grain, or even seeing it. It was basically gambling on the price of grain, whether it would go up or down. Which I guess made sense because the grain was already an idea, like paper money is just Money, unlike gold coins that actually have value in themselves.

In Moose's imagination there was a break, a snap, and then a great many things ensued with a drastic simultaneity that was the hallmark of mental events unfettered by the constraints of physical possibility: he bellowed (mentally), *"Yyyyyeeeeeeeesssssss!,"* his uvula swinging like a pendulum at the back of his throat, the prolonged, gut-heaving force of his yell loosening the support beams over his head and sending tiny fissures through the walls of Meeker Hall, which widened into cracks and gaps and then gullies, so that shortly the building was collapsing over their heads: desks, computers, books, a hecatomb of didacticism and scholarship and cruelty (toward him) reduced to nonsense by a single yell from the man they'd relegated to the basement, but that wasn't all—his yell sent shock waves through the soil in whose depths they'd forced him to work, waves that burrowed under those delicately landscaped hills and dales and dells and playing fields, so that the buildings whose halcyon views they enhanced were shaken to their foundations, and by the time he reached the *ssss* of *Yyyyyeeeeeeeessss*, a thunderous general collapse was in progress that threatened to spread indefinitely, his departmental colleagues airborne and whirling like locusts, desks, files, documents intended to effect his dismissal (he knew it! He *knew* it!), all of these separated and broke and divided until they were blowing in the breeze like the furry seeds of dandelions, and in the silence that seeped over the world following this juggernaut, a silence like the falling of night, Moose stepped from his basement hole and surveyed the wreckage his affirmation had wrought and was pleased, yes, he was satisfied. They'd had it coming, trying to bury him alive down here, and he looked at Charlotte seated across his desk, Charlotte who was on the verge of seeing, Charlotte who knew not what she saw, and said, very softly, "Yes."

And in that moment, Charlotte, too, experienced a falling away; her life fell away, her friends—they fell away. She'd been clinging to them these past weeks, wanting to be like Melanie Trier, like other people. But now she saw, or felt, that this wasn't possible. She made her choice: Moose, and Michael West. Her secret life. She gave up the rest. The relief was physical, like releasing a long tight breath that had crowded her lungs for too long, letting it go because it was stale, the oxygen was gone. Her uncle looked younger, lean and eager under his slight growth of beard: the boy in the picture again, the water-skier grinning, half submerged. And Charlotte had done it, made him that way again. She was his special student—she felt this. Knew it.

"I think we should pause," Moose said carefully, "and not read any more today."

"Actually, I was done," she said, laughing. *"The end."*

"But not the end." Moose leaned back in his chair, watching Charlotte as if she were a marvel, as if the mere sight of her had the power to restore him. They sat that way for some moments.

"Uncle Moose," Charlotte said at last. "Could I see that picture in your wallet again? Of the river?"

Surprised, Moose dug his wallet from his back pocket, opened it, removed the picture from its plastic sleeve and slid it toward Charlotte across the desk. She hardly needed to look. She knew already that it would be the same place, the exact spot where she'd first seen Michael West, last August. The same place, a hundred years ago.

It was all connected.

"Keep it," Moose said, nudging the picture toward Charlotte across his desk. "I want you to have it."

She frowned, not believing him. For as long as she'd known her uncle, he had carried that picture.

"It's yours," Moose said, and looked away.

# Part Two

## The Mirrored Room

# Chapter Ten

"*What you have* to understand, Charlotte—please don't take this the wrong way—," said Victoria Knight, friend of Lily Cabron, the hair stylist from my failed job for Italian *Vogue*, "but there's nothing inherently sympathetic about your story. I mean, most people would consider you lucky just to have lived the glamorous life you've had. The challenge for us is to open a door into your inner world, so they'll sympathize with you and root for you and want to spend money finding out more about you."

"I see," I said, which was not quite true.

This lunchtime primer in public relations was the fruit of my own arduous campaign, launched ten days earlier, after my calamitous date and failed suicide attempt. Ignoring the sage advice of Mark, the downstairs neighbor whose coitus I had interrupted, I had not slept late the next morning, but had risen early and pawed through the prior day's pockets and handbag like someone feeling for traces of life under a layer of smoldering ash. I'd been looking for Irene Maitlock's business card, out of some amorphous wish to make contact with the reporter, to speak with her. I couldn't find it. What I found instead was Lily Cabron's business card with the phone number of her friend, the alleged PR wizard, scribbled on the back.

I called Victoria Knight three times each day for nearly a week, only to be flicked away by several assistants who had a way of delivering the phrase, "She's in a meeting," as if it were an obscenity. But I kept calling (being not exactly busy). She was the only lead I had, despite a call to the *New York Post* in search of Irene Maitlock, about whom I lacked sufficient information—*Department, floor, desk, staff or freelance?* barked the switchboard operator—to locate.

And what did I want to say to her, anyway?

One night around ten o'clock, I caught Victoria Knight at her desk, sounding weary, and managed to blurt out the rudiments of my story. At which point, with a straightforwardness that seemed no less arbitrary than her prior avoidance of me had been, we made a lunch date.

"Unless—," she went on, "and I think this is something you should consider—unless we can portray your accident as being the outcome of some kind of destructive behavior pattern, like drinking or an abusive relationship, drug use maybe, something in your childhood that's haunted you—I don't want to put words in your mouth, but if we can work the story around the idea of punishment and redemption, that could be *very* appealing. Never underestimate Americans' religious fanaticism—that's something I learned early on. If you take that route, you're saying: I had it all in the palm of my hand but I squandered it and now I've got nothing. And yet, out of this wreckage, I've learned the meaning of life and can be reborn."

"The meek shall inherit the earth," I said.

"Exactly," she said, and seemed impressed.

Victoria Knight was a person in miniature (five foot one, by my rough calculation), who managed her diminutive stance with such surpassing panache that I could only stand back in awe. In brazen defiance of the popular wisdom that one should dress to offset one's defects, she wore a short skirt, a blazer with a cinched waist, patterned stockings and *flats*, all of which displayed a lovely bonsai physique. And I wasn't the only one looking: in the lunchtime furor of Judson Grill, where the air smelled of arugula and money, I sensed many eyes upon her, teasing, wondering, with a mixture of anthropology and lust, what she might look like unclothed. Her oval face was not especially small, framed by lustrous brown hair in a blunt cut. She had sapphire-colored eyes (tinted contact lenses?) and a jazzy spray of freckles on her cheeks. Her upper lip rose into two delicate points. But her greatest strength, the thing I knew I would remember about Victoria Knight even now, having barely sat down with her to lunch, was her near-midgetry. In this sense, she was a walking advertisement for her own estimable skills as a surgeon of reality.

Philippe, a tweedy, laconic Frenchman whose role at our lunch I had yet to ascertain, was taking furious notes. I'd thought at first that he was one of Victoria's assistants, but he seemed too old, and insufficiently sleek. And a fourth person was expected shortly. "My friend Thomas Keene has a lunch, but he's going to try and skip out early to meet you," Victoria had said when she and Philippe first arrived. "He has a business venture that I thought you might . . . well, I'll let Thomas explain it."

Venture smenture, I thought; this Thomas, whoever he was, was looking for an excuse to cozy up to Victoria (like everyone else at Judson Grill), to observe her extraordinary anatomy at close range.

We ordered lunch—arugula for everyone, the power of suggestion being too potent to resist. I pondered the existence of a biological link between eating arugula and earning money; what else could explain its lasting influence?

"Then there's the informational story," Victoria said. "For example, have any new surgical techniques been used on you? Any innovations in the healing or recovery process? Bottom line: Has any scientific ground been broken here? Because that's the kind of thing we could pitch as a news feature, say to the *Science Times*."

"May be shooting a little high," I demurred.

Victoria narrowed her eyes; apparently I had insulted her. "Don't be so sure."

Philippe raised a tentative finger. He was open-eared in the way a person can be open-armed, curved in his chair with a relaxed, almost sleepy mien that brought to mind a youthful Jean-Paul Belmondo. But I detected a whiff of desperation in his quick eyes, his uneven haircut; poverty, I guessed.

"PR companies have very many powers in America," he told me, in the jagged accent of someone who wrote in English more often than he spoke it. "This is the subject of my work."

"Philippe is studying us as we speak," Victoria said briskly. "He's getting a Ph.D. in Media Studies at NYU, and he's writing his dissertation on . . . um . . ."

"You," Philippe said, and grinned, unleashing a mouthful of anarchic European teeth.

Victoria blushed. I glimpsed her shadow self shrinking away from the press of Philippe's fascination, clacketing sideways like a beach crab for whom attention can only be perilous. But the apparition was fleeting, sucked almost instantly back into the undertow of her mighty persona.

"Anyway," she went on, glancing into the fray of arugula the waiter had placed at our table. "So there's the I Blew It and I'm Sorry story. There's the Scientific Breakthrough story . . ."

"I'm not sure either of those is exactly true," I ventured.

Victoria tilted her head as if it were striking her only now that I might have been brain damaged in the accident. "That's completely up to you, Charlotte," she said slowly, as if to a child. "Right now, as far as the world is concerned, you're a tabula rasa. You don't exist. But once you're positioned, you're going to have a hell of a time repositioning. I want you to pick a first move that'll get you the most coverage possible, and the kind you want."

The thinnest sheen of gold sparkled above her sapphire eyes. She was tough, tough! In my years of tormenting mousy women (Irene Maitlock being only a recent example), scourging them for refusing to take charge, dye their hair, lose five pounds and *get on with life*, it was Victoria Knight, or someone very, very like her, whom I'd held in my mind as a paragon. And yet I couldn't bear her.

"I'm sorry," I said. "Go on."

"I was also thinking . . . oh, okay. A kind of Mental Breakdown story. This would be the inversion of I Blew It and I'm Sorry; this one would go, Up until this tragedy, life was peachy-keen, but now watch me fall to pieces day by day as I try to cope with this disaster. Again, drugs and alcohol could come into this one, as you fight to stay in control. But really, you aren't in control, your life is totally unraveling, everyone knows it but you!"

"Hmmm," I said, relieved that I'd resisted the impulse to order a martini. I was trying desperately to cut back on booze while also clinging to my peace of mind and warding off Despair, whose resurrection I feared daily. It was a difficult balance to strike.

Philippe scribbled madly into his notebook. Each scenario Victoria described I watched land in his catcher's mitt face: first pity, then pity; now pity. I felt like kicking him.

"And the style—this could be really nice—sort of a diary, day by day, like *Diary of a Mad Housewife* meets *Go Ask Alice*. Call it something like, 'Faceless: My Journey into Madness.' You give us an intimate, bird's-eye view of your own disinteg—oh, look! Here's Thomas!"

A tall blond boyish person was wending his way through the fields of arugula in an olive-green Armani jacket, black jeans and scuffed white Converse basketball shoes, holding aloft a briefcase that appeared to be covered in crocodile. I sensed immediately that he'd once been overweight; he moved with a fat person's tiptoey apology, although he was lanky—or at least, tall enough to appear so. Harvard, I thought. Grew up in Greenwich or the equivalent, but with no real money behind him. He was one of those rare individuals whose shadow self—a fat, anxious boy who wanted desperately to be powerful—was more pronounced than his surface (sleek, thinnish, and in the possession of a certain modicum of power—or at the very least, a crocodile briefcase). I'd been wrong, though, about his reasons for joining us. Thomas Keene wasn't attracted to Victoria, he was afraid of her. But he needed her, too. We all needed Victoria.

"I'm sorry to barge in," he said, shaking my hand, "but Victoria started telling me about you, and I was kind of fascinated by your story."

"We're hoping it'll have that effect on everyone," I said brightly.

The waiter came, and Thomas ordered a San Pellegrino with lemon.

"How do you two know each other?" I asked.

"College," Thomas said.

"Don't tell me," I said. "Harvard."

"Actually, Berkeley," Victoria said.

My expression must have lurched, because Thomas jumped in with, "Hey, Berkeley's a great school," and I had to assure them both that I had nothing against their alma mater.

"I guessed you were from the East Coast," I explained, though in truth, I'd had no read at all on Victoria's matrix, she was that pure. You had to admire it.

"We're Berkeley brats," Thomas said. "My mom works in Admissions, and Victoria's dad is a professor."

"Logical Thinking," Victoria said, and rolled her eyes as if the very idea were ludicrous. "Listen, I'm going to make a quick call to the office." She rummaged in her purse for her cell phone and stood, bringing her an inch or two shy of Thomas's height sitting down.

Our main courses arrived, and as I tucked into my grilled salmon, Thomas shimmied his way into describing an Internet service he was creating called Ordinary People.

"It's not a magazine—it's a database," he said. "What I'm doing is, I'm optioning the rights to people's stories, just ordinary Americans: an autoworker, a farmer, a deep-sea diver, a mother of six, a corrections officer, a pool shark . . . Each one of these folks will have their own home page—we call it a PersonalSpace™—devoted exclusively to their lives, internal and external."

My knowledge of the Internet was limited to a few tentative spins on Oscar's computer at work, but I decided to bluff comprehension. "What will these . . . PersonalSpaces look like?" I asked.

Each one would be different, he explained, to reflect the life of that individual, but certain categories would be standard: Photographs of the subject and his or her family. Childhood Memories. Dreams. Diary Entries—everyone was required to keep a weekly diary, and daily entries were encouraged. Future Plans/Fantasies. Regrets/Missed Opportunities. And people could add their own categories, too: Things That Make Me Angry. Political Views. Hobbies.

"The idea is to give you, the subscriber"—Thomas swung around to Philippe, who was so flummoxed by this lash of attention that he dropped his pen and had to grub for it under the table, ass in the air (worn khakis), forcing Thomas to wait with mounting impatience to finish his sentence—". . . access to every aspect of this person, all the things you wonder, say, when you read about coal miners in the *Times* and you think, Hey, what would it be like to be a coal miner? Well, my subscribers will be able to answer that question in a totally frictionless way—they don't have to buy a book or pick up the phone or a newspaper or go to a library or download a lot of boring crap from Lexis—they can go straight inside a coal miner's life: kids, house, childhood traumas, what he ate for dinner last night, health problems, dreams . . . Does a coal miner dream about coal? I'd like to know that!"

There would be audio and video, too, Thomas assured me, so people could hear the miner speak in his own voice and watch him extracting coal from the mine.

Victoria had resumed her place at the table, and the waiter brought her steak tartare. It was genius. I wished I had ordered one, too.

"Now obviously, a slew of people are already doing this on their own," Thomas said, the very presence of Victoria having introduced a whiff of defensiveness into his posture. "I don't know if you've checked out any of these 'personal' Websites, but frankly, they're a snore. It's all the wrong people: youngish Webheads with too much free time on their hands, and who really cares? No coal miners, I can promise you."

"So why would . . . coal miners want to do this?" I asked.

"Same reasons people do everything," Victoria said. "Fame and fortune."

Philippe didn't catch it. He cocked an open ear in Victoria's direction. "Fame end . . ."

"Fortune," Victoria said, cracking the word like a nut and swallowing its soft inside.

The "fortune," Thomas explained, meant an option fee for developing a PersonalSpace, followed by a purchase price. Fame would result from the ensuing exposure. "And out of that exposure could come incredible opportunities," he said. "Movie options, research contracts . . ."

I must have looked incredulous. (I was incredulous.)

"Okay. For example. Paramount is doing an updated *Moby Dick*. Screenwriter needs to know what it's like to be a fisherman. He's a subscriber, so that gives him access to whatever we've got: say, a tuna fisherman in Maine and a salmon guy in Alaska. He reads everything in their PersonalSpaces and he still wants more. So for a negotiated fee, he can actually spend time with an Ordinary Person, say the salmon guy, on his home turf—meet his friends, go out on the boat with him, learn the lingo, maybe do some actual fishing—really soak up the atmosphere of that subject's life. *Voilà!* My salmon fisherman is now a film consultant. Who knows, maybe he winds up in the movie for authenticity, maybe they throw him a couple of lines—*voilà!* My fisherman is now movie talent. And that's just one possible scenario out of dozens; book contracts, TV appearances, expert witnessing—come on, we're the most litigious society in the world, and everyone's an expert on something! And that's not even getting into things like product placement. Believe me, Coca-Cola's gonna pay a pretty penny to get its brand into these people's homes. Now obviously we'll have to go easy on that stuff, because authenticity is everything, here. We want to get people in their natural environments, doing exactly what they would normally do, but if companies are willing to pay them to use the products they've been using all their lives, I say, Why the hell not? I act as their talent agent, that's part of the deal, and all contracts are split fifty-fifty."

I expected him to fall back exhausted (I was exhausted; too exhausted to finish my salmon, which now seemed unpleasantly linked to the fisherman-turned-movie-actor), but this sales pitch seemed to have persuaded Thomas afresh of the magnificence of his venture. His eyes glittered with a kind of madness behind his wire-rimmed glasses. Philippe, apparently having despaired of keeping up using the old-fashioned rudiments of pen and paper, had excavated a tape recorder from his floppy leather shoulder bag, and now was performing the delicate task of eating a softshell crab while holding the orange bulb of a microphone under Thomas's chin.

"But wait a minute," I said, partly to give the Frenchman, who I'd noticed made less of an effort to capture my remarks, a chance to eat a bit of lunch. "Okay, a researcher needs some information—fine. But who else is going to give a damn about some fisherman's dreams and family history? I mean, not to be rude, but that sounds like watching paint dry."

"Not at all," Thomas said, leaning into this challenge with such relish that he actually shoved the table an inch in my direction, rattling our water glasses. "But with all due respect, Charlotte, I think you may be the exception, here. Most of us are desperate for raw experience. We work in offices, dealing with intangibles; we go to lunch and talk to other people surrounded by intangibles. No one actually *makes* anything anymore, and our so-called experiences are about climbing Mount Kilimanjaro on our two-week vacations or snapping a picture of the Dalai Lama in Central Park. But we're so powerfully aware of all the stuff we're missing! It creates this frustration, this craving to get out of ourselves. TV tries to satisfy that, books, movies—they try, but they're all so lame—so mediated! They're just not *real* enough.

"Eventually, we'll take this international—a Yanomamo warrior in Brazil, a rebel in Sierra Leone. A Hezbollah suicide bomber . . . imagine if there were a way for you to hear that guy's last thoughts as he gets ready to die for his beliefs! And for him, the exposure—way beyond anything he could get from a day or two of headlines."

"It's really quite revolutionary," Philippe remarked, holding his tape recorder to his ear like a seashell, I guessed to ascertain that it was working. He cast a baleful glance at his unfinished softshell crabs as the waiter lifted them away. Victoria, who had been eating with meditational fervor, now mopped her plate with bread until it gleamed.

"So how do I fit in?" I asked. "I don't make anything, either. I'm just another New Yorker, surrounded by intangibles."

"True," Thomas said. "True. Although to a farmer—and we're hoping farmers will subscribe, too—to a farmer, a fashion model's life would be pretty damn interesting."

To that end, he'd created an offshoot of Ordinary People that he likened to Premium Pay cable: "Extraordinary People," meaning people who were undergoing unusual experiences. He'd recruited a woman on the verge of having a liver transplant, a man on Death Row, someone just elected to Congress. Like "Ordinaries," these "Extraordinaries" would use the categories of Memories, Dreams and Diary, but the focus would be on a particular situation and its effects.

"Which ties perfectly into my book idea for Charlotte!" Victoria cut in, reprising it briefly for Thomas. "Her internal struggle, day by day. Faceless: My Brush with Madness. Or something like that."

"Perfect," Thomas said. "And see, if you were one of our Extraordinaries, that book could come about really naturally. We set up your PersonalSpace, let some excitement build, then we go to publishers with a proposal that includes how many hits you've had, and we say, Look, here's a built-in readership of seventy thousand people, here's a chunk of text, and we get you half a million instead of squat, which is what you'd get otherwise."

"A quarter of a million," I said, "after your commission."

"Correct."

"Supposing I went on line and set up a PersonalSpace," I said, feeling a fledging confidence in the use of these terms, "and after a few months I wanted to quit?"

"No problem," Thomas said. "We keep whatever materials you've created for five additional years, with an option to distribute them during that time and negotiate any deals that might come of it."

"Five years," I said.

"Well, remember," Thomas said, eyeing the desert menu, then shoving it resolutely away, "it takes work to turn people into cottage industries—we wake them up to the possibilities and shape their material into a digestible form, and I think we deserve something for that. Otherwise it could be Wham, bam, thanks for helping me organize my story. Now sayonara."

"I see," I said; he'd guessed the inclination of my thoughts. Victoria's blue gaze abraded me with the texture of ground glass. She saw everything.

"But frankly, we don't anticipate a lot of drop-off," Thomas said. "Like I said, anyone can do a Website, and who cares? The whole cachet comes in being with our service. I'm not especially interested in Joe Shmoe's take on life, but if Joe Shmoe is an Ordinary Person, that means we've decided his story is worthwhile and we've worked with him to give it some definition. That's going to generate a lot more interest from subscribers and the media than he could possibly get on his own."

"So Joe Shmoe gets rich from being Joe Shmoe," I said, beginning finally to grasp not just Thomas's words, but the strange new world they described. Strange, yet familiar, too. Eerily so.

"Well, I don't know about rich," he said. "But he makes some money—more than he's making in the widget factory, that's for sure, especially if he's part-time with no benefits. But to me the beautiful part, the thing you really can't put a price tag on, is how it'll feel for Joe to know he has an audience, that people care, that they're interested. I think guys like Joe feel they're toiling away so far from the world of glamour and fame; they have no access to it except as consumers—they're the grunts who pay the bills. I'd put money on the fact that Joe's life will be enhanced in nonmaterial ways."

Since Thomas had begun his pitch, virtually all of my mental horsepower had gone into the seemingly simple (yet surprisingly difficult) task of trying to understand what the hell he was saying. Now that the gist was upon me, I felt myself reacting with a visceral throb of recognition, as if I were hearing aloud parts of my own dreams. "So . . . what stage are you at with this project?" I asked.

"So far, we've signed option agreements with about fifty Ordinaries and twenty Extraordinaries," he said, "meaning we'll develop Personal-Spaces with all of them and pay them something for their efforts. Then, after they've created their material, that's when we decide if we'll purchase."

"If they're boring, no deal?"

"Well, it's not really that simple," Thomas said. "I mean, some people you'd expect to be boring—not boring, but you know what I mean: a brick layer doesn't have to write sonnets, and if he does, no one expects him to be John Donne. We certainly wouldn't penalize him for that. But you want variety. Maybe two Ordinaries will sound similar—same fantasies, same family configuration, it happens—and one will have to go. Also, we want to strike a balance, especially with Ordinaries, between having them describe their experiences in ways that're interesting, but also keeping them representative of their type. That sounds terrible, but you know what I mean."

"Sure," I said, feeling a kind of queasiness. "Otherwise they'd be Extraordinary."

"Exactly," Thomas said. "Victoria's our publicist, and I have a partner in L.A. with directing experience"—his voice hitched slightly; with yearning? Envy?—"who's working with the film community. Hollywood's drooling for real-life stories, so a subscription with us will be industry standard, no question."

"It sounds expensive, all this," I said. "Who pays for it?"

"Well," he said, reluctantly. "Most of the start-up equity comes from Time Warner and Microsoft. But we're completely independent, all that means is that they'll have access to certain kinds of media options before anyone else."

"I guess it makes sense," I said. "Between the two of them, don't they own just about everything?"

Now Thomas looked troubled; I'd hit upon the one aspect of his venture that shamed him. "But really, I see this product as being for people," he said, a bit plaintively. "I can't emphasize that enough. I see us contributing to people's knowledge of one another and connectedness— wearing down that weird divide between folks like us, who deal in intangibles, and folks that're out there in the trenches, getting their hands dirty."

A part of me thrilled at Thomas's proposal. How could I resist the offer of attention and money, the very polestars whose gleaming emanations had navigated my existence to this point? Yet some rogue part of me, some renegade element heretofore unknown, recoiled. *Who are you?* I queried the source of this rebellion. *Do I know you?* I felt a sudden need to get out of there, the eager part of me greedy for consummation, the other desperate to escape. "Okay," I said. "Let's talk money."

I caught a glance between Victoria and Thomas, a tiny dart of elation, and congratulated myself on having managed to conceal the fact that my participation had never been in doubt.

I had nothing left to sell!

Thomas was excited again, and grateful, I think, that I'd seen the worst of it—his frightening sponsorship—and hung in there.

"For Extraordinaries—and you folks get a little more than Ordinaries, for obvious reasons—we offer a ten-thousand-dollar option against a purchase price to be negotiated after you produce your PersonalSpace," he said. "Our offer will depend, quite frankly, on how excited we are by what you do, how much access you give us to your life."

The least they had paid to purchase an Extraordinary was $80,000, he said; the most was in the $300,000 range. I would also receive an annual salary of $25,000 to maintain my PersonalSpace and keep it active to their standards. Any additional contracts—TV and film options, book deals, research consultancies, product endorsements—would be on top of that.

"Ten thousand up front?" I asked.

This quaint notion inspired a chuckle from Thomas. "Twenty-five hundred up front, another seventy-five when you deliver a completed first draft to our specifications."

"I need all ten thousand now."

"That's impossible," he said, the affable smile sitting a little less easily on his affable face. "Think about it—we could give you the ten grand and you could conceivably—not that I'm saying you'd do this—grab the money and head for Aruba."

I widened my eyes and said nothing. There was a long silence. Thomas glanced at Victoria. Philippe delicately insinuated the microphone into our midst.

"Half up front," Thomas said. "It's my final offer."

"Three-quarters," I said. "Or you and Time Warner and Microsoft will have to find yourselves another model who's had reconstructive surgery and is unrecognizable to anyone."

He grimaced. "Done."

We shook. Victoria waved for the check. Philippe shut off his tape recorder and stowed it away. One more business deal expelled its gamey essence into the atmosphere at Judson Grill.

"I'll messenger you the contract tomorrow morning," Thomas said. "Read it carefully, have your lawyer look it over. We'll cut you a check on signing."

A beautiful phrase, *cut you a check*.

It was Thomas who seized the bill when it came, thus confirming what I had already begun to suspect—that Victoria's role had been purely to deliver me to him.

"The contract specifies exactly what materials we'll need from you, and in what time frame," he said. "I think you get two months to generate the first chunk of text, and if you choose to tape rather than write, we deduct the transcription and editing costs from your last payment. But that's all in the contract!" Retrieving his credit card, Thomas frowned a moment over the tip. "And frankly," he said, eking out a round, childish signature as if he were forging it, "I'd invest in a laptop and get on line, if you haven't already. You'll need to if we purchase, for your Diary and Dream entries, all the day-to-day stuff, and you'll get a free subscription, too, so you can check out your fellow Extraordinaries and Ordinaries. We really encourage that. Our hope is that it'll be a kind of family . . . I mean, that sounds corny, I know, but so few things really hold people together anymore. Why not this?"

I made a brief, meticulous study of Thomas Keene: his smooth self and his fat shadow self, his olive Armani, his sandy hair and small round eyes. I scrutinized him for one granule of cynicism, a scintilla of evidence that at bottom he didn't believe a word he was saying. I found nothing. This ex–fat kid with a penchant for crocodile truly believed he was making the world a better place.

And maybe he was. What did I know?

We stepped from the restaurant into an overcast afternoon. The daylight felt jarring, as if I'd just watched a long movie. Deprived of the Judson Grill's warm, flattering light, Victoria's eyes were hard and pale, less blue than before.

Philippe blinked sleepily, as if he were coming to after a long nap. His eyes settled on me. "How did this accident occur?" he asked. His first question of the day.

It was so straightforward, so obvious, so entirely unexpected that I found myself at a loss. "I . . . well, I . . ." I looked beseechingly at Thomas, who leapt forward instantly to protect me.

"Wait!" he said. "Don't say a word. I want it fresh, like you're telling it for the first time! Sorry, Philippe!"

Philippe ducked his head abjectly. "No problem," he said. "Today was great for me."

"Oh, good," Victoria said with relief, and I sensed that she really was glad—that the Frenchman's happiness and entertainment weighed on her as one of a great many responsibilities. "Oh, my God, is it three-fifteen? I'm late for a meeting," she cried.

And with that, they swirled away, Thomas and Victoria bolting ahead, the Frenchman flapping in their wake like a giant crow, leather bag swinging from his shoulder.

I wandered through Midtown, bumped and jostled by people swollen to twice their normal size by winter coats. My mind felt weirdly blank, as if Thomas and Victoria had absconded with my thoughts. In their presence I'd felt buoyed by frothy excitement, a jittery sense that the events they narrated were already in motion, hurtling me inexorably along. But the excitement had turned out to be Thomas's and Victoria's, not mine; I wasn't excited anymore. I was tired. Since jumping off my balcony, I'd been sleeping ten or eleven hours a night.

So here it was: exposure. The very thing I had craved since childhood, perhaps the only thing I had never tired of or ceased to love or changed my mind about—now offered to me inexplicably, unexpectedly, over lunch. A chance to tell who broke me and how. Blab to the world and get paid. Court the audience I had always desired.

Yet I felt cowed. I could hardly read anymore, hardly write. I despised talking about myself. For years I had lied to avoid it, feinting and darting, obfuscating slyly, lying because it was easier, because I felt like it. Lying to erase the truth, though this never seemed to work. I knew I was thirty-five; I'd tried to forget, but the knowledge stayed in me. As a liar, I had failed.

I couldn't do it. This came to me on the corner of Sixth Avenue and Fifty-first Street, and the surprise of it made me go still. I stood there, sustaining frisks and jabs from behind, mutters of impatience. "Go around me," I commanded. I was trying to think. I would sign the contract, cash the seventy-five-hundred-dollar check, and that would be it. Not a bad haul for a two-hour lunch. Another few mortgage payments.

The mirrored room had opened its doors to me finally, after so long! But it was too late, I was too tired. Too accustomed to my exile.

I began walking quickly away from Midtown, away from Thomas and Victoria and Ordinaries and Extraordinaries and Future Plans/Fantasies. As I walked, my exhaustion began to lift, and I was suffused by a sense of lightness, rejuvenation at the thought of spurning the single thing I had always craved.

I headed south on Seventh Avenue, returning instinctively to the land of soot and bricks and faded signs, the land of Anthony Halliday, whom obviously I wouldn't visit. We had not spoken since our brutal parting in the taxi. I assumed we never would again.

I'm free, I thought, swinging my arms. And I felt the possibility of a different kind of life, a life in which I wanted different things.

There were no more old signs left in Times Square; they'd been obscured by new glass buildings and slick elastic tarps emblazoned with luscious photographs of models. Paint itself had been outmoded. But on a side street a few blocks south of Forty-second, I spotted the remnants of a ghostly typewriter high on a brick wall, a device reminiscent of a theater, its keys arrayed in staggered rows. "Stefani's Fine Writing Machines" was scrolled above it in faint, elegant script.

Childhood Memory: Pretending with my sister that our lives were a twenty-four-hour movie.

Regret/Missed Opportunity: I'd forgotten every line of "The Eve of St. Agnes."

Hobby: Looking at old painted blah blah blah.

And I realized, then, with fascination, with horror, that the mercenary part of me was already pacing the confines of my life, taking measurements, briskly surveying the furniture, formatting my thoughts to Thomas Keene's specifications and calculating their price.

In rebellion, I reviewed the list of other things I could sell: apartment, clothing, sectional couch. They were only things; first one, then another, then another. Then they would all be gone. But a story was invisible, infinite, it had no size or shape. Information. It could fill the world or fit inside a fingernail.

Watershed Experience: Having once come so near to fame that I knew its smell, its taste, the whir of its invisible generator.

Regret: I'd never forgotten it.

Of course I was going to do this thing. And now I was tired once again. Disappointed in myself.

I stopped at a bank to check my balance, an activity I engaged in seldom these days because it depressed me to watch my savings plummet in dizzy response to my high mortgage and one-way cash flow. But I wanted to see how long my new seventy-five-hundred bucks might possibly last. As I pulled out my cash card, Irene Maitlock's business card, that lost, irretrievable prize, dropped into my palm. I felt a shiver of significance. Irene Maitlock. I conjured her instantly, just looking at the name: her tentativeness and drab hair, her absurd sincerity—I saw her as if she were standing in front of me. She was the inversion of Victoria Knight; Victoria backwards. Victoria inside out. Holding Irene's card, I felt a jolt of strength.

If I was doing this thing, I was taking the reporter with me. Whether she wanted it or not. And she would, I told myself. She was interested in me.

I walked straight to a pay phone and called her, listening to her flat, slightly nasal voice ("Hi, it's Irene. Please leave a message?"). Irene Maitlock, journalist. I wanted to see her office, what it looked like. How a journalist lived.

"It's Charlotte Swenson," I said. "You tried to interview me about a month ago. Call me," I said, and left the number. "Call as soon as possible."

I hailed a taxi, leaned back in the seat and shut my eyes. With Irene's help, I could perform the tasks of an Extraordinary Person. She could read and write, for one thing. And I trusted her.

In my apartment, I found a message on my machine from Anthony Halliday. I called him back without taking off my coat.

"I'm sorry," I said, the instant I heard his voice.

"I'm supposed to say that," he said. And then he did. "I'm worried I hurt you."

"Impossible."

"I mean your head. After your acci—"

"Didn't even feel it." I'd taken so much Advil in the first days after my encounter with the taxi window that I'd barely felt the clothes on my body.

"Nothing was—broken or anything?"

"The opposite. You worked out a kink in my neck," came my spirited riposte, but each word was a tiny pain pellet breaking open inside me. "And you?"

"Intact."

"Still reformed?" I asked, then cringed as the retort I myself would have made, *despite your best efforts,* jeered at me.

"Knock wood," was all he said.

"I'm glad." And I was glad. "Good luck."

"And to you, Charlotte."

Still in my coat, I lay down on my couch. Missed Opportunity/ Regret: That I'd wrecked my evening with Anthony Halliday before I'd managed to pull his zipper down, to see and feel him so that at the very least I could remember him now. I imagined it, the sound of the zipper (pulling down my own, meanwhile), reaching inside, his inadvertent shiver, like horseflesh. Then ripping off his shirt in the time-honored fashion, making every button pop.

Masturbation: a word with all the sensuality of suitcases tumbling from a closet shelf, another one falling just when you think the noise has stopped. A futile and lonely act, I'd always thought, but I'd missed the boat, I decided now, misunderstood the joys to be had from declining to introduce yet another human being into one's life. New discoveries at thirty-five, or twenty-eight, whatever the hell I was, pulling that zipper down, the sound, the flinch—

Floating, waiting for my ringing ears to stop, I heard the telephone and reached for it dreamily, assuming it would be Halliday with a telephonic response to the telepathic delights I'd just administered.

"Hi, Charlotte. It's Irene."

"Oh!"

"You left me a message?"

"Yes! I did!" Feeling indecent with my pants around my knees, I wriggled to yank them back up and in the process dropped the phone, which bounced under the couch.

"Hello?" I heard her calling into the upholstery. "Charlotte?"

"Here I am!" I shouted. "Right here." Pulling. Zipping. Smoothing my hair. I dropped to my belly and fished for the phone. "Hello," I said breathlessly.

"You called me," Irene said. "I'm calling you back."

"Yes, I did call. Because I've reconsidered. I—I want to work with you on that story for the *Post*. And I really will cooperate."

There was a long silence. "Gosh," she finally said. "I've sort of moved on, actually."

"You found another model?"

"No, I just—let it drop."

"Oh, I see," I said, relieved, somehow, that I hadn't been replaced. "Because actually, there's something else. But I'd rather explain it in person."

"Explain what?" She sounded deeply wary.

"Well, it's complicated," I said. "Could we just . . . I'll come to your office if you want, or you can come here? Or we can meet at a café, or a bar . . ." I stopped, disliking the begging note that had crawled into my voice.

"There's no reason for us to meet," she said, "and I don't have the time." It was a no. She was saying no. "That's my other line, Charlotte, I have to go," she said. "Good—"

"I'm coming to your office," I said. "At the *Post*. I have your card. It's four-thirty. I'll be there in—"

"No!" she said sharply, and I thought she sounded afraid. "Don't do that."

My God, I thought, was I really that bad? Bad enough that the notion of my arrival at her office was actually *frightening*?

"I'll come to your apartment," Irene said, her voice gritty with resentment. "What's your address?" I provided it. "I'll be there by six," she said, and hung up before my ironic "I look forward to it" had landed.

I sat on my couch looking over my balcony, trying to make sense of our exchange. Something was at work here that I didn't understand, some missing fact.

I pulled open my balcony door and let cold wind scour the apartment. Then I peeled off my clothes and abraded myself against a scalding shower. The past was up for sale.

Irene arrived ten minutes late, stepping into my apartment with visible trepidation. She wore a gray wool skirt and jacket. Her tortoiseshell hair hung loose, just as before, but she wore mascara today, and light blue eyeliner which was back in style that season, though I doubted she knew it. The sight of her there in her too-dark stockings and clunky loafers and ridiculous gray wool filled me with unexpected pleasure. I was glad to see her.

I settled her down in a comfortable nook of couch and poured her a glass of water, which she chose over my offer of wine.

"So," I said, sitting across from her and cradling my first drink of the day, a Riesling that winked at me so alluringly that I felt like dousing my face with it. "What's new in the world of crime?"

She told me she was finishing a piece on private detectives.

"I know a private detective!" I cried, with bizarre urgency. "His name is Anthony Halliday."

Irene gave me an odd look. "I never came across him," she said.

"Just wondered," I said mildly. And then, without further ado, "Listen, Irene, I have a business proposal for you." I laid it out: Ordinary. Extraordinary. Options. Access. $80,000. $300,000. Exposure. Media. Soup. Nuts.

"I'm asking you to be the writer," I concluded. "We'd split everything fifty-fifty, beginning with the option. I'll get a check for seventy-five hundred as soon as I sign the contract." I felt like Thomas. Except that Thomas believed his project would revitalize the world, whereas I believed—well, I didn't believe that.

Irene's face underwent myriad changes while I spoke: confusion, intrigue, disbelief. Finally she said, "That's one of the more surreal things I've heard lately."

"I knew you would say that!"

"Charlotte," Irene said, and then sighed. "I'm used to writing things for some purpose. This really doesn't have one."

"It has a purpose," I assured her. "Its purpose is to make us rich."

"That's not enough," she said ruefully.

"But wait a minute. Remember those things you talked about before, when you tried to interview me? About identity and . . . and identity? Things like that?" I concluded feebly. "You seemed very interested."

"I am interested in identity," Irene said. "But assembling your life story for some Orwellian on-line service that'll probably never see the light of day is not a viable way of exploring that interest."

And now I saw the problem. The missing fact. With breathtaking clarity, I gleaned it: Irene didn't like me.

"It doesn't have to be my life, exactly," I hedged, determined to sustain my breezy tone despite the wounded sensation I felt. "We wouldn't have to see each other much. I'd give you the raw material and the rest would be up to you; you could tell it any way you want, you could make it up. In fact I'd rather you did make it up. . . ." My breezy tone was intact, but I'd leapt to my feet and was standing on tiptoe. Irene began to laugh.

"Come on, Charlotte," she said, burying her face in her hands. "Why me?"

"I don't know."

Rubbing her eyes had smudged Irene's mascara, and she looked perplexed. But despite these outward signals of noncapitulation, I felt an irrational quiver of hope (or was it the Riesling slipping into my bloodstream?). Irene was here, in my apartment, arguing with me. She could have been at home with her husband, or working at the *Post*, or a hundred miles away, but she was here, on my couch. I had learned enough about seductions over the years to know this: real desire, the kind that gnaws and lasts, was nearly always mutual. It seemed conceivable that whatever was compelling me to talk to Irene would also make her want to listen.

"Frankly, Charlotte, even if you get someone to do this thing for you," she said, "and for the money you probably will—I can't see you going through with it. You won't answer questions—you think interviews are a sham. You gave me a lecture about it!"

"I'm going to change," I said stiffly. "I'm in the process of changing." After a moment I said, "I've changed."

She eyed me skeptically.

I excused myself and went to the kitchen to refill my glass. I poured a glass of wine for Irene, too, just in case. Then I stood at the sink and strategized. Either I would make some headway in the next few minutes, or it was over. It was over, and I was alone in my apartment with a face full of titanium.

Back in the living room, I handed Irene the wine, which she took. Good sign, I thought. "Irene, ask me anything," I told her very seriously. "And I promise I'll answer truthfully."

It was a show of good faith, a free trial of my services. I sat on the couch and waited in dread for her to speak. There was a long silence, and then she sipped the wine. Good sign, I thought.

"Okay," she said, with disheartening indifference. "How did you get in your accident?"

I nodded, indicating readiness. Then I fought the urge to lie down, as I'd done when she interviewed me before. No, this time I would sit. I would look at her. At least a minute passed while I tried to organize my thoughts. Where were the facts? My memory, the pig, just smirked at me.

"You can't," Irene said. She was smiling now. "Look at you. You actually can't."

"I can." My body was grinding with the effort. Answer the question.

I had a frightened sensation I remembered from certain tests, foreign language tests in which the questions were spoken aloud, vanishing even as I clutched at them with my mind.

"You can't! You can't do it," she said, and laughed. Her light, laughing shadow self—there it was. I felt her relief, her eagerness to return, unencumbered, to the husband she loved.

I gritted my teeth, resisting the urge to retreat to my bedroom and shut the door. You brought her here, I reminded myself; she'll be more than happy to go. "Okay," I said weakly, and decided I would make something up. Except that sheer avoidance was my game. Feinting and darting, that was my game. Finally I shut my eyes, which helped. "I met a man," I began, my voice emerging like a bark, or a yelp, "called Z."

Breathless, I cracked an eye to look at Irene and found that her laughter and even her smile had disappeared. She was listening.

"Z," I said, and with the repetition of his name I felt myself collapse against the inside of a door—I'd taken that bit of ground. "At first, I hardly noticed him," I advanced, with great effort. "But at some point I realized he was watching me. I could feel it. Sometimes I felt it even when I couldn't see him."

I opened my eyes. She had slipped off her shoes. Good sign, I thought. They were worn and scuffed, the scarred leather inked in with a black Magic Marker.

"One night," I went on, squeezing the words from my solar plexus, "I saw a shape inside his shirt, like a shadow. It was a wire. You know, like a microphone. He'd been taping me. Taping everyone I knew, for months. I didn't know why."

I swallowed dryly. I'd heard people describe withdrawal symptoms, the dreadful convulsing of it. But what was I withdrawing from?

"I wasn't angry," I said. "Or scared. The opposite, almost."

I stopped, exhausted. After a moment Irene turned to me, her cheeks flushed. "So, what happened?" she asked, and I felt the warm reach of her curiosity.

"I was enthralled," I said. "It was like falling in love."

# Chapter Eleven

*Michael West stood* at the chalkboard in front of the words "Inscribed Angles" and watched Mary Peterson punch out a wad of blue gum between her big serrated teeth. He felt the possibility of anger in himself and glanced at her covertly, hoping it would catch. The Walther was strapped to his calf.

"Henry is correct," he said. "An inscribed angle is an angle whose vertex is on a curve, and whose sides contain chords of a circle. What does the angle do to the arc? Someone, please."

They stared at him with their helpless mouths, their freckled cheeks and moist pale eyes. "Intercept," said Marcie Blum.

"Precisely."

The lesson continued. The blue gum looked poisonous, disinfectant. Michael raked himself against it, desperate to locate the anger that had lived in him like a hot coal for much of his life. In his eagerness, he'd begun watching news reports from the part of the world he had come from: dust, rage, starved zealous faces, languages he had trained himself not to think in anymore but occasionally still did, when he dreamt. The images jogged memories of his own rage, years ago, hearing English words in the street, or spying the bustling, clandestine trade in videotapes of Hollywood movies: cloudy, illicit, the apparitions barely visible through the murk of amateur recording devices used surreptitiously, heads of moviegoers sometimes blocking the picture. Yet infused with a promise that was like the sting of a scorpion. There was no recovery. Capture desire and the rest will follow. Wars, weapons; they were messy, obsolete. Feed people a morsel of something they'll crave the rest of their lives, and you won't have to fight them. They'll hand themselves over. This was the American conspiracy.

"Are there additional questions?" he asked. Then, disliking his formal diction, he amended, as another hand went up, "Lemme guess. You wanna know if that's gonna be on the test."

Titters. A wad of blue gum. Michael lifted his foot, feeling the weight of the Walther at his ankle. He wore it often to school, secreted against different parts of himself, liking the sense of power, the implicit threat. The gun held the place where his anger used to be.

When the bell rang, they shuffled from the room in their winter boots. It was January, and the paroxysm of Christmas, that product America had packaged and exported nearly everywhere (he'd heard the streets of Istanbul were full of Santas) had subsided at last. Snow was predicted for later in the day, and Michael West looked forward to this. He had never seen it at close range.

The room emptied, and Lori Haft stood at his desk. She often required his help after class, and her scores had improved. Michael sought this avidly, to maintain good relations with her mother: the fool who sees everything. He dreaded to confront her in his present, weakened state.

"So," Lori said. She wore a tight green sweater with little rabbits woven into it. She twirled her hair on a finger. "What's important?"

"You tell me what you think is important."

"Um." Her hair was sugary, soft. Michael noticed this, noticed the shape of her breasts through the sweater, but felt nothing. Deadness. Without the anger, his desire, too, had mostly vanished.

"I guess the part about the angles . . . ?"

He crossed his legs, resting one hand on the Walther, excited by the thought of how easily he could remove it, unmask himself and cause the whole ghastly charade to fall suddenly, cleanly away. "You tell me, Lori," he said, looking into the flower of her face. "You tell me what is important."

Ricky lay spread-eagled on his back in the dead winter grass outside Paul Lofgren's rec room, holding his breath so they wouldn't see him pant. One hand on his Tony Hawk, he listened to the crack of boards against the empty swimming pool. The pool was getting repainted in the spring, so now they were allowed to skate it raw, fuck it up as much as they wanted.

The hash was making him sweat, even in just a T-shirt. He shouldn't have smoked, but it was Paul's private stash, Paul's jade-green pipe with the bowl like a wind god puffing out his cheeks, Paul yanking him into the powder room with the circles of pink soap in a white shell by the sink, yanking him in while the others were microwaving Cheeze-Corn in the kitchen. Then firing up a dense little pellet and smoking it with Ricky alone, because Ricky was Paul's man. Even though he was an eighth-grader and Paul was a junior, age was irrelevant. Paul liked him best. Ricky had stopped wondering why.

He deserved it, that was why.

He could do a backside grind on Paul's tricky pool, that was why.

"Cathouse," someone said, and Ricky muttered, *Shit*. Not that again.

He staggered to his feet, ears ringing, nosed his Tony Hawk to the pool's edge and dropped in, cold air knocking through his T-shirt. He swooped into a frontside grind on the pool's edge (metal trucks abrading the concrete) but coming back down the board squirted out from under him and he was flung into big looping steps to keep from slamming against the turquoise concrete (Paul didn't wear pads, so neither did anyone else), pinwheeling his arms, panicking for a second because the Medi-port was under the skin of his chest—what if it shattered inside him? But no, they'd taken it out last summer, which was why he could skate.

It bugged him, how he kept forgetting that.

He collected his board and hoisted himself from the pool straight into the evil beam of Jimmy Prezioso's grin. Ricky beamed back his secret weapon, a face devoid of emotion. He'd learned this trick from Charlotte back when he was going to school with no hair, half his eyebrows gone, a baseball cap over his head and so scared all the time it was like trying to carry a live hen in his arms. Charlotte told him, "No one knows what you feel—no one can see behind your face." In the bathroom mirror, they practiced: "Tell me what I'm thinking," she said, her eyes flat and narrow and mean, and Ricky said, "You hate me," about to cry like always back then, and Charlotte put her arms around him and said, "No, you dumbolt. The opposite.

"You can hide behind your face," she told him, and that's what he did. That's what got him through all of it.

Charlotte had powers, to what extent Ricky still wasn't sure. He respected them.

They dropped in one by one. Paul flew up the pool's curved side and did an air, clutching the board to his feet with the kickflip indie grab they'd seen on the Toy Machine video—as a skater Paul was egregious beyond all measure—landed hard on the board and scraped back down having nailed the trick effortlessly. Cacophonous applause, everyone flapping their boards up and down with their feet. Paul had the same things all of them had: hair, eyes, legs (he was taller than Ricky by at least a foot), but in Paul some alchemy had happened, and he was better. A king among men.

"What time does it open?" Paul, calling from the pool to Jimmy Prezioso, his slave. Talking about the cathouse, or what they thought was a cathouse.

"Sundown."

"Soon." Mark Smallwood, stating the obvious.

Ricky dropped in again, loose in his knees, riding the munchy sound of his Pig Wheels. He leaned, twisted, shimmied back up the pool's parched side and rocked the fakie, then swooped back down into the bowl, in a zone, finding lines he'd memorized—he'd try an air if Prezioso weren't standing there waiting to laugh if he slammed—up again for a frontside ollie, his body singing, dancing.

"Thought bubble: Why is little Ricky stalling?" Prezioso, of course, who hated him, who was jealous of his skating, his bond with Paul. Ricky ignored him, skating because it felt good (Paul was watching), because he felt strong and light, he was firing lightning bolts from the top of his head that spelled out the words I'M NOT SICK!

When he lost speed at the bottom of the pool, he finished it off with a little kickflip, landing softly on the board.

"Lush, bro." Paul.

"Dire." Chris Catalani, clanging his Richard Angelides.

"Egregious." Mark Smallwood, going with the majority.

"Pretty." Prezioso—who else? In a sweet, nasty voice. "Very, very pretty."

Ricky hefted himself from the pool and stood in front of Jimmy. He smoothed his face flat as a bedsheet. "And," he said. It was Paul's favorite word, his universal comment—"And"—just that, floating by itself, meaning anything, everything. Until his association with Paul, Ricky had been blind to the word's potency, its vast expressiveness.

"*And,* you look pretty."

Ricky tossed his Tony Hawk onto the concrete in front of Prezioso, where it collided noisily. He was stalling, waiting for Paul to pick a side. Jimmy waited, too. They all waited, exhaling arms of steam.

In the very long pause, Ricky heard someone sawing trees.

"Like you know Thing One about pretty, you rank mofo." Paul to Jimmy, shoving his arm, and everyone laughed, even Jimmy did, he had to. He was Paul's slave.


After school, Michael drove to McDonald's on Alpine Road and sat in his car in the parking lot. He had done this many times since arriving in Rockford, had visited all eighteen McDonald's in and around the city, including Belvedere and Machesney Park, but had never eaten the food— never in his life—having always believed the internal result would be combustive, violent. Now he longed for that.

He gazed through his windshield at the fake red-brick exterior, the debased shrubbery surrounded by wood chips. Beijing, Moscow—they were all over the world, McDonald's, colonizing, anesthetizing, and it was said that no country containing one had been at war since. Of course, they were already defeated.

Today was the day. Michael went inside and stood in the long, slow line. After surgery, the stomach had only two weeks in which to begin functioning again, or it lost the ability. People died that way. For Michael, the anger was like that; deprived of its logic, its livid energy, he questioned his survival.

"Can I help you?" A girl roughly the size of an American refrigerator. He ordered a Big Mac—what else?—a Coca-Cola—what else?—French fries and apple pie, carried the orange plastic tray to a small plastic table and peeled the foil away to expose the burger. His first thought was that it didn't look big enough, it was squashed, pelletlike, the meat gray and incidental; was this really a Big Mac or had they given him something

inferior? Then his own thoughts sickened him—greed, individualism—
and he lifted the thing to his mouth and jammed half inside.

He couldn't taste anything at first, could only think that it would
never go down, he would choke to death on this gray sweetness, dry and
sticky; he tried to swallow, his throat straining, seizing to push the clot-
ted mass down its slender duct. Finally the lump evacuated his mouth
with a tearing sensation, eased into his throat like a rat moving through
a snake. He ate a French fry, breathing hard, sweat on his face, then shoved
the second half of Big Mac into his mouth, loosening its airless compres-
sion with a slug of Coca-Cola, his body braced for the surge of rage that
would galvanize his dead insides when this affront reached them, an explosion that would shove it all back up. But nothing happened. He sat
there nibbling French fries, watching *light trucks* big as houses slip past on
Alpine, the Walther inert at his ankle, feeling the lump of food dissolve
and become part of him, its cells mingling with his own cells, dividing to
make new cells—the cells of a person who had eaten at McDonald's. Then
he crumpled the rest of his meal into the foil, a shiny McDonald's wad,
pushed it through the plastic slot of the garbage bin and stood beside it,
unsure what to do next.

He walked outside. Rockford, Illinois, flat and colorless in winter. He
was among runways of concrete and woodchips and highways, for no reason. By sheer accident. He could be here or anywhere. Michael West had
lived amidst danger for many years without ever panicking, had absorbed
the possibility of fear, drawn it in. But standing by himself in the parking lot outside McDonald's, he felt a first intimation of terror: of the land,
the crushing gray sky, the bloated strangers everywhere. Of facing this
new world alone, without an enemy.


Ellen waited in her Lexus outside the low-lying medical complex where
Gordon's office was, heat and radio on: "Baby Stay with Me Tonight," a
song whose unabashed cheerfulness made her snap her fingers. The sky
was soft and white. Snow? She hoped.

Now that she'd done it, called Gordon at his office using Charlotte's
telephone (as if that would provide some sort of camouflage); now that
he'd agreed (albeit stiffly) to meet and talk things over, a delicious calm
had befallen Ellen. Getting the kids off to school, promising Harris she

would sprinkle cured kudzu over the salad tonight (he'd been asking for weeks) for a little ad hoc market research—why had these things seemed so unmanageable before? Yesterday, she'd bought lingerie at Lord and Taylor—black, Gordon loved black, but the inky flora that glutted her drawers from their year of trysts was nubbled and stringy by now; she'd worn it to the hospital, to play squash, tennis. She'd worn it to church.

There he was. Leaving the building, striding toward her through the parking lot, not smiling, but then, these were anxious moments, climbing into each other's vehicles in public. A miracle—would he really get in? He did, bringing cold and steam. "Ellen," he said, kissing her cheek politely, the way he kissed her at cocktail parties, this man she'd screwed in bathrooms, closets, toolsheds, basements, splayed over flights of stairs, in cars (they would drive to Rock Cut Park, hardly speaking in their hurry and compulsion), in attics, outdoors in summer (just one time, it made them too nervous), in motels where they'd paid cash, and once, insanely, in an empty banquet room adjacent to a wedding reception they both were attending with their spouses. Some distillation of these memories assailed Ellen now that Gordon was so near, the smell of his aftershave, his antiseptic soap, and she was stunned by a fillip of nostalgia so sharp it felt like pain. Her hands shook as she backed out of the parking lot.

"How are you?" he asked, running a hand through his fading blond hair. "How's Ricky?"

"Off the chemo since May. Now we have this agonizing year of tests . . ." She was driving, nervous. She didn't want to talk about Ricky, kind as it was of him to ask.

"Should we grab a cup of coffee?" Gordon suggested. "We're right near Aunt Mary's."

Ellen glanced at him, startled. Aunt Mary's was a public place, a place they very well might see someone they knew. "Actually, I was thinking," she began, knowing already that it was the wrong suggestion, even as it vaulted from her, "we could drive out to Rock Cut and take a walk before it gets dark." She'd imagined them holding hands in the cold. Imagined it starting to snow.

"I don't have time to go that far," Gordon said.

They settled for McDonald's, on Alpine Road. Already the sky was fading into dark. As she waited for Gordon to bring the coffees, Ellen felt an ache of dissatisfaction; the setting was wrong, without atmosphere or romance—and yet, she reminded herself, watching Gordon's tall Nordic profile as he waited in line, their attraction never required those inducements. Had crashed forth in far less auspicious settings than this one.

The tray looked small in his hands. Silly. McDonald's was a place where everyone looked silly. Gordon sat, gathering his unwieldy knees under the table. They stirred their coffees. Something had changed about him, Ellen decided. There was a new composure, even buoyancy. She wondered, fleetingly, if he had begun an affair with someone else.

"So," he said. "You've had a hell of a time."

"Is it that obvious?" she said, dryly.

"I didn't mean that." He smiled, eyes winking inside their pale lashes. Ellen knew he didn't mean that, so why had she said it?

"It's true," she said. "For a long time, everything stopped."

"How could it not."

The coffee was sour, too hot. Ellen set down her cup. "I think I was—abrupt. At the time," she said. "With you."

"I understood," he said simply. He was making it all very easy. The problem was that Ellen hadn't come here to apologize, or be forgiven.

"Anyway," Gordon said, "soon, hopefully . . ."

"Yes. Spring."

"And then you can relax."

"But Gordon."

And now he wasn't smiling anymore. He looked away from Ellen, to her left, a tiny seizure of apprehension unsettling his face. And in that moment she saw it all: that Gordon had his old life back again—his old life minus the thrilling, crushing abstraction of another life he would rather be living. That no one had replaced her. The opposite; Gordon regretted what had happened between them and was determined not to repeat it. And at last Ellen recognized the new quality she'd noticed in him today, and put a name to it. Relief.

"Gordon, I miss you," she said.


"It's rank, but I have to get home pretty soon." Even saying it, Ricky heard the lack of conviction. Wedged in the front seat of the truck between Paul (driving) and Prezioso (smirking), Ricky aimed his unhappiness out the window as they headed south on Alpine. Smallwood and Catalani had it worse, stuck in the open back with the yowling wind and the boards, Ricky's Tony Hawk included, which he hoped they wouldn't have the nerve to touch.

He was afraid to go to the cathouse, but saying so was not an option, or else Jimmy or God forbid Paul might think there was something wrong with him because of the chemo. Jimmy had implied it. And Ricky didn't know; was he normal? Two years ago he'd seen a girl at the hospital wearing a pink T-shirt and a stiff blond wig, crying. Lisa Jacobs. She'd walked out of the girls' room, her face soaked and tired and gentle in a way that seemed beautiful to Ricky. Lisa snagged in his brain. For months she made him look forward to the treatments; he shook, sometimes, at the thought of seeing her. Lisa had the bad kind, the kind in your nervous system. She had a younger sister named Hannah and two Siamese cats. Her parents were divorced, and her hair, when she'd had it, was dark brown. "I'm a cancer blonde," she'd said, and laughed a little harshly. Ricky hadn't seen Lisa in months, and he had a bad feeling about it.

The windows of the "Glamour Health and Fitness Center" were covered with moth-colored lace and ringed with white Christmas tree lights. The little sign in its door said "Open." It did seem pretty small, Ricky thought, for a health club.

Paul parked up the block, and Smallwood and Catalani clambered from the back and surged around the windows.

"R. and me'll go first." Paul.

"Someone else can." Himself, hollowly.

"All of us, c'mon!" Mark, blundering in the door like a big cold dog.

". . . if you want to see them really laugh." Paul. And as always, a blinding nimbus of truth surrounded the fact, once he'd said it. "Anyway, R. needs the experience." This last with a barely perceptible wink—at him, Ricky thought. Or had Paul been winking at Jimmy, saying something else?

Ricky assumed a smooth, mellow face that told the world this was all exactly in line with his expectations. He glided out of the truck, heart detonating in his chest, and sauntered beside Paul to the Glamour Health and Fitness Center, whose door, not too surprisingly, was locked. Paul pushed a little pink doorbell lit from underneath, and a buzzer sounded. Paul shoved open the door.

The place was softly lit, pale pink walls and a short white counter where a bored-looking lady was sitting on a tall stool. She wore a magenta leotard top and was tan, dark hair pulled back in a ponytail and a little bit of acne on her cheeks and an upturned nose and shiny red lipstick. She looked either part Spanish or part Chinese or maybe both. "What can I do for you?" Coldly, but with a husky voice.

"We're here to work out." Paul, grinning weirdly.

"Sorry. It's members only."

There was a pause. Paul looked at the lady and the lady looked at Paul.

"And." Paul. The word floated in front of the lady, majestically suspended, but when she didn't react, it boomeranged back around at Paul. "So, uh. How do we join?"

"The club is full." She had an accent from somewhere. China? Spain?

"We won't take up much space."

"Not this gentleman." The lady eyed Ricky, and he sensed a squint of humor somewhere in her face. "You, mister, you're taking up space already."

"Well, that's just peachy, because Ricky here is the eager beaver."

Ricky gaped at Paul, who had never in his experience sounded so retarded. It was a painful thing to witness.

"Ah. So." The lady turned to Ricky, and he was momentarily distracted by the question of whether she had just spoken to him in Chinese. Then he inclined his head in a slow, easy nod. He was trying to picture kissing this lady or even doing it with her, but the effort strained his imagination to the point of blankness. She was a lady, like the ones you saw at the Piggly Wiggly stacking their carts with pints of Jell-O salad.

"He's my brother." Paul blurted this for no apparent reason. Ricky averted his eyes in distress.

The lady climbed off her stool and came closer. She wore a wraparound skirt that waved a little in some hot, invisible breeze. "How very sweet. Looking out for little brother."

"I'll pay extra."

224

She ambled to one of the windows, lifted the moth-colored lace and glanced outside. Satisfied with what she did or didn't see, she turned to Paul. "Pay for what?"

"Whatever you normally do."

"Kid like this? I take him to the zoo. See the lions."

"Whatever you wanna call it." Paul sounded easy, but underneath that ease Ricky felt something edgy, fluttery, a CD skipping—not nerves (Paul didn't have nerves), but a kind of excitement, now that they were close. And as often happened when Ricky abandoned himself to the scrutiny of Paul's state of mind, he briefly forgot his own existence.

He was startled when the lady turned to him. "Eager beaver. How come your brother does all the talking?"

"He's my spokesman." A swipe of laughter from Paul made him grin.

"One-oh-oh. Take it or leave it." Paul.

"With you watching, is that the grand scheme?" The lady, and Ricky turned on Paul, not liking the sound of this one bit. It was a test—a test for sure!

"At ease, bro." Paul, shrugging him off. "She's the perv." Smiling. But underneath it, Ricky felt the neon vibration of Paul's anger.

The lady watched them. She was going to say no, Ricky thought eagerly, and assembled his pose of stoic disappointment.

"Okay, Mr. One-oh-oh. Let's see what you got."

Paul hesitated, then produced an impressive wad of bills from his back pocket. He peeled off tens and dropped them onto the white countertop.

"Tacky." She raised her thin eyebrows at Paul, then slowly smoothed each bill flat before counting it, making him wait. Ricky felt the struggle between them the way he felt it between Charlotte and his father, himself in the middle. His heartbeat clicked in his ears.

"Say bye-bye to little brother." The lady buzzed open the door so Paul had no choice but to exit. Which he did, oddly docile now, flashing Ricky a salute as the door swung shut.

She pressed a button with one long red fingernail and spoke into an intercom. The place was so small that Ricky faintly heard her voice arriving in another room. "Anita," she began, then spoke rapidly in another language that he soon determined was not Chinese but Spanish. "This way, sweetheart." She beckoned him with a finger up a narrow flight of stairs to a second floor: several doors along a snug, dim hallway. She led the way into a small room lit duskily in pink, containing a bed, a closet, a sink. She shut the door and pushed in the lock. "Have a seat, dear."

Ricky looked around, saw one place to sit—the bed—and sat. "Uh . . . excuse me," he said, but the lady didn't hear; she had opened the closet and what sounded like a drawer within it.

"Ma'am?" *Oh, shit, don't call her that!*

"Maria." She was still inside the closet. "For Mary, mother of God. What kind of music you like?"

"Don't care."

She emerged from the closet to peer at him. "Eleven years old, you don't care about music?"

"Thirteen." Then he realized it was a trap; she'd only been guessing.

"So. What kind?"

"Smashing Pumpkins." A miserable mumble.

"Don't have."

"It doesn't matter."

"Aerosmith?"

She put on some horrible CD—Ricky despised Aerosmith, Steve Tyler's voice made his skin itch—but even now, with the music sawing away at his eardrums, Maria was still rummaging in that closet. For what? Some kind of . . . *equipment*? Ricky counted slowly (a hospital trick) to relieve the tension mounting within him—then, unable to contain it, he leapt from the bed, flung open the door (which unlocked when he twisted the handle) and bolted into the hallway.

"Hey!" Maria, startled, but already Ricky was scrambling down the hall, wrenching the handles of other doors and finding them locked (hearing—or did he imagine it?—muffled sounds of surprise from inside). At the end of the hallway there was another flight of stairs, up, up, Ricky gobbled them two at a time using hands for speed, Maria behind him now, cursing in Spanish but trying to keep her voice down. At the top of the stairs Ricky stood wondering where the hell to go next when he spotted a weight room, door open, just a few machines hunched in dim blue light, and he threw himself underneath a small freeweight bench and curled there, panting, stoned, freaked. And then he thought of Charlotte. She filled his mind: her face, her eyes. Calming him down. "You won't die," he heard her say. "You're well."

The lady was in the room now, breathing. "Listen to me. I see you under there and I'm not gonna do nothing, okay? Let's just mellow out, here, okay?"

Ricky rolled from under the freeweight bench, already sheepish. He sat on the floor and looked up at Maria, who gingerly took a seat on the bench as if he were a feral cat. "Look, your brother hired me to babysit you, and that's all that's gonna happen here, okay?"

"Babysit." He was offended.

"Sure. We're a health club, but we do babysitting on the side."

Ricky gazed into her face, trying to decode the array of messages he sensed issuing from it. "I'm not a baby."

"Joy to the world." Maria exhaled a long, rickety breath, and he knew he'd scared her. "I got a boy your age, he doesn't like babysitters either."

He thought she was kidding. *"My age?"*

"Yessir."

"Does he . . . like Aerosmith?"

"He's more into metal. Nine Inch Nails, that kind of thing? Breaks my ears."

Ricky pursed his lips to keep from grinning. "Cool."

He followed Maria back downstairs. Somewhere he heard a toilet flush, and was aware of people around him, at close quarters, people he couldn't see.

Back in the little room, Maria pointed to a deck of cards on the bed. "That's what I was looking for. You know gin rummy?"

"Sure." A hospital game.

They sat on the bed at right angles from each other and began to play, using the mattress as a table.

"Your brother, he's begging for a smack across the head." Maria.

"He's not really my brother."

"Then for the love of God, avoid him. Gin." She threw down her hand, swept up Ricky's and began shuffling again.

"He was acting weird tonight." Embarrassed for Paul.

"So, be your own man! Don't let him play you. Don't be his pet."

Ricky bridled. His *pet*?

"Oh. Wait." Maria set down her cards and fished in the pocket of her skirt. Looking at her downturned face, the little roll of flesh caught above her waistband, Ricky felt something move in his belly, a warmth that seemed alive, like an animal prowling his insides on clawed, tiny feet. He had a blurred vision of lying down beside Maria, surrounded by her arms and her smell. When she tried to hand him fifty dollars, carefully folded, he gazed at her and made no move to take it.

"Yes, yes, one half for you!" Urging the money on him briskly. "Fifty-fifty, that's it. No debates."

Ricky took the bills and stuffed them in his pocket. He and Maria resumed their play. As the animal subsided its motions, Ricky began to worry. "What should I say to them?"

"My advice, you say nothing. Not one blessed peep."

"Yeah, but I mean. They're gonna want, like. Details."

"The less you say, all the more excitement. This is human nature, my friend."

"Huh." Human nature was deeper than he normally went.

They played two more hands, which Ricky won. He wondered, though, if Maria might have let him. She was probably used to letting her son win.

Abruptly she put down her hand, as if some internal timer had sounded. She led the way back downstairs. "Study hard, grow up to be a good man and treat women with respect." This over her shoulder. "You promise?"

"Okay."

"Between us, remember? This business adventure."

Maria buzzed the door and Ricky pushed it open. She flicked her eyes somewhere beyond him, then leaned over and kissed his cheek, ostentatiously. "Smile for the cameras."

Ricky scrambled into the darkness. It was seven-thirty, forty-five minutes past dinnertime. He flung open the truck door and a half-hour's worth of pot smoke and four people's collective breath accosted him like a solid. "R. You did the deed?" Paul, sleepy.

"Look, I gotta get home. I'll go in the back, but Paul, can you get me there fast? Or I'm gonna—"

"At ease. Forget the back."

"I'll go in back—I *don't* want to hear." Prezioso. Smallwood went with him, accommodating as ever.

"In the middle." Paul to Ricky, who climbed over Catalani and retracted inside his parka, resenting the boys' weight on either side of him.

"Paul, go, or I'm gonna be in grievous shit!"

Paul glanced at Ricky, then started the truck with an air of painstaking leisure, letting the engine run a few minutes before pulling away. "With her? Or someone else?"

"Her." The lump of money was jammed against his thigh. There was bad luck in this arrangement, Ricky felt it physically, a creeping sensation of the heavens lining up in his disfavor. At last Paul was driving.

"You did it?" Catalani, incredulous. "You, like, put it in her?"

"Whoa!" Paul. "I want it in order. So I walked out the door. And."

Ricky peeped at his watch. They were maybe ten minutes from his house. "Well, she pressed this button and talked to someone in Spanish I think."

"And."

Ricky told the story in atomic detail: ascending the staircase, the hallway, room, bed, sink. To his surprise, this dodge was entirely effective; the boys listened, rapt. In the middle of it all Paul suddenly erupted, turning to Chris. "This is real. This is totally real. He fucking did it. Thirteen years old, how egregious is that!"

"Lush!" Catalani. They were eight blocks from Ricky's house.

"And."

"Well, I lay down on the bed and she opened this, like closet, and went in there and started opening drawers and stuff."

"Getting undressed!" Catalani, crowing.

"What about you? Did you get undressed?" Paul.

"For a hundred bucks, I thought that should be her job." Hilarity flocked to this retort, and Ricky experienced a swell of bravura followed by a contraction of guilt followed by relief that he was almost home.

Paul eased to the curb and killed the engine. It was a dare. They were a block from Ricky's house.

"And."

Ricky leaned against Paul with his brain. He imagined it, their brains clenched together like two sweaty wrestlers. Paul wanted something from him—Ricky still didn't know what it was. He was beginning to doubt he had it.

Ricky leaned across Catalani and jerked open the truck door, then rappelled over him and flung himself into the crackling winter air. It smelled like destiny. He looked back into the truck, every instant slow, weighted.

Paul watched him from the sides of his eyes, not even turning his head. Ricky heaved up his shoulders. "Paul, whaddya want me to do?" he begged, then heard the whine in his voice and stopped, let his face fall blank. Without another word, he turned and walked toward his house. Casually, at a normal walking pace. The truck sat there spookily; no one even shut the door. Ricky felt the eyes of all four boys fingering him from behind. Only when he was halfway up his own long driveway did the truck finally jerk away with a screech.

Ricky sprinted over the crusted lawn to the back door. In the kitchen, light bounced off his eyeballs and a faint buzz took up residence inside his head. His family was sitting at the table.

"Where've you been, son?" Dad.

He felt the hash again, warping his thoughts. They all sat there, watching him. His mother looked like she'd been crying.

"With Paul and them." Ricky slid into his chair, eyes down. Why should he say he was sorry? His father's being pissed was not high on his Richter scale of worries, which included cheating Paul of money, being possibly abnormal, and something else, too, some bad thing he couldn't fully see. His mother went to the stove and returned with a plate of beef stew and mashed potatoes, his least favorite foods on planet earth. Ricky nudged at the stew with a fork while paranoia tightened around him— Maria, Paul's hash, the fifty bucks in his pocket felt like information too unstable to contain within the confines of his head—it would pop out, strafe from the top of his skull. He avoided looking at Charlotte, certain she would know.

"You're thirteen, Richard," Harris said. "Why the rush to hang around with these older kids?"

But Harris was bluffing, assuming the posture of indignant fatherhood to camouflage his real worry, which was Ellen. Something was wrong with his wife.

"Dunno." Ricky kept his eyes averted. And now the other worry gained in size and mass until a clammy trickle issued from the base of his skull and edged down his spine toward his ass: *Tony Hawk.* In the back of Paul's truck! His magical Tony Hawk. His shimmering, miraculous Tony Hawk.

"After all you've been through, Richard, 'dunno' doesn't seem like much of an answer." Harris glanced at Ellen, enlisting her solidarity, but she seemed beyond reach.

"What do you mean, all I've been through?" Ricky said.

Harris leaned helplessly into the argument, frantic to reclaim his wife's attention, pinion her to this kitchen the way you tried to keep a person at risk for coma from falling asleep. *"I mean,"* he said, "you're lucky to be as well as you are. And you show your gratitude by hanging around a bunch of hoodlums in souped-up pickup trucks I can hear all the way from this—"

"Gratitude," Ricky objected. "To who?"

"You really need to ask?"

"You mean . . . Charlotte?"

At the sound of her name she looked up.

"No, Richard," Harris said witheringly. "I don't mean Charlotte."

"Oh, like God? Hey, thanks, Bro." Ricky lifted a hand and swerved his eyes heavenward.

"Are you hearing this?" Harris turned to Ellen, incredulous, but her face was empty. She didn't care. Or not about this.

Charlotte felt the argument edge inexorably toward herself, as conflicts involving her father had a tendency to do. Silently she recited the essay she'd read to Uncle Moose that afternoon.

**Originally, cows and sheep and pigs were herded through Chicago into railroad cars and taken to other cities to be butchered, but the animals lost weight on the trip.**

" 'Bro'?" Harris said, appealing to his wife. "From a kid this sick?"

A disaster was mounting in Ricky. He turned to Charlotte and bawled, "Tell them!"

**Then in the 1870s people started butchering the animals in slaughterhouses by the tracks, cutting them up and packing their parts in the railroad cars in pond ice . . .**

"Say it, Char!"

"He's not sick," she said, knowing it was a mistake. "He's well." And felt her brother relax beside her. There was silence in the room. "It's—it's just a thing we say," she said, nervous.

For a long moment, Harris just stared at her. "Wipe that look off your face," he said at last, "or you're excused."

"What look?" Charlotte asked.

"Harris, stop it," Ellen said.

Ah, there. At last, he'd done it—delivered his wife back into their midst—in perfect time for her to take Charlotte's side against him. Little piles of kudzu lay beside each plate; they had picked it from their salads without comment.

"*That* look," Harris told Charlotte, feeling an irrepressible twitch of rage. "The look you're wearing right now. Wipe that off or I'll . . ."

"Stop it!" Ellen said.

He was standing up. Why was he standing up?

"That's not a look," Charlotte said, sounding tired. "It's my face."

The words lingered as she stood, carried her dishes to the sink and left the kitchen. They listened (Harris still standing) as she climbed the back stairs to her room. Almost immediately, Ricky bolted from the table and scrambled into her wake.

Standing by the half-empty dinner table, Harris experienced a wave of defeat.

"You're so brutal with her," Ellen said, not looking at him.

"She's arrogant."

"She's calm. It's her personality. And Ricky thrives on that."

Harris loaded the dishwasher, then returned to the table with a bottle of Chardonnay. Ellen hadn't moved. He poured the wine and watched her take a sip. "Ellen," he said. "I'm worried."

"About what?" She sounded afraid.

"You."

Now there were tears on her face—so many, as if they'd been waiting behind her eyes. "I'm fine," she sobbed.

"Tell me what to do," Harris said, leaning close, shaken by the intensity of her grief. "Tell me and I'll do it."

She shook her head. She was ready to tell him—she was! Her despair had an authority of its own, it demanded to be recognized. "Oh, Ellen," Gordon had finally said this afternoon, hardly meeting her eyes, "I'd love to, but." Like someone declining a dinner invitation. Smiling at her in edgy apology. He looked older, Ellen noticed then, tired around his mouth and eyes. And abruptly the time had presented itself—more than three years since they had last been together. Ellen had forgotten the length of time because for her, they hadn't been years of life so much as a dreadful hiatus from life. *I'd love to, but.* Embarrassed for her because it was long over, their affair, and her query was so foolish. So inconvenient.

"Three years is a long time," Ellen told Harris. It relieved her to say it, to lean against the truth in her husband's presence.

"It's a very long time," he rejoined eagerly. "The strain has been unbelievable. And it's not over, really, not until June."

"Not ever."

"That's not true," he said. "After a year his chances are excellent."


Upstairs, Charlotte waited for Ricky to come in her room. When he didn't, she opened his door and discovered him facedown on his bed, the floor beside him littered with crushed ten-dollar bills. "What's that?" she asked.

He looked up at her, his face grooved from the spread. "Money."

Charlotte came nearer the bed. When Ricky didn't move to let her sit, she squatted and picked up the bills, flattening them in a pile.

"What's that?" Ricky asked, and she frowned. "On your chest. What you keep touching."

Without realizing, she'd been fingering the amber bead through her sweater. "Nothing," she said. "A necklace." She left it there, out of sight. It hung between her breasts, as she now thought of them.

They eyed each other, Ricky waiting for Charlotte to take out the necklace and show it to him. She didn't. And then he didn't care. Severed from his Tony Hawk, he was slowly dying.

"Where were you?" Charlotte asked.

"Nowhere."

"Ricky," she said. "You won't tell?"

He turned upon her his blankest face, the face she'd taught him herself. "Tell you what," he said.

"Maybe the stars are out," Harris said. "Let's take a look."

Ellen pushed back her chair, her face wet. She was ready to do whatever Harris told her; some tiny flame of volition, of independence, had finally been snuffed. In three years, Ferdinand Magellan's crew had circumnavigated the globe for the first time in history, withstanding mutinies and supply shortages, teasing three ships through a tortuous South American strait and then seeing Magellan killed in an internecine dispute in the Philippines. Three years was that long.

"I'll get our coats," Harris said.

Ellen waited in the empty kitchen. *I'd love to, but.* Even as Gordon spoke, the words had landed in her ears with a kind of echo. "I completely understand," she had answered—breezily, she thought. Hoped. And then she'd stood to go, surprising him. Maintaining her dignity, which was something.

Harris pulled the coat around Ellen's shoulders, took her hand and led her outdoors. She was afraid he would show her the constellations. He'd loved to do this when they first met, her sophomore year at the University of Michigan, Harris twelve years older, in business school. And at nineteen, Ellen had relished touring the stars with her boyfriend, as if they were rooms in a mansion that one day she would own.

Tonight the sky was cloudy. Thank God.

Harris put his arm around his wife and pulled her close. There was so much he wanted to say. Courage! Look around you! The makings of happiness are before us! When Demographics in America first began to thrive, when he launched his focus groups of disenfranchised machine tool workers and reconstructed farmers, when the politicians started showing up, Ellen had been electrified. If all these people were coming to him here, she'd said—*here in the middle of nowhere*—imagine what would happen when they moved somewhere central! By then, Harris had glimpsed the truth that his wife still could not accept: *this* was the center. This. The center of the world. The place everyone turned to learn what American voters and moviegoers and worshipers, investors and sports fans, dieters, parents, cooks, drivers, smokers, hospital patients, music lovers, home-builders, drinkers, gardeners really cared about. What they would buy, yearn for, dream of. Harris had those answers. Or knew how to find them. The Lord had given him this gift.

But to Ellen, they were merely back where she had started.

"This summer, let's go somewhere," Harris said. "Let's take a trip." He needed her. Needed her to look at him as she was doing now, for the first time tonight. When he woke in the middle of the night, his wife was always turned the other way. Harris would reach for her, seal her in his arms, but the next time he opened his eyes, she had always escaped.

"Africa," he said. "Asia."

She glanced at the sky. "It was supposed to snow."

"Ellen, look at me."

She did. She held his hand and looked up at him.

"Anywhere you want," Harris said.


As soon as it was quiet, Charlotte slipped from the house and pedaled madly through the cold. She looked for the moon, whose size she recorded occasionally in her notes. Tonight, a layer of violet clouds hid the sky, and the air trilled with flecks of ice.

His light was on. She pulled into the driveway on the quiet, ill-lit street, skimmed down it quickly and softly and knocked on the back door. He opened it, scanning the yard while she stepped past him into the kitchen. The shades were down.

"How are you?" he asked, his accent always most audible in those first words, when he hadn't spoken in a while. Charlotte had given up asking where it came from.

"I'm good," she said.

He poured her a glass of juice and sat across the table from her, sipping his Bud, watching her with his strange dark eyes. "Tell me what you did today," he said, and Charlotte told him: a trigonometry test (what kinds of problems? he wanted to know, competitive with Mr. Marx, her math teacher). The fight at dinner, a short version because she didn't want to think about it—she was here to forget it. She told him everything except about seeing Uncle Moose, whom she never mentioned.

She left her chair and came to him, kissing his mouth, relishing the sense of being taller, kissing down. *If he smiles, then he loves me. If he kisses back then he* but this was just habit, tiny corroborations of what she already knew.

He'd given her the amber necklace. Three nights after Christmas, pushed it into her palm while she slept so Charlotte woke to find it there, balled up and warm, a little sticky.

She kissed him, and Michael felt her pulse in his mouth, all that young, fresh blood lifting itself to him, rousing him from his torpor. At times he was hypnotized by the power of this release. Holding Charlotte's face, he came as near as he ever did, anymore, to feeling the rage he so desperately missed, rage and desire commingled; he imagined snapping her neck, crushing her skull between his palms, and the eroticism of that vision made him catch his breath. She had died a hundred different ways at his hands, but what he did instead was pull off her shirt and her clothes and do it that way, kill her as many times as she could take it.

He carried her upstairs, bouncing her in his arms to demonstrate her lightness. Charlotte heard the whistle of a train, a last vestige of that network that had revolutionized the world, cars loaded with grain or beef packed in ice cut from frozen ponds, butchered parts neatly stacked. Michael set her facedown on his bed, took her hips in his hands and eased himself inside her from behind. Charlotte held very still while he moved, while he did everything, finding all the parts of her until she moaned and thrashed in his hands, and then he turned her onto her back and began again, mercilessly, ready, the veiled tails of fish flinging shadows on the walls. She looked at his face, his dark eyes fixed on her or was it something behind her (she could never tell). He moved with absolute concentration, his breathing measured and slow, and she flailed against him, trying to get away, but he wasn't done with her yet, he could make it happen again and again until she hardly breathed. He wanted her spent, limp beneath him, and only when she was empty, her heart almost stopped, her head a can of broken thoughts, only then did he release himself with a quiet that astonished Charlotte, his body convulsing for whole minutes, it seemed, but soundlessly, like someone being electrocuted. Afterward he held very still, recovering himself, then withdrew slowly and pulled off the condom, dropped it in a basket he kept by the bed for that purpose, uncoiled his body and lay beside Charlotte as she dangled near sleep. His eyes open. She had never seen him even doze.

When the girl's modest weight grew heavier beside him, Michael pulled on his jeans and a sweater and went noiselessly downstairs in his bare feet to the living room, where he'd moved the TV after her nocturnal visits had begun. He turned it on. A shopping channel. Smiling blonde in magenta sweater. Michael relaxed slightly, letting himself drift among the images. "You can wear this all by itself or drape the cardigan over it." Drape. *You can drape the cardigan. . . .* He murmured the words to himself, memorizing.

Because even now, with no conspiracy to fight, no plan or mission or any idea, really, what to do next, the apparatus of infiltration was still alive in him, operating with an efficiency and an independence Michael was coming to find grotesque. He was a machine of adaptation, listening, memorizing, his mind gnawing like a mass of termites at the heft of all he didn't know.

He went to the kitchen, took a beer from the refrigerator and swallowed half while staring at the kitchen shade, wondering if he was developing a resistance to alcohol or had simply ceased to notice its effects.

Then he heard something faint, tinkling. A barely discernible crackle. It seemed to come from everywhere at once; Michael wondered at first if it was happening inside him.

He pushed open the back door. And there, in the light from the kitchen, he saw thousands of soft white plummeting spots. Snow. He stared, amazed to find that it looked exactly as he'd imagined, like snow in a picture. He stepped outside and a soft cold layer stung his bare feet.

He breathed in frozen splotches as he tipped back his head to look up at the trillions of feathery shadows hurtling toward him through the streetlight. He felt them on his face, in his eyelashes. They melted and ran down his neck.

For years he'd made such a common, stupid mistake: assumed the world was full of people like himself—conspirators—failing to consider that his several lives would have been impossible in such a place. He'd credited his light skin and chameleon face, his ease with languages and ability to germinate documents; his instinct for plotting a few coordinates of knowledge onto a vast, alien landscape and waiting for the strands of connection to form and proliferate, until eventually his ignorance would fragment, fall away like an island dissolving into the sea. The difference between not knowing and knowing was so slight. One fact.

But he owed his survival to none of that. Michael saw this now, tilting back his head, letting the snow ache in his eyes. He owed it to faith: other people's faith, which in most cases was so powerful that the most gigantic assumption—you were the person you claimed to be—was one they accepted at the outset.

Faith. Of all things.

It wasn't that people weren't bad. But if they were bad alone, there was no way to stop them efficiently. If the badness worked through them, then they, too, were its victims.

His feet ached, his hair was caked with snow. He opened the door and went back inside. *Screen door. Formica table. Linoleum floor.* Memorizing.

In the living room, he drove his cold feet into the cushions of the couch and turned to a cooking show. A bearded man making crêpes. "Let a small amount of batter spread evenly over the pan, and keep the flame under control." *Batter. Flame. Control.* Michael memorized the crêpe-maker's technique.

He must have dozed, because when he heard the girl come downstairs, the TV displayed a family of baboons gnawing leaves. "Homer, like any kid, makes a mess of his meal," a narrator said.

"What time is it?" she asked, her small, warm hand on his neck.

He tilted back his head to look at her. She was wearing one of his shirts. Michael encouraged this; for a day or two, the shirt would retain the smell of the lotion she wore. It reminded him of the sea. "Four," he said.

"I better go."

He followed her upstairs and watched her dress. The fish danced in their bowl. He found himself looking at them often as he went to sleep, just as she had instructed. And he slept well.

"Did you see?" she asked, pointing out the window at the snow.

"I saw."

In her tennis shoes she bounced down the stairs, Michael behind her. "Whoops," she said. "My glasses."

They were on the windowsill, beside the fish. Michael retrieved them and slipped them onto himself. He hadn't realized how terrible her eyes were, everything running together in a way that made a pain in the center of his head. "Is this what you see, without them?" he asked, emerging from the bedroom.

She stood on the stairs, laughing up at him. "Now you really look like a teacher."

An idea: clear glasses. He'd used them at other times. But whom was he trying to deceive, and for what reason?

In the kitchen she went straight to the freezer. Waffles, her favorite. He'd bought real maple syrup, but she preferred the fake kind.

"I'm making one for you," she said, dropping two into the toaster.

"No," Michael said, and pulled one out. "I had lunch at McDonald's." It relieved him, somehow, to say it.

"Lunch," she said, puzzled. "That was yesterday."

He smiled. It was true, lunch was yesterday. He raised the shade, watching the snow spin through the light on his neighbor's house. "You can ride your bike in this?" he asked.

"Of course!"

"You won't fall?"

"Please."

She pulled the waffle from the toaster with two fingers, dropped it onto a plate, buttered it and poured syrup on top. He sat beside her at the table, dreading the vacancy she would leave behind. Often he heard a thrumming sound—the whir of emptiness—and felt the possibility of panic moving inside him. But he hadn't panicked yet. Never in his life.

"One bite," Charlotte said, and held out a forkful of waffle.

He shook his head. He had covered the overhead bulb with a big round globe that filled the kitchen with feathery light.

*If he eats the waffle.*

"Come on," she said, raising the fork to his mouth. He smelled the butter, the syrup. "Open up."

# Chapter Twelve

*Irene Maitlock paused* before her computer, thinking she heard Mark on the stairs. She listened, trying to parse her husband's mood from the meter of his tread, the trochees and spondees he made while climbing the four tiers of steps to their apartment.

Jangling keys, the complaining door. Irene heard her husband wrestling his coat into the overstuffed closet, breathing hard from the climb. "Hi, baby," she called.

"Hello." Wiping rain from his big shoes. Irene swiveled around at her desk, which faced one of the two windows in the living room/dining room/kitchen/office of their tiny one-bedroom apartment, and looked at her husband, whose expression of defeat was palpable even through the gauze of her nearsightedness. "How did it go?"

"Okay." He crossed the room and hugged her in her chair, holding her head to his stomach. Irene felt him sway a little; he'd been drinking, probably from nervousness.

"Not so good?" she said.

"No, it was good. It was fine." The party had taken place at the East Seventy-eighth Street duplex of Gadi Austenhaus, a composer who for many years had been Mark's mentor and champion. Irene had stopped just short of begging Mark to let her come along—he was so shy in groups, and there had been a time when her presence had relaxed him. But now, Mark said, having her with him at such events made them harder. It was her own fault, Irene knew, for as this lean middle period befell her husband, this era when commissions were routed around him, past him—right through him, it almost seemed—on their way to other, younger composers; as a whiff of anxious isolation began to infect this man who had written his first sonata at the age of six, she found herself scrutinizing her husband's behavior more closely in the presence of his colleagues.

Physically, he had altered: in three short years, Mark's uplifted sweep of glossy black hair had vacated his head, leaving behind a saddle of baldness. And this sudden evacuation of hair revealed more than just the pallor and slight knobbiness of her husband's skull (knobs Irene kissed at night and covered with her hands to protect them)—it revealed how critical that layer of raffish black hair had been to the emphatic figure Mark had formerly cut. Now his vast height—six-four—had been reduced to another component of his baldness, the lengthy wand at the end of which his denuded pate was brandished at the world. And he'd developed an unfortunate corollary habit of shoving his hands backward over his nearly bald head with such force that people naturally must assume that this violent pawing *itself* had induced the hair loss. And so, when Mark's hands rose inadvertently to his skull while he chatted over plastic cups of wine after someone's recital, Irene would spear him with a fierce warning glance that made him feel as if his last ally in the world—his wife—had turned on him.

"Who was there?" she asked.

"Everyone. Everyone was there." He crossed the room to the half-kitchen and poured himself a glass of vodka from the freezer. "Saw John Melior."

"And?"

"He didn't bring it up."

"Did you?"

"There was no opening, really. He didn't give me one."

"But that doesn't necessarily mean it's off."

"No," he said, and lowered himself onto the piano stool. Lately, to make money, he'd been giving lessons in the apartment on nights when Irene was at Charlotte's. "But it doesn't seem good."

Incongruously, he smiled. So exceptional had Mark been for so much of his life, so unaccustomed to being ignored and disregarded, that the normal responses—anger, bitterness—seemed never to have developed in him, and he reacted to each new slight and disappointment with an almost childlike bafflement. He didn't understand. He didn't understand and there was no way for Irene to explain what she barely understood herself: that fashion was ruthless, reputations variable, that the slightest intimation of failure could drive people away. Lately she had begun forcing herself to see these things coldly, dispassionately, because one of them had to; otherwise they would be trampled underfoot by everyone else.

"If it does come through with Melior," he said, "you could quit that bitch."

"She's not so bad," Irene said, over his grunted objection. "And think about the money. If it comes through." She added, mostly to herself, "No one will know I had anything to do with it."

Mark soon retreated to the bedroom—to read, he said, but more likely he would be flattened by sleep and have trouble rising in the morning. The thrum of fear he'd brought with him into their tiny home surrounded Irene now; she looked anxiously at the familiar artifacts of her married life, the musical instruments she and Mark had bought in India hanging on the wall, two sitars, a mridangam drum, a sarod, a shruti box, the kanjira tambourine, the zither Mark could play so beautifully; all of them he could play, he lifted them from the wall and played them. But not lately. Irene taunted herself with these thoughts; they galvanized her with an energy she'd never felt in her life, some combustive agitation of love and anger and fuck you and not so fast, buddy! She wasn't Mark, exhausted by fear—she would win. Win for both of them. Hundreds of thousands of dollars. She would sail their little boat. And when Mark stopped being afraid, his luck would turn, because that was how luck worked, and then the world would favor him again, because that was the world. He didn't have to see it. She would see for both of them.

Before Mark's return, she'd been longing for bed herself. Now, thus electrified, she stared at her screen. Ten days ago she had delivered Charlotte's background to Ordinary People, but there had been no response. She'd had trouble concentrating since then, kept sliding into academic jargon whenever she tried to compose.

I, she typed. Then consulted her notebook, letting the memory of Charlotte's voice soak her mind until, with a ventriloquism that still amazed Irene, words tumbled from her in a voice that wasn't her own or

Charlotte's but a hybrid, an unholy creature that was Irene's creation, too, fed by the cheap detective novels she still gulped down when she had time. She could hardly type fast enough.

The next time I saw Z, I got near enough to reach for the spot where I'd seen the wire inside his shirt. There was nothing this time. Just the spokes of his ribs and a hard stomach. It was the kind of hardness that can mean a few things. Devoted gym attendance. Subsistence living.

He put his hand over mine and held it to his chest.

"Charlotte?" came the faint drowning call from the cistern of a speakerphone. "Thomas Keene."

"Thomas!" I said—yelled, actually, into my cell phone over the chumming of the Circle Line, which was passing close to me. Tourists lined its deck, waving merrily. I waved back. It was late April, and I was sitting in one of my new haunts: a bench facing the East River on a spit of land across the FDR from my apartment building; the same spit of land, in fact, where I had dashed in a panic last winter, shortly before leaping off my balcony.

Having switched to a regular phone, Thomas said, "So. I spent last night reading your background."

My stomach pitched. I knew Irene had turned something in—I'd signed an accompanying letter she had written in my name. "And?"

"The material was incredibly thorough, very professional."

"Good!" I said.

"Very . . . realistic."

"Good."

"There is one thing. It's—it's not a problem, exactly," he said. "It's just, I have trouble believing you wrote this, Charlotte."

I was prepared for that. "You mean it doesn't sound like me."

"No, it does sound like you. A lot like you—too much like you in a way," Thomas said. "Too much like you for you to have written it."

"What the hell does that mean?"

"See, I have no problem with you using a writer. Frankly, I'm delighted—you've saved me the job of finding someone to clean it all up at the end. But I want to get Cyrano out from behind the curtain and bring him to the table. I'd like to work with him."

"So you liked the"—what had he called it?—"material?"

"Oh, my God, it's fantastic! A thousand percent better than I expected."

There it was: the insult I'd sensed lodged in the middle of all this like an infected tooth.

"It's a her," I said. "The writer. But she won't want to meet you."

"Why not?"

"She's a journalist," I said, with pride. "For an extremely well-known paper that you probably read—"

"I get it, I get it," Thomas said. "Tell her not to worry."

"I'm not sure you—"

"She doesn't want to compromise her name. But see, I don't want to compromise yours, so we're fine. She's off the record, guaranteed."

By the time we hung up, I had promised to bring Irene to Thomas's office within the week, a promise I knew she would deplore, having told me repeatedly that she wished to remain, as she put it, a ghost.

I had come to the river that afternoon from my other new haunt: Gristede's, where I had a job bagging groceries. This unlikely turn of events had transpired for two reasons: First, I was desperate for money. Second, I was itching for something to do, being not merely jobless and friendless, but unable to afford or justify the myriad self-grooming activities that once had comprised a sizable portion of my schedule. Of course, my professional aims had initially been much higher: TV anchor, fashion editor, executive assistant. But I'd discovered the existence of traits that, in my old life, I had regarded as dull, invisible and pointless. These traits had a name, I now learned: "skills." And I didn't have any.

I knew powerful people, of course, any of whom I could ask for help. But after one disastrous attempt—lunch with a financier whose jet had ferried me to ski slopes and islands over the years, who flinched when I identified myself at the restaurant bar and glanced distrustfully at my face throughout lunch; who left me standing on the curb as he was driven away in his car, then ignored my calls to obtain the leads he'd promised—after that, I couldn't bring myself to try again. The calls from my old life had winnowed away, like calls to a prior tenant whose forwarding number has finally made the rounds. All that remained were Grace, Irene and Anthony Halliday, who called a couple of times each week, usually at night, for conversations whose main ingredient was silence. Yet I looked forward to his calls. Afterward, I felt a kind of peace.

I accepted the bagging job for minimum wage because I was tired of looking and because Gristede's, where I had shopped for years, was just around the corner. Since Sam, the waxen-mustachioed deli man, and Arlene, the cat-eyed manager, didn't recognize me as the woman they had sold groceries to for many years, there was no shame in it. I even took a certain pleasure in being an expert grocery packer, making a careful pyramid of each bag in which the most fragile items—eggs, raspberries, chanterelles—floated weightlessly at the top. And Irene approved of the job. Its jarring contrast to my prior line of work would help, she said, to make me sympathetic.

Two nights each week, she crossed my threshold, bringing with her smells of the city, the newspaper where she worked; she sat on my sectional couch with a notebook in her lap, and asked me questions. I had intended to lie as much as possible, but I was thwarted by an unforeseen impediment: I lacked the imagination to invent another person's life. My own was all I could think of. So I told the truth, first awkwardly and in a kind of agony, then ploddingly, and finally, to my own surprise, with a feeling that edged, at times, toward pleasure. I began looking forward to her visits—she was my only visitor. I tried questioning Irene about herself, in part just to change the subject, also out of real curiosity about the life of a *New York Post* reporter. But Irene was tight-lipped; she disliked talking about herself as much as I did, and she wasn't being paid to.

Shortly after I hung up with Thomas, Pluto, one of a handful of homeless people who lived in tents and garbage bags near the mouth of the tunnel, appeared at my bench carrying a sack of laundry, which he washed in a First Avenue high-rise during the shifts of a particular doorman who believed he lived there. He sat down gloomily and opened a paper bag containing eight beers from an obscure micro brewery. He offered me one, but I declined. The beers were expensive, and Pluto needed them.

"What's wrong?" I asked.

"Man accosted me in the laundry room," he said. "Says, I've got my sneaking suspicions you don't actually live here. I say back, Sir, I do my best to abide with dignity amidst more countervailing circumstances than you can shake a stick at. Should a man be punished for this? He says, Count of ten, I'm calling security. Had to pull out my whites before they were fully dry."

"Jerk," I said.

"That and more, baby," he said, gulping his beer so the Adam's apple rolled like a die in his throat. "That and more."

Pluto was a dark-skinned black man in his forties, I guessed, whose taut, striving physique seemed the very personification of human effort. I had never known a homeless person—the notion would have seemed ludicrous before the accident—yet I was impressed by Pluto's resourcefulness. Each morning at dawn, he used a handmade rope harness to lower himself from the rail of the concrete embankment into the East River, where he bathed vigorously in its icy waters and shaved before a mirror shard he'd epoxied to the embankment wall. He dressed impeccably, pressing his clothes with bricks heated over fire; read several newspapers each day, rented computer time at Kinko's when he could afford it, and on garbage days combed the Upper East Side wearing yellow gloves and a face mask, searching out products by Kiehls and Polo (his favorites), along with vitamins and antibiotics whose "best used by" dates had passed. He begged outside certain buildings, Citicorp being his favorite, and carried handmade business cards—rectangles of white paper with his E-mail address printed on them—should anyone wish to expand the relationship of donor to beggar into that of employer to employee. Yet such mammoth effort did it require for Pluto to maintain his clean, sweet-smelling, healthy and well-informed demeanor that no time remained in the day for him to put it to any real use; he longed to improve his life, but could only remain in a perpetual state of readiness. The beers, which he drank at night, ate up most of his cash.

"Speaking of the unpleasantries humans are capable of," he said, "you had a nasty look talking on your phone just this minute. Who's the lemon made you pucker up?"

In the spirit of my new life, a life in which I answered questions straightforwardly and at length, I launched into a description of Ordinary People, presuming, of course, that Pluto would be mystified. After six or seven words, he cut me off. "You're part of that circus?" he cried. "Why you hide something so critical all this while?"

"How do you know about it?"

"Never mind how I know; I've got myself a lane on that information highway. Now tell me where you're at with this thing. Tell me everything you know. Fill my ears."

After a minute or so of description, Pluto leapt to his feet, dropped to one knee on the concrete before me and gazed beseechingly into my eyes. Not for the first time, I saw his shadow self, angrier, more despairing and also more hopeful than his surface—a childish version of the rest of him. "Charlotte Swenson," he said. "There's a favor you must do for Pluto."

I thought he was going to ask for sex. He usually did, eventually.

"Find out if they've got a homeless person yet," he said. "They're gonna need one. Homelessness is a part of life."

"I'll—"

"Wait, here's what you tell them: You've got a spotless homeless guy knows this city belly up and belly down, you tell them he dresses well, he does everything he can to improve himself, reading, expanding his vocabulary, you tell them he does all this with no money, just a tent and a flashlight and a little oxygen he gets for free here at his summer residence."

"I'll—"

"Wait. You tell 'em I've been pushed, I've been pulled, stabbed, shot, I've cooled my heels in jail many a time, I've been kicked around by every Tom Dick Harry John and Julie here in this damn city and a few other ones, too, but they can't stop me. I cannot be stopped. I will not be denied."

"I'll—"

"You tell them despite a multitude of discouragements that would've stamped the spirit on any normal man into grit by now, I'm living in a state of absolute faith—I believe in the stars, the sun, the planets, the Milky Way, the American Dream, God the Father, I believe it all, cross my heart. Every day when the sun rises I say, This is the day, hallelujah.

But the higher powers got to give me some encouragement pretty damn soon, or a man's belief naturally starts to erode."

"I'll tell him," I said. "Maybe he'll be interested."

"You tell it right, he will be," Pluto said, resuming his seat and removing one of his handwritten business cards. "Tell him he can reach me directly there."

It was almost sundown, and I stood to go. "I don't want to get locked in," I said.

"Stay with me, baby," Pluto said. "Just this night."

"In a tent? Please."

"Then take me upstairs in that diamond-studded castle where you live."

"I can't."

"You can," he said. "You must. I look up there and I see you having your shower before bedtime . . . what you got, tiles in there? I'm seeing tiles. I've got visions of you and those white tiles, and it hurts. You're making Pluto hurt, I hope you know."

"Maybe someday," I said, not wanting to nurture the fantasy by telling him that my shower tiles were actually blue. "But not today."

"It's because I'm black. It's because I'm homeless. You think I've got dirt on me somewhere."

"You're cleaner than I am, Pluto," I said. "I'm just not interested in sex." And this was true. In my new life, I didn't have sex. I just thought about it.

"Hell with sex, prettygirl, I just want the use of that shower!" Pluto cried. "Hot water splashing against those white tiles, oh, Lord protect my sweet soul." He shuddered. "I'm just saying, Miss Charlotte Swenson," he called after me as I made my way to the overpass, "try not to flatter yourself so very, very much."

## 27

The next time I saw Z, I got near enough to reach for the spot where I'd seen the wire inside his shirt. There was nothing this time. Just the spokes of his ribs and a hard stomach. It was the kind of hardness that can mean a few things. Devoted gym attendance. Subsistence living.

He put his hand over mine and held it to his chest.

"Where did it go?" I shouted. We were in a club. For a change.

He shook his head. His heartbeat jumped against my hand. He had a hungry face. Dark-eyed, sharp-featured. A hungry, empty stomach. I pulled my hand away.

"Who could possibly care," I said, "what's going on here?"

"Everyone cares," he said, in his accent. "This is America."

"This?" I gestured at the room. The booths. The dancers. "This has nothing to do with America. We're all in here hiding from it."

He watched me. He'd been watching me for weeks. I'd felt the watching before I realized he was the source.

"Are you a spy?" I asked.

"Of course," he said. "Like you."

I laughed, uneasy. Mitch and Hassam were across the room. Z had come to them two months before with a business proposal. Now they were inseparable.

"Seriously," I said, moving closer, into his smell. Pepper, menthol. A not unpleasant smell, but strange. Strong. "What are you doing here?"

He smiled. Sipped his tea. He took in the scene. I tried to do the same, but I couldn't see it. I'd been looking for too many years.

He said, "I'm watching the nightmare."

### 29

I made my way from the club to the street. He was waiting. I invited him to my apartment for a drink. He suggested we walk. "I enjoy walking when the city is empty," he said.

It was June, rain drying on the streets. "Chicago," I said, when he asked where I came from.

"Chi. Ca. Go." Moving the word in his mouth.

"The Chicago area."

"Chicago." He said it easily now.

"Outside Chicago," I said. "About ninety miles west."

"Is America there? Ninety miles west of Chicago?"

"Oh, yes."

By the time we reached my building, I was sweating. It was 4:30 a.m. The doorman smiled at us. I think he'd actually forgotten that the man beside me was always a different man.

We rode the elevator in silence.

I took a brief shower, certain that Z would be riffling through my things. But when I emerged, head in towel, he was standing on my balcony. I joined him there. Desire showed its naked, greedy face.

Z's eyes never shut. Not as we kissed, standing on my balcony, not after we moved to the couch and lay down, my hands on his bare chest and refugee's stomach. His musculature was spare, military. Professional.

By then I'd been watching shadow selves for many years. They'd rescued me from boredom, from sadness. From tables full of rich, awful people. They'd given depth to the shallow, dimensions to the simpleminded. Mystery to the blatant. They were my own secret project. But Z knew about them, too. He was looking for mine.

A spy. Like me.

In my bedroom I kept the lights off, thinking now he would have to give it up (no light!). The colors of Roosevelt Island floated on his eyeballs. He hardly blinked. We eyed each other with a pressure that was like a shove. After a while I got angry. Fuck you, I thought. But there was no backing down, not until he did. We're enemies. This came to me right in the middle of fucking. We'll kill each other one day.

When I woke, the sun had bullied its way over Roosevelt Island and raided my bedroom. Z was gone. The sheets were pulled tight around me, tight as a hospital bed. Already the night was slipping from my mind. My lousy memory to the rescue.

I worked. Lingerie. Standing against a rolled color paper backdrop, resting my hand on a cube. Two men and a woman crouched below my groin, pinning the underwear to grip my inner thighs. I worried about my smell. The very fact of being alive felt tasteless. Look at this, I said, mentally. To him. And then I felt better.

Better than better. Interested.

Shooting, I wore a sweetly absent smile. A lingerie smile. It ached on my face like something heavy I'd been carrying for miles. "Turn left, not so much, back at me just a little . . . yes! Yes!" It could have been any day from the past ten years.

But I felt different, just slightly. The other model was one of the high school girls who come to New York in the summers. Her face was so fresh. So unmarked. She looked like a prototype.

Different. Just slightly. Look at this. And this. Watch the nightmare.

I perched on a stool in the unisex dressing room. I was fluffing out my hair. Two male models in jockey shorts pelted each other with sock balls. Eye job? I wondered, looking at the older one. Excitement cracked through me. I'd been discovered: someone had come for me, bringing with him a draft of something distinctly alien. Unrecognizable. But familiar, too.

He was the strange dark life I had made for myself, in human form. As if I'd invented him.

The offices of Extra/Ordinary.com encompassed an entire floor of an old factory building just off Union Square. Apart from the exposed viscera of heating and plumbing ducts, their main design feature was poured concrete. I had never seen so much concrete in my life: floors, ceilings, walls, concrete glazed and buffed, burnished and roughed, resembling, at various times in various lights, marble, alabaster, stucco, clay, fresco, paint, dirt and (creepily) human flesh.

Thomas Keene waltzed Irene and me through a brisk tour of the premises: a white sail splayed across a conference room wall as a projection screen; a small cafeteria serving organic food and juice made from prairie grass. Irene drifted behind, indignant at having been prised from her anonymous cocoon, skulking behind her hair when Thomas introduced us to members of his staff as if she dreaded to be recognized in an S&M dungeon.

Bearing mugs of Kona coffee, we retired to Thomas's spacious office, where he joined us on a gaggle of chicly utilitarian chairs set around a black disk of coffee table. Through the canted factory windows came a chop of laughter and voices from Union Square.

"So," Thomas said, and slapped his small, rather delicate hands against his haunches. He wore a midnight-blue jacket, camouflage pants and the same high-top Converse shoes he'd worn before. But these details had been subsumed by a mysterious new authority, as if Thomas had come to believe he actually *was* the person he had merely yearned to be two months ago. The fat, anxious shadow self was nowhere to be seen.

He sprang to what I guessed was a desk (black and sleek like the coffee table, only larger), seized the only object on it—an orange manila envelope—and sat back down. He waited for Irene to look at him. "This is very good."

"Tell Charlotte," she said. "I'm just the amanuensis."

But Thomas continued to gaze at Irene without so much as a glance in my direction. "What you've managed to do," he said, sliding a sheaf of papers from the envelope and fanning through them admiringly, "you've created this overwhelming sense of a life totally misspent, a person so completely benighted that every decision she makes is wrong."

I hardly listened. I was staring at the chunk of pages in Thomas's hand. There must have been a hundred of them—more! I tried to connect this wedge of paper to the sparse notes I'd seen Irene taking in my apartment; one small notebook in two whole months, and it wasn't even full. I'd urged her to embellish, true. But the number of pages confounded me.

"There's this deep sense of her life being moribund, you know, just bankrupt, almost waiting to be cast off, and then bam! Finito. When it goes, we're almost glad for her."

Irene had pushed aside her hair and seemed to be listening. I turned to Thomas. "You keep mentioning 'her,'" I interjected. "Who are you talking about?'"

They both stared at me, Irene's eyes bugging a little. "You, Charlotte," she said carefully, with a pointed, highly communicative stare that I took to mean, *Stop making trouble.* To Thomas I said affably, "Why not say 'you,' then, since I'm sitting right here?"

"Sorry," he said. "Habit from creative writing class. So anyway"—back to Irene—"I'm over the moon. You've got so much here, I love all the childhood stuff, I love what a little rebel she—whoops, you—were. The dreams are fantastic, I love how those geese come up again and again. But I was especially tickled by the Hopes/Aspirations category. 'The mirrored room'—like, what is that? But we get it. We get it without getting it. And the dog stuff is absolutely priceless."

Geese? Dog?

"Good," Irene said cautiously. As a show of good faith, I added, "I begged Irene to put that in about the dog—I knew it would add something."

"It does," Thomas said. "It shows that she can care for another living creature, which I'm not sure we'd know otherwise. And that's important, because we don't have to love her, but we do have to like her, or at least be able to tolerate her. I mean," he shifted in his chair, avoiding my eyes, "you."

There was a pause.

"So. Here's where we are," Thomas said, like a newscaster switching from genocide to sports. "We're absolutely going to buy this, it's just a question of price."

Irene and I exchanged sharp, hopeful glances.

"In fact," he went on, "the plan right now is to launch in September with a handful of Ordinaries and Extraordinaries that we think have the best prospects, media-wise. I'd like you two—if you're willing—to be part of that inaugural group."

Irene and I mashed our feet together between our chicly utilitarian chairs.

"Now, what that means is, you'll have to move quickly to finish up these materials. So to add a little incentive and buy some more of your time, I'm offering you a bonus of ten grand when you hand me a finished draft."

"On top of our last option payment?" I asked.

"Correct, on top of that." He surveyed our faces, taking in what surely were unmistakable signs of jubilation. "Now. What do I want." Thomas swept to his feet and paced his poured-concrete floor (black and sparkling, like asphalt), as if the sheer intensity of his desires made them impossible to discuss while seated. "This background is great, like I said, but as an Extraordinary, the next phase is the most important for you: action. The accident itself and what happens next." He was speaking to Irene.

"I'm—we're—working on that," she said.

"A few pointers. Number one: Drama. Excitement. I want fireballs rolling through the cornstalks. Lots of bright, rich color—find the beauty in it. Write it as one long narrative, and we'll use what we need. Then for the hospital part, the facial reconstruction, lots of medical detail. Remember, authenticity is the beginning and the end of this product. Start with the ambulance, the siren, the rain, wheeling her in . . . 'We don't know if she's going to make it, nurse.' That kind of thing. I'm not saying make anything up"—he raised his hands, fending off any such suggestion—"I'm saying *find* the drama, *find* the beauty, *find* the tension and give it to us. You may feel like you're making it more contrived, but it's the opposite. Think about the Parthenon."

Throughout this speech, Thomas's eyes never left Irene. Why, I wondered, when I was the subject, the one whose life was supposedly so extraordinary? But I couldn't think of a way to object, or even to question him, without sounding petulant. Instead I said, "The Parthenon?"

Thomas and Irene began speaking at once, then stopped. After a brief contest of demurrals, Irene explained to me that slight asymmetries in the Parthenon's design actually gave it an illusion of perfection. "That's what you meant, right?" she asked Thomas.

"Yes!" he said, surprised and a little touched, I thought. "That's exactly what I meant. Okay . . . so. Two." Then he seemed to founder. "How to put this? An accident's an accident, shit happens and all that. But, see, we don't want shit happens, we want shit happens for a reason. It sounds terrible when you put it into words . . ."

I had an inkling of what he was saying—it was the same thing

Victoria had told me at lunch—and I was burning, for once, to be the person who knew something. "He's saying her accident can't happen by chance," I told Irene. "Something in her life has to be the cause of it, so people can relate to her story and understand it."

"Yes!" Thomas hollered, whirling around and lunging to the place where I sat. "Yes. Yes. Yes." He gazed at me, astounded. "Beautifully said, Charlotte!"

"Thank you." I flushed, already loathing myself for having pandered to Thomas, feeling as if I'd sold someone down the river in the process.

"Again. I'm not saying make it up—I'm saying find the connections. Show us the buried logic. What I don't want is, I was bringing cookies to Aunt Susie and I got run over by a tractor. This is not a Raymond Carver story, if you're familiar with his work."

"It sounds more like Aeschylus," Irene said tartly.

Thomas mused a moment over this. I sensed that Irene impressed him, that he relished the abrasion of her skepticism. I was proud to have discovered her, brought her there.

"Tragedy, okay. Yes," he said. "But not Greek. Too cold. Has to be something warmer."

"Nineteenth century."

"Bingo. Hardy. The Brontës. Tolstoy. Sad things happen but they happen for a reason."

"Zola."

"Exactly. Stendhal. Or Dickens, for God's sake."

"George Eliot," Irene said. *Adam Bede.*"

"That's the one where he—"

"Gets her pregnant," she said. "And then she tries to find him after his regiment is moved to Scotland."

"Oh, my God, where she's hitching rides on carts and sleeping in the fields? That was the saddest book . . . ," Thomas said, his whole face opening at the memory. "But only the second half. The first half was kind of—"

"That's amazing!" Irene said, and she did look amazed. "I thought exactly the same thing."

"—schmaltzy."

I listened, my frustration at finding myself ignorant of these books offset by my wonder at the abrupt change in Irene; she was smiling, cheeks flushed. Books, I thought; she loved books. It made perfect sense.

"Edith Wharton," she said.

"Yes! Wharton is perfect. *Age of Innocence. House of Mirth.* Or Flaubert," he added, but then changed his mind. "Nah, *Madam B.*'s too dark, too modern."

"Too ironic," Irene said.

"Exactly, exactly. See, irony we don't want—there's too much of it out there! We just want the story without the built-in commentary."

"Ah, the universal point of view," Irene said. "Would that we still believed in it."

I sat in silence. Several times I'd been on the verge of mentioning "The Eve of St. Agnes" or "The Rape of the Lock," but I was afraid that Thomas and Irene would know these works better than I did (which was to say, know them even slightly), and I would be exposed.

As Irene scribbled into her notebook, I saw Thomas eyeing her with the faintest tinge of appraisal, and only then did it strike me that he'd won. He'd coaxed Irene out of her sulk and into formation in a matter of—I glanced at my watch—thirty-eight minutes.

"Okay," Thomas said, taking a breath that seemed to portend still greater challenges ahead. "Three." Now he turned to me, aiming his attention so fully upon me that I felt my spine extend like a charmed snake. "Three, and this is kind of a new development, but like I said, things are moving fast and changing a little, Three, I'd like you to consider—you don't have to decide yet—I'd like you to consider having a small video camera installed in your apartment."

"For security?"

"Actually not. This would be to get some raw footage of you in your natural environment. See, people are already doing this on their individual Websites, so we basically have to give our subscribers that option. Now obviously MTV's been doing it for years, but the fact of the matter is, *Real World* sucks and everyone knows it. Too fake. Too contrived! Too unlikely that these people would ever live together, much less be able to afford the kinds of apartments MTV sets them up in. But some raw footage from a real person's life—an interesting person—that might be worth watching."

"But I mean," I said, "I live alone. Most of the time all I'm doing is smoking cigarettes and looking out my window. Or sleeping."

"See, and you think that's dull. But to the cannibal in New Guinea, eating human brains is pretty ho-hum, too. You've had this terrible accident, Charlotte! People are going to expect a sense of desolation, some anomie. That's what makes it real!"

"So you'd shoot some footage and kind of . . . edit it down to the essence?" said Irene, whose literary joie de vivre had been supplanted by a look of seasickness.

"No, see, that's another mistake *Real World* made. We'd do it as a raw feed. That'll keep it from getting too constructed, too mediated. Whenever someone wants to see what you're doing at that moment, they'll click an icon—'I Spy,' I think we're calling it—and there you'll be. If you're home."

"Pardon me for pointing out the obvious," Irene said, a vibrato of incredulity, or something like it, fibrillating her voice, "but isn't this all just a wee bit Orwellian?"

Thomas's jaw clenched, and a fleeting, nearly invisible current of anger jostled his features. "You know, I keep getting that from people? And I can't for the life of me figure out why?" he said, almost joyfully. "This is the *exact opposite* of what Orwell was talking about: There, you had folks being spied on by a totalitarian government—they had no choice in the matter and no freedom. Whereas this is not only a hundred percent voluntary, obviously, but the whole thing is *about* freedom—freedom to communicate your experiences! Freedom to learn how other people live. If you ask me, it's the ultimate expression of a democracy!" Despite his best efforts at joviality, blood had soaked his round, pleasant cheeks.

I didn't even have to look at Irene to know that Thomas had blown it. It didn't matter what he said now; the camera had pushed her too far.

"Suppose I decide no camera?" I said.

"Not a problem," Thomas said, with edgy nonchalance. "I mean obviously it'll affect your purchase price, because I've got people—frankly I think it's nuts—they're willing to have the video feed straight from their bedrooms. So obviously they'll get more because they're giving more. Oh, and endorsements'll hit the roof if people can actually watch you consuming products in your own home."

"I need to think about it," I said, wanting him to feel just slightly redeemed, to restore some bonhomie to the room, now that (for once) it was within my power to do so. But even as I said it, I felt a part of me reconciling itself to the camera's arrival, embracing it, awaiting it, preparing to foist its acceptance on the rest of me.

"I'd like to see this product of yours," Irene said, in a tone of fragile neutrality. I sensed her regret at having been won over so easily by the mention of a few books.

"Absolutely. That was next on my list." Thomas rose from his chair, anxiously scrutinizing our faces. Yet even now, with his pitch having clearly gone awry, his shadow self remained strangely recessed. Why? I wondered; what was protecting the fat, nervous boy from having to come out and face the jeering world? As Thomas ushered us into a shaded room adjacent to his office, a room containing a computer whose broad, iridescent screen appeared to hover in midair, I realized there could only be one answer: he didn't need us.

"None of the domestic stuff is signed and sealed yet, so legally I can't show you that," he said, seating himself at the keyboard with Irene and me on either side of him. "But the rules are looser for the International Ordinaries, and it's not like these folks are going to know the difference."

He touched a few keys and the screen filled with the richly saturated image of a very black man standing by a yellow cow. Seeing him reminded me of Pluto. The man was draped in salmon-colored plaids that looked like tablecloths. He squinted in our direction, one hand extended to touch the velvety neck of the cow, whose horns twisted from its head like arms of a chandelier. The quality of the image was extraordinary; each yellow hair on the cow's hide stood out in a kind of relief that suggested three dimensions. The man himself was beautiful, sharp slivers of muscle in his chest and torso flicking in the sunlight. He had one of those rich, symmetrical faces you could read anything into: love, humor, rage. His hair had been woven into long thin braids saturated with what looked like red clay. On his neck and arms were strands of multicolored beads. Irene and I both gaped at the image, whose urgent realism had the unlikely result of making it seem, finally, unreal—like a hologram.

"He's a Samburu warrior," Thomas said. "I don't know if we'll end up using him—we may want to go more exotic. But he's basically a mockup, just to show our investors how the international stuff'll work." He pressed another button and the image slid into motion, the man's shy expression breaking open into a white crescent smile, the cow shifting restlessly, rousing dilatory flies that soon refastened themselves to its yellow neck. The man began speaking rapidly, incomprehensibly, and as he did, a bar of text scrolled along one side of the screen:

```
Hi! My name is Kanja Joi [spelling???] and I'm a Samburu
warrior living in the country of Kenya on the continent of
Africa . . .
```

"Translation needs some work," Thomas mused.

```
I carry this short sword in the event that I should chance
to meet any lions while grazing my cows on the grassy plains of
my country. Here, perhaps you would like to hear me sing . . .
```

The text lagged behind the warrior himself, who had already burst into song: a series of guttural, atonal sounds gouged from someplace well below his diaphragm. The sounds, like the visuals, had a heightened precision that made me feel not merely in the warrior's presence, but inside his throat.

"Here, check this out," Thomas said, moving the pointer to one of the warrior's strands of beads and clicking there. Abruptly the warrior and his song evaporated, replaced by an image of a young girl arranging wires and dusty beads on a cloth. We heard her whispery voice, and the translation box scrolled,

```
Hi, I'm Baka, Kanja's niece. I learned the art of beaded
jewelry from my maternal grandmother . . .
```

"This will all be direct mail," Thomas interjected. "You can order beads, wires, finished necklaces—whatever you want. Plus there'll be a way to donate money to the family by credit card, which I personally think is going to be the future of charitable giving." He turned to Irene. "People aren't moved by abstract concepts anymore," he said, with feeling. "They're moved by people's individual struggles. Save the Children—like, what children?"

He was appealing to us, waving the flag of his altruism in hopes of winning us back, and I felt myself awaiting Irene's reaction—Irene, who surely knew more about altruism than I did.

Another double-click, and the original warrior was restored to the screen, still heaving up his strange noises with an eagerness that verged on desperation, as if he believed he were singing for his life.

"Anyway, this is a crude mock-up," Thomas said, stifling a yawn. A heaviness had engulfed us, the passivity of three people in a darkened room, looking at a screen. "The translation's pretty bad, but you get the picture. Click on his hair, you hear about the hair. Click on his forehead, you get the thought categories: Dreams, Wishes, all that stuff. Want to guess the number one Hope/Aspiration of every single International Ordinary, bar none? Live in America. Even the ones whose governments hate us! And the beautiful thing is, a guy like this might actually get to do it—not the usual way, jammed in a tenement in Queens hawking fake Rolexes outside Tiffany's, but with the real potential to make it! Casting agents, model agencies, record producers—they're all going to be scouring our Internationals for raw material. You ask me, this guy could wind up a pop star, easy. I mean, it's hard to tell if he can actually sing, but it may not even matter. He could rap, for Godsakes."

"I just wonder," Irene said, and then stopped. "I wonder if someone might not just visit Kenya instead."

"Now, absolutely," Thomas said. "But ask yourself: how long is that going to last? I think the golden age of tourism is basically over, especially for Americans. The coral's dead or dying, you've got weird grass choking out the Med, you've got e-coli and flesh-eating diseases all over the place, you've got terrorists mowing people down in the Temple of Luxor . . . I mean, at a certain point, how much are you willing to risk for a two-week vacation? So we're thinking ahead."

As we filed back into Thomas's office, I watched Irene, trying to gauge her reaction. She seemed dazed, subdued.

"I have a question, too," I said, feeling oddly nervous as they both waited for me to speak. "I know a homeless man, and I was wondering if you might want someone like that in Ordinary People."

"You know a *homeless man*?" Thomas asked, glancing at Irene in surprise. She mimed her ignorance.

"I met him near the East River by my apartment. He's a pretty interesting guy." I knew better than to say unusual; he had to be representative of his type.

"Homeless. Homeless," Thomas mused, going to his window and looking outside. "We've talked about having a homeless Ordinary. But see, a lot of homeless people are crazy, and we already have a manic depressive and two schizophrenics."

"Oh, no," I said. "He's not crazy at all."

"How do you know he's homeless?"

"He lives in a tent, he goes through garbage cans, he begs. He's definitely homeless."

"What about substance abuse?" Thomas said. "Because again, we have two addicts—heroin and crack—plus an alcoholic."

"He drinks a little," I said, playing it down. "Nothing major."

"Huh," Thomas said. "Well, there are two ways we could go with something like this. The easiest is to introduce him as part of your daily life and see if people take to him. If they do, we consider setting him up on his own as a kind of spinoff."

"I'm not sure I see a homeless man being part of Charlotte's daily life," Irene told Thomas.

"Oh, but he already is," I said, thinking she'd misunderstood. "I mean, not a huge part. A small part."

"No, but Irene has a point, though," Thomas said. "It may be kind of a stretch."

I crossed my arms, stilled by a revelation that had been mounting in me ever since our arrival in this bower of poured concrete: that as the "subject," I was both the center of attention and completely extraneous. The feeling brought with it an eerie, stultifying familiarity; I was still the model, after all. I was modeling my life.

"He asked me to give you this," I told Thomas, and dug Pluto's home-made business card out of my purse.

Thomas frowned. "The guy has an E-mail address?"

"He uses the computers at Kinko's when he can afford it. He's trying to improve his life."

"God, I love that," Thomas said, his voice full of tenderness. "It's so moving. This poor guy. Is he relatively clean?"

"Immaculate."

"Well, I'll send him an E-mail," Thomas said. "We'll see what happens."

Irene and I gathered our things and Thomas walked us to the elevators. As we waited among the poured-concrete walls (blotched aquamarine, like undersea stone), a silence opened among us and spread. Irene fingered the worn strap of her shoulder bag and stared at the elevator doors.

"Look. I know you have doubts," Thomas finally said. "Even I wonder about this project sometimes—will it really improve people's lives, or am I just kidding myself? Couple of weeks ago I approached a guy—heart surgeon, actually—about becoming an Extraordinary, and he tells me, exact words, 'You're turning people into shopping malls.' I hardly slept the whole night, thinking about that. But finally I decided, you know what? If that's where it's going then I want to be there, making sure it's done responsibly. I invented this product, sure, but I'm not so unique—I'm part of a Zeitgeist. If I don't do it, someone else will. And maybe there's a positive to it, you know? Maybe the more interested we get in learning about each other, the less reason we'll have to do things like fight wars—we'll all be on the same side. So the next morning I come in here, no sleep from obsessing about this thing, and guess what? There's already a message from the guy. The surgeon. He wants in."

The elevator came and I turned, intending to board, but Irene was listening to Thomas. The door slid shut. "See, it's the future," he went on, with a kind of apology. "It's going to happen with or without you. But if you go with this thing, if you give yourself to it, you'll own that future; you'll be right in the heart of it. If you resist, that's when it rolls over you, and whatever you have now, you'll have less."

He was speaking to Irene, and she listened with a look of panic.

Thomas pled his case with a rueful energy quite apart from his usual zeal, as if he suspected that this future would elude us despite his best efforts. We weren't up to it. And for the first time that day, I glimpsed his shadow self—the awkward, overlarge boy I'd befriended two months before, peeping from the recesses of Thomas Keene. Not in fear, as I had expected (even hoped), but in empathy. For us. The big, softhearted boy had been summoned from the shadows by worry. And for all my queasiness about the future Thomas and his poured-concrete office embodied, worse was the thought of having no place in it—of being left behind.

Irene and I lurched from the building into skittish sunlight. "Oh, God," she said, as we made our way toward Union Square.

"I know."

It was market day in the square, bright, towering piles of lettuce, squash, marigolds, asters. I felt as if they were stabbing me. Too many colors, too much sunlight and joyous human traffic. Too many dogs on leashes and babies in strollers.

We went to an empty bench and sat. The perennial old kook was parked a few benches down with a sack of bread, which he tossed in limp handfuls to several hundred clamoring pigeons. A few overeager birds leapt onto his arms and knees, flapping their dingy wings in gratitude. If I had no place in the future, I thought—I, who had spent my life awaiting it—what was going to happen to the pigeon guy?

"He says such awful things," Irene said, "but with the gentlest look on his face." She was slumped against the bench, her face tipped to the sun. After a moment she turned to me. "Charlotte," she said, with crisp resolution, "I can't do this."

I didn't answer. What I had to say to Irene—that I knew she would do it, she had no choice but to do it—seemed cruel and unnecessary. It wasn't just the frightened expression she'd worn when Thomas invoked the steamrolling future; it was the safety pins and masking tape I'd glimpsed holding up her hems, the clumsily patched moth holes in her sweaters and cheap strawberry shampoo I'd smelled on her hair. It was the telltale orange tint of her generic panty hose; the broken plastic hairbrush in her purse, the fake leather wallet, the gold peeling off her earrings, the Bic pens. The tired circles under her eyes. Her bleeding cuticles. Irene had no choice. She would have to go through with this thing, much as she might loathe it. And loathe it she did. She was a kind and honest person (a reporter!), a person who would visit her emphysemic father in Arizona if she'd had one, despite the fact that being near him made her feel lousy and sad; she was devoted to her husband and (I had no doubt) friends, most of whom she'd probably had for years; she was immune to appearances, oblivious to the mirrored room, incapable of dissembling, fakery or bullshit, and knowing someone who had these qualities was the closest I was ever going to get, I figured, to having them myself.

"I shouldn't have stayed," she said. "I shouldn't have listened. I shouldn't have come in the first place."

But you did, I thought. You did and you will. Which means it must be all right.

Two pigeons had alighted on the pigeon man's head. His hair, I thought, must be full of birdshit. "How about a drink?" I asked.

To my surprise, Irene agreed. It was four-thirty. We crossed the square to the Coffee Shop, a perennial hangout for models and their devotees, one I'd patronized perhaps six or seven hundred times over the years, and yet, as I passed with Irene into the swill of its dance beat, strangely, arrestingly new. Something had changed, I thought, as the pigtailed hostess seated us, her bare midriff leading the way. Some restructuring had occurred beneath the surface.

My back was to the room. As we waited for our drinks, I turned and made a quick, habitual scan for familiar faces. My gaze stubbed on Oscar, seated with four people I didn't know, two of them models, in one of the prominent booths along the wall. I had walked past his table without even seeing him; more shockingly, without Oscar noticing me, flesh trader that he was, the whole of whose expertise lay in his ability to see. My impulse was to jump to my feet and bolt to his table; the inclination moved up and through me, lifting me halfway out of my chair. Then it passed, leaving me behind.

The inept waitress arrived (they were always inept), two martinis quavering on her tray. I relaxed into my drink, the incongruously buttery, milky, cream-swirling yet coldly medicinal flavor of a martini, the flavor of liquid freon as I imagined it. There was nothing more delicious in the world. "That's Oscar over there," I told Irene. "The black guy." I pointed with my chin so as not to look again.

Irene carefully set down her drink and moved her chair for a better view. Without taking her eyes from Oscar, she fumbled in her bag for her notebook, shimmied it out, flipped it open, found the page she wanted and jotted a few notes in her parsimonious style. I longed to see exactly what she was writing, to witness the alchemy whereby Irene and I merged into a woman who owned a dog and had recurrent dreams of geese.

"He looks exactly the way I imagined," Irene said. "You described him well."

"He's my best friend."

She set down her pen and looked at me. "Charlotte, we know this thing is rotten," she said. "But it's still in our hands, we can still walk away. All we will have lost is some time!" I saw the martini in her eyes—the heat, the conviction. And a strange feeling overtook me then; it flared at the word "we," a kind of vision—myself and Irene moving together into another kind of life: a life in which my choices were all different, in which *I* was different. The life of someone else. I glimpsed that woman rushing somewhere, engaged, engrossed, and a fat knot of hope snaked through me and jammed in my throat. And then she vanished. I was thirty-five. I'd made my choices long ago.

"It's too late for me," I said. "As you know."

Irene slipped her notebook back into her bag and rose unsteadily from her chair, the one drink visible in her gait as she headed for the restroom. She looked beaten. I felt it, too, but fought the feeling back. I looked at the notebook in her bag. After the briefest deliberation, I yanked it out and opened it. But my unease at violating her privacy, compounded by fear that she would catch me in the act, made me too anxious to read anything. I wedged the notebook into my purse, but it jutted conspicuously from the top. I pulled it out with the intention of returning it to her bag, but now Irene had reappeared and was heading toward me. Panicking, I jimmied the notebook back into my purse and used the silk scarf around my neck (a lingering habit from the days when I'd had bruises) to camouflage it. As I turned to wave for the check, I saw that Oscar was gone. Not even Irene had noticed.

Outside, the unseemly sun was still grinning down at us. "I'm drunk," Irene announced, and looked at her watch. "No!" she cried. "I'm a half-hour late to meet Mark. He'll think I was hit by a bus."

"He'll think you're having an affair," I said.

She looked so stunned that I genuinely regretted having said it. "Oh, God," she said. "He knows I'd never do that."

# Chapter Thirteen

*Eventually, when Anthony* Halliday refused to leave the brownstone stoop despite two requests from Mimi and one from Leeland, her lover, who tapped on the glass and spoke from behind it as if Anthony's instability made opening the door a risky proposition, as if he might attack Leeland in a feverish attempt to right the imbalance between them (namely, the fact that Leeland was living in Anthony's apartment with Anthony's wife and twin daughters); after two hours of ringing the buzzer at ten-minute intervals and reiterating, quite calmly, his refusal to depart, Mimi finally opened the door and came outside. She sat beside him on the stoop, a compact woman, athletic, a runner of marathons. Colombian. She had become a citizen when they married.

"Tony," she said. "This is not good for anyone."

"You'd do the same," he said, "if I wouldn't let you see them."

"The situations are not comparable." She accented the middle syllable of that word in a way he found sweet.

They looked together at St. John's Street, exhausted in advance by a conversation they'd had too many times, playing out the moves like a game of telepathic chess. Orange streetlight soaked the leaves. "Seven months today," he said. "Not a drop."

She touched his back. "That's fantastic, Tony."

It was the longest abstention of his adult life, excepting the five years when he hadn't drunk at all, five years that had included (it was true) the period when he'd courted and married Mimi. But the present abstention had come a year too late. A year ago, without warning—or rather, after a warning that had seemed no different from the thousands of other warnings Mimi had delivered—she had stopped loving him. It amazed Anthony how distinct that feeling had been, like someone leaving a room.

"They're my children," he said. "They trust me. You have no right to stand between us." But he couldn't bring himself to go on, so belabored and oratorical did it sound.

"They trust you, yes. *I* don't trust you. Seven months—why should I believe that? I should demand a urine test!"

Anthony took a certain grim delight in listening for the moments when the voice of Leeland, a law professor at Fordham, broke through Mimi's speech like clicks on a tapped phone line. The last time they'd spoken, she had actually used the phrase, "In any event." Yet his fascination with this audial commingling of Leeland and Mimi failed to salve the hopelessness it made him feel. Leeland Wile, a dispassionate, bearded pipe smoker whose toes pointed out when he walked, had forced himself into every crevice of Anthony's life—was speaking to him through his wife's mouth!

"Drinking isn't illegal, Mimi," he said.

"Drinking is not illegal, no. But what about reckless endangerment?" (Leeland) "What about scaring our girls half to death with your negligent" (Leeland) "drunkenness and your wild hallucinations? What about the fact that I couldn't reach you, I had no idea what was going on and the girls were panic-stricken while their daddy slept off a binge? I could sue you for emotional pain and distress and I'd probably win!" (Leeland, Leeland, Leeland).

"Stop," he said. "Please." It gave him physical pain to listen. He couldn't remember any of it, couldn't remember why he had been drinking with the girls there in the first place.

Mimi hove a sigh. "In any event—"

Anthony held up a hand and she stopped, her eyes moving over him in the orange, leafy darkness. He imagined she was looking right at the gouge of his loneliness, which he felt able to hide from everyone but Mimi. He saw the shame of it in her face.

"Can I watch them sleep?" he asked, taking advantage.

She stood without answering and opened the door. This was their compromise, the concession that, every few weeks, he was able to wrest from her. Together they climbed the carpeted stairs, every bulge in the plaster wall familiar to Anthony's hand. She turned the shiny new Fichet lock (Leeland). The musk of his pipe tobacco filled the apartment.

"Let them sleep," Mimi warned as he pushed open the girls' bedroom door.

The smell of them nearly overpowered him, a smell he missed so acutely that he forgot it instantly each time he left. The milky, waxen, fruit-tinged smell of his children. Apples, or apple juice. Damp cookies. They were asleep in their beds, six years old, red curls. His twin girls. Anthony lowered himself cross-legged onto the floor between their beds. The room was shadowy and small, neatly stacked toys and books seeming to float on the tide of his girls' breath, its peaceful rise and fall, and Anthony felt like an interloper, someone who could never belong in such a place. But gradually he relaxed into the aquarium of their sleep, their breath, their very white skin, their nearly identical faces. He spread his arms and placed one hand gently on each girl, Laura's arm, the little fin of Fernanda's shoulder blade, feeling the life under his hands even through pajamas and bedclothes, warm frantic life thrusting against them from inside. And he had helped to make that life.

For the first time in days, the first time since the last time Mimi had let him come inside and watch them sleep, Anthony felt a kind of peace, as if some perpetual discomfort, a discomfort so unrelenting that he no longer noticed it, had finally eased. They were still here, still alive, still breathing softly, and Anthony felt their life enter him through his two hands, strengthen him. Yes, he thought, yes he would hold on, he would win them back. His girls and Mimi, too. Why had it felt so impossible before? They were warm, almost hot. Laura wore her Orphan Annie pajamas, Fernanda wore Madeline. Very gently he touched their faces, kissed their folded, velvety ears.

At the sound of Mimi outside the door, he got up. He didn't want her to come in.

He left the apartment without ever seeing Leeland.

Back in Park Slope, the peace Anthony had felt among his daughters stayed with him for perhaps a block, then began to dissipate. After three blocks, he felt like doubling over. The discomfort was back, with the difference that now he was aware of it—keenly, agonizingly. He took the long way home to avoid a particular bar he didn't trust himself to resist in such a mood, then opened the door with his key and ascended three flights of steps to his new apartment, an aerie surrounded by spreading trees that reminded him of hands holding playing cards. He loathed it. On his desk lay a legal pad full of notes he'd taken earlier that day during a visit to his friends at Immigration. They'd had a few ideas about Z, nothing definite. Of course, the pictures Mitch and Hassam had given him were practically useless: a man whose eyes were always closed or averted, a man about whom the only thing you could say for sure was that he didn't want to be photographed.

Anthony's interest in Z had engaged (he'd felt it distinctly, a bolt sliding into place) during his first conversation with Mitch and Hassam, when they'd told him the address of Z's office: the same Seventh Avenue building where Anthony's own office was. Five floors down. What were the chances of that? In a space virtually identical to his own (shared among several anxious looking men with import-export connections), he'd found Z's desk and computer, all of it empty, bereft of files. Anthony dusted for prints, knowing he wouldn't find Z's; it had all been carefully wiped. Not a single ragged edge, not a clue as to who had been there. Except one: a business card placed neatly inside the top middle desk drawer, a card that read, "Z," the letter tiny, a phone number leading to a voicemail box that had turned out still to be active. He'd called it right there, on Z's still-connected phone, sitting in his chair, and had been greeted by the man's voice, his light, indistinguishable accent. He sounded as if he were smiling. As if he had known Anthony would trace his steps this far, and meant to say, Yes, I was here, there's no mistake. He was a man who didn't make mistakes. And Anthony was all mistakes, mistake after mistake, and the damage they had wrought would surround him forever.

He unlocked a drawer in his own desk and pulled out the birth certificate he kept there, its county seal in relief. Ralph B. Goldfarb, a Caucasian two years younger than himself. Born in Pittsburgh. Murdered six years ago, walking his dog on the West Side highway. Anthony had snagged the birth certificate in his first year as a detective, going through the man's possessions. That was shortly after he was fired from the DA's office—one of his biggest mistakes. Fired for drinking, of course, the single mistake that underlay all the rest. Except that it wasn't a mistake. It was the thing he loved most.

He held the birth certificate in his hands and let his mind run. To disappear, leaving not one single ragged edge. To clear out, as Z had done, whoever Z actually was (and Anthony would find out eventually—he was a good detective, despite everything). To begin again with a new name, in a new place, a place where he hadn't made a single mistake, and wouldn't. He could do it. All you needed was a birth certificate.

One birth certificate. It could spawn a whole life: Social Security number, bank accounts, credit cards, loans. All of it, from so little. Almost nothing.

The fantasy of disappearance had been with Anthony for many years, but since his abrasion with Z it had become more insistent. He found himself clinging to the search even now, when Mitch and Hassam had decided to cut their losses and stop paying his retainer. He had something to learn from Z, he was convinced. Something that would help him.

He brought the phone to the next room, lay on his bed and called Charlotte. He had no idea why the urge to call her overtook him so often at night—was it her connection to Z, or a sense that she occupied the same dark stratum as himself?

"Hi," she said. She always seemed to know who it was.

"Did I wake you?"

"No. I was watching *Unsolved Mysteries*."

Her voice, rough from cigarettes in a way that reminded him, incongruously, of a child's, had the power to relieve him. Even when she lied, as she nearly always did.

"How was your day?" he asked.

"Busy," she said. "I'm a TV anchor now."

"Think I saw you. Six o'clock news?"

"That was me."

"You move fast," he said, closing his eyes.

Charlotte laughed. She had the saddest laugh he'd ever heard. "What about you?" she asked.

"The usual. Trying to separate the good guys from the bad guys."

"Is there a difference?"

"I have to think so," he said. "It's a matter of faith."

There was a lengthy silence, a silence of several minutes. He heard the match as she lit another cigarette, heard the voice of the *Unsolved Mysteries* guy in the background.

"Sweet dreams, Charlotte," he finally said.

## 34

July. Z was everywhere. I looked for him in the crowds of people waiting to cross Sixth Avenue. Short dresses, gold lamé sandals. Men in shirtsleeves, jackets hooked to one finger. Gold mist dusting the air.

I searched for his outline behind the windows of limousines slowly turning corners. The streets were riotous. He was everywhere, places I couldn't imagine him going. Sitting in outdoor cafés. Applauding a bawdy comedian in the fountain at Washington Square. Looking down from fluorescent cubes of office windows against a neon-blue dusk. Looking down. Instantly picking me out.

I did the things I'd always done, but with a new excitement. A fever that reminded me of childhood. Adulthood as children imagine it.

Dinner at ten with a man visiting from Europe. I'd known him for years. Added my bit of color to parties at his villa in Antibes. At lunchtime, an old English servant would wheel a cart to the water's edge. Starched tablecloths thrown over yellow rocks. Grilled fish, white wine. The Mediterranean went purple in the afternoons. Twice I was burned by a stingray.

This man was married now. A father. But still eager to see old friends, as he put it. While the others laughed around us, his hand drifted to my leg. "When are you going to get married?" he asked.

"Never," I said.

The hand wandered, inquisitive. "Then what? This, on and on?"

"Of course not."

Something else was going to happen. I was right up against it.

## 37

Z and I pretended we were strangers. No one knew. That secrecy was the hidden pulse. The buried engine.

We were at our best with a room full of people between us, linked by a glittering strand of mutual awareness. His presence made the air sing. Made me loopy. Buoyed me up on a reckless swell of freedom I hadn't felt in many years. I threw my arms around people and shouted into their ears. I jumped onto tables and danced. I expanded, trying to fill my exaggerated outline.

He watched me. I was showing him something, but I didn't know what it was. I was leading him someplace.

He came to my apartment a few more times. Alone in a room, he was hard to take. Too goddamn serious.

I was getting impatient. To begin! To play my part, whatever that was! I imagined drugs, crime. Spy missions. Weapons trading. But only in the most sketchy, cinematic terms. None of it really made sense. I think I didn't want to know. Even as I boiled with frustration.

I'd never liked mysteries. Except on television.

He felt the frustration, too. Once, in the middle of fucking, he slapped my face. I hit him back, socked him right in the head. I heard my knuckles on the bone.

And then we kissed. It was a relief.

My name was printed in small block letters on the cover of Irene's six-by-nine steno book. Looking at it gave me a tiny flick of pride, but each time I opened the cover, I felt dread.

Dread of what? I didn't know. Maybe it was as simple, as childish, as the fear that she'd written nasty things about me.

On the day of our next appointment, I brought the notebook with me to Gristede's and then to the river, where I sat on my usual bench. I opened the notebook. Irene's writing was cryptic, streaky, illegible at first. Upside down it looked the same as right side up. I flipped among the pages, half relieved that I couldn't read them. Then I deciphered *Saved $*, followed by (the words seemed to tumble toward me) *Bought apt. 198— v. proud, esp. sect. couch.* This was true, I thought; I was proud of my couch (it was an excellent couch), but reading it in someone else's hand made that pride seem ludicrous. I made a mental note not to refer to the couch again in Irene's presence.

And then, by degrees, other words yielded themselves to me, painstakingly at first and then in a kind of rush, as if I were pushing through a wall: *tough pose dev. early. Why? Hurt?* Later I found *sms completely isolated. Exile. Self punish? Ask abt religion.* And I remembered Irene questioning me about religion, describing the Lutheran church where I'd gone each Sunday with my parents, blah blah blah. It was unsettling, now, to read the original question. All of it was unsettling, like hearing the other side of a conversation I only dimly recalled my end of. There were doodles: a sailing ship, a woman lying in bed covered with a blanket, her stomach bulging in pregnancy. Several long lashed eyes. Trees. Chess pieces. I found lists. *Laundry,* scrawled in one margin, and beneath it, *buy: Windex, pap. towels, plant food, cereal, ravioli, shoelaces.* Another list, *Re: Mark 1. Invite J. M. to dinner. 2. Ask L. abt. commission 3. Apple composer prog—how much $$$?? 4. Mark—shrink?*

Poor Mark. I knew the feeling.

Despite these proofs that Irene's mind had strayed to other topics during our conversations, I experienced relief. There was nothing really bad. At one point, she had even written *Less bitch than 1st seems.* That was toward the beginning—the second page. I returned to it, and now a few other formerly indecipherable lines tipped open to me: *Doesn't want to talk. Needs $$. (Why me?)* and then, a few lines down, *Jackpot,* followed by *lying before, did know Z.* In the margin she'd written a phone number that looked familiar. I flipped ahead, then returned uneasily to that page. What did she mean by lying *before*—when was before? My eyes drifted again to that number. I opened my cell phone and dialed it.

"Mr. Halliday's office," his receptionist answered.

I hung up confounded, my brain straining to conjure a scenario whereby a connection between Irene and Halliday made sense: they'd met recently, by chance; she'd hired him for some reason. I myself had written his phone number in the margin of her notebook and forgotten. It had to be recent, because weeks ago I had mentioned Halliday to Irene, and she'd denied knowing him; I remembered that distinctly. And when I'd impersonated Irene in Halliday's presence, he had betrayed no recognition of her name. My mind gyred harriedly, eagerly among these possibilities, but in the end I found myself staring at that word *Jackpot*, an ominous sensation lazing through me like a stench.

Pluto was back, hovering to my left with an air of frenetic insistence. I hardly saw him through the blur of my distraction; I had to finish this. I pressed redial, and this time Halliday picked up.

"How do you know Irene Maitlock?" I asked, not bothering to identify myself. "The *Post* reporter?"

There was a long pause, a completely different sort of pause from the ones that took place during our nocturnal conversations. This pause was filled with the creak of Anthony's thoughts. "She interviewed me," he said, "about three months ago."

Pluto was standing directly in front of me. I ignored him.

"I sent her to you," Halliday said quietly.

"Why?"

"I could tell you," he said. "And I will, if you want. But I'd rather give Irene a chance to do it her way."

I felt strange, tingly. Sick. My new life was so small; together, Anthony and Irene made up the major portion of it. And they knew each other—had from the beginning, but kept it a secret. Foreboding fastened leathery wings around me.

But when I thought of Irene, the foreboding eased. She wasn't capable of deception; she was too transparent. Too honest. It simply wasn't possible.

"Okay," I said. "I'll talk to Irene."

"Will you call me, Charlotte? After you're done?"

"What an excellent question."

I closed my phone and sat numbly, staring at the water. Pluto could contain himself no longer. "You find yourself in the coveted position," he declaimed, dancing beside me, "of having a human being owe you his blessed life. Fill my ears with what that feels like."

"No one owes me their life," I said.

"Oh, yes," he said. "Oh, yes, Pluto owes you his." He pulled from his immaculate pocket a check I recognized, a check for $1,000. From Extra/Ordinary.com.

"Randall Joseph Smith," I read.

"That's the name I had back when I got named."

"Wow. So they signed you up." I did my best to sound enthusiastic, despite my seismic uneasiness.

"All these years of waiting, and something finally happens," Pluto said. "Because of you."

"Stop saying that." He was starting to make me angry.

"I love America. I love this crazy damn country. Where else does such beautiful insanity enter the realm of the possible?"

"He's doing it for himself," I said, "not you."

"That's the only reason I've got any modicum of faith whatsoever!" Pluto retorted. "If he's doing it for me, he won't do it. He's doing it for himself, there's some possibility it'll actually get done."

"Just don't trust him."

"Trust," Pluto scoffed. "You're telling a homeless guy that's been kicked around by every man woman and child got legs to kick with not to *trust*? I read every word of that contract before I set my John Hancock to it. Brought my specs and read it right there in his damn office. Took me over an hour."

Having not read a word of my own contract, I could only be impressed. "He paid me a lot more than he paid you," I said.

That stopped Pluto for a moment. Watching him hesitate, I felt a grinding cruelty whose single goal was to take this pleasure away from him. Because it was false; all of it was phony and false, and he shouldn't believe it. "More than seven times as much," I added.

"Well of course he did," Pluto said, regaining his composure. "You're worth more at this particular point in time. We'll see in the end; I've got every intention of being their number-one guy." He cocked his head at me. "I know what you're up to, prettygirl, but you can't hurt me. Don't you see? I'm impervious—it's just not within your power, powerful though you may be." He went to retrieve his laundry bag from his tent.

"The irony of it is," he said, returning, "all this silly money in my hand and I can't even rent a room. I've got to stay homeless until I'm filthy rich. Then I'm gonna buy me a palace with tiles in the shower like you've got. Portuguese tiles, that's what I'm thinking, with little paintings on them. Each tile, I want a different historic scene, the Greeks and the Babylonians, the African kings. I want to stand in my shower and look at the whole mad fantastical evolution of the human race. I want to ruminate over mankind all at one time, with hot water splashing down my back."

"You've never seen my shower," I reminded him, but he had already walked away from me, grinning.

Irene arrived punctually at the appointed hour; I'd left the door open as usual and she locked it behind her. She wore a plaid dress that contained the color orange and smelled of mothballs. I liked it on sight.

I held up the notebook.

"Oh, I'm so relieved!" she cried. "I called Thomas, I called the restaurant, I've been . . . where did you find it?"

"In your bag."

She'd been on her way toward me; now she stopped. "You took it from my bag?"

"In a sense."

"What do you mean, in a—? You either—"

"Yes."

"Charlotte, why?"

"I wanted to read it."

"What kind of fucked-up thing was that to do?" she said, in the first volley of profanity I'd ever heard from Irene. It jarred me. "All you had to do was ask. I would have shown it to you gladly. Why sneak around like that?"

"I don't know," I said. "I don't know why a person sneaks around, but I'm looking forward to finding out." And then I told her: The phone number. Halliday. *Jackpot.*

She looked away, exhaled and sat down heavily on the piece of furniture I had determined not to mention in her presence.

"He said you would explain," I said.

Irene didn't answer. For a long while she seemed to be thinking. "Okay," she finally said. "I'm going to start with the worst part, right up front. I'll just say it, okay?" Still, she hesitated. Since entering my apartment, she had actually gone pale. "I'm not a reporter."

She blurted this out, then seemed to wait for what devastation might follow.

"Huh," I said, careful not to react. But I was shocked. More than shocked, I couldn't believe it. I couldn't imagine her as anything else.

"I'm an academic," she went on, "a professor of comparative literature. An adjunct," she added quickly, as if saying the first without the second amounted to further duplicity. "My area is cultural studies. Specifically, the way literary and cinematic genres affect certain kinds of experience." I sensed her straining to put this in language I would understand. "For example, the Mafia. How do cultural notions of the so-called wiseguy affect the way people like John Gotti dress and move and speak? How does that extra layer of self-consciousness impact experience? The same for cops; they watch cop shows, too. And how does their experience of those shows affect their experience as cops?"

"Detectives," I said, addressing the cigarette in my hand.

"Exactly. Detective stories. The genre is almost as old as the profession, the two have been intertwined practically from the beginning."

"Detectives write books," I said ruefully.

"That's right," she said. "A surprising number try to write detective novels, as if writing books were a corollary of the experience of being a detective. So . . . well, you know where this is going."

She had interviewed Halliday for a paper she was writing on detectives, then asked if she could spend a couple of weeks observing his work. He'd called her a few days later, spur-of-the-moment, and offered her an opportunity to experience his work from the inside: to interview a reluctant witness in a missing-persons case. So she'd invented the phony story about being a reporter who was looking for a model with a brand-new face. She'd phoned around until she found my agency and pitched the story to Oscar, who, desperate on my behalf, had lunged unthinkingly into the trap. Then she'd fabricated a business card on one of those self-service machines and shown up on my doorstep.

"At that point you weren't real to me, Charlotte," she said. "It was all just a goofy experiment, a slice-of-life kind of thing."

During our "interview," she'd felt cushioned at first by the several layers of disingenuousness that separated us, but with time those had seemed to burn away, leaving her exposed and at my mercy. And then a queasy sense of impropriety had made itself known within her. "I don't know if you remember this," she said, "but you said something like, Can you look me in the eye and swear on your husband's life that everything you're saying is absolutely true? I was like, Oh my God, get me out of here."

Afterwards, she'd felt crummy about the whole thing—so crummy that although she did write the paper on detectives, she'd found a different one to observe rather than work with Halliday. "He was very sweet about it," she said. "He felt badly that I felt bad."

"So there was no article?" I asked, still not fully able to grasp it.

"Well, there was an article. But not about models. And not for the *Post*, that's for sure. I don't even read it!"

"And the business card wasn't real?"

"It was all fake, Charlotte. That's what I'm telling you."

"But how did you think up those questions?"

Irene looked at me with concern. "I just made them up. I was trying to get you to talk about Z. I mean, granted, I wasn't very good at it—I had no idea what I was doing."

"I see," I said. But I didn't. Irene Maitlock the reporter I trusted implicitly; this new woman I was having trouble believing.

And then, she said, I had called her out of nowhere, wanting to meet again. She'd tried to wriggle out of it, but when I announced that I was on my way to her "office" armed with her phony business card (a card she was fairly certain she had made illegally, with her real phone number on it), she'd dashed to my apartment to stave me off. And once she was here, practically the first words out of my mouth were about the very person Halliday had been looking for.

"I listened," she said, "I was curious, obviously, I remembered that this was the guy who'd disappeared. But afterwards, when I got home, the whole thing seemed too neat. And I wondered if Anthony was somehow behind it—if the two of you were in cahoots, trying to mess with my head."

I knew the feeling. Because now, at last, I saw it all, like the final, critical moves in a game of solitaire. Halliday wanted information on Z. He'd sent Irene to get it. And, in the course of two short months, I'd told her everything.

"So you called him," I said pleasantly.

"I did."

"You told him what I'd said."

"About the wire. Yes."

"And?"

"And I could tell by his reaction that he hadn't set it up."

"He was excited. He finally had some information."

"He was . . . interested. But I told him he was on his own from there on in. That was the last time we spoke."

"And there's a bridge in Brooklyn you'd like to sell me, if I'd be interested."

Irene sighed. "It's the truth," she said. "You can believe it or not believe it."

"You little bitch!" I cried, jumping to my feet.

She looked frightened, just as the other Irene—the reporter—would have looked. But I wasn't fooled anymore.

"Charlotte, I wanted to tell you," she said. "I felt shitty about having lied. But the longer I waited, the harder it seemed, the weirder it got, and finally I thought, Look, what does it even matter? This thing we're doing is about you—what does it matter exactly what I do for a living?"

"Oh, it matters," I said. Already she seemed different to me; bolder, less restrained. I wondered if what I'd mistaken for reticence, reserve—for *honesty*—had merely been the fact that she'd been hiding something.

"I would even tell myself sometimes that you, of all people, would understand," she said. "If you knew."

"I do understand," I said. "I understand that you're exactly like everybody else. You lie, you say whatever you need to say, you're one more calculating bitch in a world that's full of them."

"Like you?"

"Yeah, like me. The difference is, I don't pretend to be anything else."

"Neither do I!"

"You did! You do! Look at you, with your odd hair and your ripped hem and your genius husband who obviously can't earn a dime. You come off like someone who could never tell a lie; the last Honest John left on earth."

"You invented that person," she said angrily. "That was never me."

"I liked her better."

"Then find someone else to play her," she said, standing up. "I'm done."

"Go," I shouted. "Take the apartment. Take the couch. Is there one fucking thing I have left? Take that, too." I knew I wasn't making sense. I felt on the verge of passing out.

I stormed into my bedroom and flung myself on the bed, facedown. The room was dark. I heard buzzing in my head. There were certain fights I'd enjoyed in the course of my life, riotous collisions and clamorous dissolutions, but this one felt sickening. A loss I couldn't afford. After a few minutes, Irene came in. "I'm sorry I hurt you," she said in a tight voice, from somewhere to my right.

"Hurt me," I snorted.

"Well, disillusioned you."

"This happened long ago."

"I'm sorry I'm not the person you thought," she said sadly. "I have a feeling I used to be."

"I'm sorry I believed you," I muttered.

There was a long silence, so long that I wondered if Irene was still in the room, or had left. I wasn't going to look.

"Anyway, there are a million reasons not to do this thing," she finally said. "Now it's a million and one."

I opened my eyes just as her silhouette vacated the doorway. I heard her gathering up her belongings as if she were doing it inside my skull—jacket, bag, notebook—footsteps whispering on the carpet toward the door, whose many locks she unfastened effortlessly now. She checked it after it closed, making sure the lock had engaged.

I lay there a long time, such a long time that when I finally sat up, I felt the imprint of the bedspread on my cheek. Irene was right, whoever she was—we were more alike than I could have believed. She had done exactly what I would have done in her place, and I was stunned by what a bitter, almost intolerable disappointment this was. I didn't want Irene to be like me. I wanted her to have the qualities I no longer had—perhaps had never had—so that in her company, I would have them, too.

I called her. In fact, I called her even before the lumbering crosstown bus she took to the West Side, where she lived, had delivered her home. Her husband answered the phone. We had never spoken.

"Charlotte?" he said in an anxious, threadbare voice when I asked for Irene. "Isn't she with you?"

In the midst of explaining myself, my other line beeped. It was Halliday. "Charlotte—" he began.

I hung up without saying hello.

# Chapter Fourteen

*"Up there?" Charlotte* asked, squinting through her rain-spattered glasses north along the river and teasing into focus, among the vectors of railroad bridges, a sheet of falling water. The dam. It looked like the skin of a bubble. "That's it, right?"

Moose nodded, standing close to her in his orange plastic rain poncho. "Built when?"

"Eighteen fifty-three."

"By . . . ?"

"The Water Power Company."

"One of the first companies to use it?"

"Clark and Utter."

"Their most famous product?"

"The Manny reaper."

Satisfied, Moose lunged into a brawl of wind that rousted his poncho halfway over his head, bounding north along the slippery riverbank with an urgency Charlotte noticed more and more often in him as the weeks passed. It was April, late afternoon. She fought to keep up with him.

Near the Morgan Street bridge, a factory building was still in use, two workmen in blue jumpsuits avoiding the rain in a doorway. The men flicked their eyes from Moose to Charlotte in a way that pleased her. She was flattered when people mistook them for a couple; it helped to redeem the fact that she could never be seen with Michael West. Two weeks ago, she had gone to Baxter pretending to look for her friends, but really to see

him—see what would happen when they met in daylight, in that familiar place. She'd walked the halls until she glimpsed him in a classroom,
talking with two younger boys at his desk. She stood in the doorway and
waited for them to finish. *If he smiles, then he.* Michael had looked past the
boys, turning on Charlotte a cool, stranger's face. "Can I help you with
something?" he asked, his voice so persuasively that of a teacher she had
never seen before that Charlotte froze, disoriented, wondering if she knew
him after all. "No," she said, and left the school shaken, without even
finding her friends, whom she hadn't seen in many weeks.

He never mentioned the incident, nor did she.

Her uncle stamped onto a soggy spit of pebbles and mud thrust out
among the brothy waves of the Rock River. He pointed left at Kent Creek,
a snaking, muscular arm that parted the land, then angled out of sight.
"You know what that is . . ."

"Of course I know," Charlotte said, but withheld the information,
teasing.

Moose grinned at her. Rain dripped from his longish hair into his wet
brown eyes and back out again, coursing like tears through the stubble of
his beard. "Oh, yes?"

"Yes!"

"Would you care to, as they say, back that up?"

"Midway," she said. That was the name Germanicus Kent had chosen
for his settlement in 1834, because it was midway between Chicago and
Galena.

"Keep it coming," Moose said.

"Lewis." That was Kent's slave, a man who had followed him north
and earned his freedom after four and a half years.

"You're getting there."

"Eighteen thirty-eight." The year Kent built his sawmill—Rockford's
first industry—in the woods along the creek, just yards from where they
were standing.

"Bingo," Moose said.

Of course, what surrounded them now were not woods or sawmill but
abandoned factory buildings and empty lots, weeds erupting from fissured
pavement, idle smokestacks, piles of old garbage and rotting tires and

occasional desultory human workers in tall black boots. The old Water Power District, on the west side of the river just south of downtown, where Clark and Utter had made a foundry, where John Manny built his reapers, where threshing machines and wood lathes and drill presses and gas stoves and socks and paper and paint and pianos had all been manufactured at one time or another. Last spring, Charlotte had sat on this same section of riverbank, drinking Old Styles with Roselyn and some guys from school. Then it had seemed a blank, empty place: no place. This was hard to remember, now, so dense were her surroundings with clues and artifacts, winking from every direction like ore in a mine. There was a kind of thrill in just standing in a place she had seen so many times on her uncle's maps.

"So over there is where the millrace was." She pointed north across the creek to an area that was now mostly parking lot.

"Exactly," Moose said.

"And right on the corner there was the Central Furniture Company, founded in eighteen seventy-seven—"

"Good!" Moose interjected with surprise.

"—by E. R. Herrick and L. D. Upson—"

"Very good!"

"—after Upson's other furniture plant burned down."

"Excellent!" Moose cried, and favored Charlotte with a look that was purely her own; fond, sweet, a look she began to pander for when she hadn't received it in a while.

It was easy. Her mind trapped information and held it—she had always been that way. She knew more about Rockford's history than she did about tropical fish; facts itched in her mind, looking for ways to be said. Their meaning was secondary, sometimes altogether absent; history was the idiom she and her uncle could speak. They joked and teased each other in history; they sparred, snapping it back and forth, or else let facts float between them desultorily, like sweet nothings. Moose challenged her, poking factual questions as if Charlotte's mind might have wandered (which often it had), and she reassured him with facts applied gently, soothingly. For Charlotte, it was like entering a state of hypnosis. At times she had trouble switching from the language of history to the language of everyone else.

"Let's backtrack," Moose said, and led the way onto Morgan Street. The Illinois Central tracks sliced through it at an angle, one of four lines that still bisected Rockford, stopping occasionally to pick up freight. "We can follow these right to the old depot," he declared, and charged between the rails.

Moose was thriving, kinetic, infused with a new vitality that made him seem in a state of constant great haste. Charlotte had trouble remembering the man who had flopped at his desk looking pained and half asleep as she read to him. Now he paced, he stalked, sometimes marching from his office and continuing his declamations from the basement hallway at a shout. Or he and Charlotte went out, canvassing the dregs of Rockford's past like detectives: the old Swedish neighborhood on the east side of the river around Kishwaukee Street; the Esterline Whitney factory, one of the last machine tool factories still active in Rockford. The Industrial Hall at Midway Village, where Moose had narrated for Charlotte a tour of Rockford's industrial products with such booming authority that the entire population of the hall (namely, four visitors from Des Moines and two from Cincinnati) politely asked if they, too, might join.

Each Friday, when she appeared on his doorstep (she'd been coming on a weekly basis since January), a kind of stunned happiness would float across her uncle's face, and Charlotte would feel a pulse of anticipation that made her head ache. Eventually Moose would reveal something to her, she felt this keenly: the solution to the deepest mystery of all, which had nothing to do with Rockford. The mystery of himself.

Her uncle hounded the tracks onto Main Street, crossed the bridge over Kent Creek and hurried to the old railroad depot, abandoned now, surrounded by cyclone fencing, windows either boarded or broken, ringed with icicles of glass. "Northern Illinois Central Freight Station" was still faintly visible on its yellow brick.

"Trains changed the shape of ladies' skirts from hoops to bustles," Charlotte said, by way of conversation, "so they could get down the aisles more easily."

Moose murmured in reply, "At one point, twenty-three passenger trains stopped in Rockford every day."

He glanced at Charlotte in a knowing, particular way, as if alluding to a shared understanding between them so axiomatic that she couldn't bring herself to ask what exactly he thought she understood. Charlotte did her best to return the look. She hated disappointing him.

"Did you ever catch a train here?" she asked.

"Oh, yes," he said, and pointed through the cyclone fence at a more modern structure, also vacant, closer to the tracks. "That was the passenger depot."

His mind pitched into memory: rocking over the railroad bridge and Grape Island, spying into people's backyards at their flailing laundry; bolting through crossings where the same group of children seemed always to wait astride bicycles, waving. But Moose wasn't going to talk about this. He had to be careful—Charlotte would always try to make it personal. It was the reigning habit of mind in this land without history, this era when all relationships of time and space, of cause and effect, had been obliterated by the touch of a key. And so people were adrift, lacking any context by which to orient themselves, seeking to fill the breach with *personal history*, that diminutive, myopic substitute.

"Did you go with your mom and dad?" she asked. "On the train to Chicago?"

"Just my dad," Moose said.

Those long-anticipated visits! The University Club, on Michigan Avenue—first a swim in the ancient pool, where chlorine fumes lazed like ether from the milky water, where yellowish old men swam their laps, mouths agape at each breath. And afterward, lunch with his father in the wood-paneled dining room, Moose's eyes foggy from the chlorine, the silver heavy and cold in his hands. Raspberries for dessert, raspberries served in a silver bowl over ice shaped like scrabble pieces.

But he wasn't going to talk about this. Or think about it. His mind was fuddled from lack of sleep. An old problem, resurgent in recent weeks: lying awake, counting Priscilla's breaths, or else pacing a living room blanched by moonlight. Some nights he left his apartment and walked along State Street for miles, trudging east through vast empty superstore parking lots toward the interstate (the older parts of town were dangerous at night); walking without sidewalks to walk on, his clothes and hair suctioned to him by the backdraft of passing twenty-four-wheelers. Since January—nearly four months, now—Charlotte had teetered on the brink of sight. And as Moose waited for her to slip, tip, tumble irrevocably into the chasm of comprehension, the vision's maelstrom, his eagerness had come to eclipse nearly everything else.

Meanwhile he was talking, feeding his niece facts about this particular railroad line: "Illinois Northern and Central . . . first reached Rockford August fifth, eighteen eighty-eight, after a series of skirmishes known as the Railway Wars . . . first cargo was a load of yarn from Georgia headed for the Nelson Knitting Company . . . watermelons from Texas . . ."

The old tracks ramified into the distance with a thready shimmer that was not unlike the gleam of circuitry—odd how they looked the same. Moose's distrust of a world remade by circuitry brought a corollary nostalgia for trains; their noise; their visibility; their physical existence. Again and again he spoke to Charlotte of *things*, watermelons and grain and cattle and string, reaper-mowers and harvester combines, chisel mortisers and scroll saws and flue stops and piston rings and grain elevators. Objects existing in time and space. But things had lost their allure generations ago, shunted off to countries where people would make them for less. And information was the inversion of a thing; without shape or location or component parts. Without context. Not history but personal history. Charlotte hadn't seen this yet, Moose knew. She was too happy.

Flushed, smiling up at him in her bright yellow rain slicker. Kicking stones. And oh, the grind of impatience he felt—an old, dormant anger that had a shivery boil to it, like sinking his teeth into wood, or ice, or aluminum foil. He had reached a point in his life, he'd told Priscilla last night over chicken pot pies (his wife listening with a look of worry that annoyed him), when he no longer could wait. He'd been too passive since the incident at Yale, too accepting of the limitations imposed on him! Yes, he'd imperiled the lives of twenty-four undergraduates plus himself: a methodological catastrophe, Moose was the first to admit. But his method had improved—witness Charlotte! So close, so very close! And so now the time had come to accelerate.

"Uncle Moose," Charlotte said.

"Yes!" She was shivering in the heavy rainfall. Not kicking the stone anymore, which was something. "Yes, let's keep moving."

They walked north along Main Street—once the prime artery of

Rockford life, now an empty thoroughfare lined with parking garages and parking ramps. Cold rain had eked its way inside the neck of Charlotte's raincoat, her jeans were caked to her legs. Ahead she noticed a seedy-looking bar, a worn-out Old Style sign suspended above its door. She wished Moose would take her there.

But her uncle had veered into a vacant parking lot, sections of old brick grinning up from beneath its retracting asphalt. He was loping toward the river's edge. They were north of the dam; Charlotte heard the giddy plummeting crush of its waterfall. And suddenly she was tired, drained by her uncle's relentless stamina. Tired and a little defeated.

"Come on," he called to her through the rain. "From here we can look right over the dam . . ." He was heading along a wispy trail into desiccated shrubbery, branches festooned with garbage, a child's soiled undershirt—the sort of place where you found people dead. And a wall of stubbornness came down in Charlotte.

"Uncle Moose," she called to him, folding her arms. "I'm cold."

Moose turned, saw that his niece was not behind him and backtracked through rotting foliage. She peered at him, glasses fogged, arms crossed. Resisting him. And Moose was disconcerted by a paroxysm of impatience with his niece that was very nearly rage, a ruthless, bodily urge to crush her innocence. Sweep it away. The feeling stunned him. No, he thought, no. He wanted to save her—save her from the blindness of the world. And now he was beset by the obverse of his rage, an urge to sweep Charlotte into his arms and cleave to her, fend off those who might wish her harm.

"You're cold, you're cold. Of course," he said, returning to her side. "Let's go somewhere warm, let's find a place . . ." Shaken, half dizzy from the force of what had just transpired within him.

Charlotte pointed at the bar.

Her uncle's disappointment made a weight between them as they walked, and she was sorry; she hated not to please him. "Gas lights came to Rockford in eighteen fifty-seven," she offered, but he was too distracted to reply. "Telephones in eighteen-eighty. And the first electric streetcar company in eighteen-eighty also."

Finally he turned to her. "Telegraphs?"

"Eighteen forty-eight. And the phonograph in eighteen seventy-seven."

"Standard Time?" She sensed him beginning to relent.

"Eighteen eighty-three," Charlotte said, with passionate relief, "because of the railroads. Because before, if you went from the East Coast to the West Coast, you had to change your watch two hundred times."

"So you did," Moose murmured, still unnerved by that seizure of rage. It wasn't his; he disowned it. "You did indeed."

Compared with the emptiness of the streets, the room was thick with life. Perhaps two dozen workmen in blue jumpsuits milled at a broad humid bar, heads tipped at a White Sox game unfolding someplace sunny on an overhead TV. Charlotte's entrance with Moose made a ripple of awareness. Her uncle stood inside the door, squeezing rain from his hair and rolling his poncho into a slobbering orange ball.

"Moose," the bartender said. He was a stringy man with thinning hair, a blond mustache, and a slight concavity to his face—a suggestion of missing teeth. "Long time."

For several perilous moments, Moose looked at the speaker without recognition. Then he said, "Teeter" (to Charlotte's relief), and smiled uncertainly. "How odd to see you here."

"Odd?" Teeter ejected the word like a seed. "Been here fourteen years come June. I'm part-owner now."

Moose made the introductions. Jim Teeter. My niece. "We went to high school together," he told Charlotte in an ironic, quizzical tone that came across as obnoxious, but in fact meant her uncle was uneasy.

"Your niece," Teeter said. "She better be older than she looks."

Her uncle frowned; Charlotte sensed the comment landing in his mind with an unpleasant weight. "I just wanted a Coke," she rushed to assure the barman. "We just came in to get out of the rain."

"One Coke," Teeter said. "How about you, Moo-man?"

Moose winced at the epithet. "Beer," he said. "Whatever you've got."

"Old Style do you?" Teeter was already pulling the tap. "So where you been all this time?"

"I teach history over at the college," Moose said, with great effort. "I'm married for the second time."

"How many kids?"

"None, actually."

Teeter glanced at Moose, then slid the beer and Coke across the thickly varnished bar. Moose lifted the glass to his mouth with trembling hands. Charlotte had forgotten how ill at ease he was with other people. "Do you have kids?" she asked Teeter, anxious to lift the burden of conversation from her uncle.

"Three," he told Moose, sounding downcast. "Wife's looking out for number four. Guess I'm supposed to plant a money tree out back." Moose said nothing, just rested his eyes on the ballgame. "Economy's gangbusters, right?" Teeter went on. "Every day you got a new millionaire. Guess I forgot to pick a number."

"Tell me about it," Moose said suddenly. "I'm driving a 'seventy-eight station wagon."

"Mine's an 'eighty-two," Teeter cackled. "Green, looks for absolute shit."

"Mine's blue," Moose said, and grinned. "With *paneling*."

"No way, aw shit! You got me on that," Teeter cried, and they laughed together with a kind of relief. Then Teeter said, "Look at us, right? Thirty years later and so what."

Moose seemed taken aback; Charlotte felt him straining to grasp Teeter's meaning. Finally, with deliberation, he said, "If you're talking about high school, we graduated twenty-three years ago."

"Twenty, thirty."

Moose downed the last of his beer and planted the heavy glass against the bar. "Right," he said in a tight voice. "So what."

"You oughta order up some soup. It's cats and dogs out there."

"Let's sit," Charlotte suggested. She wanted to get her uncle away from Teeter and farther into the bar. She was the only female in the room excepting the waitress, a middle-aged lady in skirt and sneakers, pink lipstick bleeding into a barbed wire of creases around her mouth. The density of men roused in Charlotte an unfamiliar sensation of girlishness; she felt like girls in the lunchroom at East, their breasts and bracelets and feathery hair folded around them like the leaves of a tree. She felt this now about her glasses, the wet tips of her hair. The amber bead, which she fished from inside her sweater and let dangle between the lapels of her raincoat. As she led the way to an empty table, her gaze locked with that of a young black man seated across the room, and she smiled at him.

The waitress arrived with battered menus and a second beer for

Moose. Charlotte wiped her glasses and left them off, letting the room cave in around her. "So, you and Teeter were at East together?" she ventured.

"Yes," Moose said dully. The encounter had drained him. "We played football, both of us."

"Did you win a lot?"

There was a pause. "We won the state championship. My junior year." And now he smiled, unexpectedly.

"Wow," Charlotte breathed, imagining it—those long halls at East, everyone cheering him. "That must've been like being God."

"I guess it was," Moose said, and he smiled again. "God of a fishpond. God of a lily pad. Of course," he added, "you think it's the universe."

The waitress brought his beer and Moose ordered another on the spot. "And then what happened?" Charlotte asked.

He took a long sip. "I opened my eyes," he said. "I opened my eyes and it disappeared. Pop."

He'd never said anything like this before. "It sounds scary," Charlotte said.

"Terrifying." He was looking right at her. "Terrifying, but beautiful, too. Because my head was clear."

"How old were you?"

"Twenty-three. I was sitting by the interstate, looking down. For no reason. I pulled over for no reason."

He was watching her with eyes so bright and distinct that Charlotte saw them clearly even without glasses. Moose took her hand in his. Hot. She had never touched her uncle's hand before, or any part of him. "Charlotte," he said, softly but with great urgency, "I need you to concentrate. I need you to think very, very carefully. Will you do that for me? There's so little time!"

What do you mean? she wanted to ask. So little time for what? But the part of her that monitored her behavior with Moose, eliding all evidence of incomprehension, censored the query.

"But Uncle Moose," she said, leaning close, glancing in Teeter's direction, "how did you change from being like *that*, to now?"

It was the question she had always wanted to ask, the question everyone wanted to ask—her mother most of all. What had happened? Moose clutched her hand. Charlotte felt the tension in her uncle as he struggled to make an answer.

The table joggled slightly, startling Moose so he flinched, nearly upsetting their drinks. Instantly he released Charlotte's hand. She looked up and saw the black man she had noticed before squeezing past their table toward the exit. He smiled at her in recognition. Disoriented, Moose fixed a resentful and suspicious eye on the man as he moved past. Meanwhile, the man's friend, a freckled redhead who was following behind, planted himself in front of their table and waited for Moose to meet his gaze. "You got a problem with Pete?" he said.

"No, I don't have a *problem*," Moose said, in his mocking, nervous voice. "What kind of *problem* would I have?"

"I got no idea. Maybe you're racial."

"Come on, Allen," Pete called back through the crowd. "Say we rock and roll here."

Moose and Allen eyed each other with lush, expectant hostility.

"He can't seem to tear himself away from our table," Moose said loudly, though whether he was speaking to Charlotte, to Pete, or to Allen, his new enemy, was not clear.

"Take your eyes and put 'em someplace else," Allen instructed Moose.

"You want a ride, Al? 'Cause I'm outta here."

"What choice do I have, with you looming over my table like some weird dirigible?" Moose asked.

A silence was falling over the room in gentle phases, as if a speech were about to begin. Charlotte didn't know what "dirigible" meant, but the longer the word hung there, the worse it sounded. "Uncle Moose," she said, and touched his sleeve. He didn't notice.

Moose rose from his chair, a terrible energy coming off him like heat. He was bigger than Allen, but Allen looked stronger, white freckled arms dangling like wrenches from the rolled-up sleeves of his shirt.

Suddenly Teeter was fluttering in their midst. "Whoa, hey, come on kids," he said cheerfully. "You gotta play nice in here, that's the rules. I don't want no trouble." When no one responded, he slung a collegial arm around Moose's shoulders. "C'mon, Moo-man. Aren't you getting kinda old for this shit?"

Moose sloughed Teeter off with a single shudder of impatience. "I'm getting extremely tired," he told him, in a quiet, menacing voice, "of having you tell me how old I am."

Teeter went red, and Allen turned to him. "You know him?" Indicating Moose.

"Sure do," Teeter said sourly. "Stolt my girlfriend in high school. Then he cracked up, if I heard right. Set off a bomb or some such hoo-ha."

Moose punched Teeter in the face so abruptly, with such unequivocal force that the bartender somersaulted backward over a table and clattered to the floor without having uttered a sound.

"No!" Charlotte screamed as several men jerked toward her uncle, a band of anger contracting around him. "Stop!" And then she was plucked from their midst—Pete yanked her out of the way and seized her shoulders to keep her from running back in. "Nothing you can do . . ." he murmured, ". . . gotta play itself . . ."

Moose lunged heedlessly, longingly into the violence, lobbing punches at Allen's face and stomach so the redhead fell, holding his eye, then flinging blows at two or three other men, cuffing them away almost playfully, filling the air with the rusty stench of their blood. He was riotous, free, joyful as Charlotte had ever seen him—as if the excitement she'd felt building in her uncle these past weeks had at last found its perfect expression.

By now, Teeter had heaved himself to his feet. He swiped dirt from his legs and arms with studied indignation, then came at Moose, fast and mean, kneeing him in the gut and dislodging a groan. Moose doubled over. And now the others set upon him ravenously, too many to one, some holding his arms, others assailing his bulk with fists and feet so that each time Moose tried to stand, another blow crumpled him. Charlotte flailed in Pete's grasp, but he clamped her shoulders down as she watched her uncle slide to the floor, screaming, "No! No!" certain he would die, until finally she did twist free, writhed like a newt from Pete's hands and thrust her skinny way into the fighters' midst. She draped herself over the prone heap of her uncle, begging, "Stop! Please! Leave him alone," but she couldn't cover all of Moose, he was far too big and they were still kicking him, getting in where Charlotte couldn't stop them, until Allen went for Moose's head and Charlotte blocked his boot with her wrist.

The pain made her shriek, knocking tears from her eyes. And that stopped it. The men stood back. Charlotte heard Pete, ". . . it's done, just let it go . . ." talking to the others the way she'd heard people whisper into horses' ears to calm them. The pain in her wrist nauseated her, and she held very still, trying not to be sick.

Her uncle felt dead beneath her, mountainous, insensate. Charlotte's uninjured hand was still cupping his head, the chaotic tangle of his hair, his blue-white cheeks. "Oh, God," she kept saying. She was afraid to get up, to leave him exposed. "Oh, my God."

"Shhh. He's gonna be fine," Pete said, and pried her off Moose. Allen and the other brawlers had slunk ineffably away, back into the crowd at the bar, or outside. Teeter, his eye socket already going gray, carried ice packed in a towel and held a few cubes to the back of Moose's neck until he stirred. Then Teeter and Pete together hoisted Moose off the floor and propped him in a chair, where he drooped semi-conscious, blood running from his nose, one eye swollen almost shut. Teeter stuck the towel full of ice in Moose's hand, bent Moose's arm and pressed the ice pack to his swollen eye. He gathered the stray pieces of ice and held them to his own.

Charlotte knelt at her uncle's side. Already she was calmer; he wasn't dead, and he wasn't going to die. "If you give me Aunt Priscilla's number," she said softly, "I'll call her at work."

"No," he said sharply. "Don't."

"But you're—"

"No."

They sat for a very long time, Moose draped in the chair, Charlotte kneeling helplessly beside him while the bar lapsed into willful amnesia, erasing the fight until Charlotte herself could hardly believe it had happened. Pete had gone and Teeter was behind the bar again, black eye and all, pulling the tap. The White Sox scored and everyone clapped. Charlotte felt exiled, heart chattering in her chest, wrist throbbing in her lap.

When Moose was strong enough, they left the bar and walked back through the Water Power District to his station wagon, still parked on Main Street beside the bridge over Kent Creek. The sky was beginning to clear, pink fingers of sunset nudging the dark clouds. "Should I drive?" Charlotte said, amazed at the sound of her calm. She felt scared, strange.

"No," he said. "I'm fine."

She crawled inside his station wagon, pushing aside the old coffee cups and pizza containers that seemed to reclaim the seat each time she left it. Moose started the car and they sat, engine running. A thick, guilty silence packed the car, as if they'd gotten in some awful trouble together, as if it were Charlotte's fault, too. *I did something wrong,* she kept thinking, and felt a queasy shame. Her wrist ached.

"Charlotte, if you wouldn't mind," Moose said at last, stiffly, "I'd prefer you not mention any of this to your mother."

"My mother," she said, stung. "I don't tell her anything."

# Chapter Fifteen

*When the ushers* arrived with their brooms and trash bags and rousted Michael West from his seat, he repaired to the crowded lobby and idled there, gazing at the synthetic red carpet, inhaling salty lungfuls of artificial butter smell while around him moviegoers coursed from other theaters and dispersed. Watching movies left him weak, porous to the world in a way that felt hazardous, as if his skin had been removed. Usually he waited for the feeling to pass before venturing outdoors. It was almost dark, a groggy smudge of pink beyond the shaded windows, puddles of rain suspended on the asphalt.

"Michael?"

A tumble-haired woman in a raincoat: Abby Reece. Michael wondered how long she'd been standing there. "Are you waiting for someone?" she asked.

He smiled, adjusting. "No, I'm just—hanging around. Killing time, I guess."

They had avoided each other at school for many months—or rather, she had avoided him. Michael looked at her sad gray eyes and tried to remember what exactly had happened between them.

"Which movie did you see?" she asked, a bit nervously, and he told her the name. "Any good?"

"I had a mixed response," he said. "I liked the basic premise of a man who plunders deep-sea wreckage for treasure, but I thought Tom Cruise seemed too kind to seize gems from the skeletal necks of the drowned. I did enjoy his conflict with the salvage operation, and I thought Jennifer

Aniston was an unlikely but interesting choice for his adversary and eventual lover. Of course their discovery of a fully furnished bedroom two hundred meters below the sea was preposterous."

Abby nodded, studying him, and Michael wondered if he'd gone on too long. He'd had little practice discussing movies with other people, though nowadays he consumed them heedlessly, rapturously—the moment school ended, after a faculty dinner; all day, sometimes, on weekends. Even the poorly made ones kicked him open effortlessly, invading him with their light and motion and noise, their burning planes and sinking ships and couples destined to find one another and marry after a designated number of hilarious mishaps. He'd become a connoisseur, a seasoned arbiter of car chases and court-martials and crises aboard 747s, a discerning appraiser of talking animals, of drug busts and fistfights and tearful reconciliations, sex scenes, death throes, and simulated high-speed travel in outer space.

"I was going to grab a bite to eat," he told Abby. "Will you join me?"

At the sound of the horn, Charlotte ran from her house and plunged into the melty backseat of Roz's father's Park Avenue, a vaporous tank of hairspray, sour candy, body heat—the smell of her friends—a lost, familiar smell that enfolded her like bathwater the precise temperature of her body. Roselyn twisted around and blew her a kiss. In the backseat, Laurel hugged her tightly. Only Sheila, twitching the radio dial, failed to acknowledge her entrance.

"Whawhawha," Roz said, slapping Sheila's hand away. "I like Oasis."

"Hi, Sheila," Charlotte said, eyeing her friend's slumped shoulders and pale blond hair. She was eating Rollos.

"What happened to your arm?" Laurel asked Charlotte.

"I fell off my bike."

Her wrist had been so sore by the time her uncle dropped her at home late that afternoon that she'd actually shown it to her mother, who examined it carefully. Just a bruise, she thought, but if it was worse tomorrow they would drive to Rockford Memorial for an X-ray. She swaddled Charlotte's forearm in an Ace bandage, whose pressure relieved the pain. Ricky was having dinner at the home of his new—his first—girlfriend, Allison Jones. Charlotte had planned on going to Michael West's tonight; she nearly always did, after seeing Moose. But doing her homework she felt restless, anxious. Strange. Her uncle kept raiding her thoughts, flinging ecstatic punches, then buckling to the floor, spent. She found herself calling her friends for the first time in weeks. They were at Roselyn's, all three, getting ready for a party. "Please," Charlotte told them. "I have an urgent need to be kidnapped."

Now she said again, "Hi, Sheila."

Laurel began hissing into Charlotte's ear, ". . . was supposed to visit her dad in New York but he canceled at the very last minute pluswhich now her mom's selling the—"

Sheila swooped around, her lovely face grimed with fury. "Don't tell my shit to her!"

"Her," Charlotte retorted, indignant. "Who's her?"

Sheila turned back around and ate another Rollo.

"You're so dark," Roselyn scolded Sheila. "It's like, callous."

"Sor-ry," Sheila said, with hostility. "Just because she has five minutes to spend, we're supposed to like fall on the ground with happiness?"

Michael and Abby drove in separate cars to Chili's, where they faced each other across a slab of varnished table and ordered frozen margaritas. The food arrived sizzling on black cast-iron trays, and Michael set upon his ravenously. He'd grown fond of Chili's; the enormity of the portions, the sense that there would always be more regardless of how much one ate— even the predictability of the food instilled in him a deep comfort. He'd developed a monstrous new appetite; it had driven him back to McDonald's many times, where the cheap food stuccoed his insides, plugging the holes of his hunger. He'd eaten at Burger King and Wendy's and Arby's and Taco Bell, had drunk nondairy shakes that were said to contain flour, gobbled onion rings, chicken nuggets, fish sandwiches, synthetic ice cream, until all that remained of his old revulsion was a slight frisson of wickedness as he gorged himself. A new layer of softness had begun to float above his bones where once the skin had stretched tight. Not fat, but a harbinger of fat. He would stand before the mirror and study this new stratum of himself, a widening and settling in his face that amounted to natural disguise. Soon he would begin to exercise, jogging along manicured sidewalks, huffing among rows of tulips, running in circles and then straining to lift hundreds of pounds of weights, cultivating muscles that would adhere to him like expensive clothing. And then his infiltration would be complete.

Abby was studying him over the broad saucer of her margarita. "You seem different, Michael," she said. "I can't figure out how."

"Really?" he said. "I feel the same."

But she was right; at last there was movement within him, a plan taking shape. He experienced it as a burrowing, the tunneling of a small industrious creature wakened after long sleep. He would survive without his anger, after all. More than survive—would thrive, for the absence of anger had left him, in moments, with an almost delirious sense of freedom. And when he glimpsed the part of the world he had come from (occasionally, on the evening news), soaked in rage, locked in anguished and protracted wars, it all looked forced, overwrought. He studied the faces mashed by suffering, the skirmishes and tear-gas clouds and people stunned by rubber bullets and wondered, seriously, whether all of them were pretending. How could anything matter so deeply?

"Wait," Charlotte said, "so now you're all pissed at me?"

No one said anything. The delicious bathwater of her friends' proximity had turned coolly gelatinous.

"I heard you were at school? Like two weeks ago?" Roz said.

"I was, but—" It was the time she'd seen Michael West, or the person who resembled Michael West. "I was."

"You just, like, disappeared at a certain point," Laurel said, with apology.

Charlotte said nothing. After the violence of her afternoon with Moose, her friends' anger felt unbearable, toxic. She knew they were right. She pictured getting out of the car right there, in the middle of traffic, just walking away.

There was a long silence.

"So . . . why tonight?" Sheila said acidly. "You had nothing else to do, so you thought, I'll like spend time with the little people?"

Charlotte flung open the door. They were stopped at a red light on State Street, in a middle lane, almost at Aunt Mary's, where they'd been headed for dessert. She heard the little thump of their surprise as she got out, then ambled calmly among panting Ford Explorers toward the curb.

Roz began honking her horn. She maneuvered into the outer lane and drove next to Charlotte, slowly. She kept honking, and soon the cars behind her were honking, too.

A window slid down. "Get in."

It was Sheila. Charlotte didn't even glance at her.

"Get in, or I'll take shit for it all night."

"That's a reason not to get in."

"Chari?" Sheila said. "Will you please?"

"If I get in, will you get out?"

Charlotte turned to the car. Sheila was grinning.


A universal truth: people loved to speak of their children. "Tell me about your kids, Abby," Michael said. "How're they doing?"

"In Los Angeles, right now. Visiting their father." She rolled her eyes, only partly offsetting their sudden, lustrous cargo of tears. Yes, he remembered now: The husband who had run away to Los Angeles. The little girl whose toes had suctioned to him like a lizard's to a wall.

"Then he hasn't come back."

"Come back?" Abby said, and shook her head. "He has no intention of coming back. He's gotten into the movie business."

Michael received this information with the whole of his body, as if he'd been shoved. "Really," he said, and set down his drink.

"Producing, whatever that means. Some kind of movie-Internet-multimedia-blahbiddyblah."

"What *does* it mean?"

"Who knows? He's optioned a book, he's got someone writing a script. Keeps saying all you need to know is how to tell a story. Which sounds a little pat, but on the other hand, if Darden can do it, or convince people he's doing it, then frankly it can't be all that hard."

Michael smiled, holding very still. "He's making movies?"

"So he tells me."

"He went there without training?"

"He's a litigator! I put the guy through law school!" She smiled, baring anger and white, imperfect teeth.

Michael's whole body tingled, a forest full of breathing animals. "How does he describe it?" he asked carefully.

"Tediously," she said. "He goes on and on about how there's a revolution happening. Keeps talking about cross-pollination and globalization and channels of communication and new media. And 'Renaissance,' that's my favorite. *This is the new Renaissance,* he'll say, like he has the remotest idea what the 'old' Renaissance consisted of."

"What else?"

"*Everything is about to change,*" she intoned. "*In ten years you won't recognize the world we live in. People's lives will be totally different* . . . yeah, right. Like having some life-sized computer screen in your living room showing interactive horror films is going to bring you closer to God. I mean, how about feeding some hungry people? How about paying some attention to the Third World, or even just dirt-poor Americans trying to survive without welfare? For them, life *is* an interactive horror film!"

She looked beseechingly at Michael, and he nodded gently, sympathetically. But he hardly heard her. He was memorizing Darden's phrases.


"I don't have friends there," Charlotte said. "I don't."

They were sitting in a booth at Aunt Mary's, a spectral wariness still flickering among them as they forked their desserts—all but Laurel, who was dancing in "The Corsair" and had ordered a fruit cup. She cut open each black grape and removed the seeds before eating it.

"Bullshit," Sheila said.

"I mean it."

"Then it's a boy," Roselyn declared, with carnivorous approval.

When Charlotte didn't deny it, Roz shrieked until Laurel clapped her mouth shut with the flat of her hand.

"The screamers," Sheila explained to Charlotte, rolling her eyes. "They got bigger, and now she has to have an operation."

"*Might,*" Roselyn corrected her. "Might have to have." She was speaking very softly now. "At East?"

Charlotte hesitated. How to explain her secrecy, her failure to produce the boy for their collective inspection? "No," she said. "He's older."

"College?"

". . . No."

303

The implications of this disclosure sifted over them gradually. "Wow," Roz breathed. "So he's like, a man."

They stared at Charlotte, and she felt herself suspended, afloat in their collective amazement. And guilty as it made her to smuggle forth these bits of contraband, the pleasure of release—of bragging aloud, of telling someone, finally, *what the hell was going on*—more than compensated.

"Is he like . . . married?" Laurel asked.

"No."

"Divorced?"

"Don't know."

"Would we know his name? If you said it?"

Charlotte paused again. She should lie, of course, but she didn't want to lie; she wanted to say the name aloud—finally, to someone. To say it and hear it said. "Probably."

The girls looked baffled. There was a long, circuitous silence.

"Is he . . . famous or something?" Laurel asked, in a small voice.

Charlotte laughed, but the others regarded her with wistful awe. Anything had become possible. "That's completely screwy," she said. But watching her friends, she felt the tiny strands of their conviction affix to her like silk. For an instant she saw herself differently—someone glamorous, whose life was crammed with remarkable event. A person she herself would envy. And Charlotte grasped something then, for the very first time: people would believe almost anything.

"Look at me," she said, serious now. "You guys? Yoo-hoo. Look."

They did, all three. In thoughtful silence.

"She's blushing," Sheila said.

"Meanwhile, he did come out here and pick up the kids," Abby said. "I wouldn't send them alone on the plane, they're just too small. And that was great. I mean, they need a dad." And here she looked away.

"How long have they been in L.A.?"

"Four days," she said. "They're in love—they don't want to come home." Again, that quivering brightness; tears, Michael thought, and hoped they wouldn't fall. "Colleen says on the phone, 'Mommy, it's warm every day here. You should come, too.' I guess he lives right by the ocean."

"Maybe you should," he said. "Go there, too."

"Never!" Abby said fiercely, and the pressure of her smile finally shoved the tears from her eyes, a single strand veering haplessly down each cheek. "The people out there have no souls. They're not really people—they've got plastic in their faces, their legs, their breasts. Even the men, they put it in their calves to give their legs a better shape. I mean, these are not human beings in the traditional sense." She blotted her eyes with a napkin. "How could I live in a place like that?"

Michael crammed a last bit of fajita into his mouth and washed down the chicken and green peppers with margarita slush. The food made sweat prick to the surface of his face. He was tired of Abby, of her anger. It felt tedious, like something not just he but all the world would soon be rid of.

"The good news," she said lightly, as if in apology, "is I'm finally getting some money out of the guy. I reupholstered the entire living room, even the rocking chair! Now I'm redoing the outside, putting flower beds in the front, and in back? That big concrete patio with the grill? I'm having them jackhammer that away, and I'm putting in grass."

Michael listened with approval. He remembered the area, and she was right, grass would be far, far better than concrete. He swilled the last of his drink and wiped a napkin over his hot, pounding face. Then he had an idea: "You ever thought of doing prairie?" he asked.

He walked Abby to her car under a black sky, a big spongy moon off to one side. He kissed her cheek and received in exchange a puzzled look, as if she were remembering before, and wondering why—or why not.

"Thanks," he said, "for keeping me company."

"Thank you for dinner. It was perfect timing—I've been a little lost without the kids."

How did she survive, Abby Reece, with her transparent face? How had the world not stamped her into pieces and ground her to a fine, glittering silt? Yet here she was, intact, tears in her eyes and a heart so tender that Michael imagined he overheard its gentle beating; she had survived, and showed every sign of continuing to do so. And there had been a time, he knew—perhaps just a moment—when exhaustion had tempted him to lay down his small bundle at the threshold of Abby's flat yellow house, to uncoil himself among the modest dimensions of her life. And then the girl had come along and startled him, distracted him. Yes, he had Charlotte to thank for the fact that now, as a plan amassed within him, he would not have to leave Abby Reece and her children behind, not stun them with his sudden, inexplicable departure.

"Howard told me you aren't coming back next year," she said, looking up at him in the darkness.

"No." *A revolution is happening.*

"You're teaching somewhere else?"

"I'm not sure," he said. "I think . . . probably not."

"What will you do?"

"I haven't decided. Something different. Something new." *Everything is going to change.*

"That sounds exciting," she said.

Michael nodded, looking into her eyes. He was eager to be rid of her. At last she got in her car, and he waved to her as she pulled away.


Charlotte could hear the party, a bass line seeping up through the car, thumbing her insides. Laurel opened her shiny pale blue purse, whose hue exactly matched her fingernail polish. After some feral digging, she excavated a lipstick and applied a blossom of color to her lips. She offered the lipstick to Charlotte, who shook her head.

"Aw, live a little," Laurel said. And with breathtaking precision, considering that Roselyn was parking the car in which they sat, Laurel seized Charlotte's shoulder with one hand and used the other to push the soft nub across her mouth.

"Gimme," Sheila commanded from the front seat, clutching for the lipstick. "Hey," seeing Charlotte. "You've got lips."

Laurel was applying her blusher, a lunar, sepia glitter in the streetlight. "No," Charlotte groaned, recoiling as her friend came at her with the brush. It grazed her cheeks, soft as mink.

"Mascara next. Hush hush," Laurel said. "Or your face'll be totally debalanced." It was hard not to flinch—Charlotte's eyes felt so exposed without her glasses. But there was a clean divide in her, one part simulating disgust so the other could accept the mascara with impunity.

"Nuh-uh," Laurel said, swiping Charlotte's glasses away when she tried to replace them. "That'll wreck it."

"You realize that I'm totally blind," Charlotte said.

"There's nothing to see in there anyway."

They left the car and wandered toward the music among ranch-style houses and waxen golf course pines lit from below, past open garage doors exhaling smells of motor oil and cut grass and rindy walnuts still in boxes from last fall. They paused under a tree to relight Sheila's half-joint. The pot, in conjunction with Charlotte's uncorrected eyesight, made her feel like a stand-in for herself. Laurel brushed Charlotte's hair with a small neon-green plastic brush, and she felt it lift slightly from her head.

Michael stood alone in the parking lot, an asphalt version of the empty sky. A clear, cool night, a smear of light to the east, where Chicago was. The emptiness of this land and sky had ceased to trouble him; they no longer felt empty in the way they had. The plastic signs were everywhere—Mobil, Holiday Inn, Kentucky Fried Chicken—holding him like the fingers of a hand that would reach as far as he might wish to go. He pulled his car onto State Street, heading west, then took a right, then another right onto Squaw Prairie Road, still amazed at how quickly civilization yielded to countryside: fields, tractors in silhouette, long rows of freshly turned soil, other fields abandoned, still crowded with last year's dead stalks. Old barns like ghost ships. He crossed over the interstate and soared beyond it, heading for a building site he'd visited once before. It glowed: a cloud of low, flickering light. A condominium village at an early stage of construction that was weirdly akin to devastation—the sort he'd once dreamed of causing himself.

Michael parked his car and went to look at the development. Nothing had changed since his last visit: four sample condominiums were poised among acres of dirt and curved, sparkling sidewalks. The houses were jaunty ersatz Victorians, each one distinct in size and shape but accented with identical festive trim, mailboxes saluting out front. A vast constellation of Victorian lampposts haunted the empty sidewalks, leaking a faint lunar glow from their flame-shaped bulbs.

Michael followed one of the sidewalks to its desultory end, then kept walking, trudging through loose, turned earth that worked its way inside his shoes, until eventually he reached three strands of barbed wire demarcating the outer limit of the development. Beyond these lay a planted field, rows of shoots just lifting their heads from the soil. From planted crops to condominiums: three strands of barbed wire abridging a gap of millennia. Wind cackled around him. *Cross pollinization.* No. Pollination. *Cross polliniz—*no! *Globalization, pollination. This is the new Renaissance.*

*All you need to know is how to tell a story.*

Well, that he could certainly do. That he'd been doing all life.


The door to the party house was open. Inside flourished the sort of event made possible only by a blanket absence of parents, not an out-for-the-evening absence but an out-of-town absence. A primordial murk, a loamy, humid stench of beer and carpeting, a ravaged kitchen where four guys were playing soccer with a beleaguered cantaloupe. A stereo heaved up the Verve's "Bittersweet Symphony" at disorienting volume. Charlotte was astonished to find it all still here, undiminished by the passage of months or her own lengthy absence. Head down, she avoided people's eyes at first, then discovered that she couldn't see them even when she looked. The world slurred, buckled, smashed pleasantly, the lashes of her eyes felt heavy, coated like sticky buds, and her lips and cheeks were hot. As she moved among the unrecognizable faces, her hesitation yielded to a marvelous detachment, a sense that she wasn't herself anymore, so none of it mattered. She carried her face like an object newly made, still wet, in danger of smearing or losing its shape as she followed her friends downstairs to a basement rec room populated by boys in baggy attire who nodded their sparsely bearded chins in accord with the rap music stomping from a boombox. And here was the keg, the party's faulty, intermittent heart, a guy squeezing out cup after cup of foam, complaining bitterly about the pump.

"Yo, Tupac!" someone bellowed.


Stories? You want stories? I got a doozy, said the voice of a Hollywood producer as Michael envisioned him, a voice cribbed from movies and TV, a man who took meetings beside a pool with slices of fruit on his cheeks and chamomile teabags over his eyes. *Listen,* he said,

We've got a guy from one of those crappy parts of the world where people get shot up every other day—Lebanon, let's say, but hell it could be anywhere, Sri Lanka, Nigeria. Sudan. Say Lebanon's southern coast—Tyre—cute little tourist town until everyone started gunning it to pieces. He's from a middle-class family, Shiites. No, you clown, *shee*-ite, two syllables. It's one of those Muslim sects. Now our guy, he's a prodigy. Math whiz, gobbles up numbers like most kids eat M&Ms. Goes to college in Beirut, honors in every class, brilliant career ahead of him yadda yadda. Gets married, has a kid. Then bam. Chucks the whole thing. It's the early eighties, the Israelis're in South Lebanon trying to clear out the PLO, and our guy joins a bunch of Shiites that's trying to get rid of the Israelis. Hezbollah, you've heard of them. Scary folks. Extremists in the extreme. But our guy *wants* that—see, he's mad. Pissed. Becomes a fundamentalist, starts baying at the moon or whatever the hell they do. No booze, no girls in bathing suits. Then poof, he disappears. Wife, kid, folks, they all wait terrified. Never hear another word—finally they figure he must be dead.

Is he really dead? No, he's in Iran. It's a Shiite majority over there so they like Hezbollah, send 'em money, ammo, whole bit. Our guy gets noticed by the higher-ups because he's got this knack for languages, picks 'em up like that, accents, jargon, dialects, the whole tamale, plus he hates—*despises*—America. Thinks we've got a plot to control the world with our "cultural exports," which you know what that means: how come our nice girls start whipping off their head scarves every time Brad shows up on the screen?

So these Iranians, they've got an extremist chameleon on their hands who hates America—but hates it. So whaddo they do? Set him up somewhere, Africa, let's say—Kenya—gets married all over again, new name, new history, starts a business doing import-export. But really, he's part of an intelligence network, people who let's just say our health and happiness aren't real big on their priority list. But our guy gets restless fast, he's got all this hate inside him and it's eating him up and he wants to *do* something. Wants action! So when Hezbollah doesn't move fast enough, he disappears again. Poof, can't find him. Hooks up with some more splintery types, coupla rich guys in the deep background pulling strings. They want to send him to America, do some real damage. Horse's mouth, right?

Whack the Holland Tunnel, whack the White House. Hey, don't kid yourself—this stuff goes on! He relocates to Libya, Afghanistan, wherever. Doesn't matter. New name, new wife. Then at a certain point the guys in the shadows say go. To America. Poof, he's out the door. Doesn't look back. Buncha phony documents in his hand. And where does he wind up? One guess. New fucking Jersey—how about that?

Charlotte followed Roz through sliding glass doors to the backyard, tonguing her cup of foam as she stepped into a familiar grind of wood against concrete, a sound like an electric saw in reverse. She made out a swimming pool girded by slouching, comma-shaped sentries, boys without jackets spurting one at a time up the sides of the empty pool and landing on its rim. Charlotte wondered if Ricky might be among them, her blurred eyes fumbling in search of her brother, but no, he'd lost his skateboard back in January and refused to buy another, even though Charlotte had offered to help pay for it.

Resting her screamers, Roz was uncharacteristically quiet.

"Whose house is this?" Charlotte asked her.

Okay, I know what you're thinking (said the voice), I'm reading your mind as we speak. What's this story about? You're thinking, God help us if it's terrorism, because *Nightmare in Gaza* tanked and *Middle East Massacre* barely broke even, including international.

("Paul Lofgren's," Roz said.)

You're thinking God forbid this is some kind of history of the Arab-Israeli conflict, I mean not even Spielberg's taken that one on, and he can make just about anything taste sweet. You're saying, How can we root for this guy? He's a jerk, a fanatic. A loony. What kind of guy walks out on family after family? It's not human, right? Okay, look. The movie's got nothing to do with history. Wigs, horses, sex scenes where they have to paw through all that lace—this isn't like that. This is about *self-discovery*. It's one man's personal history!

And sure enough, Charlotte made out Paul Lofgren inside the pool, grinding up against the edge. Roz's sort-of-boyfriend came outside and bit her cheek and she went away with him, leaving Charlotte among the bevy of skateboarding spectators, one of whom, the guy beside her, was starting to look familiar. Charlotte stared at him with the brazenness of the nearly blind until at last he looked back. "Hey," he said, and she recognized the voice. Scott Hess.

Charlotte turned back to the pool, mortified.

"Hell—o—o." Scott was waving an arm in front of her eyes. Except the arm was not an arm, but a white triangular shape. An arm in a sling. "We're twins," he said.

She'd forgotten about her Ace bandage. Now she lifted it, returning his goofy salute. And realized, then, that Scott Hess had no idea who she was.

"Happened to your arm?" he asked.

"I got caught in the middle of a fight."

"No way," he said, admiringly. "Mine's from sliding into second. It's not a break, just a really bad sprain. But I'm probably out for the season, 'cause swinging a bat is like totally out of the question."

"Mine's just bruised," Charlotte said, and smiled a little helplessly.

"Could be a sprain," Scott mused. "It's a fine line between a bruise and a sprain, I mean basically it just comes down to inflammation. You get much swelling?"

"Not really."

"Mine? The first day? It was like, three times the normal size at least. My girlfriend was like, don't come near me with that thing."

Charlotte laughed, but it sounded like someone else, as if her makeup were laughing.

"What's your name?" Scott asked, and she hesitated, still afraid this was all some multilayered joke at her expense. "Melanie," she finally said, and experienced a thrill that gave her gooseflesh.

"You don't go to Baxter."

"No," she said. "East."


Self-discovery! Hear me out. Who is our guy exactly? He hates Americans, that's all we really know. But see, where does he make sense? Where does he fit? Over in Europe, they're still yammering about who took out whose castle three hundred years ago, who's got the nicest accent. Who cares? We're heading into the twenty-first century. With us it's the opposite: Build your own castle, make up an accent if it rocks your boat. Start from scratch. And that's our guy to a T! That's what he's been doing from the beginning. Don't you get it? He's *American!* He's been American all his life, the whole time he was hating our guts! Which is what he finally figures out. The self-discovery. Which is what this movie's about!

"I'm Scott."

"Hello, Scott."

And now he was shaking her hand, injured arm to injured arm, exchanging with Charlotte a secret intimate handshake of the fallen. She went along, laughing a little uncontrollably.

"How long you have to wear it?" he asked.

"I don't know. I haven't even gone to the doctor."

"Oh. Hey. Mel. Lemme give you some advice." Scott was serious now, with serious warnings to dispense. "I know how it is," he said, "no time and all that, you're like hey, everything's fine, whatever, but freshman year? I twisted my knee and I didn't go to the doc for like two weeks . . . ?"

(Now the boisterous narrator went abruptly silent, blew away like dust, leaving Michael West alone beside the barbed-wire fence.)

". . . and no shit, they said if I waited *one more day*, I could've had permanent damage in the cartilage."

"Wow," Charlotte said. "Permanent damage!" She was gulping laughter, inhaling it, popping it with her ears, blinking it back inside her head. She felt the old excitement of talking to strangers, except that Scott Hess was the opposite of a stranger: he was the boy who'd taken her virginity in under five minutes, then tossed her out of his car. But Charlotte wasn't that girl anymore. She'd cut ties with that humiliation, and was Melanie now. Who wore makeup. *She* was the stranger. Scott Hess had nothing on her.

"And as it is, the doc says I might end up with knee problems later on, you know, like when I'm older and stuff, from the injuries and also just the wear and—"

"Scott," she interrupted, "that's enough whining for one night."

He peered at her, startled, then laughed—a nervous, wheezy laugh. "Funny," he said. "Very funny, Melanie."

"Actually, I'm serious," she said, but she was laughing, too. She and Scott were laughing together. "I have to get out of here," she said.

The voice gone, its garish performance complete, Michael found himself alone at the edge of a condominium development surrounded by perfect silence. And here came the terror, raw, wild: a panic whose shadow he'd sensed flickering near him these past months was on him, now, at last. He scaled the barbed wire and began to run across the planted field, sprinting over acres of loose earth, running anywhere, away, the opposite direction of where he'd come from. They'd won, stamped out his anger and filled his head with this poison—*listen to it! Listen to it.* The scorpion sting had erased his real thoughts and replaced them with a plan to go to Los Angeles and *make movies*—exchange plots for plots! Spread the poison even further. They'd won! Running, he tripped, fell sprawling among short green stalks and lay there whole minutes, heart punching the soil. Then he turned his head to look at the moon, cooler now, white, the precious moon; "Listen to it," he whispered, beseeching the moon, "they're controlling my thoughts." But in English, always in English. He thought in English, dreamed in English. It was too late. The other languages were gone, his past was gone and so was his rage, it had vanished with the conspiracy. Because there was no conspiracy—no "them" in this nation of believers. Only us.

Charlotte left the swimming pool and pushed open a sliding glass door at the far end of the house. She slipped inside a white-curtained master bedroom, elongated shapes of skateboarders flung like shadow puppets over the walls. From the bedroom she reached a hallway and began opening doors, looking for—what? A place to laugh, except her laughter was gone, had burned away, leaving a little pile of ashes in her throat.

She opened doors: A girl's room, four people gurgling over a bong amidst hundreds of stuffed animals. A boy's room—Paul's? Paul's brother's? Did Paul Lofgren have a brother? It was empty. Charlotte went in and shut the door and sat on the bed, breathing the odor of teenage boy, sweat, cedar, mildew, Juicy Fruit. Something herbal—pot maybe. She lay back on the bed and shut her eyes.

---

Slowly, Michael rose to his feet. The panic had passed through him and gone. He began walking slowly back through the planted field toward the nimbus of light that first had drawn him there.

Charlotte pulled her glasses from her purse and wiped them clean, restoring them to her face so the room crashed into focus, a dresser crammed with trophies, silver soccer balls affixed to feet, gold hockey sticks soldered to hands, Blackhawks posters attached to walls along with several Baxter flags. The world remade itself, and she was Charlotte Hauser once again, from Rockford, Illinois. Who wore glasses. Scanning the reconstituted room in which she sat, she noticed a familiar shape beneath the dresser and knelt on the carpet to pull it out. A skateboard. A Tony Hawk, in fact. On its underside, in neat, felt-tipped capital letters, the name "RICKY HAUSER."

Charlotte hefted the board under her arm and departed Paul's room, shutting the door behind her. She left the house, navigating among boys who floated aside like inner tubes on a lake to let her pass.

Michael climbed back over the barbed-wire fence. Beyond it he saw the sample Victorian houses, the fake gas lamps with their flame-shaped bulbs. In the distance he made out his car, parked where he had left it.

Outside, Charlotte walked some distance from Paul's house before setting down the board and tentatively mounting it. She'd ridden Ricky's skateboard before, and it wasn't that far to her house. As Michael made his way toward the sparkling sidewalks, a calm began to rise in him. Yes, he thought. He wasn't lost. His car was right there, in the lamplight.

Charlotte pushed off, working her legs, feeling the wind along her arms, holding them out like the scarecrows you still saw, sometimes, in the fields of corn.

He wasn't lost. He was home.

# Chapter Sixteen

*Excepting last August,* during the accident, I had not been back to Rockford in seven years, following a visit I'd terminated prematurely after a shouted exchange of insults with my brother-in-law during Roast Beef Night at the country club. Yet the drive west on I-90 from Chicago to Rockford was intensely familiar: the rusted, jiggling trucks that looked hopelessly irreconcilable with the digital age, tarps fastened over their cargoes of dirt, of old tires; the freestanding mirrored office cubes that seemed not just postindustrial but posthuman; the overpasses with their old beige McDonald's built in the sixties, when fast food was still racy, cosmopolitan. Every few miles, a thirty-cent toll basket would materialize before me like a recurring dream, and I would toss thirty cents down its mechanical gullet and wait for the barrier to rise.

"How does it feel," Irene asked, "making this drive again?" She sat beside me, fiddling with the radio on the cherry-red Grand Am we'd rented at the airport. The Chicago stations were just beginning to fade.

I tried to consider the question. How did it *feel*? But almost immediately, the breathless narrator who had taken up a pampered existence in one lobe of my brain (red curtains, ostrich feather slippers) began piping in her own treacly reply: `It had been nearly a year since the devastating event, and oh, the pain Charlotte felt on returning to the scene, the anguish of seeing those same fields scarred by terrible memories . . .` and as she spewed this dreck, tilting her face for the overhead camera, I felt not just unable to speak, but unable to feel. "Like nothing," I said. "I could be absolutely anywhere."

Irene didn't write, which disappointed me. When many minutes passed without the scratch of her pen, I felt a mounting sense of urgency.

We were visiting Rockford this afternoon in early June at the behest of Thomas Keene, "gathering visuals," as he put it. An all-expenses-paid trip to the middle of nowhere, so Irene could photograph and videotape the house where I grew up, the cemetery where Ellen Metcalf and I used to smoke, my grade school, high school, country club; Dr. Fabermann in his surgical scrubs, Mary Cunningham and her moss-crammed fishpond, and most vitally, the stretch of interstate where the accident had happened—the field where I'd landed in my burning car.

Last week, Thomas had sent a professional photographer to my apartment: Randall Knapp, a solemn, beturtlenecked fellow with a single earnest crease running straight up the middle of his face, beginning at his cleft chin, advancing along the points of his lips and concluding in two deep grooves between his beseeching eyebrows. "Let's try it without the smile," he'd importuned woefully as I sat smoking on my sectional couch. "Remember, you've lost everything. You don't know how you're going to earn a living. There. Good. Hang your head," all in a gentle murmur that seemed calibrated to coax a reluctant partner through a sequence of daunting sexual positions. "Lose the pose," he crooned in the bathroom, shooting close-ups of my face as I parted my hair to rub vitamin E oil onto my surgical scars, when in fact I'd stopped doing this months ago. "There's no glamour here," he chided me softly, "this is sad, this is a sad, private moment. Yes. There. Looking in the mirror like, Who am I?"

I was so disheartened by the time we adjourned to my balcony that I shuffled to the railing and stood motionless, staring at the river below. A berserk cry jackknifed me into a cringe, nearly pitching me over the edge. Shaken, clutching the railing, panting fearfully, I turned to find Randall Knapp in extremis behind his camera. "Yes! Great!" he yelled, shooting madly through his ululations, "Like that! Frownier. Bunch up your hands on the rail. Awkward, frightened—like that! Beautiful! Yes! Despair! God! Yes! Yes! Yes!"

I endured these indignities for a reason that was infinitely complex yet capable of being named in a single word: money. Staggering quantities of money were shortly to come my way, according to Thomas; the media potentates before whom he'd dangled my story were responding to my "character," and phrases like "bidding war," "TV series" and "publishing tie-in" (which apparently meant a book) had been uttered in conjunction with my name. As the sphincter of other people's excitement tightened around me for the second time in my life, I spoke to Thomas as often as I once had spoken to Oscar. The sensation was familiar, of course, from my earlier brush with fame, but with a difference: then, I had existed in a state of pure giddy anticipation, but now I felt a constant twitch of anxiety, as if something ominous were stirring in my peripheral vision. When I tried to stare it down, it vanished, but no sooner had I glanced away than it was back, skittering in one corner of my eye.

After Elgin, the mirrored buildings melted away into fields—bright, iridescent green corn, burnt-orange soybeans. Each one appeared haphazard, disorderly until you hit that angle from which the secret of its perfect geometry was revealed—a dimly remembered pleasure from my childhood—long clean lines like spokes of a wheel extending outward from my eye.

"We're getting close," I told Irene. "Close to where it happened."

"I was thinking we'd save the accident until later," she said. "Unless you want to stop."

"We can save it forever," I said, applying this toward the quota of ironic, curmudgeonly remarks that I now understood were typical of me. Sure enough, Irene took a note.

When the feathery plaint of a cell phone issued from her bag, her face underwent a contraction of unease. The caller was nearly always Thomas—he'd given her the phone so he could reach her easily, now that her spring-term teaching had ended and she was writing not just me but two Ordinaries. "Hello?" she answered with apprehension, but already a shiny simulacrum of cheer was hardening over her hesitancy, culminating now in the utterance "Hihowareyou?" A bright disk of greeting.

"Hihowareyou?" It was Thomas.

"Yes," Irene said, "we were just . . . are we getting close to Rockford? We're fairly close." Then she lapsed into silence, as was usually the case when she spoke to Thomas. Listening.

One of Irene's new Ordinaries happened to be Pluto. "I have three words for you on Pluto," Thomas told her during one of our many recent visits to his office. "Dickens. Dickens. Dickens."

"You mean . . . victim of circumstance," Irene said.

"Exactly."

"Living below his—"

"You got it."

"So his fortunes will improve. They have to."

"Bingo," Thomas said.

Irene was starting to scare me.

She wouldn't talk to me about Pluto—said it was breaking his confidence—but Pluto and I gossiped tirelessly about Irene: Was she as straitlaced as she seemed, or was some shock of wildness hidden in her? Was her husband really a genius, or just a loser? What color were her bathroom tiles? And why was she so quiet lately; had we started to bore her?

Irene folded up her phone and sat in silence. Contact with Thomas left her disoriented, as if she'd been jostled by a crowd. "He still wants to come," she finally said.

"Why?" I objected. "What's he going to do, give me a tour of my hometown, which he's never seen in his life?"

"I cannot imagine," she said, in a tone of wonderment that Thomas often induced in Irene. "He keeps talking about movie cameras."

She leaned into the heels of her hands and shut her eyes. I had thought, after our fight and reconciliation, that Irene and I would become closer, like sisters. We hadn't. Something had shifted or fallen or failed between us, and what we had become, instead, were professionals. Fellow employees of Extra/Ordinary.com—comrades, yes, but not friends. Our very employment seemed to isolate us from each other in a way that brought to mind my professional beauty days, when I'd been too beholden to the rich homeowners who made my life possible to afford an allegiance to someone else as beholden as I.

I exited the interstate onto East State Street, the five-mile tentacle

Rockford had extended over many years to greet it. *"Voilà!"* I told Irene. "Feast your eyes."

Even as a child, riding home with my mother and Grace after a Saturday in Chicago, new dresses and Frango mints from Marshall Field's packed carefully in our trunk, lunch at the Walnut Room still alive in our minds—even then, when the drive between Rockford and Chicago had encompassed the entire trajectory of my known world, arriving at State Street's outer reaches, at that point practically rural, had roused in me not the lilt of home but a flat dead drone inside my head. Even then, I experienced my return to Rockford as a submersion, a forfeiture of the oxygen of life. And with every subsequent return there had been a flattening, an incursion of dreariness, as I remembered what I had come from and faced it again.

Except now. Today, a silly joy flopped at my heart as I drove past the Clocktower Hotel with its "Museum of Time," past the "Welcome to Rockford" sign, past the Courtyard Inn, the Holiday Inn, the Bombay Bicycle Club, Burger King, Country Kitchen, Red Roof Inn, Gerry's Pizza, Mobil, Century 21, Merrill Lynch, Lowe's Gardening and Home Depot. I felt proud of Rockford for appearing on cue and playing its part with such conviction. I had told Irene it would be blighted, bloated, vacant, and now Rockford heaped upon us a quintessentially awful American landscape, the sort of vista that left Europeans ashen-faced: flat, hangar-sized windowless buildings; a swarm of garish plastic signs; miles of parking lot crammed with big American cars throwing jabs of sunlight off their fenders and hubcaps. It was a land without people, save for a few insect-sized humans sprinkled among the parking lots like stand-ins from an architectural scale model, humans diminished to quasi-nonexistence by the gargantuan buildings and giant midwestern sky, pale blue, dotted with tufts of cloud, vast and domineering as skies in Africa.

At last Irene's pen was moving. Pool-o-rama, Tumbleweed, Stash O'Neill's, Happy Wok . . . I felt proud! Proud of my hometown! Of its hokey ethnic restaurants, of its meticulous obliteration of the natural world. Of the vertiginous sense that we could be anywhere in America and find these same franchises in this exact order. Of Rockford's scrupulous effacement of any lingering spoor of individuality, uniqueness!

I had booked rooms for us at the Sweden House, nearer the river on East State Street and always the motel of choice among my visiting relations. After Irene and I checked in, I gazed out the window of my single room at the Sweden House's faux-alpine façade, its little flags bearing generic coats of arms. I breathed smells of carpeting and Lysol and old cigarettes and braced myself for the familiar sensation of entombment. The Rockford thud. **She sensed the possibility like a proverbial shoe waiting to drop, and it added fuel to the already smoldering fires of her uneasiness as she paced the room like a caged animal . . .** Oh, shut up, I thought.

I knocked on Irene's door, which was next to mine. She was sitting on her bed beside her unopened suitcase, doing absolutely nothing. "Are you okay?" I asked.

"Fine," she said, with a blank look.

"Feel like going for a walk?"

"Sure."

"Actually," I said, "people here don't really walk. But we can try."

It was a misty, humid day. The air smelled of motor oil. We left the Sweden House and walked alongside several lanes of traffic toward Alpine Road. "Is this the downtown?" Irene asked, opening her notebook.

"No, no," I said. "That's west, across the river. But no one goes there anymore."

"So . . . is there a center?"

"Not really," I said, and she took a note.

Aunt Mary's, my favorite diner and bakery in Rockford, had undergone a disappointing facelift since my last visit, its big flabby booths replaced by glass-topped tables accented with slender bottles of olive oil. When we'd ordered, Irene smiled at me and said, "So, how is it, being back?"

This sort of exchange had become so routine between us that I hardly noted its friendly packaging; it registered simply as: "What've you got?" And now the lepidopterist to whom I'd subcontracted the job of preserving my thoughts and memories for delivery to Irene appeared with her samples pristinely embalmed, iridescent wings pinned flat against velvet: Driving into Rockford as a child. Seeing the perfect geometry of the cornfields. The Walnut Room, the Frango mints. The Rockford thud. Nowadays I remembered things constantly (I was being paid to remember); I panned, I grubbed, I fished, I lunged for recollections with a net; I plundered my own thoughts as recklessly as any oil baron ramming his way through pristine landscapes, convinced there would always be more. And in the moment of speaking these memories aloud, I disowned them. They sounded false to me—invented, exaggerated. They reminded me of advertising.

Irene took notes.

Her cell phone rang, provoking the usual spasm of dread in her face. "Hello?" she answered, and I knew instantly that the caller was not Thomas but her husband. "Hi, baby," she said, the phrase a tender bundle of sadness and worry packed inside something mysterious, something that brought to mind warm rooms with curtains pulled. Intimacy, I guessed.

I left the table so they could talk in peace. When we'd first come in, I had noticed a man who looked familiar; now I took another pass at him. He sat alone, two coffee mugs and several empty glasses vying for space at his table amidst an open book and a yellow legal pad, upon which he was furiously writing. It was Moose. He appeared much the same—still handsome, though heavier; older now, of course. I veered toward his table preparing to say hello, to laughingly reintroduce myself, but even as I approached, I felt tremors of misgiving. Moose seemed altered. On a Thursday afternoon in the fortyish year of his life, he was alone at Aunt Mary's, in rumpled clothes, scribbling in a kind of frenzy. And whatever story it was that I'd heard about him began wafting back. Some bizarre episode of violence.

By now I was standing at his table. Moose jerked up his head and looked at me fearfully. I had slept with him, of course, but I had no memory of that—what I remembered was my first glimpse of Moose on my front lawn, in slanted sunlight, tossing our sprinkler head in the palm of his hand with an air of bemused investigation. I scanned his skittish brown eyes for some link to that regal, confident boy. Nothing. And I, of course, was unrecognizable. We stared at each other, two strangers. "I'm sorry," I faltered, and moved away.

Back at the table I sat, breathing shakily. "That was Moose," I told Irene. "Ellen Metcalf's brother. Something happened to him."

Irene turned to look, taking notes. I composed myself and used her phone to call Grace, from whom I learned, to my amazement, that Frank's grudging willingness to let us photograph his home had blossomed inexplicably into an invitation to dinner. This rash of hospitality I could only attribute to the power of the *New York Post*, which Irene and I had invoked rather than try to explain what we were actually doing here. In fact, we'd resurrected the same bogus pretext she had originally used to dupe me: a story about a model with a damaged face; her background, her feelings, her struggles to adjust. And it was only now, at Aunt Mary's, as Irene and I hammered out the final details of this lie ("Okay, we'll say I called your agency." "We'll say it's a story about identity."), that I was struck by the fact that it was no lie—the story did exist, Irene was writing it; there was even talk of newspaper serialization!

"You know, I think maybe you're clairvoyant," I said, regarding Irene in real astonishment. She smiled, avoiding my eyes. "I'm serious," I said, "Have you ever done that before, made something up and then it came true?"

"Jesus, let's hope not," she said, glancing out the window. Light fell across her face from one side, making deep shadows. And as she pushed the hair behind her ears, I glimpsed a catastrophic change to her shadow self: a degeneration from the dancing sylph of months ago, when we'd first met, to a lank, dreary presence—resigned to some deep unhappiness. This apparition so shocked me that I set down my glass and forced myself to look again—No, see? It's gone, I told myself. I was staring.

Irene turned away. "Knock it off, Charlotte," she said.

My sister's new home, which I had seen only in pictures, was part of a brand-new development known as White Forest. "East of the interstate?" I'd exclaimed when she told me where it was. "You'll be practically in Beloit!" But east of the interstate was where people were building these days, Grace informed me, now that the older farmers were dying off and their children were selling the farms to developers to avoid the taxes. A twinkling sign amidst the cornfields alerted us to a freshly paved road, which we followed into a saddle-shaped oasis of verdant knolls whose bright grass offset the scalding whiteness of perhaps two dozen columned colonials. There were no trees yet in White Forest, but a legion of skinny saplings no higher than my waist cowered under a scourge of wind that lashed at them from the miles of flat surrounding landscape. We nosed along a serpentine drive in search of my sister's address.

My brother-in-law appeared first, his gut leading the way with the burly insistence of a face. In my mind, Frank Jones embodied a certain physical crudeness: hands like shovel heads, side-of-beef face, a ditch where his navel should have been, so I was always startled to behold the nearly adolescent delicacy of his features. He was a roofer, or a roofer-cum-businessman who now managed several roofing franchises to the tune of two hundred grand a year, according to Grace.

"Hiya, Charlotte," he said, not bothering to kiss me hello, which I appreciated. He introduced himself to Irene, who greeted him with her new, inscrutable cheeriness. I had a feeling Frank would like Irene; she wasn't stylish enough to offend him.

Grace and the kids came tumbling from the house, Pammy and Allison sealing me in their arms without quite looking at me, hesitant to behold this reconfiguration of their glamorous Aunt Charlotte; Jeremy, the youngest, whom I'd never seen in person, swerving away and attaching himself, limpet-like, to his father's chest. The wind set upon us with a roar, yanking conversation from our mouths, making the hair leap from our heads as we fought our way into the house.

"Wind's godawful," Frank apologized to Irene, "but once these trees get some height, they'll stop it dead."

Indoors, Grace pulled me into a laundry room and stared rapturously at my face. "I can hardly believe how much better you look!" she said, seizing my hands. My younger sister was one of the few people in my experience who was genuinely capable of beaming, and she beamed at me now in her jeans and pink sweatshirt whose white decal read "Sexy Moms." The wedding ring hung loose on her thin red hand. "You look like nothing ever happened," she said. "It must've been that second operation."

"Oh, Grace. Do you think so?" I asked, fending off the flock of acid replies I felt beating their wings against my skull: *Tell that to all the people who used to be my friends,* or *I guess that's why your daughters can't face me.* Instead I just hugged her, too hard, so we bumped together and Grace laughed. This hug of mine was sloppy, inexpert, prolonged (How did you end a hug? Who began the ending of it?) because I felt so grateful to Grace for believing I looked like myself, purely because she loved me.

Frank and the girls were leading Irene on a tour of their new house. A kitchen spangled with fresh appliances, a spotless living room. Irene wore on a strap around her neck the Nikon Thomas Keene had lent us, having heeded my advice that she should get what pictures she needed immediately, in case Frank and I blew up and we were banished thereafter from his house. My history with my brother-in-law was a barren vista of enmity punctuated by occasional monuments of horror: the time I accidentally knocked him off the deck of his powerboat into Lake Michigan; the time he found out I'd slept with his best man on the eve of his wedding to Grace; the time he called me a bitch at the country club—shouted it, after too many Canadian Clubs—inciting a voluble exchange whose dreadfulness, in my memory, issued not from the public embarrassment we'd caused, not from our forcible ejection from the club or even the fact that we made my sister cry and my nieces cower beneath the table, but from the verbal constipation that had stricken me at that crucial juncture. "You . . . ," I'd begun, and whole minutes seemed to float past before I heaved up, "dope!" with a monstrous effort, the sheer volume of devastating truths I wished to unleash having clogged my throat, "You dum-dum!" "You g-g-g—." Hours drifted past, seasons changed, children grew up and had children of their own. "—goofball!"

Even after our ejection from the club, I persisted in my anguished ravings as Frank hustled his sorrowful family into the car, convinced that if only I could loosen this momentary constriction, I would give silver-throated voice to my loathing for him, its textures and filigrees and chiaroscuro, but at that point I lost altogether the power to make words. "You gagrraglegh! You msnnnsgulums," I bawled, aiming these wads of gibberish at a car window flecked with the sputum of my exertions, Frank shaking his head behind it as he drove away with his family, with Grace and the girls, leaving me alone in the parking lot with a panicky teenage attendant.

The following summer, being no longer welcome in my sister's home, I persuaded her to bring the girls to New York. We spent the weekend in what the three of them perceived as a swoon of decadence, sleeping until ten, ordering stacks of pancakes at Delphi, the Greek diner, Rollerblading to house music in Central Park in the arresting company of some very attractive black men. On Sunday night, Grace called Frank to say she was extending their visit by two days. I brought the girls to a shoot, where they curled their hair in my electric rollers and availed themselves of my various lipsticks; I let them eat popcorn in my bed while they watched MTV. I didn't have to suggest a second deferral; Allison and Pammy did it for me, Pleasepleasepleaseplease, they keened, and that time, Frank's objections were audible across the room. But Frank had lost his hold; they were mine, I thought greedily, I'd won, pried them from his shovel-handed grasp, and that night we used an extension cord to cheat the blender onto my balcony—frozen margaritas, virgins for the girls—we danced on my couch to the Jackson Five, and at last the girls fell asleep watching *Murder by Death* in my bed. I slept between them, a drugged sleep thickened by opiate smells of their hair and skin, a sleep so entangled that I never even heard the phone; it was Pammy who answered when the doorman called shortly after dawn to announce that Frank was downstairs (having driven through the night). Allison shook me awake with terror in her lovely eyes—*oh no, oh no, Daddy's here,* and I barely had time to yank on my silk kimono and light up a Merit before his fat finger was trouncing my doorbell. I admitted him without a word. Frank made a spectacle of himself, hurling Chrysler building keychains and Statue of Liberty mugs into suitcases, Grace hovering near him, swerving between guilty consternation and giddy explosions of laughter. I sat on my balcony and smoked in a state of deep calm. I barely heard their commotion, so attuned was I to the silence they would leave behind.

Allison was almost fourteen now, with long amber hair, freckled skin that would age terribly, poor thing, but at present was flush with succulent youth; small breasts enhanced by what looked to be a mildly padded bra, light green eyes and a whooping laugh. Leonardo DiCaprio's feline visage squinted from the walls of her bedroom, and from her closet she pulled a dress she would wear to a school dance the following week: a short-sleeved sheath with black and lavender stripes.

Pammy, two years younger, still had the star-shaped hands and mushroom haircut of a little girl. She eyed the dress warily, as if knowing instinctively that it portended her neglect. I remembered how frantic Grace had been when I'd first begun to exclude her out of some notion I had of a more grown-up life, how afraid she'd been to face the world without my protection. And I had felt no sympathy at all—just impatience, resentment at the idea that I would hold myself back for her, for anyone. Ever in my life. "What about the movie?" she would plead. "The movie starring us?" Finally, weary of the question, I'd told her (the lepidopterist advanced, chloroform in hand, wearing her exterminator's smile), "You're not *in* the movie anymore. The audience liked me better."

"Here!" Frank called to Irene in the next room over the staccato of the Nikon. "If you go out onto this balcony, you can get the whole room," and, "Wait, let's move this vase—oops, hold on, pillow's crooked!"

I put my arms around little Pammy, and she folded against me. "How would you like it if I trimmed your hair?" I whispered in her ear. "If I cut it like mine?" She looked up at me, solemn bird's eyes blinking, and nodded.

At seven we fought our way back through the gauntlet of wind to our cars. The girls rode with Irene and me, windows down. The wind shook a wet, musky smell from the fields around White Forest, the smell of early summer as I would always remember it. Heading west on Squaw Prairie Road, we passed dilapidated barns, a pen full of sheep whose velvet black faces I could actually see.

"You know," Irene said, "this is really sort of beautiful."

I'd been thinking the same thing, exactly. But I said, "Don't get carried away." One for the quota basket.

Giovanni's, my favorite restaurant in Rockford, was a flat, windowless behemoth fronted by a capacious parking lot that the girls and I crossed arm in arm to the flash of Irene's Nikon. Inside, a carpeted foyer gave onto a piano bar in one direction and several dining rooms in the other: tables the size of small dance floors girded with engorged diners who made instantly credible the nation's statistics on fat. I saw wonderment in Irene's face as she stood in the lobby, holding her notebook. "It's like another country," she said.

But another country was precisely what it was not; I had fled to other countries to escape the gigantism of these dining rooms. Yet each eyesore, routed through Irene, now emerged as a triumph of picturesqueness. See? I found myself thinking, as I watched my brother-in-law jawing with the hostess, rocking on the balls of his feet. *See?* Frank Jones was the avatar of authenticity—he was an ordinary person! I felt something perilously close to admiration.

At the table, the aproned waitress took our cocktail orders: hard liquor, Cokes for the kids, white wine for Irene, a mistake first-time visitors to Rockford occasionally made. When the booze arrived, Frank raised his glass. "To Charlotte. For guts in the face of adversity," he said, and tears swelled in my eyes—not because a tribute from my nemesis meant anything to me, not because I had always secretly sought Frank's good opinion, not even because I believed I was courageous and wanted my courage acknowledged. Because I understood that with my new face, I was no longer a threat to him.

"Charlotte and I've had our battles over the years," Frank told Irene.

"Battles over what?" she asked, in a winning impersonation of ignorance.

Frank and I exchanged glances, caught together under a net of shyness. "Just your basic dislike, I guess, wouldn't you say?" he asked me tentatively.

"I guess that's really it," I agreed.

"I don't remember a beginning." He rattled the ice in his glass. "Just seemed like it was always there."

"I loathed you on sight," I concurred amiably.

Like taffy pullers, we worked back and forth until our topic acquired texture and resistance. "She pushed me off a boat," he told Irene. "Right into Lake Michigan during a storm watch."

"That was an—"

"Yeah, yeah," he said, waving the waitress for another Canadian Club. "Like those guys they find in cement shoes are accidental drownings."

"What happened was," I explained loudly, "I turned around suddenly—"

"Holding a tray!" Grace jumped in.

"Exactly. Holding a tray of sandwiches, and I hit him *accidentally*—"

"In the stomach. With the tray. Food all over my shirt."

"And for some—"

"Pastrami on my feet."

"—for some reason, maybe having to do with the twelve or thirteen Michelobs he'd drunk that afternoon—"

"Now hold it there—"

"His balance was a teeny bit off," I said, "so he somersaulted backwards into the lake. Feet right over his head."

A shining silence while everyone waited. "Pastrami and all," I couldn't resist adding.

Grace's eyes jumped between her husband and myself, afraid lest we perform our own backward somersaults off this ledge of retrospect into the furor of conflict itself. And in the moment of recognizing her fear, I realized that such a relapse was inconceivable. In barely two hours, Frank's and my enmity had lost its bite and become quirky, anecdotal. We shared a responsibility to our audience, whose mere presence had transmuted fifteen years of mutual loathing into the jaunty esprit of collaborators. Like the restaurant, like Frank—like all of Rockford—I, too, had become picturesque.

"The real fireworks—hey, don't go now," Frank cried as I rose from my chair, "—were at the country club. Listen to this . . ." but I excused myself, in part to escape a reprise of my tragic verbal performance, and for another reason, too: despite the joys of reconciliation, the cozy bonhomie—despite these dulcet pleasures, something was wrong. I felt a trill of discomfort, some deep agitation in my gut. I sat on the toilet, listening to the prolonged tinkle of old ladies pissing around me, and wondered what it could be.

Anxious. I had never been so anxious in my life.

Leaving the restroom, I stepped around a group waiting to be seated, the majority humpbacked and silver-haired—such were Rockford's demographics. When a man in a suit spoke my name, I lifted my head with the utmost reluctance, bracing myself for the specter of some boy I'd chased at fourteen (no hair, several hundred children). It was Anthony Halliday. In a suit. The juxtaposition of the detective, thus attired, upon Rockford, Illinois, was one I couldn't accommodate at first. For a full minute, it seemed, I stood mute, then finally blurted, in a moment of extreme creative failure, "What are you doing here?"

"Working," he said, eyes moving over my face.

"Don't make me pretend to believe you."

"And I wanted to see you," he said.

I hadn't spoken to him since the day I'd learned of his deception with Irene. He'd been using me to get to Z, I understood then; that and nothing else. It was a mystery why I cared—normally I was all in favor of mutual usage—but I couldn't forgive him. Each time Halliday called in the weeks that followed (and it was remarkable how long he held on, how desperate he managed to sound toward the end) I set the phone in its cradle the instant I heard his voice.

"But—how did you know I would be here?" I asked, even as the term "rising indignation" made an appearance in my mind ("I'm a detective," he reminded me), **a state of rising indignation led her to retort with scorching indifference,** "I don't want to see you. Anywhere. Ever again," and turn—"Can we just?" he said, **turned on her heel,** "Can I just—" carpet sponging under my feet as **she stalked back to the table in a huff, giving him what for and not taking any guff from that moralizing hypocritical schmuck,** yet oddly, at that point the angry part of me seemed to peel away from the rest, stalking and huffing picturesquely, and I returned to the table wishing I'd stayed to speak with Halliday.

And here was the problem, here was the worry scrabbling like mice behind these brightly painted panels of picturesqueness: I was peeling apart in layers. I was breaking into bits. **She was coming apart at the seams . . .** my head buzzing with a confusion of junk noise, white noise, space junk, a junkyard of noisy thought that made me long instead for a lovely, petaled silence.

"And we came back from Wisconsin?" Jeremy was recounting to the table in his breathless, gulping voice, "and we came in the house? And Ally said, Hey, where's Saucy . . ."

I was itching to tell Irene about Halliday; I wanted to give her a jolt.

It was only with difficulty that I managed not to interrupt, so accustomed had I grown to handing over my experiences to her recklessly, indifferently, neurotically (I wanted her to take notes).

"So we ran in Pammy's bedroom? And Saucy was right in her drawer where she keeps her socks? And she was having kittens? And we saw them come out!"

"What did they look like?" Irene asked. Strangely, she was taking notes.

"Little pellets," Pammy said.

"I thought they were dead," Grace admitted.

"Wish a few had died," Frank said. "Now we're absolutely crawling with—"

"Daddy!!!" all three children shrieked.

But no, I decided, when the fracas subsided. There was no reason to tell Irene about seeing Halliday.

Our salads arrived on a rink-sized tray, and as the waitress dispensed the cut crystal bowls, Irene left her chair to get a couple of shots of the family at dinner. As she focused the camera, I glanced into her open notebook, prising apart the knots of her script to see what she could possibly have found to write about Saucy the cat. *lost,* I read. *intense and piercing sadness.* Further down the page, I saw *fantasy of drowning.*

"Smile everyone," Irene said, and I did, I looked into her despairing eyes and I smiled.

"Tell about New York, Auntie C.," Allison enjoined as we began to eat. "Tell about the stuff you've done."

"Gosh," I said, with a quick backward glance at the months since my return: the unrequited passes, foiled suicide attempts and baffling forays into the world of PR. In the end, I went with the quota basket, tossing in another thirty cents. "Drinking," I said. "And smoking way too much."

The girls tossed back their heads—this was the glamorous Aunt Charlotte they adored. "Remember the time when we slept in your bed, Auntie C.?" Pammy asked. "When we went to New York?"

"You bet I do," I said. "It's been empty ever since."

Frank shifted skeptically in his chair.

Irene took a note. *Auntie C.,* it said.

---

A warm tide of goodwill lifted us from the restaurant and carried us into the parking lot, where we said our goodbyes and promised to speak the next day. Crickets creaked in the fields. Irene drove the Grand Am back along State Street (my night vision still being lousy), whose garish plastic signs were now lit from within. After a few remarks on how well it had gone, we lapsed into silence, our camaraderie loosening, falling away as it often did in the absence of other people, replaced by a mutual knowledge that was deep, but not warm. I wanted to talk about what I'd read in her notebook, to understand what was wrong with her—whether the same thing was wrong with both of us. But the engineering of such an exchange required conversational skills I simply didn't possess.

Back at the Sweden House, I scanned the lot for an idling car. In the lobby, I checked the empty chairs. The air rocked with shouts of plump children cannonballing into an indoor swimming pool that was visible beyond a sheet of Plexiglas.

Sitting together on Irene's floral bedspread, we consulted our schedule for the following day: *C. chldhd home 9:00* A.M., it began, and went on to detail a rigorous itinerary of locations from my past. We agreed to meet at 8:00 A.M. in the lobby and drive to Aunt Mary's for breakfast.

As I pushed open the door to my room, it hissed over a slip of paper. "I'm outside," it read.

I sat on my own floral bedspread, flicked the TV on and channel-surfed. *Unsolved Mysteries.* A chef who vanished from the steakhouse where he worked; close-up of a filet left sputtering on a grill. After ten minutes or so, I dropped the volume to a purr, slipped on my jacket and crept from the room with the exhilarating sense of wriggling through a crack, ducking around curtains of picturesqueness, leaving behind an entourage that I was finding increasingly claustrophobic: a breathless narrator mugging for an overhead camera, a lepidopterist bearing tools of death, and of course Irene. Joyfully I tripped along miles of wet-smelling carpet past the blue-white nimbus of a soft-drink machine, down a flight of steps, out a side door and into the parking lot.

He was leaning against a car, arms folded. Angry though I was at Anthony Halliday, he appeared to me now as a rescuer, the clever mastermind of my escape.

"You came," he said, as if he couldn't believe it.

We didn't speak. I was trying to ascertain what had changed about the detective, beyond the fact that he was wearing a suit. There was definitely something.

"You were a witness in a case," he said with exaggerated care. It was the beginning of a speech. "You were unwilling to talk, so I asked Irene to—"

"All this I know," I said. And I moved closer to Halliday, not because I found him physically attractive; not because a car was crossing the lot and required that I get out of the way; not because it seemed the most graceful manner of accepting what was obviously meant as an apology. Because I thought I smelled booze on his breath.

And when I'd finished stepping closer, I knew that I did. "You're drinking," I said, incredulous.

He relaxed, now that I'd seen it. "Sorry to disappoint."

"Disappoint, hell," I said, "I've waited months for this." But it was a bald untruth. I felt crushed, a crushing disappointment. For him.

He laughed. "You told me," he said, a bit haltingly, " 'I'll see you on your way. Back down.' "

"I was bluffing," I said. "And anyway, you said you'd see me on my way up."

"We were right," he said, and mimed a body shrug, a who's-to-say-what-makes-the-world-go-round gesture that requires either sobriety in the gesturer or drunkenness in the gesturee to work. And Halliday was right, I wasn't drunk. I was rarely drunk anymore. It was technically impossible to lose yourself in drink when a breathless narrator was panting into your ear: **She was losing herself in drink, the shroud of her alcoholism having obscured all else . . .** It was literally sobering.

Some obscure automotive law apparently required that every rental car in Rockford be a Grand Am. Halliday's was blue. He opened the passenger door for me. "I would be honored," he said, "if you would join me for a nightcap."

"I'll drive," I told him. The blind leading the sloshed.

The nightcap was apparently to be vodka neat, judging from the unopened fifth of Absolut that Halliday cradled in his lap, still in its liquor store bag. As I drove west on State toward the Rock River, I sensed him waiting, ticking off the seconds until he could unscrew the lid. I parked in the lot outside the YMCA—the same lot whose pay phone I had used to call Halliday for the very first time, almost a year ago. It was nearly ten o'clock, but the riverside park was still lively; the Y's doors were open, leaking fluorescent light and a trickle of workout music. Walking north along the path, we passed joggers, mostly young men with heads down, sweat dangling like icicles from their faces. Halliday carried his bag discreetly. I felt a grim complicity, walking beside him. The night was humid but cool, the sky full of thick clouds and weird bright light.

Some distance from the Y, we settled on a bench by the water. Halliday opened the bottle and took a long, ravenous swallow of the sort I had seen only in movies, when the booze was actually water; vodka churned, convulsing in the bottleneck, his throat seizing three or four times before he finished, gasping, wincing, and handed the bottle to me.

"Wow," I said, as he wiped his mouth on his sleeve.

I took a sip, then held the bottle in my lap, but he took it back. He wanted to hold it. "Why?" I asked. "Why now?"

"I felt it. Coming," he said, teeth chattering, "Did everything I could. To stop it."

I rested my eyes across the river on National Avenue, blurred, beautiful houses with little docks reaching into the water. In one I caught the festive stirrings of a party, an aura of white light, streamers of music. "You were in a hospital," I said. "Last August."

He glanced at me, startled, then lifted the bottle again. It was the sort of drinking you really couldn't watch.

"Why?" I asked.

"Alcohol—" he gasped from his exertions, "induced psychosis."

"Meaning . . ."

"Midgets with enlarged heads. Climbing out of my toilet. Among other attractions."

I laughed, he drank. "So you dried out?" I asked.

He nodded. "But they were scared. To see me."

"Your girls."

He was looking straight ahead, at the river, though I doubted in his state that he could see it. So his daughters were there, I thought, while he raged at the midgets, and I found myself imagining it—how terrified they

333

must have been. "No," I said, wresting the bottle from his grasp when he tried to lift it again. "I want to hear this."

He went on, speaking with enormous effort as whole sections of his brain began shutting down—I could see it happening, like blocks of light switching off in a skyscraper. "Hanna office. Downstairs. Desk, com-purr . . . nothing. I thought, Whassisecret?"

"Whose secret?" I asked. "What are you talking about?" And then I realized that he must mean Z. Always Z. "What makes you think he had any secret?"

"I thought," he said, with great effort, *"He can help me."*

"Anthony," I said. He was trembling, shuddering as the poison raided his bloodstream. I put my arm around him and tried to hold him still. "How could he possibly help you? What could he say that would make any difference?"

There was a long pause. I felt Halliday struggling physically with some thorny abstraction, wresting it into speech. "Tell me. Don't. Drink," he finally gasped.

For a moment the words hung there, golden, strange, and I saw a jerk of clarity in Halliday's eyes.

"See?" I said, taking his hand. "You already know it."

But the poison had emptied him, and he reached for the bottle again. I released it, but it lazed from his hand and dropped on the grass. He struggled to his feet and careered onto the path. "I hava. Get."

"Whoawhoawhoa," I said, seizing his arm and steering him back along the path in the direction of the Y. Some vast concentration steadied him as we walked, as if he were carrying suitcases full of Venetian glass. But halfway there, he doubled over, clutching his gut. After a minute or so he straightened, panting, then bent in half a second time. He waved me away, staggering toward the river.

I let him go, watching the shadows enfold him, then waited, stand-ing on the jogging path, expecting any minute to hear a splash. Silence. And then I heard vomiting, a wrenching, helpless sound tinged with panic, as if a ferocious animal were clawing its way out through his skin. Then weeping, sobbing intermingled with yelps of pain. I walked away, up toward the old train tracks, inhaling the smell of grass and trying to steady the wire of fear jumping inside me. I sat by the tracks and put my hands on the iron rails, imagining the sound of the train, its distant vibrations, the promise of that faint, rhythmic clacking.

After a long time, I descended the hill and found Halliday lying by the river, unconscious. Vodka and vomit fumes hung on the air. I had the absurd thought that the grass in that area would not survive.

"Come on," I said, shaking his shoulder, but he was out cold. I considered leaving him there, dropping the car keys in his pocket, calling a cab from the Y, serve him right to wake up at sunrise, shivering among disapproving joggers. But even as I entertained these thoughts I was bullying him into a standing position, "Up. Up. Come on. Let's go," seizing his hands and yanking, hauling, dragging, heaving him onto his feet, all hundred and eighty pounds, or whatever the hell he weighed. He drooped on my shoulder, a sleepwalker reeking of vodka puke as we walked, my spine trembling with the effort of holding him up until somehow we reached the car and I emptied him into the passenger seat. I got in and rolled down all four windows.

"Anthony!" I shouted over the wind as we headed east. "What hotel are you staying in?"

"Courtyard," he said obediently, his eyes shut. I knew where the Courtyard was—I'd passed it today, driving into town on State Street. Halliday leaned against the door, either sleeping or dead. "Room number," I yelled as we approached, but he was out again, so I pulled into the parking lot of the Courtyard Inn and extracted the key stick from the inside pocket of Halliday's jacket, checking it for vomit flecks before I presented it at the front desk. A girl in desperate need of a diet was eating Doritos and watching Jay Leno. "Forgot my room number," I sang. "Halliday." She managed the impressive feat of looking up the room number and telling me how to find it without once compromising the connection between her eyes and the TV set.

In the car, Halliday hadn't moved. I drove to the parking area nearest his room, pried him from the car and herded him up a set of outdoor stairs to the second floor. He walked heavily, doggedly, sensing he was almost there. His room was roughly interchangeable with mine: two large beds, garment bag open on one of them. I steered him to the bathroom and turned on the shower, adjusting the water so it wasn't scalding. Then I left, shutting the door behind me. "Take a shower and brush your teeth,"

I instructed through the door. "And drink water. Lots and lots of water. You can do it in the shower if you want." Why bother? I asked myself, even as I spoke. What did I care if he felt clean when he woke?

A long time passed before I heard any evidence of a human mass beneath the spigot. I flipped on the TV and found *Unsolved Mysteries* again— a teenage girl who disappeared while walking her dog; close-up of a scampering terrier dragging its leash. Her remains found one year later in a limestone quarry. A high school yearbook photo: Blue eyeshadow, lopsided smile. Too much mascara.

By the time Halliday emerged in a towel, soap and toothpaste smells perfuming the bathroom steam, I had pulled the leaden curtains and turned down the bed. He looked awfully good to my male-starved eyes: lean torso, lots of dark hair. I did my best not to gawk. He climbed into bed without a word, pulling the covers to his chin.

"Take off the towel," I said, but he didn't react. His eyes were shut.

I turned off the light, slipped my jacket back on and left the room. A light rain had begun to fall. I walked through the parking lot toward State Street, watching the garish lights crackle against the sky. I remembered driving past this very spot earlier this very day, and feeling pride. I remembered the feeling, but I couldn't find it. Or even imagine it. I was alone in the middle of nowhere—worse than nowhere: the place that had made me. And now the depression, the Rockford thud whose arrival I had awaited from the moment Irene and I first drove into the city, blanketed me in its crushing, airless weight.

"You again," I said.

My old friend.

*I can't bear to see you alone,* it said.

Shivering, I stuck my hands in my pockets, where one of them collided with Halliday's car keys. I'd forgotten to leave them. An uplifting discovery; I could drive his Grand Am to the Sweden House and return it in the morning. But I didn't want to go to the Sweden House. And when further burrowing revealed that his room key, too, was still in my possession, I headed back at a trot, drawn by the pulse of warmth I imagined radiating from Halliday's sleeping body. I hadn't lain in bed with a man in so long: even a comatose one would be a luxury.

The room, of course, was exactly as I had left it. I showered and dabbed dry my face, wishing the towel were softer because my bones ached, bones held together by pins; the rain made them ache, I was sure. I wished I'd brought my special lotion; I knew the cheap motel brand would sting. When I looked at myself in the mirror, I regretted having showered. Without makeup, there was something too exposed about my face, broken-looking even though the cracks were hidden inside my mouth, under my hairline. This new face gave too much away; it was that, and not the absence of beauty (though perhaps they were related), that I would never get used to. Still, if I left before Halliday woke, he would never see my face. I went naked to his garment bag and found an undershirt and some boxers, the most delightful exhaustion lapping within me as I slipped them on. I switched off the light and climbed into bed beside him, my stomach to his back. After a minute or two, I pulled the undershirt over my head. It wasn't often anymore that I felt skin against skin, and I wasn't going to squander a chance.

Sometime before dawn, Halliday took a long piss in the bathroom. Water, I noted dimly, he drank the water. I faked deep slumber on his return, doubting his enthusiasm over my uninvited naked presence in his drunken bed; but then, guessing he'd dispensed with the towel, I cracked my eyes for a peek. The room was too dark. When he'd settled back down and was breathing evenly again, I slithered out of the boxers. I hadn't lain naked with a man since that one right after I came back to New York. Paul Shepherd. His name streaked through my mind, a name without a face. Paul Shepherd from Hong Kong.

The next time I woke might have been ten minutes later or an hour. Halliday was facing me, sound asleep, the towel unquestionably a thing of the past because I felt his erection against my leg. This was a lovely sensation indeed, and for a while I just lay there, enjoying my good fortune, until a certain restlessness set in, a wish to parlay this good fortune into better fortune still.

"Anthony," I said, but he didn't stir. I tweaked a hair from his head and he murmured, shifted. I reached down and touched him, took him in my hand, to which he sighed and tensed, pushing against me—I'm just taking advantage of what's in front of me, I told myself, I'd be crazy not to—the question was how to do it without waking him. Technically I supposed it was against the law, having sex with someone asleep, so waking him up to insist that he wear a condom seemed a poor move, strategically. But I could live without that, I decided, it was worth it to me (such was my desperation), I was premenstrual, I'd be fine; he'd been married, so he probably didn't have AIDS. I began formulating excuses in the event that he should wake to find himself in a compromising position, as they said, such as: *I didn't know you were asleep! You spoke, you said, Charlotte, let's make love,* or better yet, *Gosh, I've been asleep, too, you mean we—?* or hey, why not this?: *Nothing happened, you dreamed it all up,* rolling these possibilities through my mind as I pondered an architectural model of our prospective union, a model whose two engineering objectives were sexual intercourse and the preservation of the inebriated slumber now engulfing the male participant. After some tentative essaying of legs and knees and hands I made my choice, awkward and ludicrous though it surely was, for it involved suspending my left leg midair while bending the right knee over Halliday's side so as best to avail myself of the crucial part of him, which I guided inside me with the delicacy of someone loading a nuclear missile into its silo. Now he began to move, playing his part—one hell of a dream you must be having, I thought, and stepped up the prattle of excuses, *I didn't know, I was asleep, too, I have these waking dreams I've seen doctors about them,* this mantra of exculpation clacking through my mind as I mashed myself against him, afraid he would come before I did and then where would I be? Yes. There. No. Yes. There—in a heedless deviation from my architectural model, I seized his ass and shoved him against me and came, long and tortuous and mostly silent, at which point he did, too, with the startled cry of someone slipping off a ledge; his eyes burst open, but I'd sensed that possibility and shut my own at the very same instant, feigning sleep, awash in satisfaction, the drift of tides, sounds of distant barking dogs, telling myself there was no way he could prove it, I was asleep, *I've been asleep the whole damn time you can't tell me I wasn't, I have proof, I had dreams . . .*

But as I floated toward sleep, Anthony's arms loosely around me, I found that I couldn't relax. An object was lodged in my chest, caught there; a fist-sized object that had to be expelled, an object consisting of words, a very small handful of words. I didn't want to say them. I was afraid to.

"I love you," I whispered into his doomed, unconscious ear. "I love you, Anthony Halliday."

There, I thought, it's gone. I said it and it's done, it's gone.

But of course it wasn't gone. It was indestructible.

# Chapter Seventeen

*The first night* Charlotte discovered the math teacher's house dark, she ped-aled home unfazed; it had happened before, several times. She was always careful not to allude to these failed visits, preferring to let him think she'd been off doing other things. But had it ever happened two nights in a row? She stood at his back door the second time, hand almost touching the knob, but was stopped by the thought of how angry he would be, if he knew. Anyway, he would never leave a door unlocked.

On the third night, a bead of anxiety hardened inside Charlotte's chest, small, dense; she noticed it when she breathed because it hurt, like a stitch. She stood astride her bike in front of the dark house in plain sight (breaking every rule) for twenty minutes. It was midnight.

After that, she waited five days before going back. It was early June, school nearly out—Baxter had ended last week. Charlotte didn't feel like going outside. When she wasn't studying for exams or working at Fish World, she burrowed into her room with the shades down, reading about Rockford's industrial triumphs before and during the wars. When the First World War began, it was "furniture city," the second-largest maker of furniture in the country (after Grand Rapids, Michigan), not to men-tion the largest producer of hosiery—the Nelson "Seamless Sock" having captured the market in the 1880s. Her mind rustled, meanwhile, tallying proofs of his love: the amber bead, of course, but other ones, too—cars that had rounded corners exactly on cue, *and exactly the right color,* to prove it. Rockford's machine tool factories thrived during the wars, making aircraft propeller governors and air-control valves and hydraulic transmissions and air-cooled aircraft engines, yet some aspect of love still eluded Charlotte—a smell or a taste, a hidden texture, something she sensed she should know, but didn't. This worried her.

She went to her desk and opened the calendar where she'd kept the coded records of her visits.

It was strangely empty. She'd gotten lazy in recent weeks, taken few notes, and now she lacked any map against which to measure the meaning of that empty house three nights in a row. Well, she would start with last time. Ten days ago. She'd left the house at twelve-nineteen (she made this up). A warm night, unusually warm for the start of summer, she hadn't worn a sweater. He'd seemed glad to see her (she made a note of this). They lay with his window open, warm air spiraling in from outside, and as Charlotte was slipping toward sleep, she'd asked, "Can we go places now, if you're not a teacher anymore?"

He turned to her. He was no longer thin. This fact had presented itself without warning a couple of weeks before, and Charlotte had been shocked, feeling she didn't recognize him.

"What places?" he asked.

"Anywhere. Like a movie. Or Chili's." Just once in a while, she was thinking, like friends. Like other people.

He didn't answer, but he took her hand (she made a note of this).

"I'll be seventeen in three weeks," she said. She'd been looking for a way to mention her birthday. She was hoping for a gift.

And rather than get up, as he usually did before she was even asleep, Michael lay there watching her—Charlotte felt his gaze even through the sheath of her eyelids. So comforting, to be watched as she dropped into sleep, the safety of it. As if he were holding her. She squeezed her eyes, willing herself to sleep now, fast, before he left. *If he doesn't get up before 1 . . .* It was automatic.

Michael lay there, watching the girl. He wanted to say something to her, a particular thing he'd rarely said before, to anyone. His mind swarmed with memories now that Rockford was fading around him, a fresh set of documents harvested, his next move finally clear: a last exodus in what had revealed itself only now as a steady migration in one direction (west), whose endpoint he had very nearly reached. Los Angeles. For years it had hovered before him, a flickering mirage awaiting his arrival. He would make movies. Build a white house overlooking the sea.

He remembered the reek of meat. A humid, bloody, gagging smell, mysteriously sweet, that had soaked the Jersey City apartment from a Halal butcher one floor down, suffused the mattresses and sheets, imbued the splintered floor and the foam-rubber couch, so there was no relief from it.

How easily she slept! An American sleep; the sleep of those who believe they will never be alone, or forgotten, or lost. That they are always safe. A sleep he was coming gradually to enjoy himself.

He remembered the waiting. Hours of watching sunlight twist through coils of the gasoline pumps at the filling station where he'd begun working one day after his arrival in America. More than a year ago, now—March—wet and icy but stubbornly without snow, which Aziz (as he was known) longed to see. In the filling station office he listened to sounds of trucks, waiting for the phone to ring—his UN contact, a man whom Aziz believed was his inferior and so despised. But he himself was a fugitive, a dead man who lived, who carried three false passports, and so could not be slipped onto one of the lower diplomatic rungs, as others were.

To empty his mind he prayed, prostrated himself in the strangely dilute American sunlight, sun dissolved in water, sun filtered through leaves. On the grimy floor of the filling station office he knelt, facing east, and looked for a rhythm in this waiting, this emptiness, a way to inhabit them. But as the days wore on—days, then weeks—he began to seethe with boredom and anger and restlessness.

At the end of each endless day, he crept up the rungs of a swerving fire escape and looked at Manhattan from the roof of the building where he and nine other men shared two rooms, distant cousins by birth or marriage (as they believed him to be) all sleeping in shifts; where each night Aziz shook another man's hairs from the sheet: Ali, his ghost twin, who worked overnight driving a limousine. Aziz almost never saw Ali, but he was on intimate terms with the smell of his Ralph Lauren cologne, the stenciled hieroglyphics his gelatin-pumped Nikes imprinted on the kitchen linoleum.

At sunset, Manhattan shimmered like a single thing, a beaten piece of gold or some mythical animal flicking its pink feathers in the sun, and beside its ravishing silhouette the steps Aziz and his compatriots were taking seemed too small: amassing drums of nitroglycerine and ammonia and fertilizer in a nearby family's basement; stacking them behind an upended plastic swimming pool in whose turquoise basin they would eventually fold them into gallons of petrol, using a canoe paddle to stir. Bemoaning the fact that Wall Street had been made a pedestrian zone to protect it from suicide bombers. Collecting bits of pipe for detonators. Useless. Useless and small. Like Jersey City itself, which had looked so near to Manhattan on the map as to be the same place, *as good as there,* Aziz had told himself in English, practicing, but that had proved an error of perspective that you could only make from afar.

At night, they watched TV. Aziz and his gaunt compatriots crammed together onto a foam-rubber couch that stank of Ralph Lauren cologne and butchery; they huddled like pigeons, craving the anesthesia that issued from that screen, the tranquilizing rays: cars animate as human faces; breakfast cereals adrift in the whitest milk Aziz had ever seen; juice erupting from phosphorescent oranges. And girls: ribbony girls whose hair floated and danced, girls who winked at each occupant of the foam-rubber couch individually, eliciting a chorus of exhausted sighs. And even as the anesthesia worked upon Aziz, even as his mouth fell open, eyelids splayed helplessly to admit these sights, hands curled like an infant's, he was aware of the rage waving like a flag near his heart, reminding him that this hypnosis was a conspiracy at work, whereby a seed of longing was implanted forever in one's thoughts. Aziz had been seduced by his rage years ago, caught in its swooning thrall until everything else in the world seemed faint beside it. At times he felt gouged by all he had given up to fight this war, whittled down by the many years of effort, as if the anger had chewed something away in him. But if fighting the conspiracy had reduced him, that loss merely strengthened his grim and patient will to destroy it.

First visit to Manhattan. From across the river the city had looked dense enough that Aziz pictured it being all center; he would see the cars, the oranges, the girls. The famous people. But when the bus rolled into its slot at the Port Authority, he found himself among hustlers and addicts and victims of birth defects and malnutrition. He walked gingerly south on Eighth Avenue in a frigid wind, expecting at each corner to tilt his head and see the beautiful and the famous. What he saw instead were men in African garb, various Asians and Central Americans; foreigners speaking languages Aziz could not identify, many hawking items clandestinely over card tables or blankets thrown across grime-encrusted sidewalks: watches, belts, used radios, stereo equipment, along with (Was it possible? he wondered, standing closer, disbelieving) the same bootleg videos of Hollywood movies that were sold throughout the world!

Not me, Aziz thought.

"Pen. Pen. Pen. Pen. Pen. Pen." A frantic looking Sikh, brandishing a tattered box. Aziz sailed past without glancing at him. Not me, he was thinking. Notme. Notme. Notme. Notme.

He needed money. American money, that green whose metallic glint all the world panned for among the rainbow frills of other currencies, a green whose monochrome merely amplified the phosphorescent fantasies it had the power to enact. Conjuring green. And here, everyone had it, the hustlers, the hucksters, the toilers, the tourists in bright shorts and visor caps, the men who sold hot dogs on corners—they handed it out in wads, in bouquets, in plain sight. Aziz was finding little methods of siphoning some away, a few dollars from the envelopes of cash that came to the apartment through the auspices of a charity, an occasional ten or twenty from the filling station. Three weeks from now, an overseas wire would arrive at a Canadian bank (where such things were watched less closely), and he was determined to be the one who would drive across the border and retrieve it.

"Yo, brothermine, what's yo' name?" A black with a looping, swaggering prance fell into step beside him. An American, but so excluded from the conspiracy that had enticed these foreigners here that he was forced to lie in wait for them, to prey upon their surprise and confusion and disappointment. "Step this way and behold a thing I guarantee you ain't never seen the likes of in all your sweet life on earth." The man's eyes were bright and antic, desperation dancing just behind the mirth.

"No thank you," Aziz said.

He traversed the dark streets south of the bus station, dark with soot and the shadows of tall buildings blocking the already weak American sunlight, dark with the faces of toilers pulling racks of clothing over soiled, uneven pavement, people too far removed from the conspiracy even to know they were its victims. Aziz trolled for bits of conversation: "The guy was a Froot Loop," and "I started seeing, like, funny shapes," and "I gotta go play my mother's numbers," words and phrases catching in his mind like burrs—"Too rich for my blood," and "Knowhamsay?" One word. Aziz whispered it: "Knowhamsay?"

His next visit was one week later. This time he brought a guidebook with a laminated map attached. Already his English had improved, words begetting words even as he slept, a proliferation that was not unlike the obstinate and furious activity of life itself. **For architecture buffs, we've rated the city's treasures on a scale of one to four, with "1" meaning Miss at Your Peril!** He was able to read most of the guidebook, though all he really wanted was to identify the different neighborhoods and canvass them. He walked north to the "Upper West Side," which appeared to be the exclusive domain of children and babies along with their bedraggled mothers or tranquil Caribbean nursemaids. Sidewalks jammed with strollers five abreast, the air moist with phlegmy cries. He fled to Central Park, where the babies had reached adulthood and were exercising their bodies with a rigor that appeared brutal, expiatory. On the "Upper East Side" he emerged into the last phase of this fore-shortened life cycle: an abundance of ancient bejeweled ladies crushed into wheelchairs only slightly larger than the prams across the park, pushed by the same Caribbean nursemaids through an embalmed and moneyed silence. It was April; Aziz prowled the streets in his lush beard and immigrant's garb of obvious synthetics. No one looked at him, and this was convenient; it allowed him to stare at people unhindered, conduct his search for conspirators beneath a mantle of invisibility.

The soles of his cheap shoes were paper-thin, he felt grains of pavement under his toes. He turned, heading south on Madison Avenue **(The window shopper will find much to savor, but the bargain hunter may be disappointed!),** when a long black car eased toward a curb, tightening a string around Aziz's heart. A slight blond woman emerged among a cordon of attendants, her familiar, striking face tipped down, dark glasses sealing off her eyes, the mere intimation of her physical presence impacting everyone within range like lightning stunning a pool full of swimmers. People froze, clutching shopping bags, they turned and strained to glimpse this woman as she slipped with her entourage inside a lavish department store. Aziz followed invisibly in his torn shoes and brown polyester, vaulting through the heavy, parted doors to keep his famous quarry in sight.

Inside, the intensity of light and perfume and glittering objects made him gasp; he stopped, wavered, stared into a foam of blond hair and brightly painted faces aimed at him like spears. Indoors, he no longer was invisible! He stood, caught in the brightness, caught on the prongs of the women's stares as a guard approached, a gentle-eyed black in a uniform with gold piping. "Sir, may I help you?" this man began politely, and Aziz bolted back outside, shamed by the piteous spectacle he made even as he knew that it was temporary. Necessary.

Still, he'd learned something critical: America's conspirators were no different from overlords elsewhere in the world, encased within bullet-proof cars and crusts of bodyguards, all the usual accoutrements of oppression and injustice. Of course you didn't see them on the street! As Aziz peered through the store windows, the rage that lived inside him like a second beating heart awoke with a jerk that stirred his lower parts, rousing him. Exciting him. Rage and desire were a pair, joined somewhere deep within him. He cut short his search that day, consumed by a need to return to Jersey City and stand behind the blue plastic shower curtain (the bathroom door didn't close) and masturbate.

Next time, Charlotte went to the house in daylight. She saw a "FOR RENT" sign in the front window and was instantly lifted away, spirited from inside herself to a safe and padded distance. From there, she watched herself push the front doorbell, which she hadn't done since that first night when she'd brought him the fish. The sound of the bell clattered through the empty house.

Still, she pretended not to know, and not knowing lent a drenched, sensuous quality to the next several minutes. She walked behind the house to the back door, overwhelmed by the humid, sour-sweet smell of mown grass, bees panting in the bushes, the air thick with sunshine you could practically eat. And behind it all the eerie chime of locusts.

The door was unlocked. Charlotte pushed it wide and stepped inside the kitchen. In daytime it was a different room. So light! But airless, too. She went straight to the freezer, found a half-empty box of frozen waffles and felt a lurch of hope. But the refrigerator was bare, a carton of sour milk, dry sandwich meats. No one had been here in days.

Upstairs, the bed was stripped. On the windowsill sat her fishbowl, empty. He took the fish! Charlotte thought, grasping for some encouragement. Window and screen were wide open, big flies butting at the walls. The kumquat tree had fainted. She carried it into the bathroom and watered it in the sink. Everything looked slightly meager in daylight. She went in his office and opened desk drawers in search of a note, a letter addressed to herself, some explanation that would include her. She felt it in the empty house: an intelligence. Some deeper fold in the mystery. But there was nothing in the desk. She trudged downstairs to the living room and clawed between the cushions of the couch, threw open drawers in the kitchen but found just the same dented cutlery. She looked inside the waffle box. And gradually, the inoculation she'd received outside the house began to fade, and she felt a pull of fear.

She ran back upstairs to the bedroom and wriggled her fingers under the mattress, slid her palms over the bottom of each dresser drawer, collecting a fine layer of dust on her fingertips. Then she sat on the bed and touched the amber bead at her neck. She took it off and held it. It was real, it was in her hands. But the exotic smell of the leather had faded. Now it smelled like nothing, like herself.

She was supposed to have been at her uncle's office twenty minutes ago—the first appointment of their new, twice-weekly summer schedule. She'd written an essay describing the changes to Rockford after World War II: the construction of the Northwest Tollway in 1958, five miles east of downtown, and the subsequent drift of the city in that direction until miles of commercial strip replaced miles of cornfield which in turn had replaced miles of nine-foot-tall blue prairie grass. She'd detailed the construction of malls, the closure of downtown theaters and vaudeville houses in the 1950s when people started watching TV. Charlotte knew she was late, but she couldn't seem to move. She was afraid to. As long as she was here in this house, some possibility remained alive. She lay face-down on the bare mattress, listening to the strange, chattering locusts. **The** furniture industry was dying out because the trees were long gone, even the trees in Wisconsin were depleted . . . Occasionally she heard a car. The first two times, Charlotte bolted into his office, whose windows faced the street, and each time, she felt some terrible knowledge preparing to lift from her like a page, to peel away, an unhappiness whose full weight she sensed only in those moments of believing she would be freed of it. And then the car would mutter out of sight and the page would fall back down and she would release herself to the suction of that mattress. She wanted to cry, to be consumed by convulsions of innocent grief. *My love affair has ended,* she baited herself, *My boyfriend has left.* But her chest stayed dry and tight.

The sun completed its trip, curtsied, vanished. Shadows crawled inside the room. Charlotte heard people coming home from work, but she no longer jumped to her feet. She imagined her uncle waiting for her at his desk, nervously checking his watch, lifting the shade on his window to peer above the dirt. When two hours had passed, she was relieved to think that her time with her uncle would be finished. He would be home now, or heading home, carrying his Smith-Corona. Bits of speech from other houses flecked the quiet, church bells specked the distance. Charlotte tried to picture Michael West, what he might be doing: driving with the radio on, or else riding a bus, or lying on a bed somewhere, hands behind his head. Or sitting in a park, as he'd been doing when she met him first. His arm in a sling. But she couldn't imagine any of it. What she saw instead was her uncle traversing State Street, a lone figure weaving stolidly among fenders and hedges.

At sunset, Charlotte hauled herself outside. She didn't want to see the house in darkness. She would never see it again, would forget where it was, felt herself forgetting even now. She walked her bike around to the street and got on, then hesitated, standing in front of the house, dogged by a sense that she was leaving something behind. Gently she rested her bike on the curb and went around back. Beneath Michael's open bedroom window she squatted in the grass, thinking *No,* even as she teased apart the strands. *Don't.* But she kept looking, propelled by some thrust of dread, until she found them—two out of three, anyway. Fish were almost all water, so they dried to practically nothing in the open air. Little husks.

Charlotte lifted them out of the grass by their membranous tails, dry and delicate as butterfly wings, amazed that they had always been so small inside their floating veils—nothing really, just seeds, those feather-shaped seeds that twirled from the trees each fall. As she sat in the grass, holding the fish, she felt her memories of Michael West begin to shrink, to dry away, leaving behind a chilly desolation that bore a faint trace of relief. As if some mammoth effort had at last been suspended. She dropped the fish in her shirt pocket and rode away.

Five weeks after his arrival in America, Aziz unveiled his proposal on a Jersey City pay phone to one of the several puppeteers who believed they were controlling him from afar. If the collective goal was *to be seen*—to saturate the airwaves with images of devastation that would serve as both a lesson and a warning—why not strike at the famous people themselves? Were they not at the conspiracy's very heart, its very instruments? If the goal was symbolism, how could leveling a bridge or a tunnel or even the *fucking White House* (this in English) approach the perfect symmetry of his idea? Thus he argued in a forcible hiss, then lowered his voice as a man his compatriots believed was an FBI informant moseyed toward him through the icy dawn.

It was an idea, the puppeteer conceded. The main thing was not to act precipitously. Aziz understood his caution—rogues were a serious worry. Witness the World Trade Center fiasco; only seven people dead of the many thousands who worked in those buildings, seven including an unborn child! Structural damage completely underground. In short, nothing to see! Nothing to see but hundreds of people coughing and weeping. Yes, Aziz agreed about rogues and their dangers. And now he cajoled the puppeteer by putting on accents, a Jersey accent, Brooklyn accent, Queens, Haitian, black American; he dangled expressions, *A face like a hundred miles of bad road,* and *I'll hurt you bad, motherfucker,* he donned and doffed voices like silly hats until at last the puppeteer snickered, then laughed outright. And then, with the man's laughter tickling his eardrums, he broached the topic of who should drive to Canada and collect the money to be wired there.

———

Charlotte called her uncle to apologize for the missed appointment. I'm sick, she told him, unable to push the despair from her voice. But her very sorrow seemed, oddly, to enliven Moose, for his voice shook as he assured her, "I understand completely. Completely. Call when you're ready."

At home no one noticed. They were concentrating on Ricky's one-year bone marrow test, which was later that week. School was out, and Charlotte spent hours on her bike, taking the measure of the strange, empty new world where she lived. She rode in search of people, strangers—anyone. It was hard to find them. They were all in their cars, afloat in air-conditioning. She crossed the river to the west side and rode downtown to the old water power district, that glittering wreck she'd plundered with Moose only weeks before, but she found just various forms of emptiness, parking lots and parking garages, parking ramps, solitary drinkers slumped on benches. Twice she rode past Teeter's bar, but didn't go inside.

The riverfront park was still the most populous place—her old haunt, where children wobbled on training wheels and flabby guys played volleyball on rectangles of orange sand. The water twitched with motor boats and jet skis. She rode north to Shorewood Park and the water-ski jump, then south to the YMCA, her stomach seizing each time she approached it because she half expected to see Michael West sitting cross-legged by the river. His arm in a sling. She craved this—to begin the story again, like re-entering a dream. But it wouldn't be the same. Something had shifted, broken in her. When she thought of herself a year ago she remembered a girl flush with outsized hopes, a girl who believed the world had made secret arrangements in her favor. Charlotte hated her.

On a Saturday night six weeks after his arrival, Aziz wedged himself among the others onto the foam-rubber couch and closed his eyes prophylactically, shielding himself from the television's stupefying rays. Then he waited, eyelids fluttering, for anesthesia to befall the rest. When they were fully prone, mouths ajar, eyes crossed, he shimmied out of their midst, slid from the room and broke free of the apartment.

Across the river, Manhattan glittered like a gold mine.

At Port Authority, Aziz threaded his way among the desperate stragglers, the drug-baffled wanderers and empty-eyed travelers, then walked straight across Forty-second Street to Fifth Avenue. But the avenue was empty, jewels in windows replaced by photographs of jewels, skinny faceless mannequins semaphoring in linen dresses—empty, empty, newspapers lazing on the air.

He stood on a corner, debating where to go. By now he had gathered intelligence in all of Manhattan's neighborhoods except those mired in poverty, where victims of the conspiracy lived. Greenwich Village was home to a handful of conspirators; dank, empty Tribeca housed an even greater concentration. The East Village had practically none, although now and then they visited to buy narcotics. Soho was the hardest to assess; at first, Aziz had believed it consisted solely of famous people, but he'd come to see that its inhabitants were merely sympathizers of fame—they darted from black cars with exactly the feinting, coded motions that famous people used.

He took the number six train downtown and got off at Spring Street, where the Geiger counter of his anger began to signal instantly. He walked to Broadway, searching out the source of his excitement among the multitudes of young-looking people in black, men with small round glasses, women whose belly buttons winked at the warm night; intentionally scruffy people whom he had only recently learned to distinguish from actually scruffy people like himself. Finally he began walking north, then east, guided by a pulse from within the city's depths.

He reached a narrow street with a contortion of activity at one end—a crush of taxis, a phalanx of long black cars, a beseeching crowd yearning toward an unmarked door where two bulky blacks and one bulky white were keeping order. He fixed his eyes on the individuals going inside, heartbeat flailing in recognition: *There,* the famous misbehaving boxer! *There,* the young actress who resembled Grace Kelly! *There,* the red-haired girl from the shampoo commercial! They parted the crowd as if it were sea foam lapping at their knees, floated indoors and out of sight. A convocation close enough to touch! He'd stumbled upon them! And although Aziz knew he should regroup to formulate a plan, still he thrust himself invisibly among the throng of seekers, the welter of anxious devotees, unable to stop himself until he'd reached the front of the line and massaged the velvet ropes with his fingertips, ascertaining that no electric current ran through them; they restrained the crowd through sheer symbolism. He hung there, enjoying the beat of his rage, half pleasure, half sickness, until one of the black door guardians confronted him, a tilt of amusement to the man's face as he flicked his eyes at the chaotic whorls of Aziz's beard, his synthetic raiments. "You on the list?" he asked (skeptically), and Aziz shook his head, swallowing back his anger, shamed by his own abjectness, so pronounced in this setting, and worse (he realized now) fully erect inside his polyester pants, a fact not lost upon his inquisitor, who shook his head muttering, "Call a doctor, man," before his eyes shuttered over and Aziz felt himself to dematerialize. And only then did he notice the peculiar din made by other petitioners calling out to this man. "G!" they cried, "Over here—G," entreating his attention with the urgency of drowning victims begging for flotation. And as Aziz detached himself from this crowd, melting back into the shadowy darkness whence he had emerged, those plaintive cries caught in his ears: "G! . . . G!"

G.

Heading south along the river, Charlotte noticed someone waving from a bench. Two people. She had taken to riding without glasses, blurring the emptiness around her into something almost lovely, and now her helpless eyes fumbled at the waving shapes, searching for the outline of Michael West. She braked, sliding the glasses from the collar of her shirt. But by then she knew. It was Ricky and her mother.

"Wow," she said, pulling over beside them, weak from that spasm of hope. "Is everything okay?"

"Ricky thought we'd find you here," her mother said.

But Ricky wasn't talking. Ricky was grinning, arms folded at his chest, big feet nuzzling his skateboard like two hands, sliding it lovingly back and forth across the grass. He was looking at the river and looking at Charlotte, too, from the edges of his eyes.

"The tests," she said.

Now Ricky let his eyes flick in her direction, the grin half breaking his face.

"And?" Charlotte said. "And?"

And Ricky grinned, her beautiful little brother grinned like a knife. He looked older. Something in his jaw, his eyes. The proportions of his face. Charlotte noticed this now, for the first time, and it shocked her.

"Everything came back negative," Ellen said. "It was absolutely clean."

She had said this again and again, silently to herself and aloud with no one in the room. Back and forth with Harris on the phone, both of them silly with the news. "He made it!" and then, "So far."

"We made it."

"For now."

"It's over."

"For the time being, anyway."

"I don't think I realized how awful it was until I knew it was behind us."

"At least for now." Again and again they swapped the roles of exultation and sobriety. Their son was well—for now he was well, and probably forever.

Across the river, a pink sun nudged the ashy remains of downtown. Ninety percent. Even to Ellen's pessimistic ear, ninety percent sounded awfully good. As she sat with her children, watching the sun, she thought of Bartholomeu Dias, the Portuguese sea captain whose ship was blown around the Cape of Good Hope by a storm—the first time a European had rounded Africa's tip. But his crew refused to go on to the Indian Ocean, and it was Vasco da Gama who retraced his steps and reached India and famously subdued it. Eventually Dias died in a shipwreck, sailing for another captain. But he'd done it. Ellen looked at her children: Ricky, who was well, Charlotte, whose heart was broken. It was impossible not to see; Ellen knew the signs too well.

And always, too, there was an absence, an empty place she was holding with her mind. Moose. An explorer who hadn't returned, who remained on a strange, distant sea. Ellen could barely keep her brother in sight anymore, but she did, she would forever. As she sat on a bench, her children near enough to touch, the sun in her eyes, Bartholomeu Dias rounding the Cape of Good Hope, she felt something pooling inside her. Peace.

Ricky went to the river's edge and began flinging stones at the water.

When he found a flat one, he skipped it. "Careful of the water-skiers," Ellen warned, enjoying the luxury of fretting over something so tiny.

"I'm not even close, Mom," Ricky snorted—in the same spirit, she thought—miming with her the gestures of a mother and son with nothing more urgent to think about.

Ellen moved close to Charlotte, narrowing the space between herself and her daughter. She reached an arm around her shoulders. It was a bold move, and she half expected Charlotte to shake her off. But Charlotte didn't move—too depressed, Ellen thought, self-mockingly. They sat together in the gaudy sunset.

Charlotte watched Ricky throw stones, his lithe silhouette against the brown water. Early settlers had written joyous tributes to the Rock River: its leaping fish, its sweet taste. Ricky was well, just as Charlotte had promised him. He was growing up. Soon he wouldn't need her anymore; she saw this now with a pitiless clarity. At the touch of her mother's arm she had an impulse to withdraw, hold herself apart; preserve herself for the special fate she had always believed was awaiting her. But that mystery had shrunken away; there were no more shortcuts, no shimmering paths through the darkness. She had made them up. Her uncle's picture of the Rock River was of no particular spot; Charlotte saw this, now, each time she looked. It could have been taken anywhere along the riverbank.

She leaned into her mother's arm and gazed across the river. Old houses, weeping willows. *Evidence,* Moose had said. Evidence of what? Charlotte narrowed her eyes and tried to imagine today in black and white, pale and shrunken in her hand: this river, this bench, this afternoon in 199–, and for a telescopic instant, she felt how long ago it would all seem one day. The vision shook her, like peering through a crack and glimpsing some alien, furious motion. She opened her eyes, relieved by the brightness around her, the colors of the setting sun, her brother whipping stones across the water's skin. Her mother's arm. And something scratched to life in Charlotte, then, as if she had very nearly lost these things. She held them with her eyes.

The next time Aziz approached the velvet ropes, three more weeks had passed. Colored tulips fringed the streets. He wore a suit designed by Helmut Lang. He was clean-shaven, with short, neatly trimmed hair spiked up slightly from his head, and very small eyeglasses containing yellow-tinted glass (his vision was perfect). He concealed in his hand two crisp hundred-dollar bills, which he palmed to the doorman, along with a business card that read "Z," with the telephone number of a voicemail box he had rented using cash that very morning.

"Thank you," he murmured in a faintly European accent, and floated through the doors.

He had settled on these details of attire and mien by milling outside the club on a different night each week (excepting Fridays, which he spent at the mosque), standing invisibly, observing in punctilious detail which of the conspirators' sycophants and admirers were allowed to accompany them inside. He studied clothing, a jacket thrown over an arm, an upturned label above the neckline of a ladies' dress. He studied haircuts, beard stubble, possession of an earring or lack thereof, shoes, glasses (if any), wristwatches, beepers, cell phones, moneyclips. Neckties were certain doom. He dredged the premises for listless chat and repeated phrases to himself before the bathroom mirror. He filled his pockets with debris from the sidewalk and street: business cards, cigarette butts, a tiny spoon, a hair clip, cards advertising other clubs, two earrings, a nail clipper, three small glassine bags, a ribbed red condom still in its package, a playing card with two phone numbers on it, both of which he called, listening to the style and tone of their outgoing messages.

Archaeologists were right. You learned the most from people's garbage.

To effect these drastic changes in appearance and demeanor without alarming his Jersey City compatriots, Aziz had rented, first, a locker in the Port Authority in which to conceal items of clothing as he acquired them, then a room in an Eighth Avenue hotel (paid for weekly, in cash) whose selling point was its full-length mirror, admittedly speckled with mold, in which he studied and made adjustments to his ensemble. The money had come from the Canadian wire, which he'd depleted by nearly half on the pretext that the puppeteers had instructed him to buy weaponry. But there would come a time—soon, he guessed—when no further explanations would suffice, when he would seize what cash remained and vanish.

He felt no guilt over this. He'd turned his back on people he owed far more than he did these compatriots, had walked away from people he actually loved, without a backward glance. Again and again. Aziz did everything possible not to think of those people now, the lost loves he'd abandoned for the thrall of his rage, but occasionally a memory would flinch awake and startle him with its slice of pain, a glimpse, a blurred glimpse of some other life he'd once enjoyed. A squall of velvety limbs across a room: his first son, wet from the womb, kicking in sunlight. A boy who would now be fourteen. His tired wife smiling at him from tousled sheets. All this and more he'd given up to fight the conspiracy, and so he had to win. Had to, or these forfeitures would have been for nothing.

Inside the club, he took several long breaths and looked around through his yellow-tinted glasses. He was pressed among a crowd in what appeared to be a restaurant. Waiters fought through a mob amassed before a spectacular bar, spare, colossal, backlit, crowned with textured squares of something deeply red, while music jerked up from beneath the floor, hijacking his innards. The conspirators were seated beyond the bar at round tables and booths, identifiable by the concentric rings of admirers inclining toward them, and by the noose of scrutiny they dropped around everyone else. The room was filled with hundreds of the most beautiful girls Aziz had ever seen, girls from television, the makeup and shampoo girls all gathered here in such abundance that it was impossible to look at any one without his eyes slipping inadvertently to the next, as if they existed collectively rather than singly: the very medium in which the rest of it was suspended.

So much beauty in one place made the equivalent of brightness, and Aziz shut his eyes, struggling to organize his impressions. He recognized this place as the referent of every crummy disco in the world, every cinderblock room with colored lights and a mirror ball missing half its chips, every girl with a cheap, shimmery blouse pulled over her scrawny arms, nodding her chin to a synthetic backbeat; Cairo, Mombasa, Beirut— all were concentric ripples of a disturbance generated here, a hunger whose signal had reached virtually every cranny of the earth.

Still, the basic questions eluded him. Who was in charge? How were the cheap dreams tested to ensure their effectiveness? Was headquarters actually here, or did the plan of subjugation arise from some more remote place? The girls distracted him, glowing like marine life from the phosphorescent reaches of the sea, girls like unicorns, their impossible, faceted faces making him dizzy. How he loathed them. And standing in their midst, Aziz felt the peculiar, dizzying pleasure of hating a thing so purely you'll do anything to destroy it, anything, a pleasure that was indistinguishable from the wish to be destroyed himself. Consumed.

As he scanned the room for some articulation of the conspiracy, his eye fell upon a woman he'd already looked at several times, a short-haired brunette who was the same physical type as the other girls, but older. Familiar. He seemed to remember her from years ago—TV, perhaps, some commercial or photograph that had wended its way through the locks and sluices of telecommunication to his remote patch of the world. She seemed to call to him from his own youth, when the conspiracy had worked upon him without his knowledge or consent. Unlike the other girls, who were purely visual phenomena, this one had an air of consciousness. She was seated at a conspirator's table, but seemed not to act in tandem with the rest. She sipped her cocktail, bracelets sliding down her arm, a chill in her eyes as she surveyed the room, appraising these trappings of her life. She was waiting. And Z smiled, recognizing her.

He'd met her before, countless times. Every social structure contained such a figure: the disillusioned one who knew the system but no longer cared, no longer believed. Who was waiting. Sometimes money was required to turn such people, but often not; often, attention alone was enough, the appearance of love, or helplessness, or strength. Mystery or straightforwardness. Z recognized her, and in that instant, his hatred and lust and longing to destroy, his regret over all he'd gouged from himself in the process, affixed themselves to this woman with a heave and thrust of connection that obscured the room's din, an eruption whose radiance blocked every brightness around him. He imagined sinking his teeth into her lovely white arm, pulling off those bracelets and breaking them between his jaws. As he watched her, the woman looked up (had she really, or did he only imagine it as he watched this young, sleeping girl in Rockford, Illinois?), looked up as if alerted, somehow, to the chaos within him, the heaving and crashing. Her eyes sifted among the crowd inevitably toward his own, which Aziz imagined fulminating like stars, and broke there, resting on him very lightly (he leaned over the girl's sleeping ear, lips almost touching it, and whispered, "Good-bye"), eyeing him with something too mild to be called curiosity as she sat, luxuriating in this tyranny. ("Good-bye," he said again.) They watched each other for a full twenty seconds, a period so prolonged that Z was relieved when at last the woman's eyes drifted past him, carrying with them her boredom, her indifference.

"Good-bye."

But of course, Charlotte couldn't hear him.

# Chapter Eighteen

*"Pluswhich," Roselyn told* Charlotte, emerging from behind the counter in her little paper hat to mop a swath of Orange Crush from the white linoleum floor, "if you worked here, we could be homies all summer long."

"Aren't we now?"

Roselyn wielded the mop in silence, letting Charlotte mull that question over for herself. Laurel had gone off to ballet camp for the summer, and no one knew what Sheila was doing. Their quartet had ceased to exist and Charlotte was to blame—in disappearing, she had cut the knot of her friends. Everyone seemed to agree on this.

Folded into a booth, she tipped her head, watching Roz swab the Crush and then wring the mop into a bucket of inky water. She'd come to TCBY straight from Fish World, where she had worked alone among salt-water and seahorses and starfish and chunks of live coral, interpreting for customers the mute, elastic motions of fish. Gradually, she was breaking the habit of picturing them dead, as they would look after days in the open air. Charlotte handled herself very carefully. She came to TCBY without her glasses, with blusher on her cheeks and eyelashes drooping with mascara; she sluiced her lips with a tube of crimson, strawberry-scented gloss Roz had given her, and in performing these ablutions she unburdened herself of the other Charlotte Hauser, the one the boys from Baxter had despised.

Often they would appear, these boys, amassing at TCBY before or after jobs in other places: Magic Waters, where a lot of them worked at

359

night manning the water rides, the food court at Cherryvale. They accreted on chairs and tables inadvertently, like ice forming on windowpanes; they perched atop their skateboards and kneaded them back and forth across the floor, occasionally cracking one against a wall until the manager shooed them away. At which point they roused themselves and shambled outdoors to skate the handicapped ramp. Charlotte took unexpected comfort in the presence of these boys; they didn't know about Michael West. They didn't know, and so he was erased.

"How can I quit?" she pleaded with Roz. "It'll take Mrs. Holenhaft so long to train someone else, and she's already old."

"*Por favor,*" Roz said, nudging the bucket back around the counter with her foot. "For once in your life." She had a new soft voice, fluttery, tender, a voice that turned her most ribald remarks into sweet, delicate patter. Charlotte hadn't even known about the operation.

"For once what?" she said.

"Be like everybody else?"

The computerized bell on the glass door tolled the arrival of two guys dragging pockets of heat from outdoors like parachutes. Roz acknowledged their cuteness with a forked glance at Charlotte and a crack of green gum. The yogurt machine shuddered to life.

Sunlight leaned through the glass door. Charlotte checked her watch. She was meeting her uncle for the first time since the missed appointment two weeks ago, the belated start of their intensive summer schedule. She'd prepared encyclopedically for this encounter, reviewing everything he'd taught her until her brain quivered with facts like a thousand racehorses twitching at a starting line. She wanted to stun Moose, delight and overwhelm him, redeem the missed appointment and all the days she'd spent not thinking about Rockford's history. She hungered for the jolt of his proximity—the sensation of slipping with Moose through a hidden door into a strange, secret world.

At the same time, she was anxious—afraid, almost—to see him.

"I can hold him off maybe one more day," Roz called from behind the counter, heaping chocolate sprinkles onto spires of yogurt. "Then he's gonna do the 'Help Wanted' thing." Behind her sweet new voice there was a gap: indifference. She expected Charlotte to refuse.

"Got it," Charlotte said, uneasy. She gathered up her books. "I'll think about it tonight."

"Thinking is a good thing," Roz said.

Charlotte stepped outside into the heat. Paul Lofgren and Jimmy Prezioso were skating the little flight of steps that lifted from the parking lot to the shops. Charlotte glanced at them quickly and raised a hand hello; she'd become a shy, demure girl in their presence, polite and sweet, asking nothing, deeply tentative without her glasses, fearful of tripping or colliding. And in exchange for this reticence (and the makeup, too, she supposed), the negative charge she had borne had at last been canceled. They waved back at her, easy.

Away from them, she replaced her glasses and pedaled fiercely up Alpine, facts swarming her mind as she went—crooked bridges, surveyor's sticks, twenty-four-hour stagecoach to Chicago, horse races over the river in winter before the chemicals stopped it from freezing—

The campus felt sullen, aquatic, bushy with leaves, vacant of all but an occasional listless summer school student. Charlotte locked her bike on the rack outside the history building. Descending the steps to her uncle's office, she was mugged by a despondency she hadn't felt in many days— it emptied her of everything but a wish to lie down and close her eyes. By the time she reached her uncle's open door, she felt faint.

"Hi," she said, setting her books carefully on the floor and collapsing into an orange plastic chair.

Moose was standing at his desk, backlit by a few feelers of sunlight that had made the long descent into his office, shy emissaries of the brightness above. He wore an uncharacteristically seasonal ensemble: khaki pants, a pale yellow shirt open at the neck, a blue-and-white seersucker jacket that tugged noticeably at the shoulders. An artifact of Moose's old life, it looked like.

"Charlotte," he said, beholding her. "Charlotte. Charlotte," uttering her name with such resonant clarity that she felt as if this were the first time she had ever heard him say it.

"You're happy," she said.

"It's a beautiful day," her uncle said, smiling at her. "It's . . . it's summer."

"Hot," she sulked, crossing her arms.

"Oh, it's not so bad. But it's gloomy down here. It saps the spirit, being underground! Let's get outside, let's get up into that . . ." He pulled down his shade, choking off the light, then patted his pockets for keys. ". . . that beautiful sunshine."

"Sure," Charlotte agreed. She was eager to escape the basement, to shake this sudden weight of sorrow. For the first time in days, she pictured herself in Michael West's empty house, where there was no card, no note. Where her many proofs had come to nothing.

They climbed the stairs, Charlotte carrying the books. Stupid, she thought, as they stepped together from Meeker Hall into the tacky air— why bring the books outside? But it seemed too late to turn back, to resist her uncle's cheery momentum. Hundreds of yellow dandelions flecked the grass. They looked delicate, bright. So alive. Moose pounded over them in his big black shoes, leaving juicy prints as he flattened multitudes. Charlotte wished he would be more careful, but then, what did it matter? Dandelions were weeds.

They reached the athletic field, wide as a lagoon, white skeletal goal posts tottering in the heat, bald patches at the baseball diamond. More of those yellow dandelions, thousands of them. Her uncle stamped onto the field, buoyed by the restless vigor that had come to seem his permanent demeanor, each of his jouncing steps leaving Charlotte weaker. He was whistling. And now she stopped—stopped to watch him walk. Stopped to rest. The books felt like an anchor in her arms; she wanted to set them down in the grass but was afraid they would get lost, or wet—that the sprinklers would detonate without warning. Moose charged on, swinging his arms, trouncing dandelions, until finally (and it was odd, she thought, how long this took) he noticed that she wasn't beside him, and stopped.

He turned. He was alone in a field of weedy summer grass, alone and filled with a nearly indomitable urge to laugh. To sing! Leap! Sob! Because at last, at the outermost margin of almost too late, he had managed to impart the essence of his vision to another human being! Moose had known it the moment he'd heard Charlotte's despairing voice on the phone two weeks ago, after she didn't show up at his office.

He'd been afraid, of course, that she would never come back. In the days after her call, Moose had subsisted in a state of nearly lethal anxiety, pacing his living room unable to so much as read. But Charlotte had phoned this week, sounding much improved, at which point Moose's fear that she would bolt in response to what she had seen was supplanted by a more fundamental doubt (had she really seen anything?) and a new spate of anxiety had thus commenced, until Moose lay limp, spent, helpless upon his couch.

Only just now had his doubts been dispelled. Charlotte looked changed. Tired, pained, older (in a span of two weeks!), her features newly delineated, some darkness around her eyes, as if the vision had shocked her into a more final version of herself. To Moose, these changes amounted to a sudden radiance—beauty, even—and this impression took him aback.

Charlotte watched her uncle notice she wasn't beside him and turn. He looked back at her for what seemed a very long time, and then slowly he lifted his arms, raised them over his head so the seersucker jacket splayed open and spread out on both sides of him like a pair of pale blue wings.

"Come in," he called, arms aloft. "Come in, come in—the water's fine!" sun on his teeth, and he was the old Moose again, waving to Charlotte from the wheel of a speedboat, arrayed in his splendid musculature, coaxing her into the Rock River's mysterious depths.

And then he wasn't anymore. He was just her uncle, standing in a field of dandelions.

Charlotte proceeded toward him, still carrying the books. She walked into a river of dread, felt it closing around her, an apprehension that tightened with each step. It wasn't her uncle she feared; Moose had never looked more benign, more welcoming. It was her own clear thoughts.

"Uncle Moose," she said, when she reached him. "I—I have to tell you something."

Moose took a long breath, the yellow shirt straining at his chest as he inhaled mightily, herding oxygen into his lungs until Charlotte marveled at their sheer capacity. "I know," he said, exhaling with evident relief.

Charlotte looked up at him, a broad silhouette against the sun. In her uncle's face she saw an urgent pulse of pain, some naked suffering she'd never seen in him before, or not directly. "Do you really?"

"You mustn't be afraid," Moose told her.

"But I am," she said. "I'm afraid you'll be hurt."

Moose came to Charlotte and embraced her, something he'd never done before, enfolded her in a clumsy, lumbering hug, girding Charlotte and even the heavy books she was holding with his arms and chest and seersucker wings, a hug that smelled like pizza and medicine and dust. She breathed this smell of her uncle, who was all around her, blocking out the world so nothing could touch her and at the same time hoarding her, saving her for himself alone—all this Charlotte sensed, and understood that it was love: this, more than anything else she had known. This was what love felt like.

Like this. Like this.

"You don't understand," he murmured, arms still tight around her. "I see it, too—every day of my life. It's terrifying, I know. But the blindness is worse."

His voice broke, and now Charlotte began the tortuous process of departing the warm enclosure of her uncle's arms, extracting herself blindly, fumblingly from among the folded wings of his jacket and the dusty smell of his love to look at his face. It was tense, euphoric, some ecstasy crushing him from within. "I've waited so long," he whispered, peering into her eyes. "My whole life."

Now the dread poured back around her, dread mingled with confusion: What was he talking about? What was he always talking about when he looked at her with that weird knowing? Still, Charlotte felt an old quickening in her uncle's presence. A single tear ran from each of Moose's eyes; he wiped them away with the backs of his fists and she waited, looking up at him, half believing the moment had come when at last her uncle would reveal himself.

When he didn't speak, she blundered on. "I need to take a—a break from studying. With you."

Moose nodded, shoving his hands deep inside his trouser pockets. "I understand," he said, "and that's a perfectly reasonable wish."

So he did know. Knew and understood. Charlotte rushed on, relieved. "I mean, I've learned a ton, but." Moose nodded, eyes still wet. "I want to spend more . . ." The sun bit her face, the books felt so heavy in her arms. She shut her eyes, swaying a little in the heat.

"Of course," Moose told her softly. And then, with a kind of apology, "But there's no going back, exactly. It isn't like that."

Her eyes jumped open.

"I'll take care of you," Moose pledged in that same soft voice. "You won't be alone, the way I was."

"Wait, what do you mean I—?"

"It's too late." He spoke these words with a terrifying mildness, the mildness of doctors, oncologists talking to children. "It's done, Charlotte. Nothing that happens now can change that."

"I don't understand what you're saying," Charlotte said sharply.

"Wouldn't I have walked away years ago, if that were possible?"

"Walked away from—?"

"You're strong, Charlotte," he exhorted, with glittering eyes. Never had he said her name this many times; the effect was incantatory. "Stronger than you think! Stronger than I am in so many ways!"

There was a certainty in her uncle's voice that frightened her. Something had been decided, something to her disadvantage.

"Uncle Moose. Listen to me," she said, raising her voice. "I don't want to study with you anymore. The Rockford stuff. I want to take a break from it."

Moose nodded. Empathy, pity, sorrow—she saw it all in his face.

"I want to do other things instead," she insisted, but the words emerged plaintive, quavering, as if she were begging her uncle's permission. "Things with my friends."

"And you can!" Moose rejoined eagerly. "And you should, for as long as that's still possible."

"Stop talking like that!"

Her uncle leaned forward, his face very near to Charlotte's, and once again she was silenced, trapped in the vise of her lingering fascination. "It's a gift," Moose said, with a faint tinge of reprimand. "I've given it to you, Charlotte, no one else. In all these years."

"What kind of a gift?" she asked, tentative again.

"I think you know," Moose said. "Or have a sense."

He was looking into Charlotte's eyes with impatience, with appraisal, and again she felt a brush of fear, as if she were begging her uncle for her very life. She pictured herself and Moose marooned together, surrounded by maps, far from other people and without hope of escape.

"I don't want to be like you!" she said, recoiling. "I want to be like everybody else."

"Not true," Moose objected, and something caught in his voice. "You don't want that."

"I do!" Charlotte shouted, angry now—the anger rammed her, knocking her awake, restoring her strength. She flung the books on the grass. "I want to be like other people, like normal people," she cried, crabbing her hands into fists.

"It's too late for that," Moose insisted, a flicker of anger, or possibly fear, now active behind his creamy patience, and something moved in Charlotte then, some apparatus of control slipped her grasp and suddenly she was shrieking. "I don't want to be like you, I don't! I'd rather die. I'd rather kill myself!" the words heaving from her in a kind of mass, without logic or sense. "Leave me alone," she screamed. "Stop talking to me."

She doubled over, crumpled among the scattered books, sobbing for the first time in months, the first time since she'd sobbed in Michael West's kitchen, letting despair and helplessness shake her. It felt good. For a while it felt good, but with time, her uncle's silence bore down upon Charlotte, asserting itself in anxious increments that made her draw out her crying a bit longer than she needed to, rather than face him. But eventually she did. She stood upright and looked at him.

"I see," Moose said. He sounded disoriented. He was gazing somewhere to her left. "Yes, okay, I—you're right. Yes. I think that's something different."

And although his voice was flat, robotic almost, Charlotte noticed minute changes to her uncle involving his color, his posture, the hands trembling at his sides, the leakage of sweat into the fabric of his festive yellow shirt, which was rendered translucent, a cloudy yellow window onto whorls of dark chest hair that Charlotte couldn't stand to look at; the shuttering over of her uncle's eyes and slackening of his mouth—changes that amounted to a prolonged and cumulative collapse. She was afraid he might be dying, that she'd given him a stroke or a heart attack or made something burst inside his brain, and this enraged her yet again. *Stop doing that!* she wanted to scream as she watched her uncle founder before her, but she was done with yelling, done with crying—she wanted nothing but to flee this man who had given her the power to destroy him without her even knowing. I can't, she thought, I can't do this anymore, and she turned and walked away, leaving the books splattered on the grass, her uncle standing amidst them, she turned and she walked, and immediately Charlotte felt relief—the promise of it. So quickly. She could walk away and not think about Moose anymore, forget him as she already was forgetting Michael West, wiping the thoughts from her mind. She walked away and felt calmer instantly, the way shutting a window cuts off a sound.

At the perimeter of the field, she turned and looked back. The density of dandelions made her uncle appear to be standing in a golden field, a bright yellow sea. He was watching her, but when she lifted a hand, he didn't respond. Nor did he look away. His eyes never moved, as if he were unconscious behind them. And Charlotte realized, then, that her uncle had not been looking at her after all. Not really. He was watching something else, something Charlotte couldn't see—something behind her or above her, beside her, maybe. She didn't know where. It didn't matter. She left him there.

# Chapter Nineteen

## 48

It began, like so many disasters, with something very
small. So small that I don't remember what it was. Or when
it happened, exactly.

I was at the wheel, and everything was more or less all
right. Then the mood turned. It started to rain. And things
began to go haywire.

I found it disorienting to read my own words, or something like
my words—not my words at all, actually, but a ventriloquism of Irene's
that for some reason even I believed—typed neatly onto a page, like a
document. I was resorting to it now because the alternative—that hundreds, thousands, even hundreds of thousands (according to Thomas) of
computer-fondling strangers should read this stuff without my having
done so first—seemed immeasurably more awful.

The trip began spontaneously. "Do you have a car?" Z
asked. It was late at night. We were in a club. He was talking from one corner of his mouth, looking somewhere else.
Pretending not to know me.

I do, I told him.

It was an excellent car. New. A blue BMW convertible.
Extracting it from the parking garage of my building at

```
that hour was not easy. I feigned an emergency. Thrust a mas-
sive tip at the sleepy attendant.

   Z and I got in laughing. The sheer adventure of it.

   "So," I said. We were heading south in the long, empty
chasm of Second Avenue. "Where?"

   "America," he said. "The heart. I haven't seen it."

   I considered. New Jersey. Rhode Island. Upstate New York.
"It's a big place," I said. "America."

   "Chicago. Where you come from."

   "Wow," I said. "Now that's a drive."

   I'd brought nothing with me. Not a toothbrush. Barely
a purse. Z had an attaché case, I noticed. It sat at his
feet, one of those strong cases people hurl from airplanes
in movies. Later, someone finds them, still intact. Full of
contraband.

   And then I understood. This trip was not spontaneous at
all. He'd had it planned.

   A story was unfolding.

   "I'm not
```

Thomas Keene tapped on the window of the Grand Am, and I buzzed it down. "Char, we need you out here a second," he said.

Since his arrival in Rockford two days ago, Thomas had begun chummily abbreviating my name, as if seeing a person's hometown were like seeing her naked—an intimacy that allowed for subsequent endearments. I nodded coolly and finished the page.

```
   "I'm not from Chicago, exactly," I said.
   "Ninety miles west," Z corrected himself.
   He had an excellent memory.
```

I set the manuscript aside, flipped the keys to turn off the air-conditioning and stepped from the car into the raucous heat. The Grand Am was parked on a yellow dirt road that began at a right angle to I-90 and led up a slight incline through miles of shimmering, iridescent corn.

It was the very field where my accident had taken place ten months before.

I looked for Irene and spotted her up the road, cupped around her cell phone. Talking to her husband—something she'd been doing more and more as our trip dragged on into its second week. Thomas stood at the edge of the road, looking through a sixteen-millimeter camera mounted on a tall, spindly tripod anchored to a metal frame. In his droopy khakis, sand-colored boots and pale blue baseball cap, he appeared to have been dressed by a stylist from Patagonia. But dressed for what? What role was Thomas Keene to play, here in Rockford, Illinois? This question had dogged me throughout the drama of his arrival: his debates with Irene by phone over the merits of reenacting climactic moments of my story on film (a staple technique of *Unsolved Mysteries*); the multiple bulletins concerning his travel; finally, his incongruous appearance at the Sweden House wearing khakis and cap, his facial pores and nasal hairs more exposed, somehow, beneath this broad midwestern sky.

Yesterday, he'd driven Irene and me in his rented Saturn to visit the farmer of our chosen field. I had expected one of those famished red barns you saw languishing along I-90, but the farm compound was ultra-modern: a metallic barn that looked like a hangar, a vast aerated vegetable garden that the farmer's rabbity son controlled by computer. While Irene and I drank coffee from mugs imprinted with the words "Lead me, O Lord, to Thy Heavenly Kingdom," Thomas negotiated a price for removing a single row of corn and digging a long narrow trough in its place, as well as clearing a twelve-by-twelve-foot square of field on which to build a bonfire.

"Darnedest thing," said the farmer, a twinkly man with hands the size of pork loins. "Young lady rolled her car off the interstate just last year, landed right there in that same field, bit farther down. Oh, but it was a mess. Like the Fourth of July, all those emergency lights. Believe she passed away, God rest her soul." And some communal shock, or shyness— some confusion as to which of us should correct him, followed by a sense that we'd waited too long (as the farmer moved on to a lusty diatribe against the Monarch butterfly and foes of genetic engineering), kept any one of us from imparting to him the happy news of my survival.

Later, using Irene's motel room as a kind of headquarters, Thomas had worked the phone and eventually hired a film crew from Chicago. This morning they had met us at the site: Danny, Donny and Greg (along with two production assistants who went nameless), a trio whose midwestern wholesomeness so entirely subverted their piercings, brandings, ponytails, tattoos, scarifications, shaved heads and other countercultural accoutrements that they might as well have been called See No Evil, Hear No Evil and Speak No Evil.

"Char, could you walk through the field to where Donny's standing?" Thomas asked. "Then just turn around and come back toward me."

I stepped gingerly into the corn. It reached my waist, trembling around me like the surface of a green lagoon. The leaves were slippery and sharp, rolled around tiny ears of corn that weren't visible yet.

Donny met me in the middle of the field, where the proposed bonfire site had been delineated with white string tied to thin splints of wood. Studs and earrings and small gemstones trembled on Donny's face like a swarm of insects. It was not yet noon, but the throb of locusts was like a chant.

"Okay Char," Thomas called from the road. "Come back toward me slowly. Careful not to damage the stalks."

The rows of corn were about a yard apart, but the plants themselves were so bushy and dense that I had to walk carefully, pushing aside the leaves. A gamy heat rose from the reddish soil. At the mouth of the green tunnel I saw Thomas squinting into the camera, panning slowly over the field. See No Evil, the camera operator, hovered beside him wearing a battery belt. Eyeing this tableau, I had a sudden epiphany—I understood why Thomas had come to Rockford: for all his fund-raising abilities and management abilities and entrepreneurial genius, his dexterity as a salesman of ideas and gift for answering the collective prayers of the Zeitgeist, Thomas Keene wanted something else entirely from his life. He wanted to be a director.

By the time I emerged from the corn, Irene had reappeared beside him, her hair frizzy (the humidity) and drooping from a clip, sleepless fingerprints under her eyes. To say she had resisted Thomas's midwestern sojourn would be to insult the heroic energy with which she had opposed it—on ideological grounds ("Why not let consumers use their imaginations? Why this need to give them a picture, when—"), on egotistical grounds ("Look, it's obvious you don't think my writing can stand on its own, and frankly I—"), on psychological grounds ("Don't take this the wrong way, but your presence has a stymying effect on Charlotte, which means—"), on sympathetic grounds ("You have so much to do, Thomas. Why add this to the—?"), on marital grounds ("I'm extremely eager to get home. No, nothing's wrong, I'm just dying to get—"). When none of it worked, when Thomas decided to come nonetheless (a fact that I believed had never been in doubt), Irene collapsed onto her Sweden House bed and did not rise for nearly twenty-four hours, during which she consumed nothing but Fresca. But by the following day, when Thomas arrived, she had managed to pull herself together, and welcomed him with a good-natured resignation whose primary ingredient was relief—the relief of giving up, of throwing your arms around the very thing you've done everything in your power to avoid. The relief of no longer having to fight.

But I wanted Irene to fight. A ghostliness had overtaken her since Thomas's arrival, so at times she seemed to meld with our surroundings to the point of translucence. Even her anguished shadow self appeared muted, faint. Or perhaps I was losing the power to see it.

"Good, okay. Looks good," Thomas said. "Danny, we can start to cut. Let's run the saw off your generator, if the cord's long enough. Irene's ordered sand, that should be here around one." He checked his watch, then leaned over Irene's shoulder with a familiarity that made me bridle. Together they studied her notebook. "What else?" Thomas asked.

"Well, there's the ditch," Irene reminded him.

"Oh, man. Who the hell is going to dig that ditch?"

Irene lowered her voice. "We could ask Danny if the PAs might be willing to do it."

"I feel weird asking them," Thomas said. "We're talking hours of heavy physical work. We need, like, laborers."

"Ditch diggers," I interjected with a smirk.

"Is there such a thing as a temp agency for manual labor?" Thomas asked Irene. "Would they have something like that around here?"

"I'll work on it," she said, betraying no exasperation, if she felt it. But I was exasperated—for her—having made it my dubious bailiwick to sustain the reactions I was certain Irene would have had, were she not presently a ghost. *She teaches at New York University, okay?* I mentally upbraided Thomas. *She doesn't have time to be your secretary.* But apparently Irene did have time.

"Then makeup," she said, consulting her list again. "Your nieces are all set for that, right?"

"Grace is bringing them over after lunch," I said.

"And what about kindling?" she asked. "Bonfire stuff."

"Oh, the farmer's kids are going to handle that," Thomas said. "Which reminds me." He paused, looking uncomfortable, then resumed somewhat plaintively, "Irene, is there some way you could possibly write the farmer into the script? Throw him a line or two? He's been amazingly helpful with this whole thing, and I kind of—I guess I implied there might be a part for him."

To my stupefaction, Irene said mildly, "Sure, I'll write him in."

"Whoawhoa," I said, wheeling around to look at her. "Explain how a farmer fits into my accident?"

"He can call the ambulance."

"Perfect," Thomas said. "That's nice. And it doesn't take anything away from the authenticity."

"Except that it didn't happen," I pointed out.

"Well, it could have," Irene said. "You don't know who called the ambulance."

"I know it wasn't that farmer!" I said, but I didn't want to argue with Irene. I wanted to understand Irene. I wanted to become her—to hold her place, guard the coordinates of her personality until she could resume it.

"It's noon," she said. "Should I drive into town and buy lunch?"

To hell with this, I thought, and walked away.

Back in the Grand Am, I cranked the air-conditioning to high. I didn't care about wearing down the battery; what difference could it make? A dead battery wasn't going to halt this project—nothing had that power, not Irene, not Thomas; certainly not me. It was bigger than all of us. As I searched for my place among the printed pages, the whine of an electric saw rose from the cornfield and the sound of locusts seemed to sharpen in response—a fierce, rhythmic chatter, like a legion of monkeys.

## 49

Once before, I had made the drive between New York and Rockford. Thirteen years ago. In my stalling green Fiat. Coming to Manhattan for the first time.

Now I was going home. In a car I loved too much to let anyone drive it.

Eventually the sun rose. We were in Pennsylvania. A slouching, cruddy landscape. Old factory buildings, broken windowpanes. They looked like abandoned redoubts (I made a "?" next to that word.) from a forgotten war.

Z was transfixed. He liked it. These ruins of America.

I was driving. And waiting, my body alert. Waiting for him to explain who he was, what larger structure he was part of. What we were doing. And most of all, why he had chosen me. What qualities he had recognized as being unique, or uniquely suited to his purposes.

Moose stood at his cubbyhole in the history department office, clutching his mail while summer's skeleton crew of receptionists (namely, one) watched him with her demonic personality fully hoisted. He glanced in the direction of his colleagues' doors in search of someone to talk to, someone with whom to exchange a few moments of capricious banter, because even an interaction so awkward and fraught (for Moose) seemed preferable just now to descending to his basement office.

Of course, most of his colleagues were incising Lake Michigan with powerboats or driving their children through the Grand Canyon or laying bricks around flower beds. . . . But there, an open door! A fellow summer straggler! Jim Rasmussen, reading at his desk and gently massaging his scalp. Moose lunged toward his colleague indiscriminately, singing "HEL-lo, Jim" from the doorway just one or two seconds ahead of the recollection that Rasmussen was his flagrant enemy—that he'd tried more than once to get Moose fired and referred to him as a "Looney Tune" in a recent faculty meeting. Rasmussen wheeled around with a frightened look. A mistake, a mistake. Moose saw the confusion in his colleague's eyes.

"Moose," Rasmussen muttered, suspicious of this uncharacteristic and unnecessary—indeed, interruptive—salutation. A mistake! But now, having clanged hello, Moose felt compelled to follow up with something more. *Speak,* he commanded himself as a purple heat filled his face. Talk about the weather or a sport or some departmental matter (what did people talk about?). "So, ah," he finally said, "you reading anything good, there?"

Rasmussen squinted at him, awaiting the catch. Several agonizing moments passed, and finally he held up a book. An eighteenth-century man was Jim Rasmussen, and Moose braced himself for a monograph detailing the succession of Spanish kings, or a biography of Robespierre, a history of mining in England—prepared himself to respond with some query about the evolution of sight, about glass and its uses, but what Rasmussen brandished aloft was something Moose had trouble deciphering at first: an unauthorized biography of Jennifer Lopez.

"Uh," said Moose, uncertain who she was, but mortified for Rasmussen purely on the basis of her picture.

"I'm crazy about her," Rasmussen said defiantly, slapping the embarrassment right back at Moose, refusing to accept it. He wouldn't pay—Moose would pay. "Just crazy about her."

"Huh," Moose said weakly.

"Can't get enough."

"I'll, ah, let you get on with it, then."

"Nice to see you, Moose," Rasmussen said, baring teeth, and Moose sprang away from the door and fled the debacle, unsure how extensive a debacle it really was, fighting a sense that with this bungled effort at fraternity, he had at last clinched his academic ruin.

Silence fell in around him like clods of earth as he descended the steps to his office. Turning the key, Moose smiled, demonstrating to someone (who?) that all was well, that everything was under control, that really it was a good thing the campus was so empty because he had an awful lot of work to do, and for that reason it was probably all for the best that—

But he wasn't going to think about Charlotte. Moose had made that promise to himself a week ago, when it happened, and since then had managed (mostly) to banish his niece from his mind. He hadn't even told his wife—hadn't mentioned Charlotte's name even once—though Priscilla had asked him repeatedly what was wrong.

Hands trembling from the Rasmussen imbroglio, Moose collapsed into his chair and set down his mail, a slender quantity bereft of the creamy professional envelopes he craved. He sorted through it nevertheless, purely for something to do on this desultory day. And then he stopped. A change had occurred in the atmosphere around him, a change as simple yet dramatic as a cloud occluding bright sunlight, with the crucial distinction that there had been no sun (metaphorically speaking) in Moose's life for several days. No, he was too little in the sun for that metaphor to serve (not that any did), so Moose excluded sunlight from his figuration of the shift of mood in his office, a shift like those icy currents he'd encountered on occasion while swimming in warm water: a tentacle of cold that brought with it an intimation of the ocean's vastness, its depths, its darkness, the unfathomable creatures abiding in its nether reaches.

Moose rose from his chair, went to the window and lifted the shade. In nosed a few streaks of sunlight. He gazed at the path, half hoping that someone would walk along it and lift his faltering spirits—but who would come? Who but more Rasmussens, an infinitude of Rasmussens bent on thwarting him?

But he wasn't going to think this way! Moose went to his file cabinet, opened it with his key and looked down at the musty mass of his manuscript—the history of Rockford, Illinois, which so often had the power to cheer him. He lifted a sheaf of pages and held them in his hands, straining to mobilize the worn and rusty machinery of his optimism. Perhaps the problem was that he didn't get out enough. He should do as his father had done, drive into Chicago once a month or take the train (except there was no more train), have a swim and lunch at the University Club among polished wood and expensive tailoring, raspberries for dessert, served over ice and topped with a clump of whipped cream. Chicago.

Chicago!

The consolidation of these signals and notions into a plan was a physically galvanizing event; Moose replaced his manuscript with great care, locked the drawer, then strode from his office without pause, kicking shut the door, ascended the stairs and left Meeker Hall without so much as a glance in the direction of Rasmussen's office. Then he huffed his way from the deserted college campus along serpentine paths drenched in the sur-real rhythms of locusts.

One-half mile later, awash in sweat, he found his station wagon parked in its designated spot outside his apartment at Versailles. For per-haps fifteen seconds, he contemplated going indoors and leaving a note for Priscilla, who was at the hospital, explaining his unscheduled departure for Chicago. But no. That would impede his present momentum, and mo-mentum was so hard to sustain. Go, he thought. Go! He had his wallet and his Visa card—hit the road, Jack! The very idea of departure made him giddy, and Moose struggled to calm himself, to anchor his mood like someone trying to peg down an unruly tent in a very strong wind (how he loathed metaphors, their coupling of unlike things into grotesques, like minotaurs), but the tent was too big, the wind too strong—his good mood continued to billow and flap untethered as he pulled out of Ver-sailles with a whoop, punching the radio dial until he found an oldies sta-tion, music from the seventies, hey this was great; Moose sang along with "Hotel California" as he careened down East State in his low-slung station wagon, finessing his way around Lincoln Town Cars driven by white-haired ladies whose faces were only inches from the windshield. Eventu-ally he circled onto the interstate. Ah, what happiness came of sheer motion, just letting it rip. No wonder the highway was an American icon for freedom! To hell with pills, Moose thought. Motion therapy—why not? *Mutatio loci!* And it wasn't just that a voyage such as this reminded him of the blind, easy days before his transformations—it was simply that moving felt good.

The phrase broke across Moose profoundly, *moving feels good,* a phrase that was not only inarguably true (proof being his present fizzing state of near hilarity), but (better yet) whose truth was blessedly independent of the minotaur of metaphor. Moose scrabbled in the glove compartment for a notebook in which to write—someone was honking, oh, shit, he'd swerved out of his lane—he tooted his horn and grinned, he was so happy! Splayed the notebook between his thighs and wrote, or hoped he was writ-ing, *Moving feels good,* la-dee-dah, heart racing, skipping beats. *Motion—curative?* he scrawled, then was distracted by signs for O'Hare airport to his right, signs that reminded him of his plan, as yet unrealized—undivulged—unresearched—to take Priscilla to Hawaii. Would he ever do it? Could he? These questions affronted Moose like a flock of blackbirds flapping so near to his face that he wanted physically to bat them away (and they were only metaphors!). And now here came the ominous sensation once again, an icy premonition of doom. Moose fought it back—*I am a fighter,* he thought. Surely the problem was that he was out of practice, not having traveled anywhere in so long. A trip to Chicago would be the best way to start—get his feet wet, as it were, go to the lake with its chalky limestone rim, go to the places his father had taken him as a child—yes, a melting sensation of relief notified Moose that this was indeed the right choice, the best choice, and, best of all, *the choice he had already made.* He was halfway there! And if that venture proved successful—he was accelerating again, fleeing the contortions of O'Hare airport for the refuge of motion itself—if all went well in Chicago, then perhaps he would be ready to attempt Hawaii.

By one-thirty, a twelve-by-twelve-foot square of corn had been mowed, cleared, tamped, doused in water and buried under a layer of bright orange sand—a tiny patch of Technicolor beach secreted among verdant farmland. The farmer's two sons began dragging load after bristling load of sticks and twigs and kindling wood with their heavy work gloves, piling it onto the sand into a thorny tower that reached higher than the surrounding corn.

Somehow, Irene had managed to find two men to dig the ditch. They arrived in a pickup truck, one tall (Mike), one short (Ed), their sad, floppy faces like diagrams of the damage wrought upon human skin by prolonged exposure to sunlight. As they climbed from their truck, shovels in hand, Thomas sidled over to Irene, who was standing beside me. "They look a little," he said, and moved one hand ambiguously.

She nodded, watching the men. "I'm surprised," she said. "The one I talked to sounded."

"The heat. We don't want."

"I couldn't tell."

"Voices," he agreed.

"Is this an actual conversation?" I asked. "Do you really understand each other?"

They both looked startled. "We're just saying the men are older than we expected," Irene said, coloring slightly.

But Mike and Ed were ready for work, needed work—for the money, of course, but also because this job had emancipated them from an afternoon of the computer courses they'd been forced to take since the banks got their farms: how to create a file, write a letter, make a chart. They took the classes to please their frightened, crabby wives, who somehow expected them, at fifty-eight and sixty-one, to reinvent themselves as middle managers. All this I gleaned from listening to them talk while I waited for Irene to return with the Grand Am (she was buying lunch), so I could crawl back inside it. Thomas stood near me, eyeing the ditch diggers, wincing at the whistling noises their lungs made (smokers both, packets outlined in their breast pockets), the way their sclerotic bellies strained the belts of their work pants.

"How you guys doing?" he asked, with anxious friendliness. "You feeling okay? You want to take a break? It's pretty hot out . . ." But Mike and Ed were fine, they said, just fine. Dirt shot off their shovels and sweat veered among the exotic tributaries of their faces.

Irene returned with sandwiches and sodas and potato salad, which she arranged in the open back of the film crew's van. This makeshift buffet, along with a few curious spectators who had joined our ranks (friends of the farmer and his children) began to make our escapade feel like a real shoot. As we ate, sitting cross-legged along the edges of the cornfield, swatting flies, Grace's car turned off the interstate and bobbled up the dirt road, rousing clouds of dust. Halfway up, she stopped, and Pammy and Allison got out along with Allison's new boyfriend, a youth whose startling beauty brought us briefly to a standstill.

"Who the hell is that kid?" Thomas asked me, nearly choking on his tuna sandwich.

"I have no idea," I said. "I mean, he's a local kid. He spends hours on the phone with my niece."

"What a face," Thomas said. "He's a star, look at him. *Look at that face!*"

The teenagers trudged up the road, the boy awash in those same baggy pants I'd seen on kids in New York, clutching a skateboard under his arm. With perverse anticipation, I awaited what I knew was coming next:

"We've got to find a way to work him in," Thomas muttered.

"I don't really see how."

But already Thomas was up and away, sandwich abandoned to the dust, hightailing it over to Irene (eating a BLT alone inside the Grand Am, talking on her cell phone), whose job it had become to grant his wishes.

I rose to greet the kids. With touching formality Allison introduced me to the boy, whose name was Ricky. He grinned as I shook his spindly hand—a sweet, irrepressible grin that he yanked away a moment later and folded inside an origami of teenage caginess. He was olive-skinned, with bright dark eyes set wide apart, white teeth inside a broad, mischievous mouth. Yet his beauty was irrespective of these features; it was more, somehow, ineffable. In the middle of a cornfield, a drop of beauty had landed. And despite all that I knew, I could not help feeling that this boy was numinous, an articulation of some deep wonder that would fill his life. He wandered off with the girls, then mounted his skateboard and leapt in the air, kicking the board from underneath him in an apparent effort to perform some trick. He landed on his knees in the dirt, waving that grin like a flag.

I went back to the Grand Am and kept reading.

### 53

We drove—I drove—into the next day and through it. Occasionally we paused for food. Never at McDonald's, though. Z refused.

As the hours wore on, I got tired. Then more tired. Then catatonic. But something made me put off stopping. The mood of expectation was delicious. It tingled between us all the way through Pennsylvania.

Finally, an hour after we crossed the line into Ohio, we stopped at a motel. In the weak, dusty daylight, we slept.

I woke three hours later. I turned on my side and watched Z sleep. His stern, gaunt face.

"Who are you?" I whispered. "Who is Z?"

The world felt right. The miles of highway, the trucks howling past. Scraps of voices from the parking lot outside our window. A child crying, an engine thrumming to life. "Honey, is Angie's Ponzy doll in the back seat?" Step step step.

I couldn't see these people. Just a shin, a hand between the blinds. Within minutes they would be gone. Off to live out their lives.

I was smiling.

Then Z woke. Flinched awake, eyes grabbing at the walls. "Hey," I said. "It's okay." I touched his shoulder.

He stared at my face. Through it. Then he sprang from the bed and stood naked. Slim, tense. The cheap, drab room all around us.

"Hey," I said. "Relax."

Moose rolled into Chicago reluctantly, before the pleasures of driving had nearly been exhausted. If only it were farther away! He had considered staying on I-90, but while the thought of continued driving was viscerally appealing, the thought of doing so without any clear destination made him profoundly uneasy. So he exited I-90 onto Belmont and soon found himself surrounded by Chicago's achingly familiar outskirts, a crowd of old friends he hadn't seen in years: flattish limestone buildings the same yellow as castles, cast-iron bridges crawling across overpasses. Young black kids in the street—Chicago!

Ah, the lake! Moose's heart stretched inside his chest at the sight of it, the beautiful smiling lake encircled by a necklace of the most exquisite high-rise buildings he'd ever seen, some long and slender as spinal cords, others gleaming coolly behind gray-blue Bauhaus glass. Moose was hurtling south on Lake Shore Drive, grooving to the Stones' "Miss You," full of mission, full of purpose, Jesus it was hot, like the bready exhalation from inside an oven door. "Ah ah ah ah ahahah. Ah ah ah ah ahahah," he mooed along with Mick. It was 3:00 P.M., the lake flecked with boats.

He exited the drive onto Michigan Avenue and drove past the old yellow water tower that had survived the fire of 1871, anticipation roiling within him as he approached the Chicago River, that sulky waterway whose opening had continually filled with sand in Chicago's early days and had to be dug out; a river that had flooded each spring, along with much of the city, until eventually Chicago raised its streets by as much as fourteen feet. And of course the old railroad lines, depots where the first grain elevators were built—Moose felt himself borne aloft by a nearly unbearable excitement at the thought of spending the day exploring these relics, basking in their gritty afterglow, and yet, even as his station wagon hurtled into the Loop, toward the University Club and its rattle of silver and stooped, elderly waiters who had worked there more than half their lives, even as he ploughed toward raspberries and defunct slaughterhouses and meatpacking plants now refurbished as riverview lofts, an exhaustion overcame Moose without warning, as if he'd already done and seen it all too many times. The railroads, the raspberries. Enough.

Moose passed over the Chicago River, rumbling metal under his tires. A column of greenish water, old stone skyscrapers, the Wrigley Building, the Tribune Tower, and then they were gone and he was riding into the dark, shady Loop toward the Art Institute. He made a sudden left into Grant Park. Something had shifted in his mood, he was slipping, falling, sliding, but it wasn't the icy current so much as this exhaustion augmented by the feverish activity of the park itself: picnic blankets, children, grass, Buckingham Fountain with its trumpets of water, Jesus get me out of here, Moose thought, finally easing onto Lake Shore Drive and turning around, heading north, back in the direction he'd come from, fleeing the Loop, where he had arrived only minutes ago in triumph.

The icy current had wrapped one tendril around his ankle, and Moose accelerated to escape it. Time to get out of the car. He could go to Fullerton Beach. And the memory of it—perhaps twenty visits to Fullerton Beach stretched over his lifetime—assailed Moose in one dense pellet of sensation: hot dogs, Milk Duds, fishy sand dappled with cigarette butts, the roar of children—gone, he'd bypassed that enjambment of sensation along with the beach itself. Now he imagined turning off Lake Shore Drive and heading west into Old Town, and was bombarded with another compressed anthology: burning charcoal, ivy shivering over brick, the laughter of girls, that sweet, colored juice that came inside shapes made of wax—gone. But leaving a mark, a dent. Like the apple bruising Kafka's beetle, each of these pellets of recollection lodged in Moose's flesh, releasing its cargo of memories of all the things he had lost—

"Not lost! Gained!" Moose thundered aloud, but now, mercifully, that debate (lost or gained?) was supplanted in his mind by the proximity of Belmont Harbor and the yacht club. Yes, this was the place; Moose eased the station wagon into a parking space, desperate to free himself of its chassis, whose sole purpose, it now seemed, was to hold him still so that these bullets of memory could assault him, enter his flesh and release their shrapnel of foolish and unreliable nostalgia.

He didn't even lock the car, so glad was he to be rid of it.

Hoofing it north alongside Belmont Harbor toward the totem pole, however, was not exactly a cure for reminiscence. The heaviness of the trees, the smell of them, the tint of paint in the playgrounds, the *phrix* of wind over the lake, all of these transported Moose directly to childhood, visits to the city with his father that he'd anticipated days in advance. A quiet, distinguished man, his father, the sort of man who counted out his change to make sure he hadn't been given too much, a man with hands like catchers' mitts, big and warm and soft. But something strange had happened—now Moose's own hands had grown enormous and clownish, and the little boy who had held his father's hand was gone, swallowed by this mass of Moose's present self. So intense was his memory of that boy that it seemed to him now that they were walking side by side—Moose and Moose the boy—walking together past the gleaming white fiberglass hulls, Moose holding the boy's hand in his own mitt-sized hand.

"Come on, let's go to the water, let's look at the lake," he found himself saying aloud to this boy, coaxing him, trying to win his happiness the way one courts the fickle pleasures of children. "This way," he said gently, wheedlingly, rallyingly, and they walked, Moose and his diminutive companion, around the edge of Belmont Harbor, past the totem pole, up toward the bird sanctuary and then to the edge of the lake, the great flickering oceanic lake that could look milky and tropical in sunlight (as now) or greenish-gray beneath clouds, that during storms could rage in tones of purple-black. And Moose finally did what he'd been longing to do: climbed over the seawall and perched on a cube of concrete with the boy beside him, that mischievous boy he had been, that happy, blind boy, looking out at the sunlight striking the lake with sparks, listening to sounds of locusts although there were none, they had ended with the cornfields. Clicking noises, amoebic phantoms waving their tentacles from the sky; Moose observed these phenomena, which he recognized as hallucinations induced by the excited state of his thoughts, observed them in part to avoid looking at Moose-the-boy, who was watching him. Moose felt the boy's eyes on his face, a prolonged stare that would be rude in anyone but a child, a stare Moose put off returning for as long as possible because he knew it contained a question he could answer only with the greatest expenditure of energy (and right now he was so tired), and perhaps not even then: What had happened to him?

At three-thirty, the film crew tested its rain machine, which malfunctioned spectacularly, spraying sideways in thousands of gushing projectiles that inundated camera, crew, sound equipment, spectators, the remains of our lunch, and Thomas, who was howling into his cell phone an instant later. "What's this ca-ca you've sent me?" he shouted, sounding ready to weep. "It soaked my—fiddle with what? Look, I'm not a mechanic. I need rain! Without rain, I'm totally f—"

Irene tapped his shoulder and pointed at the sky, where sallow, ambiguous clouds had begun to loiter. Thomas nodded, taking this in. "The what? Okay. Okay. Now look, supposing it actually did rain? We could shoot, right? Yuh, with this equipment. No? What if we bought . . . no? Even with—no? Okay, okay . . ." He glanced at the film crew, who had gathered around to listen. "Well then you better figure out how to get another friggin' rain machine over to . . ."

He paused. Hear no Evil was sending him a signal, although the density of his facial appurtenances made expressions difficult to isolate. "I, uh . . ." Thomas said, and paused again. We all paused. "Lemme call you back." He folded up the phone. "What?" he yapped at the sound engineer.

Hear No Evil was looking at the sky. "That's one old mongo storm you got coming," he said, a lick of anticipation in his voice.

"Yeah, but according to your boss we can't . . . unless you . . ." Thomas cocked his head with sudden interest.

"Fuck the boss," Hear No Evil said, tongue flashing metal. "Let's shoot in the rain."

The other two instantly concurred. "Let's. Let's fucking do. Shoot in the. Rain, rain," they murmured. And at last, in this mutinous accord, the wholesome boys' wish to rebel, to resist the old hierarchies and pioneer new ways of living in the world, found its full and perfect articulation. Thomas nearly swooned with relief. "Danny, you're the boss," he informed See No Evil. "Tell us what you need."

And Danny did, along with the others—even the nameless PAs—all of them issuing orders with clipped authoritarian zeal that raised immediate questions about the genuineness of their nihilism. Irene duly transcribed their commands into her notebook: tarps, stakes, umbrellas, clear plastic. When volunteers had been dispatched to purchase these items, Thomas helped the crew to wipe down its wet equipment. Then he swallowed three Advils with Dr. Pepper and joined Irene beside the narrow ditch where Mike and Ed were still digging away. The men had ceased to talk, and now there was just the tinny crunch each shovel made as it broke the earth, a faint jingle as it flung off a streak of dirt that hovered midair like a bit of cursive, then dissolved and fell to the ground. Thomas turned to Irene. "Alas—"

"I know, I know," she said, and smiled. "I was thinking the same thing."

At four o'clock, we gathered around the Grand Am for a script meeting, using its hood as a kind of table. Allison, Pammy and Ricky stood at the outermost reaches of earshot, gazing into the distance with extravagant indifference while they eavesdropped.

"Okay, everybody, listen up," Thomas said, surveying a few pages where Irene had blocked out the action. "Here's what happens before the camera rolls: Charlotte's car goes out of control on the interstate. It spins, flips, rolls, lands"—he waved in the direction of the tower of brambles, where Speak No Evil raised his motley of tattooed arms to the sky—"in this cornfield. Car goes up in flames. Charlotte gets out . . ." Now he paused, turning to Irene. "Wait a minute. How does she get out of the burning car?"

"The Good Samaritan," Irene replied.

Thomas frowned. "The . . . ?"

"Someone pulled her out of the car. She doesn't know who it was. It's right here!" Irene rapped him on the head with the script. "You haven't been doing your homework."

I stared at Irene, assailed by a brief, hallucinatory sense that the gesture I had just witnessed—rapping, accompanied by scolding—belonged somewhere in the vast family tree of behaviors known as flirtation. But no, I decided. That simply wasn't possible.

"Thomas?" I said. But he wasn't listening.

"Good Samaritan, okay. So in that case we'll need another actor!" he said, a helpless grin routing his face as he simulated a genuine search for candidates among our ranks. "Hey, what about you?" he called to Ricky, who was standing on his skateboard, immobilized by the pebbly dirt. "Want to be in a movie?"

"Thomas," I said again.

"Doing what." The kid was wary, expressionless.

Thomas ambled over to the gaggle of teenagers. "Well, see, you'd be helping Charlotte get from her car, which is supposedly out there in the field where that guy with the tattoos is standing, between the rows of corn"—he indicated the ditch where Mike and Ed were digging—"to that camera over there, where Danny is. But what you've already done, what we don't see," Thomas went on, "is you've pulled Charlotte out of the burning wreck and saved her life. Which I guess makes you the hero. You'd be playing the hero."

"Subtle," the kid said, allowing himself a modest smile.

"Hel-lo-o!" I called, waving my arms. "Thomas!"

"Char." At last I had his attention. A look of pure bliss had encompassed his face. He had the kid. The beautiful kid was his.

"Not to burden you with details," I said, "but how do I walk through a cornfield when I'm completely unconscious?"

"Where does it say you're unconscious?"

"I don't care what it says," I said. "I'm telling you. I was unconscious."

Irene began to explain, but Thomas raised a finger and came around the Grand Am to where I was standing. He put one arm around my shoulders and walked with me down the road a bit, away from the others.

"Char," he said, when we were alone, "if I could rewrite history, if I could turn back the clock, I'd have us all set up in that field with cameras and lights and sound all ready to go when you landed there the first time. That would have been a thousand percent better, no question, because it would have been real."

I pondered this odd picture and said nothing.

"But the fact of the matter is, we weren't there." He said this with a kind of apology, as if he had promised to do a job but failed to complete it. "So we're coming at this in retrospect, trying to evoke the essence of what happened," he said. "What've we got to work with? We've got an event that only you saw and can remember, and frankly, you don't re- member very much—"

"Because I was *unconscious*," I couldn't resist pointing out.

"Fine. You were unconscious. Two," he was ticking them off on his fingers, "two, we've got this chance now to start over, create the event from scratch—to improve on it, if such a thing is possible. Not that it wasn't better the first time—" His hands rose, fending off any such sug- gestion. On their descent, they seized my shoulders. His face was so close to mine that I smelled Dr. Pepper on his breath.

"What am I saying? I'm saying forget all that, Char. Forget what happened. *This* is what happened, and it hasn't even happened yet! It can happen any way we want!" His eyes crackled with evangelistic zeal. "And for our purposes, I think it's infinitely more dramatic if you walk out of the cornfield with that drop-dead gorgeous kid. As your agent, as your manager, as the producer and director of this project, that is my advice to you. Am I making sense?"

What could I say? Thomas always made sense. "Yes."

"Okay." He gave me a little coach's pat and we returned to the Grand Am, where a separate colloquy had apparently taken place in our absence.

"Ricky wants his sister to play the Good Samaritan," Irene sang out, with a cheeriness that betrayed her dread of Thomas's reaction.

"What sister?"

"She's seventeen," Ricky said. "She just, I don't know, it like fits her better than me."

Thomas gaped at him, unable to believe the kid was slipping through his fingers. He seemed completely at a loss. Ricky tried again to explain. "She's the type who would actually save a person's life, know what I'm saying?" he asked. "Like, she could really do that."

It was sweet the way he said it. He loves his sister, I thought.

"Okay, how do we find her?" Thomas sighed, then added under his breath, to Irene, "Let's just pray they look alike."

"She's at work," Ricky said. "TCBY. I don't know the number."

"That'll be easy," Thomas muttered to Irene. "There's only one every fifteen feet."

"Highcrest Mall," Ricky said sullenly.

Irene called information, wrote down the number and handed it to Thomas, along with the phone.

"Name?" Thomas called as he dialed.

"Charlotte."

"I mean your sister," Thomas said, his voice brittle with impatience.

"Charlotte. Her name is Charlotte. My sister."

Thomas shut the phone. For a moment his head hung in a kind of bow, and when he lifted it again, his face had been rinsed of anger and harassment and was brimming instead with an awed delight that made him look about six. "Your sister's name . . . is *Charlotte?*"

"Ding ding ding."

Thomas grinned—a grin that was like curtains flung open, a grin I couldn't help mirroring, despite the fact that I loathed him, rued the day that our paths had crossed and (briefly, in moments) wished him dead.

Thomas touched two fingers to his lips and raised them to the sky. "Kismet," he said.

Somehow, without Moose's even realizing it, the hazy blue sky of mid-afternoon had clouded over and swelled with what suddenly looked to be rain clouds. How long had he been sitting here? Moose wasn't sure, having fallen into a sort of trance as he gazed at Lake Michigan. The water had been light, aquamarine when he'd first sat down, but now it was gray-brown and opaque, the color of waves in nineteenth-century paintings of gun battles at sea. Moose pretended to study the lake and its variegations, pretended the way a person might pretend to whistle merrily during a stroll through Chicago's South Side—to conceal his awareness of some danger close at hand. The ominous presence was lurking behind him, a presence whose vast and imposing shape Moose could not ignore for very much longer. Finally he turned, slowly, nonchalantly, turned as if to look back at the park, the distant tennis courts whose *thop, thop* he faintly heard from where he sat. There was no one behind him. Or anywhere near him. He was alone except for a few joggers and one or two loping Labradors the color of chocolate. He was alone. And what exactly was he doing here?

Moose rose to his feet very slowly, as if awakening from a nap, his every move calibrated to conceal what was actually going on inside him: an incipient roar of fear at finding himself in Chicago—so far afield! How would he ever get back? The distance between his present location and the tightly framed world in which he passed his days felt beyond negotiation; the relative spontaneity and lightheartedness of the visit was lost upon him now, as he slowly—painfully slowly—began walking back in the direction of his car beneath the bruised and swollen sky, a sky on the verge of some violent discharge. Alone, Moose was alone, no one even knew he was here! All around him, in those glass apartment buildings overlooking the lake, lived a legion of strangers, people who didn't know, who couldn't see, and Moose was alone because his vision had divided him from these people—had altered him internally so that the child he'd once been, the little boy who had walked alongside him earlier today, by the lake, when the sun was out, no longer recognized him.

And only now, as Moose huffed toward his car past sailboats rocking in Belmont Harbor like cradles in the rising wind, only now did he permit himself to turn his mind to his niece and her defection. "I don't want to be like you," she'd said, "I want to be like everybody else." And a worse thing, too, a thing whose exact contents he mercifully could not recall, the gist of which was that she would rather die than live a life such as Moose's own. And even as he recoiled, half staggering at the impact of these memories, Moose understood.

The car, the car—he limped toward it, collapsed behind the wheel and began to drive, but driving failed now to relieve him as it had earlier today; a worrying thought intruded as he nosed into traffic on Lake Shore Drive, the traffic of beachgoers fleeing the impending storm. A worrying thought: he'd gotten into this car intending to go to the University Club for lunch as his father used to do, but he hadn't been able to. In fact he'd barely managed to drive into Chicago and sit by the lake. Or rather, he'd done it easily enough but now wished he had not; it had taken too great a toll. *Simple things were becoming so much harder to do.* Would he ever don a suit and spoon those raspberries from a silver bowl? Why did this seem a fantastical wish?

The answer lay in the vision itself: a different man than Moose was the one who thrived in this new world, a sociopath who made himself anew each afternoon, for whom lying was merely persuasion. More and more they ruled the world, these quicksilver creatures, minotaurs who weren't the products of birth or history, nature or nurture, but assembled for the eye from prototypes; who bore the same relationship to human beings as machine-made clothing did to something hand-stitched. A world remade by circuitry was a world without history or context or meaning, and because we are what we see, *we are what we see,* such a world was certainly headed toward death.

Moose drove west on Addison toward I-90, forcing himself to move slowly, slowly, though he wanted desperately to flee. Only this studied languor could halt his progress into panic. Because Moose and his ilk were not part of the great glittering future that everyone seemed to believe was now upon them; they crouched in its cracks, its interstices. They had before them a herculean task of persuasion: warning people without souls, people assembled from parts like shoes or guns of a hundred years ago, that a world populated by such as themselves was doomed. And Moose had failed—failed in all these years to explain to even one human being what had happened to him that summer afternoon when he was twenty-three, driving home from Hank Sternberger's parents' house in Wisconsin. A moodiness had been on him for weeks, a deep preoccupation whose catalyst was a tourist pamphlet on Venetian glassblowing he'd flicked open while watching football in someone's rec room. Clear glass, perfected in Murano circa 1300, glass that made possible windows, eyeglasses, mirrors, and eventually microscopes and telescopes. These simple facts, mentioned in passing, had hijacked Moose's imagination. The birth of clear sight, of people's awareness of their outward selves—these seemed the origins of a phenomenon whose reach extended all the way to the present day—screens, frames, images—a world constructed and lived from the outside.

He'd been alone in the car that day, or he likely wouldn't have noticed something amiss on the grassy embankment beside the interstate, would not have pulled over onto the shoulder in the first place. A bitch nursing a few pups, it turned out to be—a cur, a mutt—what was she doing there? His car on the shoulder, the dog and her wretched pups sprawled panting in the longish, blighted grass, and for some reason (and here was the gap, the stitch, the missing step in Moose's *personal history*) for some reason, rather than get back inside his car and continue home, rather than haul dog and pups into the backseat and drop them off somewhere more hospitable, Moose had left his car parked beside the interstate (dangerously) and climbed the parched, grassy slope that hugged the overpass, climbed without knowing why, then sat immobilized looking down at the traffic, hypnotized by the flux and flow that had surrounded him only minutes before, a crush of humanity in whose midst he had subsisted blindly, unreflexively until that moment. Hours passed, so many that when he looked again, the bitch and her pups had vanished. He lay on his back in the grass and let the sky push against his face. From somewhere came the whistle of a train. And Moose had understood that it was over: the trains, the factories—the world of objects was gone and imagery was ascendant, whirling over tiny filaments of connection he could actually *hear* amassing hungrily, invisibly beneath the soil. Wires that weren't even wires. Information that lived on the very air.

Now Moose drove so slowly that the cars behind him began to honk. It was starting to rain, big sloppy drops spilling onto the windshield. No thunder yet. His driving was stymied by a clobbering sensation of loss. But what exactly had he lost? Himself as he had been, firm-bodied and flabby-minded? Some clarity of vision he once had possessed? Or was it the old, dormant chamber of his bicameral mind calling out to him, reminding him of the days when rocks and trees and statues had spoken with the voices of gods?

———

We showered. Wriggled back into our clothes. Stepped from our motel room into the empty parking lot.

It was dusk.

Sleep had made an end to the previous day. The day when driving to Rockford, Illinois, together had seemed like a good idea. Or even a reasonable idea. An idea that was appealing in the smallest possible way.

I filled the gas tank. Dust and squashed bugs and bird shit were baked onto my beautiful blue car.

We had ridden in silence before. Top down. A brimming, windy silence.

This one was vacant. It roused in me an urgent need for talk: "Road." "Signs." "Sky." "How was?" "Where were?" "Radio." "Temperature." Forced conversation hovering over a void.

Z listened to my efforts with a dazed look. With each word, I was becoming less the person he imagined.

I saw this clearly. But I couldn't stop.

I read, sitting in the Grand Am with the light on in hopes that the battery would expire, a subversive impulse I was having more and more as I observed the mounting juggernaut around me. Each time I looked up, I saw volunteers returning with gigantic blue plastic tarps, which the mutinous production assistants began tying to stakes in preparation for rain. There was no question now of a storm; the tarps bellied and rattled in the rising wind, and clouds like three-dimensional bruises were bearing down, leaking occasional drops. Lightning bit at the edges of the sky.

By now, a multicolored chain of cars reached all the way down to the interstate, and spectators continued to amass, milling about under flowered umbrellas, waiting for something to happen. When Thomas knocked on the window of the Grand Am and asked me to test the ditch, these onlookers pressed toward me with interest. I left the car and walked the length of the ditch. Now, at last, I discerned its purpose: to lower me three feet below the surface of the field, so the corn would tower over me as it would have last August, presumably, had I been able to walk.

"Beautiful work," Thomas commended Mike and Ed when I emerged from the ditch. "Smooth. Even. You guys are real professionals." The men nodded politely, sucking their Winstons, but when Thomas turned away, they shook their heads.

And then the girl arrived. Charlotte.

I recognized her instantly—before I saw her, it almost seemed, as if some part of me had remembered the name, or her brother's face from the photographs in Ellen's dressing room. She parked down the hill and came into sight on foot, walking briskly up the slight incline, her narrow frame silhouetted against the dreadful sky. She looked different, I saw this even at a distance. No more glasses. The dreamy quality I remembered had burned off, leaving in its place what I guessed was maturity, though it registered as sadness. No one seemed to notice her, and as she scanned the group for a face she knew, our eyes touched briefly, then hers moved past without recognition. Of course, I thought—that day I had looked like no one, wrapped in a scarf, sunglasses and pancake makeup pasted over my bruises. But even as I congratulated myself on having eluded identification, I had a feverish impulse to speak with this girl, to remind her of our previous meeting.

"Sis," Ricky called. He went to Charlotte and brought her to Thomas, who was adjusting the camera. I watched Thomas turn and see her, watched the crestfallen look he tried unsuccessfully to mask as he measured the distance between sister and brother. He nodded, smiling frozenly. He was at my side three seconds later (I counted). "We've got to lose the girl," he said.

"I like her."

"It'll be easy," he murmured, thinking aloud. "I'll just say it has to be a guy. I'll tell her you have to be carried."

"You think that scrawny brother of hers can carry me?"

"I'll tell her . . ."

"Thomas. She came all the way out here and found us."

Thomas cocked his head and peered at me. "I came all the way out here from frigging New York," he said through a tight smile. "I'm the one spending money to get this shot exactly right. And that girl is not going to be in it."

"Fine," I said. "Neither am I."

He stared at me without comprehension.

"Use my niece," I told him, "she's better looking. God knows she's younger. She can fall in love with the Good Samaritan at the end." I longed to walk away, but the sight of genuine alarm catalyzing in Thomas's face was too great a pleasure to forfeit.

"Hey," he said. "I know we're both tired."

"I mean it. I quit," I said, the very words unleashing a vertiginous sensation of freedom. "It's your movie, great. Do it without me."

I knew I should walk away, but I couldn't.

"Charlotte," he said. "Charlotte, Charlotte." He'd reverted to my full name, which was something. "Charlotte, you're everything," he said, taking my hands in his (hot, moist), and gazing into my face. "You're it. The sine qua non. Without you, the whole thing is nothing. All this"—he waved an arm at the sky, the corn, the audience—"is just empty. And if I haven't been appreciative enough, if I haven't made you feel how crucial you are to this project every minute that we've worked on it, I apologize. I honestly do. Maybe it's just—maybe it's some perverse side of human nature that we take for granted the things we value most."

Where did he come up with this stuff? And yet even as I listened distrustfully, disbelievingly, I felt the words seeping into me like some witchy potion, flattening my rebellion into a thin wafer of complaint. I stood before him pouting. "I want Charlotte to play the Good Samaritan," I said.

Thomas swallowed and looked away. I saw how hard it was for him to yield—even now, with the threat of my defection immediately before him. He was a tyrant: a tiptoey, apologetic tyrant. "We'll keep talking about it," he said. "And I promise"—he held up a hand—"the last word is yours."

He smiled at me. I smiled at him. "You've already heard it," I said.

Moose drove slowly, slowly. The rain had retracted, sucked back inside the clouds; tornado weather, he thought, then wondered if the tornado was real or metaphoric. This thought came to Moose innocently enough, a moment of literary-critical speculation, but in passing through his mind it raked against him in a way that felt damaging, a tiny tear in an astronaut's suit. In Shakespeare's plays, thunderstorms accompanied crescendos in human affairs, but those storms were metaphorical, of course. And here was the ominous sensation back again—oh, yes, closer than ever, a very large body passing so near to Moose that it lifted the hairs from his head. Was it the whale? Had the whale returned after a long metaphorical absence? Moose searched for his notebook, digging for it in the crack of the seat; not finding it, he finally wrote on the leg of his pants with a black Magic Marker, *Thought, sensation, whale, tornado,* realizing as he wrote that he was getting it backward; the tornado had come first, generating the original thought, which was—what? Oh, oh, he had to remember; Moose swerved in his lane as he rummaged metaphorically in his mind (which was crammed with metaphors), desperate for that thought—yes, there, he seized it like a rope, realizing only as he did so that it was a troubling rope, a troubling thought, a rope pulling him toward thoughts perhaps better left unthought, but it was too late. He was holding rope and thought. Thought: what proof did Moose have that his vision was not, itself, just a metaphor? His mind wheezed like a bellows as he attempted to grasp the implications of this query: that the revelation he'd devoted his life to understanding might not exist in itself, might be a metaphor for something within Moose—a mistake, a mutation, a disorder of the brain. That the vision was not the cause of his isolation, as he had always supposed, but merely an expression of it.

"*No!*" Moose shouted at his windshield. "No! I reject that vision, that antivision. I reject the accusation of solipsism because I know I'm right. I know I'm right. I know I'm right!" He was yelling, battling the beast, wrestling with an apparition from the icy sea that was also a minotaur, not to mention driving a 1978 station wagon through incipient rainfall. Really, it was a feat! But one he probably could not sustain much longer, especially if the lightning he saw gnawing the horizon was actually headed this way.

I sat on a folding chair in the cornfield, away from the reaching eyes of my audience, which now included some hundred Rockford teenagers and swarms of their parents, all drawn to this field as if by a heavenly sign, some gleaming emanation of Hollywood. I sat under a small tarp held aloft by Charlotte and Ricky, rain prattling at the plastic with an eerie restraint that was irreconcilable with the fat, lowering sky. I held the manuscript in my lap and read sporadically in the jaundiced light.

Pammy, who was acting as Allison's assistant, held up last Halloween's issue of *Seventeen* (they saved them all) so her sister could see it. "7 Easy Steps to a Wretched Bloody Mess," I read amid a pinwheel of girl-faces so white and clean they resembled bars of soap. Many years ago, one of those faces had been mine. My nieces began Step One, which involved making wavy lines along my cheekbones with a set of soft purple crayons.

"I heard these guys from school?" Ricky told his sister, inclining his head at the mass of spectators. "They're like, Charlotte Hauser's in the movie? No way, how'd she get to be in it? They're on me: Bro, how come your sister's in this movie? I'm like, At ease, she has her ways. So now they're in awe."

Charlotte laughed. "That'll be new," she said.

I fought to keep my eyes open as Allison and Pammy rubbed the soft crayons over my face. It was a relief when Allison finally said, like every one of the hundreds of makeup artists before her, "Close your eyes."

With my eyes shut, sounds seemed to magnify: rain tapping the corn, leaves sliding wetly, a distant grinding of thunder. "Donny, can you hold it higher?" I heard Thomas yelling to Speak No Evil as they tested the boom. "We're getting static from the wind." All of it broke, scattered the way children's voices churn and shred in a playground, folding into the wet leaves, the sour, animal smell of the earth. My scalp tightened, prickling over my skull.

60

By the time we approached Chicago, we'd been driving more than twenty-four hours. My back hurt. My eyes stung. The car reeked with the smell of us.

I felt bad in a way I associated with coming down from drugs. A glittering apparatus, dismantled piece by piece.

Z stared into the darkness. I felt him looking for some reprieve, some escape. Of course there was nothing out there. Just plastic signs.

Allison was dripping fake blood onto my face, testing her various brands: "Dr. Spooks' Blood Bath," another called "Ghoul Gush" and a batch she'd made herself from a recipe in *Seventeen* that reeked of peanut butter. "Which is best?" she asked the group. "Or should we do like a combo?"

They gathered in around me, Ricky and my nieces, brows pursed at the import of their task. "Char, what do you think?" Ricky asked, deferring to his sister.

The girl leaned in, crouching a little, her eyes moving over my face with the intensity of hands smoothing every last wrinkle from a bedsheet. I felt something flare up in her—surprise, I thought—and was certain she had recognized me. But she gave no sign.

"The peanut butter one," she told the others. "Definitely. Because it's all clotty."

"I saw your picture," Z said. His first remark in hours. "A long time ago."

"Not that long," I hedged. "I mean, I'm only twenty-eight."

"You were selling something," he said. "Makeup, I think."

"That's possible."

"I remembered you. When I saw you again, I remembered you from before."

He was trying to tell me something. I listened very carefully. Scraped each word for the meaning underneath.

It was starting to rain.

"I thought you could help me," he said.

"I will," I said. And felt a tiny click of excitement. "I want to."

Z shook his head. "You can't. You have no idea what you're doing."

I was offended.

"You don't know," he said, with a kind of amazement. "None of you. It happens without planning, like the rain. Like the fire no one lights."

"What are you talking about?" I asked. "*What* happens?"

"The conspiracy."

The word hung there. Coiled, sibilant. I felt another click. Hadn't I known? Felt its presence around us from the beginning? A gold, shimmering net.

"Tell me about the conspiracy," I said.

Z turned to look at me. In his eyes I saw something alive for the very first time. Pain.

"It's a dream," he said.


My face dripping with gore, I borrowed little Charlotte's umbrella and crept among the cornstalks toward the blue Grand Am I'd seen wobbling up the road a half hour before. Halliday was there, leaning against the hood in faded jeans and a black T-shirt. He was taking in the scene with a look of some amusement.

He flinched at the sight of me: a broken, bloody figure emerging from the stalks. "Christ," he said.

"Relax," I said. "It's mostly peanut butter."

He ran a finger over my cheek and sniffed it. "I'm on my way to the airport," he said. "Thought I'd stop by and see what you were up to."

"How did you know we . . . ?" But I let it go. He was a detective.

I moved nearer to Halliday, holding the umbrella over both of us, snuffing subtly for booze. But the peanut butter smell was too strong.

"I've stabilized," he said. "If that's what you're trying to figure out."

I smiled. "I'm amazed you're still here."

"Had a setback or two," he said. "As you saw. Some work to finish up."

I glanced at him, curious. He seemed uncertain whether to continue. Finally he said, "He flew the coop, our missing friend. Again."

"Your friend," I corrected him.

"My friend," he said, and laughed.

"Good riddance."

There was a long silence. Halliday and I watched the commotion, swaths of movie light bleaching the cornstalks to white.

"Looks like you won't need that detective job after all," he said.

"Apparently not," I said. "This face of mine is full of surprises." After a moment I asked, "Was I in the running for it?"

"You were my top candidate."

By now a few spectators had caught sight of me—a person in movie makeup—and begun moving eagerly in my direction. More cars teetered up the road from the interstate.

"I better get out of here," Halliday said, "before your fans box me in."

He slid into the driver's seat. I stood by his open window, holding the umbrella, my other hand gripping his car. I couldn't seem to move it.

Halliday lifted my hand in his own and kissed it. Twice. "You were an angel that night," he said, with difficulty. "I'm grateful."

"The pleasure was mine," I assured him.

Now it was raining, oh, yes, now it was finally coming down. Moose by-passed Rockford, heading farther west, rain punching his window, rendering useless his less-than-perfect windshield wipers. But the imperative of continued driving overshadowed all of that—the urgent need to return to the site of his first transformation, which alone had the power to dispel the terrible thought of some minutes back. The overpasses all looked alike, but Moose never had trouble finding the one in question—there it was; he recognized it even through this crush of rain, and felt a pull deep within him, a rising up. There were tears in his eyes as he eased the station wagon onto the narrow alley beside the interstate—dangerous, he knew, in a storm, so he left his headlights on, cautious Moose, then lumbered from his car and began climbing the steep embankment, rain hugging him, blinding him, mud pasty under his shoes. Moose slipped, he skidded—slopped, flopped, fell once and landed on his rear, but slowly, slowly he fought his way to the top of the hill. Rain heaved from the sky, soaking his head, the fabric of his shirt and pants, lightning scudding across the sky like skipped stones—this was no metaphor, Moose thought, with satisfaction, this was a bona fide summer storm!

Already he was relieved. Here was the link between his old self and his present-day self—the boy and the man—here was the place that gathered them together. He was whole, had everything he needed, and yet, even as Moose bathed in this sense of completion, he was assailed once again by the terrible contents of the vision itself: it was there before him in the howling trucks, the roar and hum they left in his ears, the terrible acceleration of human history, combustive, exterminating, violent and blind, blind—no one could see, no one could see what Moose had glimpsed then and saw today: a headlong forward motion that was inherently catastrophic. Moose hunched on the windy hill and felt the icy stream rise through his body in a giant, heavy sob that shook his exhausted frame. He felt in his pockets for his pills and jammed a few into his mouth. He took them every day, oh, yes, pills and pills, trying to calm his addled mind while he worked furiously to identify the cause, the mistake, the wrong stitch that had spun such devastation.

"It's the end of the world!" he bellowed into the wind, using all of his voice. He hollered it again, down at the oblivious cars. And again, roaring with every last filament of energy he had left. *"It's the end of the world!"*

No one cared; they had eyes only for the camera's lens, these madmen who were no one, who were nothing but a series of impressions. Who were *information*, jumbled and soulless as the circuitry in which they mostly lived. And Moose was alone, bellowing into the wind. He would grapple with the harrowing task of trying to forestall a doom that only he and a few unstable others could see while the rest of the world beckoned it, a doom visible not just in the soaring temperatures and rampant extinctions, the dying coral and heaps of garbage lying in the deepest reaches of the sea, the mysterious expiration of frogs—these were things anyone could see—but a devastation that was a simple by-product of motion itself. Einstein had it wrong, or only half right, there was another equation that foretold the destruction, but Moose had forgotten it. Perhaps he'd touched on it earlier today, while driving. *Moving feels good.* It did—too good. They will move for the sake of it, he thought, they'll move with an excitement they cannot know derives from their proximity to an end. And now Moose, too, was seized by a will to move into the end, his own end, to relinquish this burden of seeing and knowing, this terrible responsibility. To set it down.

"Please," he sobbed aloud. "Please."

The traffic below called lovingly to Moose, big wheels sucking over the rainy asphalt, the brute mechanical gnashing gallop of it all, and he moved toward it helplessly, a few paces down the embankment, feeding himself into the machine, a shivering anticipation in his mouth at the thought of collision, impact, then peace. "Yes," he said. "Now. Please."

But no. The answer was no—not now, not yet—because somewhere inside of Moose, stretched between his mind and his heart, was a tiny silver thread, a thread no bigger than a hair whose contents was plain strength, a will that endured within him and had survived all these years, albeit slenderly. And even now, Moose felt a protectiveness toward that silvery wisp, a need to shelter it from every other thing as if it were a last match untouched by the rain, and he lowered himself onto the mud and lay down, lay back in the wet earth to remove from his vision the motion that was provocation and temptation both, the problem and the solution, lay back to conserve his energy, what little he had left, his mind cupped around that single strand of strength. He closed his eyes and slept.

There was a crack of thunder, and then the sky opened and emptied its contents on top of us. "All right, *move,*" Thomas shouted from the road. "Everyone. Places. Get the Charlottes over to the fire. Are they there?"

My face was slathered with gore, my wet hair viscous; fake blood and peanut butter oozed into my eyes, half blinding me as we cut through the corn to the fire. It had just been lit, and six volunteers held a tarp above it to shelter the flames. They stared at me aghast. "It's fake blood!" I told them, "It's made of peanut butter, can't you smell it?" But the storm inhaled my voice.

Little Charlotte held her umbrella over our heads as we waited to begin our long gallop between the cornstalks toward the camera. I'd begun to feel strange, slurry, drifty, as if everything were happening sideways. Lightning strobed the cornfield, making a daguerreotype from a hundred years ago. The girl watched me quietly, a pressure behind her stare like a touch.

"I know you," she said finally. "You were in my house."

"That's right," I said. "We met in your mother's closet." And I laughed, for the memory seemed to me hilarious—leaping from among her mother's dresses, the smell of that Chanel. Recalling that day, I felt an odd twinge of happiness—not because of the meeting itself, which I hardly remembered, but what had happened since, something I recognized only now: I had freed myself from an onerous existence.

The girl didn't laugh, or even smile. "How many years ago was that?" she asked.

"No years," I said, grinning through my gore. "Not even one."

"It feels like so long," she said wistfully. Then added, "I never told my mother."

"Not a problem," I said. "Probably for the best."

"You could come back."

"Sure," I said lightly, batting this away, but then I felt the idea dig into me. Ellen Metcalf. To see her again, to find out who she had become.

"Actually, she's here. My mom," the girl said.

"No kidding," I said mildly. "Here here?"

"Somewhere." She turned to look. "She came to watch. My dad, too. I told my mom it was you."

"You told her," I said, swallowing. "And what did she say?"

"She said, 'Oh, my God.' "

This struck me as tremendously funny. "Oh, my God," I said, and laughed. *Oh, my God.* I could hear her, exactly.

"When I saw you before," the girl said, "your eyes were bright, bright red."

"I'd just had an accident," I told her. "The same one we're starring in now, believe it or not."

She was watching me with her strange clear gaze. "I met a man by the river," she said. "Right before I met you. He had an accident, too."

I said nothing.

"His arm was in a sling," she went on, excitement lifting her voice. "He had a big cut on his face."

"Did he," I said.

"His name was *Michael West*," she said, the words wresting free of her and opening like a flag, as if she'd never said them aloud and was relieved, at last, to do so. Through the rain I felt the quick heat of her breath.

Mercifully, Thomas's voice reached toward us through the storm: "Fire," he bawled.

At instructions from one of the mutineers, the tarp holders tossed handfuls of explosive pellets into the flames and then stepped away with military unison, unveiling the fire at precisely the moment that it reared back on its hind legs, snapping, grabbing at the sky, disgorging a bale-sized whorl of black smoke that rolled toward the clouds.

"Gorgeous!" Thomas hollered. "Ready, Charlottes?"

"Ready," we called in unison from the narrow, spindly ditch, which was already half full of rainwater. The wet corn snapped above our heads. Charlotte held the umbrella over me to protect the small microphone affixed to the collar of my shirt, whose wire ran along my belly to a receiver in my pocket.

"Boom!" I heard Thomas cry, and I barely made out his shape under a tarp beside See No Evil, who was prostrate behind the camera.

"Boom!" called Hear No Evil, directly to our left.

"Charlotte Two, you lead! Charlotte One, you're going to do what?"

"Scream," I answered. We'd been over it a dozen times.

"Scream!" Thomas cried. "Scream like you've never screamed in your life. Scream like the naked girl running in that picture. Mouth wide open—wide, wide, got it? Three . . . two . . . one . . . Action!"

### 63

"Still," Z was saying, "it can't go on as it has."

We plunged into the night. His disappointment was so intense and embittered it felt like hate. The road was empty. Lined with tasseled crops.

Rain spattered the windshield.

I leaned on the accelerator, finding relief in the speed. It felt like tearing. Like breaking.

"It won't be allowed to go on," he said. He was watching the window. "The people will rise up and throw off these dreams you've used to imprison them."

I tried not to listen. I was an idiot. A lost and desperate idiot. But these facts seemed to melt away as I watched the speedometer climb.

The car smashed through the rain.

"It will end," he said. "It will end with fire. And the artifice will burn away, and the truth will be left. Slow down," he added.

But I couldn't slow down. I listened, uncomprehending. Clenching my teeth.

"It will end without you, without me. An explosion of violence you can't possibly imagine, sheltered and spoiled as you are."

I couldn't talk. I couldn't hear. I could do one thing: push the accelerator toward the floor. Plucking strings on a giant harp one by one. No, the sound can't possibly climb another note, I would think. But it could. It did. And each increase rippled through me with unbearable sweetness.

"Mountains will move and fall. Oceans will overflow, and you and the others will know how small this petty domination of yours really was. Please slow down," he added.

"Let it," I said. "Let it end."

I wanted nothing but escape. From my wrong decisions. From the lost time. From the fact that I'd wasted my life. Thrown it away.

"Slow down," he said again. Less politely.

I pushed harder. The car could do one-sixty. I'd never gotten near it.

Cold metal kissed my temple.

"Take your foot off the gas," he instructed. His hand trembled behind the gun. Trembled like the car, which felt on the brink of explosion.

Gently he said, "I'm counting to three. One . . ."

But it was too late. It felt too good. We were at one-thirty and climbing.

"Two . . ."

The gun nudged my skull. I didn't care. It seemed perfect that we die together. A monument to the randomness and desperation that had united us.

"Three."

I hit the brake and yanked up the emergency brake at the

same time. A wind was blowing. In retrospect, that wind looks like Self Preservation. A squall of hope. Memory. An obstinate will to live that rushes in when we least expect, saving us. Drawing us back.

But in fact, it was the wind from his open door.

He had already jumped.

We crashed through the corn, little Charlotte and I, my useless eyes squeezed shut, my mouth a gigantic *0* that dredged up from within me a sound unlike any I had ever made before, or even heard. We slipped, the girl dragging me along the wet, soggy bowl of the ditch; my legs buckling, folding under me as I fell against the bars of cornstalk. The journey felt endless, blind, doomed, but the girl kept me going, strong despite her thinness, apparently used to hauling people along rain-filled troughs between rows of corn, or so it seemed; lifting me, dragging me, heaving me through the mud. We'll never arrive, I thought each time I paused to yank in breath. It will never end.

And even when it had, when it was all over and people were around us, something still was wrong. I heard it in the panicky flicker of voices, in the fact that so many hands were touching me, soothing me. I felt heat coming from somewhere—the fire has leapt its moorings, I thought, there wasn't enough sand, not enough rain, the fire has broken free and is raging somewhere, destroying the farmer's fields.

I was lying down. I heard mention of a doctor, an ambulance, all from a great distance, all muffled by some other, unrelenting sound; something was wrong, I knew (despite Thomas in the background, muttering, "Beautiful, gorgeous . . ."), I knew from the scamper of running feet, the welter of voices—Irene's, Allison's, Pammy's, little Charlotte's—and then Grace, my sister, louder than everyone, coming closer, crying shrilly, "What's the matter? What's the matter with her? What's going on?"

Someone answered from very nearby. A familiar voice. Yet strange, new. Old. A voice I hadn't heard in many, many years surrounded me, now, familiar as my own. It was Ellen's voice. Ellen Metcalf, my old friend.

My old friend.

She was holding my hand, I realized, and her voice sounded calm, calm and very near, so near that I wondered if I might be lying in her lap. I felt a warmth around me—yes, I thought, relieved, the Good Samaritan is here, the Good Samaritan has finally come.

"Charlotte can't stop screaming," Ellen said.

In near darkness, Moose lay in the mud and marveled at the silence. The thunder had faded, a bully moving on to other schoolyards, and the rain was a light patter now, a gentle dousing, warm and friendly. The whispering sounds of traffic might have been the sea.

He was aware of a presence nearby, but for some time he waited, just feeling it there, trying to surmise its mass and weight, its goals and intentions and allegiances, before opening his eyes. He had no more strength for enemies.

When finally he looked, he found Priscilla beside him. She sat hunched on the embankment, hugging her knees, dressed in blue shorts and a blouse with little red rosebuds on it. Her hair and clothing were wet. She was looking down at the traffic, crying.

Moose sat upright. He felt confused, baffled, guilty, caught among the dregs of some unspeakable debauch. "Darling," he said, and put his arms around Priscilla, his sodden arms around his slender wife, who smelled of wet carnations. She sobbed quietly, her smooth and lovely face reversed, showing its rough, nubbly underside. "Edmund, why?" she said.

"I can't explain."

She sniffled, wiping her eyes. "I know," she said.

She was calming down, Moose noted with relief. She was becoming visibly calmer. She was very nearly calm again, his Priscilla.

"You didn't come home," she said. "I was scared."

"I'm sorry, baby."

He was sheepish, unsure himself what had happened exactly, why his pants were streaked with black ink. With Priscilla beside him, the paroxysms of the past several hours seemed already to have folded into something very small.

"Did you take your medication?" she asked.

He nodded, seizing her hand. His wife. It seemed impossible to Moose that she could really be his. The world felt so quiet, the traffic sounds hushed and sibilant as prayer. And amidst this stillness, Moose managed to assemble courage, peace of mind, reason, logic—those scattered, blinkered troops who for the past several hours had rampaged without a general—marshaled them into formation, took a long, very deep breath, and told his wife, as evenly as he could manage, "Charlotte doesn't want to study with me anymore."

"Oh," Priscilla said, her whole face parting in sympathy at this news. "Oh, that's so disappointing. It must be." Stroking his muddy head, and when Moose heard her reaction—disappointed for him, yes, but calm, presuming of both their continued survivals—he felt relief.

"Let's go home," he said.

It was dark. The lights of his car were still on, but dim. Moose flicked on the hazards, locked the car and climbed into Priscilla's Capri. She drove, legs wet with rain. At home, she would call Triple A to pick up his car. She'd done it before.

She would serve him Campbell's tomato soup with saltines and put him to bed. For the next few days he would feel tired, peaceful.

Yet even now, as they drove along the interstate toward home, sorrow clung to Priscilla, a veil so thin it was nearly transparent. A cobweb. She was sad, he had made her sad. Again.

"Should we go to the movies tomorrow?" Moose asked, working to find some joviality in himself. "It's Saturday."

"I have to work."

"The next day, then."

She nodded without conviction. A scrim had appeared between them, and it frightened Moose.

"We need milk," he said. "Should we stop at the Logli?"

"I did."

Minutes passed. A terrible silence spun open.

"When I'm feeling better," Moose said at last, haltingly, "when all this is behind us, I—I'd like to take you on a vacation."

His wife said nothing.

"Just the two of us, somewhere nice," he forged on. "To unwind, to relax."

And as he blundered heedlessly, desperately into this disclosure, this secret plan he'd hoarded for more than a year, Moose recognized that in speaking it aloud to Priscilla he would make it real. There would be no possibility of retreat.

"I was thinking of . . . of *Hawaii*," he said, the very word a yelp of fear. Moose leapt, threw himself from this cliff. "How does that sound to you?"

There was a long pause, during which he fell, fell, swiveling his limbs in the open air. But when Priscilla looked at him again, he saw renewal. Resurgence. A flame lighting her face. Faith returned to his wife like a soul reanimating a corpse. Moose sank back in his seat and shut his eyes.

The world was saved, after all.

Priscilla took his hand. "Hawaii would be wonderful," she said.

# Part Three

## Afterlife

# Chapter Twenty

*That woman entertaining* guests on her East River balcony in early summer, mixing rum drinks in such a way that the Bacardi and Coca-Cola labels blink at the viewer haphazardly in the dusty golden light—she isn't me.

That woman whose sponsors have included Doritos, Lean Cuisine, Frigidaire, Williams-Sonoma, O.B., Sea Breeze, Q-tips, Clairol, Mac Cosmetics, Lubriderm, Vidal Sassoon, Bayer, NyQuil, *TV Guide,* Calvin Klein, Johnson & Johnson, Panasonic, Goodyear, Raisinettes, Windex, Tide, Clorox, Pine-Sol, Dustbuster, CarpetClean, Mason Pearson, Dentine, See's Candies, Scope, Nine West, Random House, General Electric, Tiffany, Flossrite, Crate & Barrel, Fruit of the Loom, Scotchgard, Apple, the *New York Post*, Hanes, Odoreaters, Frame-o-Rama, Kodak, Rubik's Cube, Day Runner, FTD, Sam Flax, *Encyclopaedia Britannica*, Roach Motel, Reebok, Blistex, Braun, Levolor, Xerox, the Door Store, Right Guard, Panasonic, D'Agostino, Rubbermaid, K-Y jelly, and the services of Dr. Raymond Huff, obstetrician—that woman whose veins and stomach and intestines have opened their slippery corridors to small exploratory cameras; whose heart, with its yawning, shaggy caverns, is more recognizable to a majority of Americans (according to one recent study) than their spouses' hands; the first woman in history to both conceive and deliver a child on-line, before an international audience more than double the size of those assembled for the finales of *Cheers* and *Seinfeld* combined—she isn't me.

I swear.

The breach between myself and Charlotte Swenson had its antecedents well before Ordinary People's now legendary debut and the attendant tsunami of controversy, hysteria, opprobrium from pundits who swore it would be the end of American life as we knew it, and of course, history-making numbers of subscribers; before the rocketing fame of the "Ordinary Thirty," the original American subjects, many of whom, like Pluto, are brand names today—before any of that, I had begun to feel, as I went through the motions of my life, that I was someone other than that woman, Charlotte Swenson, in whose skin I had lived for so long.

To be sure, public life widened the fissures between us. And in the year following the debut, my public life burgeoned exponentially: the development of the TV series, *Accidental Charlotte*, a situation comedy about a woman whose reconstructed face renders her unrecognizable, resulting in all sorts of complications and mishaps ("*Mary Tyler Moore* meets *Sex and the City* meets *X-Files*," to quote Thomas Keene); the movie *Eye of the Storm* ("*Thelma and Louise* meets *Fatal Attraction* meets *Face Off*"), which I'm told was a disaster, though I never saw it; the doll "Charlotte of the Many Faces," essentially Barbie with four interchangeable heads; the video game "Z," in which players must spot and eliminate the terrorist impostor in an array of situations before he eliminates Charlotte; the release of my book (*Faceless: A Diary of Recovery,* Knopf, 199–) with accompanying shoots for *Vogue* and an assortment of other magazines I hadn't gotten within spitting distance of for many years; my appearances on *Letterman* and *The Today Show* and *Larry King*; my appointment as honorary chair of an academic symposium, "The Semiotics of Physiognomy in Post-Deconstructive Visual Discourse" (of which I understood not a word)—during that period, a chasm developed within me, a sinkhole of massive proportions dividing me from Charlotte Swenson. I was someone else.

In the second year after the debut, when my status as a pop cultural icon of personal transformation solidified, a second wave of projects began to break: an "unauthorized" biography (commissioned by Thomas) that dug up and printed my modeling pictures along with commentary from scores of old lovers (Hansen, to his credit, refused to talk); the development of "Metamorphosis," my clothing and swimsuit line, now sold in Neiman Marcus stores around the country, and my perfume, "Incognito"

(Bijan meets Poison); "Renaissance," my skin-care line specializing in distressed, wrinkled, sun-damaged and posttraumatic skin (which the marketers cleverly figured would cover just about everyone) whose crown jewel, "Alibi Scar Erasure," is sold in freestanding displays at gas stations around the country; my cameo roles in several motion pictures, usually enigmatic walk-ons that would prompt from the protagonists remarks like "She looks familiar . . . I've seen her somewhere before," or "I thought she was someone I knew . . . but I guess not"; the so-called lifestyle projects, many of them cheapo book tie-ins to the TV show: *Charlotte's Pop-Tart Diet; Charlotte's Cocktail Recipes for All Occasions; Charlotte's Guide to Pleasing a Man . . . and Being Pleased; Burning Up the Dance Floor with Charlotte* (a boxed set of my favorite club hits from the eighties and nineties); and of course, "The Charlotte," a spillproof sectional couch sold exclusively at Crate & Barrel.

The more notorious I became for my transformation, the more gapingly fraudulent this transformation began to feel. I hadn't transformed; I had undergone a kind of fission, and the two resulting parts of me reviled each other. I was a ghost sealed within the body of a fame-obsessed former model from whom I had to strenuously guard my moods and thoughts, lest she find some way to cannibalize and sell them (*Charlotte's Anti-Suicide Techniques, Charlotte's Poems for Depression*). I crept through my life, hoarding my occasional dreams and what few memories she hadn't already plundered, camouflaging my hopes and future aspirations in a palette of utter blandness lest they be caught in the restless beam of her overhead camera and broadcast to the world. Once or twice I swore her to secrecy, but Charlotte always betrayed me ("Public Star Weds Private Dick," *New York Post*, July 199–), and her disclosures left me enraged, despondent, and bent on escape.

It was during this period of subterfuge and treachery that I dug up the contract I'd signed for Thomas Keene and read it through for the very first time. On a page of attached clauses, I came upon one headed

**23. Transfer of Identity:**
Subject may at any time no less than thirty (30) days before expiration of the Term of this Agreement notify the

Service of her election to sell her Identity Rights, as defined in Paragraph 7, to the Service. Notification shall be in accordance with Paragraph 11 of the Agreement. In consideration for the sale of the Subject's Identity Rights, the Service will pay a mutually agreed upon lump sum payment due on the effective date of the sale. Subject will thereafter be released from her Subject's Duties and Obligations under Paragraph 13. The Service will, as of seven (7) days following the date of sale ("Transfer Date"), retain exclusive rights to any and all property both tangible and intangible relating to the creation and maintenance of Subject's Identity, including but not limited to her name, image, possessions, domicile, personal history, photographs, private correspondence, diaries, travelogues, financial records, medical records, and any and all additional data pertaining to Subject's Identity. . . .

As of the Transfer Date, defined herein, said transfer is irrevocable and any action by Subject or anyone acting under her direction to resume her Identity including but not limited to the use of her name or the retention or attempt to reclaim any personal property shall be deemed a breach of the Agreement subject to any and all recourse permitted under the Governing Law and Venue set forth in Paragraph 41. . . .

I sold Charlotte Swenson for a sum that will keep myself and two or three others comfortable for the remainder of our lives, although not (I'm told) for nearly what she was worth. I dyed my hair, changed my name and walked out the door of my twenty-fifth floor apartment for the very last time. I stepped empty-handed onto East Fifty-second Street and hailed a cab, leaving closets, desk and kitchen cabinets full. I wriggled from inside my life like a sheep shorn of too many winters' wool, pink skin tingling in the brusque, immediate air.

All you need is a birth certificate.

Now, a team of 3-D modelers and animators creates my likeness and superimposes her onto my balcony, my sectional couch, my kitchen, my bedroom. From the little I've seen, they're miraculously good: That delivery scene at the hospital? Even I believed it!

As for the text—diary entries, dreams and so on—I assume they're still written by Irene, or one of her employees. As the first "new new journalist," Irene Maitlock is something of a legend, though by now scores of others have followed her example. Her company, miglior/fabbro.com, has prospered unfathomably, and she's a celebrity in her own right. I saw a picture of her recently on the arm of Richard Gere, which I guess means that her marriage didn't last. She looks so different, thanks to her much chronicled makeover; without the name, I wouldn't have recognized her.

As for myself, I'd rather not say very much. When I breathe, the air feels good in my chest. And when I think of the mirrored room, as of course I still do, I understand now that it's empty, filled with chimeras like Charlotte Swenson—the hard, beautiful seashells left behind long after the living creatures within have struggled free and swum away. Or died. Life can't be sustained under the pressure of so many eyes. Even as we try to reveal the mystery of ourselves, to catch it unawares, expose its pulse and flinch and peristalsis, the truth has slipped away, burrowed further inside a dark, coiled privacy that replenishes itself like blood. It cannot be seen, much as one might wish to show it. It dies the instant it is touched by light.

Once or twice a year I still call my old voice mail, just to see if the outgoing message is the one I recorded myself. My hand shakes as I dial the phone, and I wonder who will answer.

"Hi, it's me," comes her childish, cigarette voice from the digital void. "Leave a message, but keep it short."

"Hello," I say. "It's me."

# Acknowledgments

During the years I spent writing *Look at Me*, certain individuals and institutions provided me with a tincture containing one or more of the following essentials: editorial assistance verging on collaboration; encouragement when I lacked confidence to proceed; time and space in which to work; career advice; funds; some fleck of inspiration; access to a crucial area of knowledge or expertise. I am hugely indebted to all of them.

David Herskovits, Kay Kimpton, Professor Barbara Mundy, Nan Talese, Amanda Urban, Lisa Fugard, David Rosenstock, Elizabeth Tippens, Ruth Danon, Monica Adler, Don Lee, Tom Jenks, Deirdre Fishel, Peter Mezan, Elisabeth Robinson, the Corporation of Yaddo, the John Simon Guggenheim Foundation, Dr. Sarah E. Friebert, Dr. Jack Owsley, Dr. Bryant Toth, private detectives Jonathan Soroko and Lawrence Frost, attorneys Alexander Busansky and Christina Egan, the Frary family, two former FBI agents specializing in counterterrorism who shall remain nameless, Jon Lundin's *Rockford: An Illustrated History*, and William Cronon's *Nature's Metropolis*.

# Afterword

I wrote *Look at Me* over the course of six years. In that time the novel went through countless revisions, the last of which I completed in January 2001, when America, and certainly New York, were in some sense different places than they are today.

In that final revision—a light one, since the book was scheduled for publication in September—I spent several days working on the character of Z. My editor felt that his humanity didn't come through quite as strongly in the section describing his perambulations in New York City as it does later, after he has transformed into Michael West. I welcomed the chance to take another pass at him; of the many characters in *Look at Me,* Z had always worried me the most. I was afraid no one would find him credible.

I've written elsewhere about the preoccupations that led me to develop such a character, and the research I did. My purpose here is to remind readers that, while it may be nearly impossible to read about Z outside the context of September 11th, 2001, I concocted his history and his actions at a time when the events of that day were still unthinkable. Had *Look at Me* been a work-in-progress last fall, I would have had to reconceive the novel in light of what happened. Instead, it remains an imaginative artifact of a more innocent time.

Jennifer Egan
April 4, 2002, New York